THE UNDER HISTORY

KAARON WARREN

VIPER

This paperback edition first published in 2025
First published in Great Britain in 2024 by Viper
an imprint of Profile Books Ltd
29 Cloth Fair
London
EC1A 7JQ

www.profilebooks.com

Designed and typeset by Crow Books

1 3 5 7 9 10 8 6 4 2

Printed and bound in Great Britain by
CPI Group (UK) Ltd, Croydon, CR0 4YY

A CIP catalogue record for this book is available from the British Library.

Paperback ISBN 9781800812048
eISBN 9781800812055

Praise for *The Underhistory*

'Eerie, atmospheric, full of suspense and surprises, this is a brilliantly constructed, suspenseful gothic tale'
Guardian

'The most intriguing horror novel of the year so far… Reads like Shirley Jackson or Catriona Ward at their most gothically playful. It's a wholly unique intellectual exercise and a deeply compelling page-turner'
Esquire

'A gothic-tinged tale of supernatural horror and Scheherazade-like storytelling, with all the suspense and menace of page-turning crime fiction'
Sydney Morning Herald

'An original take on the secrets that houses keep, with every page drenched in foreboding. *The Underhistory* has all the hallmarks of a contemporary gothic classic'
Erin Kelly, author of *He Said/She Said*

'A heartfelt and chilling gothic tragedy. Unbearably creepy, original and devastating'
Chris Whitaker, author of *We Begin at the End*

'An inventive, layered haunted house novel, where ghosts reside amid the dust and each room holds its own message for the unwary visitor. Kaaron Warren is one of a kind'
Alison Littlewood, author of *A Cold Season*

'What an absolutely brilliant book this is! Superbly written, completely unique. Haunting, smart and provoking'
L.V. Matthews, author of *The Twins*

'A unique jewel box of a book – tense locked-room thriller meets haunted house gothic, pulled off with immense skill'
Lizzy Barber, author of *Out of Her Depth*

'A remarkable tour de force of a novel from a master storyteller. The structure of the novel is innovative and the tension never flags, while Pera is an extraordinary and satisfyingly ambiguous narrator. Startlingly good'
Leonora Nattrass, author of *Blue Water*

'Eerie, menacing and totally original'
Philippa East, author of *Little White Lies*

'A fascinating and unnerving character study of a house and its sole survivor. A sinister, tense and satisfying read. I absolutely loved it'
Carole Johnstone, author of *Mirrorland*

'Strange, sinister and marvellously written. A box of gothic delights'
Anna Mazzola, author of *The Clockwork Girl*

'A vivid gallery of melancholy, joy and horror... A vibrant heroine, loathsome villains and a compelling setting make *The Underhistory* a haunting treasure, written by a master of her craft'
Daniel O'Malley, author of *The Rook*

'Hauntingly creepy, this twisty, layered thriller will upend your expectations and spin you deep into a house of dark secrets. I utterly lost track of right and wrong, and was gunning all the way for my new favourite heroine'
Rachael Blok, author of *The Scorched Earth*

'Warren wraps the reader in a fabric embroidered with tragedy and story, loss and memory. She enchants us with whimsy and lures us with hope, anchoring the past to the present with ordinary objects. *The Underhistory* is a triumph, intricately woven and mesmerizingly told'
Sulari Gentill, author of *Paving the New Road*

'Suspenseful, evocative, dark and original. Highly recommended'
Diane Jeffrey, author of *The Silent Friend*

'A wonderfully weird and creepy journey through a haunted house, peppered with moments of proper darkness'
Tariq Ashkanani, author of *Welcome to Cooper*

'Hauntingly dark and beautifully written, *The Underhistory* keeps you on edge throughout. There are moments of humour interspersed with tragedy and fear. A brilliant read with a wonderful protagonist'
Guy Morpuss, author of *Black Lake Manor*

'Sinuous, slippery, and wrong-foots you at every turn. I've never read anything like it'
Tim Glister, author of *A Loyal Traitor*

This research was supported by the Australian Government under an Australian Prime Ministers Centre Fellowship Program, an initiative of the Museum of Australian Democracy at Old Parliament House.

PART I

THE TOUR

Ike calls most of them DW (Dead Weight), to be discarded. He tells them it stands for Dark Warriors and they are all stupid enough to believe him.

He's told them all they are the chosen ones, You'll be the one coming with me, *he tells them all but they won't. He'll take Devon, because his family are loaded and can bankroll the escape. Davo, who had a handy flair for violence. Wayne, because he knows where the old lady's house is and what's inside it. Chook, because he looks ordinary, a middle-aged white man, and you need one of those. And Alex, who is willing to commit extreme violence at any time, because you need one of those, too.*

He'll owe Byron for this, of course. For picking them up outside the jail and driving them to safety. But what are big brothers for?

Even a big brother like Byron.

1

SINCLAIR HOUSE, 1993

Looking back, Pera figured out that at the very moment Ike shot his first victim in the jailbreak, she was cleaning up the blood spilled by a visitor who fainted after seeing the rat king. It wasn't a big spill, but she knew from past experience that even a small amount of blood would smell bad in a couple of days. It was always the Underhistory, the cellar, that got them. Sometimes it was fright, or tiredness, or the closeness of the air. But if someone was going to collapse, that's where they'd do it.

It was the second-to-last Sinclair House tour of the season, and admittedly her heart wasn't in it. Usually she'd pack up and leave after the last tour, to be away during flood season. But she was tired. This year, she would stay at home.

After that tour, she had gone into town for the last time, pulling into a parking spot right in front of the hair salon and giving herself a cheer. You never wanted to be late for an appointment with Marcia.

Pera had walked through the door with minutes to spare. Marcia glanced up and rolled her eyes.

'How are you, Marcia?'

'Running behind, as usual. Everybody's always late.' Marcia had ideas about herself and cutting hair in this small country town wasn't amongst them. Pera cursed Claudia for being away; usually a haircut meant a house call and an excuse for gossip and champagne. Pera wasn't keen on Marcia's cuts but she had been desperate; she looked like an old hag. And Marcia had a loser for a husband, so Pera tried to be kind to her. 'So, what miracle do you want me to perform today?' Marcia said.

What Pera had seen in the mirror was not who she was. At heart, she was thirty-three. She dressed young but the wrinkles? There was little she could do about them apart from a face-lift and she didn't want that stretched leather look.

She had picked out a new lipstick from Marcia's selection. 'Bit bright for your age, isn't it?' Marcia had said, and Pera had said, 'You know how much I like colour!' primping at her hair. She wasn't bothered by these slights; they said more about Marcia than they did about her. Pera never left the house underdressed. She had a lovely silk scarf she bought in Dublin, shoes from Italy and her Chanel suits she would not be without.

The previous customer paid up, grumbling, and Pera had waited until Marcia gestured her into the chair, where she poked Pera's hair. 'Had a go at this yourself, did you?' She had started combing Pera's hair, tugging at knots Pera didn't think were really there.

'You're hurting me,' she had said. 'Marcia? Can you be a bit more gentle?'

'Jesus Fucking Christ,' Marcia had said.

'Is everything all right, Marcia?'

The phone had rung and Marcia had answered it, launching into a tirade. Pera had decided she'd rather wear her hair in a bun until Claudia came back than let this woman cut it in this state of mind, so she had removed the apron and sidled out of the shop without Marcia even noticing. She had too much to do to waste her time sitting there.

There were conversations every step as she did her shopping, with the wonderful Gwennie – seventy-five, bright and lively, she still cleaned her own gutters – and with Mrs Robertson, dressed as ever as if she were going to the opera; tailored jacket, silver and pearl brooch, diamond-studded watch. She carried a mahogany walking stick but mostly used it to wave at people.

Pera liked her small town; here, people knew her. Elsewhere she was old and could wait and wait and not be noticed in a shop. She was invisible. Here, she was still Pera from Sinclair House, the sole survivor, their famous girl.

'I thought you were off to Melbourne?' Mrs Robertson had asked. 'Your annual?'

'New Zealand, actually. Stocking up on non-perishables so I have things waiting for me when I get back.'

'I hope you've let the district nurse know. You know how awful she gets when she doesn't!' Mrs Robertson had eyed the milk and cheese but had said nothing. 'You enjoy yourself,' she said, patting Pera's arm. 'Did you hear? Mrs Bee's Wayne is getting out of jail. She's had a phone call from him. She's that pleased!'

'I hadn't heard,' Pera had said. She had written to Mrs Bee, telling her the lie about New Zealand, feeling bad about it but knowing it was all part of the deception.

'Didn't our Marcia go out with him for a while? Lucky escape, that one! For him, I mean!' The two women had chuckled.

'But between you and me, I think Mrs Bee is confused. They're not letting that boy out. They locked him up and threw away the key for what he did.'

On the way out with her shopping bags Pera tripped and fell, cutting her knees badly on the corner of the kerb and twisting her ankle as well. Everybody fussed, wanting to call an ambulance.

'No, no, I have a tour coming,' she said. She did have one last group.

Later, when Pera had arrived home, the man from the stables had come to take her horses away. 'Off for a month, are you? Where is it you're going?'

'New Zealand! Lucky old me. I'll send you a postcard,' Pera had said. The lie had come smoothly off her tongue, after weeks of convincing people she was leaving town. 'One more tour and I'll be off to the land of the long white cloud.' She travelled most years. She'd planned to go back to Greece, but that seemed exhausting, so she'd booked New Zealand, but even that felt too much. Instead she had decided to stock up on food, barricade herself in and sleep, read, rest.

'I'll take good care of these beauties,' the man had said, stroking the mane of one of her horses.

'You always do,' Pera had said. She knew she should just let him keep them for good, but they provided her comfort. If she heard a whicker or neigh, she could be sure it was a real horse out there, not a ghost.

*

The blood in the cellar was cleaned away and the preparations for the last tour of the season were nearly done. On the third floor, Pera shifted the dusty mannequin dressed in a bloodied butcher's apron to the side, pushed a panel and opened the concealed door to her private stairway.

She'd added the secret door because people had no boundaries. No matter how many 'Private: Do Not Enter' signs she put up, people stamped up the stairs looking for her, wanting things, asking questions. She loved her apartment; so bright and sunny, so different from the rest of the house, which was full of history and stories. Up here there was simply the present and that was refreshing. It was a perfect space for a single person, making a small fourth floor. She had two bedrooms and too many closets, full of books, jewellery, memorabilia and clothing.

She spent a moment gazing out the window at the astonishing lawn full of flowers, all of them grown from the tributes she'd laid out there decades ago. She called Mrs Bee in Queensland, worried about the gossip she'd heard about Wayne getting out of jail – he always caused her grief – but there was no answer. Pera left a message and promised herself to call back in the evening.

Then she showered, spending too long but unwilling to leave the hot, comforting pressure of the water. She sang in the shower at the top of her voice, Puccini's '*O mio babbino caro*'. It always calmed her.

That calm left when she saw herself in the mirror. She again cursed the fact that Claudia, dear friend and hairdresser who would usually come to her to do her hair, was away, and that bloody Marcia in town, the cow, had been so bad-tempered she hadn't had the haircut and dye-job she desperately needed. She washed her hair, then brushed it back. She'd tie it in a bun and play the little old lady for this tour group.

They never minded that. Her ankle was sore from her fall, so she took a cane out of the umbrella stand. Even better.

When she had a tour going through, she could mark off hours reliably. If not, only the clocks marked time and they were not trustworthy.

Just this last tour, then she could rest.

2

THE DRIVEWAY

Pera walked down her long driveway to unlock the rusting gates. They wouldn't keep anyone out who wanted in, but keeping them locked did make people stop and think, realise they were entering private property. It was one of the little tricks she'd learned to try to keep her home her own. It was raining lightly and she was glad she'd had river stones raked over the driveway, to counteract the mudslide it could become.

Back at the house she put the kettle on and waited for the cars to arrive.

There was only one; a family of five, in a minivan. Mum, Dad, two boys, a girl. The kids all looked over ten, so they'd be more fun to frighten. Mum was last to leave the minivan, resting her head on her arms for a moment before the older child helped her out.

The final guest was a man who hiked up on his own, a small rucksack on his back, armed with a camera and a notepad. He was either a sceptic or a believer; she'd soon figure it out. He was a neat man who smelt of Fabulon; there was not a crease on him.

Six was a small number. Too many and there were gigglers at the back of the crowd, spoiling the fear. Too few and they thought she was one of them, a friend or a mother, wanting more of her than she was willing to give. Six was at the limit of this, but she was sure she could manage them.

The family were laughing and enjoying themselves, even as they stumbled in the drizzling rain over the already-swampy parking area, so they'd be good company. Tours always started out full of enthusiasm. A few minutes ago she'd felt a momentary temptation to hide until they all went away. Now, though, she was looking forward to being part of the family, if only for ninety minutes. She shivered, suddenly cold.

She stood waiting in the small copse of trees at the base of the fire stairs, her hand resting on her cane.

'Welcome to Purgatory Tours at Sinclair House, where time stands still. Although we are strictly limited to a ninety-minute tour! Most people find that's enough for a first visit. And a happy Mother's Day for yesterday to you!'

The mother smiled, and the girl hugged her. 'And many more,' the father said, kissing his wife.

'Lucky I made it,' the single man said. 'I wasn't sure. It was confusing, trying to get a ticket and finding out times and that.' He looked around at the others, hoping for confirmation. None came. 'You had to call for the time. And there weren't any tickets.' So, a believer; they wanted everything to be perfect. 'You need to be more organised than that.'

Pera leaned harder on her cane. In her mind she nicknamed him Lucky. It was a trick she used for forgettable men; name them after the first thing they said. 'I do apologise. I'm not so good with watches, or with being organised. Never have been, but it is getting worse as I get older. Don't be surprised if your watches stop. It's partly me, but it's partly the house. People say the house is trying to stop time, that it is trying to recapture its era of greatness. Who knows? The tour is ninety minutes long, regardless. I'll keep track, don't worry.'

They liked that.

'Just you, is it?' the father asked. 'Looking after everything?'

She wasn't always on her own. She had part-time employees who sometimes came in to manage the tours and the money. She'd given them all the month off, though. She said, 'Just me and ghosts today! I like to say this place is like a railway station and the ghosts get off and on, then travel from room to room.'

The parents shivered.

'In an old house, human heat or breath can do damage. Just by their presence, people do damage. They change the room conditions. These changes are like ghosts. It's like leaving a shadow of yourself behind. Something of all of you will remain here forever – as long as the house stands. The house is a sum of all who walk through her.'

Pera smiled. 'Do you want to continue? Many don't, once they hear what I have to say. You can wander the grounds instead if you like. Get a feel for the place that way. Dangle your feet in the pond. You'll leave intact, no risk. Only the brave continue.'

They almost always all continued, even though she gave the impression otherwise. Every now and then someone *would* stay outside; those who continued gave off an air of slight superiority. The person who stayed outside would be anxious, looking for a change in the others. Something missing. Something less. Or something more.

'There are ghosts even here, in this small copse. Would you like the tour to begin before it begins?'

'Of course,' they all said, feeling treated. Special. She hated ruining the illusion that they were invited guests, so didn't like asking for the entry fee at this point. She would sort it out when they got to the Mint.

The copse had once been perfect, long ago when they had a caretaker who also acted as a gardener. He was a wise old man, she'd thought, but she was only nine then and anyone tall seemed wise. She walked with him collecting wood sometimes, and she remembered him saying, 'I call this layer in the copse the understorey. Useful stuff but if you don't keep it under control and a fire comes through, oomph.' He slammed one palm against the other as if he was mimicking a rocket taking off. 'Always a use for it, anyway.'

She thought he meant 'understory', that there were stories under the leaves and twigs. Things she shouldn't hear. Like when she smelt butter and golden syrup and followed her nose to the kitchen, and the cook emerged with her cheeks bright red and gave Pera a plate of biscuits. Oats and chocolate with a tiny bit of peel.

Pera told her family about the understory, and they adapted the name for their cellar. They called it 'the Underhistory', because all the secrets lay under the surface.

They liked to have funny names for many rooms. Pera followed in the tradition when she rebuilt the house.

3

THE UNDERSTORY (THE COPSE)

'Would you like to hear about the caretaker's ghost story? He was the one who tended this copse, as well as the rest of the grounds, and the house. This is his cautionary tale about deserting your family.

'He knew my father in the First World War, and afterwards, when Dad offered him the gardening job, he took it in a flash. Times were tough, then. Thing was, though, and he admitted this later, he abandoned his wife and daughter. He never sent money back, not even a letter. It was like he wanted to pretend they didn't exist. Certainly my dear old dad didn't know about them until after the accident.' She always called it the accident, long after it was proven a deliberate thing.

The caretaker had sometimes got confused and thought Pera was his daughter. She felt sorry for him, and he was always kind to her, so she let him. He made treacle toffee on his small stove.

He'd tell her things, about the copse floor and what lay beneath, and about how to get ahead in life. He told her, 'If you can make a person feel guilty, you can get them to do anything.'

Pera told her tour group, 'It was only after he died, and they were trying to figure out who would get his things, his money and his medals, that they found out that his family even existed.'

The father shook his head. 'Terrible. Who does that? Didn't he care about them at all?'

'Not long before the accident he disappeared for a while. I found out later he went home to find his wife and child. He wasn't fully in control of his senses by then, and he'd started to scare us, staying up all night raking leaves, disappearing for days at a time, that kind of thing. What I heard was that he went home and stood in the street calling for them, until someone told him, "Don't bother, mate. They're long gone." That's what we heard. Whether or not it's true, we never knew. Maybe they just moved away? Maybe she married again? Nonetheless, he came back believing his neglect had caused their deaths.

'After that he was worse than ever, getting drunk and lashing out. He still did his job, though, and he and my father had helped each other a lot in the war, so he stayed on. So, he was here. When it happened.' She paused and nodded her head. 'Now his ghost haunts the copse. His guilt keeps him here, anchored to the place he pretended he belonged.'

'Sad,' the mother said. She had deep lines around her eyes, although she was quite young. She was tired; Pera wondered if it was parenthood and life, or something else as well.

'It is. He's always here. He usually shows himself to girls the age of his daughter.' Pera looked at the young girl. 'You'll feel a kind of shimmer in your eyes, and you'll feel sudden heat, as if there is a fire at your back. If you feel warm all of a sudden, that's why. He's there, trying to give you a hug. That one last hug he never got.'

The girl stepped closer to her father and hid her face in his side, and Pera knew this would be a good group. You only needed one suggestible one for it to work. She may have overestimated the girl's age, though. The boys were perhaps thirteen and twelve, and this girl eight, she thought now.

'Shall we go inside? Watch out for the ghosts on the fire stairs. We start our tour near the top of the house, so it's a bit of a climb. I hope you can rug up. It gets very cold in this old house. Don't worry, I've got fires in some rooms so we'll be cosy enough.'

Once upon a time she'd always lay out ghost traps for tours. Tricks and mirrors to make them believe. She didn't do it much, these days. Too tired. She felt energised by this group, though.

She let the boys go first up the stairs, calling, 'Be careful' when one, then another tripped. Lucky wiped his hands on his pants; she hadn't warned them about the flaky paint.

'Now,' she said as they climbed the fire stairs past the second floor. 'Be careful here. People often say they feel a push in the back. Hold on tight. The ghost only goes for the strongest in the group.' She used to say weakest, but no one ever owned up to that. Once she started saying the ghost only went for the strongest, *voilà*! Suddenly men felt a firm hand in the small of the back.

4

THE LOFTY HEIGHTS (HAZEL'S ROOM)

The mother was panting by the time the boys reached the top. 'Let's wait a bit,' Pera said. She was fit herself, but there were a lot of stairs. She unlatched the glass door that led inside and said, 'Welcome to the room at the stop of the stairs. Or, as my family always called it, the Lofty Heights. We were a funny lot, gave silly names to some of the rooms. This room is dedicated to my sister Hazel, because she was the first of us to become an angel.'

The six tour members crowded into the small room. Their movement raised the dust, and with the sun coming through the high windows and the glass door, it really did look as if angels were dancing. A bed with a crocheted blanket lay along one wall, with a knotted rug covering most of the floor. A dressing table with a large round mirror and a neatly placed brush and comb sat near the internal door. A small fire burnt in a hearth along the fourth wall and a modern water cooler sat in one corner.

'When did your sister . . . become an angel?' the mother asked.

'So, so long ago. Nineteen thirty-six. I was only around five.'

Pera didn't really understand it as a child. All she heard were snippets, that her sister had died 'in obscure circumstances in a St Kilda alleyway' according to the newspapers.

Everyone knew who killed Hazel. It was her boyfriend Simon Sheely. There wasn't any mystery; he was found with orange peel in his pocket (he ate oranges constantly, as another man might chew gum), and there were more pieces in Hazel's fist, flattened, all the pieces matching together like a jigsaw puzzle.

'He was locked up for life, becoming a Catholic and confessing all and atoning for the murder before being beaten to death by another prisoner, so you'd think there'd be no likelihood of him being here to haunt us, what with all that repentance. But what I say is that some people are all talk and no truth, when it suits them.'

Pera had never been to St Kilda, not in all her sixty-two years. There was something about the name that frightened her; she knew it was those early stories. She misheard it as 'Saint Killed Her' and pictured it as a place dark and terrifying, where holy men waited with weapons and women's screams were not heard. She knew that wasn't true, but still she saw no reason to go.

Pera had adored her sister Hazel, who was twelve years older and so sophisticated. Sophisticated enough to leave home without her parents' blessing and work at the telephone exchange. As an adult, Pera realised her family were trying to protect her from grief by not giving her all the details, but all it did was make her more curious about the truth. Her imagination filled in details that weren't there.

There were gaps in her mother, spaces where Hazel should have been.

'We rarely spoke about Hazel after her murder, and her room, here at the top of the fire stairs, was kept locked when I was a child. My sister Justine, who was mad for ghost hunting, had all of us terrified of even passing the doorway, because she said that killers always hid out in the victim's bedroom and they liked to come back over and over for new victims. I pretended I had no fear; I'd stomp about outside the closed door calling "Oh, Mr Killer, are you there? Or are you hanging by the neck until you are dead?" Such is life. I was going through a Ned Kelly phase then.'

The girl laughed. 'I *love* Ned Kelly!' she said.

'Remind me later. I have a little present for you. A souvenir of his life,' Pera said. She kept a store of such things, matchbooks and miniature models, shards of bone.

Pera poked at the glowing coals of the open fire with tongs.

'I can smell oranges,' the girl said. Pera nodded and winked at her. 'Not everyone does,' she said. 'That's your gift, I guess.' The others sniffed, hoping to smell it too, and they all did, now it was mentioned. Pera loved this moment, when they smelt the dried peel she'd stirred into the fire and the trick worked.

'It's not my sister who rests in this room, but the man who killed her. I don't think he feels guilty. I think he is waiting for her to come up the stairs. Many ghosts are benevolent, lonely or lost, looking for something they never found in life. A killer, though, who is tied to the place his victim most loved? They can make you feel as if you are drowning. As if you can't draw a breath.'

They called it 'obscure circumstances' because he had drugged Hazel, beaten her, drowned her in a bathtub, and then dumped her in an alleyway, and they didn't know which of those things killed her. They only caught him because one clever policeman had matched the orange peel pieces, and managed to draw a confession out of him.

Sometimes, if Pera was lucky, the water cooler would gurgle at this stage, giving them all a fright. Today it didn't happen, although one or two of them coughed in the dry, dusty room.

'Help yourselves to water,' she said, and the cooler did gurgle then, but there was no menace to it. 'This isn't Hazel's original room, of course. That burnt down with the rest of the house. As I said, my parents used to keep it boarded up, left exactly how it was. Isn't that sad? It was the only room I wasn't allowed in and it frightened me. I hated it. I can see why now, in retrospect. They knew things that I didn't, and I felt left out, but they didn't want a child to hear stories of violent murder. If you want, you could take the children out into the corridor. They could look at the funny cartoons on the walls. Done by famous people, don't you know.'

The father led the youngest son out; the daughter refused to go. 'We're going to have a surprise party for Mum after this,' she whispered theatrically. 'Don't tell her!' Pera put a conspiratorial finger to her lips.

'Most of the items in here are things we found in the rubble of the original house. I didn't recognise them all, but friends of Hazel told me these things belonged to her.' Pera took a silver ring holder from the dressing-table drawer, turned it over in her hands. 'I think if my mother were alive, she'd have changed the room as the years passed, to reflect the life Hazel could have had.'

The mother sniffed and Pera saw she was crying. 'That's very sweet, dear. You have a great deal of empathy.' She drew the woman in for a comforting embrace, enjoying the scent of her, the perfume Giorgio, Pera thought. Brand new; a Mother's Day present, she assumed. She sighed. 'Of course, I never had children myself, to my sorrow.'

She led them to the staircase and down to the kitchen on the ground floor. The range had been heating to a high temperature and she opened the oven door and slid in the tray of scones she had ready. There was a pot of soup on; she always had a pot of soup on.

5

HOME OF THE RANGE (THE KITCHEN)

'There were men posted to my house during the First World War. Before being sent to the Front. I wasn't born then, and my dad was in Egypt, "taking the record", he called it, watching men march off to Gallipoli and the Western Front. There were lots of bedrooms spare in the house. We call them men but they were only boys. Some of them as young as sixteen.'

'Only a few years older than you guys,' the father said, touching the youngest son on the head, letting his hand rest there until the boy slumped to the ground in an exaggerated joke that made them all laugh.

'They trained every day, marching around the grounds. If the weather came in they'd march around inside the house, single-file, doing a circuit of some of the rooms you'll visit today, the replicas at least. The kitchen – it might even have been one of them who nicknamed it Home of the Range – the waiting room, laundry, the boot room, back veranda, conservatory, foyer, back to the kitchen. If you looked closely in the old house you could see the path they wore.

'They all got called up to the Front. Half of them thought they were in love with the girls from town who came up to help out, so there were tears, long, sad farewells. Lots of "see you soon" and "when I get back". The butcher's daughter was even engaged to one of them; there was a photo of them together. Young and bright and surrounded by light. That got burnt in the fire, of course. One of those ladies worked here for years, putting on the teas when I had a big party. She still comes up the hill sometimes but I don't make her cook anymore. She's eighty-seven years old! None of those soldiers came back.' This statement, while untrue, always entertained.

Lucky said, 'What were their names? Is it a matter of record?'

'I have a newspaper article about it in one of the rooms. Remind me when I get there.' He nodded. Pera actually didn't mind his type; they were keen, dedicated and interested, if annoying. She said, 'We had a lot of them going through. Group after group after group.' She didn't add 'they all died' this time. It seemed an exaggeration he might perhaps call her on.

'The first time I saw their ghosts was my first night alone in the house after my husband died in 1963. A brain haemorrhage. I was sitting at this kitchen table, feeling very sorry for myself, as if no one had suffered like I had. Then I thought I heard men marching. Had I left the radio on? I didn't have the energy to find out. Have you ever felt that way? So sad it makes you weary in every joint? You can hardly keep yourself upright. So I stayed put, and the sound of men marching grew louder.'

She stopped talking, allowing the silence to settle. The grandfather clock in the hallway had a steady, heavy beat, like footfall. The father, a clear cynic out to prove a point, stepped out to look. 'It's the clock!' and his wife chuckled, relieved. 'We've only been here five minutes!' Lucky sighed.

'No. I didn't have that then. That was a gift from . . . well. From the grandson of one of those who died when the original house was destroyed. They're always leaving me presents. So no. I stayed put, and before long I saw them. On their circuit. Twenty young men, staring straight ahead, handsome and neat in their uniforms.

'The thing is, they were sunk to their knees in the floor. Because the floor in the new house is a foot higher than in the old. Rubble underneath, you know. So they were marching where the floor used to be. If you feel a throbbing in your ears, that's them marching. Even if you can't see them, you can feel the thrum of their feet.'

Even the father was quiet, staring at her, entranced.

'That poor butcher's daughter never did marry. She ended up training as a nurse and dying young, but I don't know what of. I like to think she is reunited with her soldier-love. That she marches with him, hand in hand, through my kitchen.'

The oven buzzer went. It was an old-fashioned bell, a contrivance people loved to hear.

'Scones?' she said. There was whipped cream in the fridge, and the table already set with jam, plates, neatly ironed napkins and cups for tea. She never charged extra; she liked to provide it as a treat. Made Pera think of the big raucous afternoon teas she'd shared with her sisters and parents and whoever else was around. They always had plenty of visitors.

Sometimes she heated the kettle in the fireplace, to impress, but it was too much effort today.

The mother bustled to help, and Lucky did, too, helping to tip the scones into a basket. Pera felt bad for calling him Lucky but it was too late; the nickname was set.

'If we were having a more formal meal, we'd move all this into the dining room. We'll go there next.'

'Are there ghosts in the dining room?' the older son said.

'Only the ghost of cabbage past!' Pera said, and they all laughed.

6

THE UPPER ROOM (THE DINING ROOM)

Pera had found the dining table at an auction. It was as close a match as she'd found to the one her family had owned. There were decanters on a drinks trolley in the corner, and predictably the dad opened the stopper and had a sniff.

'It's only coloured water!' Pera said. 'Otherwise I'd offer you one.'

'That's a shame,' he said, and she relented, reaching underneath for a bottle of brandy. Pouring herself a large glass, she said, 'Who wants? Kids?' and they all laughed. The father took one, and Lucky, who almost seemed about to faint as she passed him the glass.

The daughter touched her fingertips to the wallpaper. 'Don't peel at that!' her mother said. 'Don't make it worse!'

'Isn't it stunning? Designed by Florence Broadhurst. My husband knew her. They all knew each other in the art world. It still cost me a thousand pounds just for this room. That's about $20,000 in today's money! Can you imagine?' She never lit the fireplace in here for fear of smoke damaging the paper.

The group gathered around the large dining table. 'Take a seat,' she said. 'Once upon a time we'd have dinner for twenty at a time here! Wonderful parties!'

Pera loved the smell of alcohol even as a child and she loved the way it made the adults so bright and funny. She tended to hide when her parents had a party so she could watch them. They did get annoying sometimes and insist on calling her Temperance. Or Tempe. *Tick tock*, they'd say. And *Tempus Fugit*, wisely. Or they'd say *Pera* but make fun of it. Her sisters had far easier names: Faith, Hope, Charity and Justine (because both parents had hated the sound of Prudence). Mostly she hid under the dining table, where she'd hear all the gossip and goings-on. She'd look at all the shoes and decide who each person was.

The tour group were looking at the items laid out on the dining table: postcards, letters, books, and other personal items.

'Okay, I'll bite,' the dad said. 'Why's it called the Upper Room when it's on the ground floor?'

'It's a fair question,' Pera said. 'The Upper Room is the site of the Last Supper. This room is where I shared my last supper with my family. So it is to remind me of that last meal and all the other lovely ones we shared.'

20 JUNE 1941

'Lots of notable people coming, Winnie,' her father said to her mother. 'Spruce up, shall we?' He kissed his wife on the forehead. Mother always looked fine, but she had none of the glamour the girls admired in other women. She wore flat, sensible shoes –

always well made – and the same for her clothes, and she said she wouldn't wear lipstick again until the war was over and all the young men were back home safe and sound. Pera's father would say, 'But, my dear, they can't all come home. They can't.' He himself was far too old. He had 'lungs'. Pera had lungs like that, too. Prone to pneumonia.

It was Pera's father's fiftieth birthday tomorrow, and they were hosting a three-day gathering in his honour. This meant the visitors would be staying for two whole nights, a situation all five of the girls found horrendous, because it meant they had to be polite at breakfast as well, which they all thought was above and beyond the call of duty.

Mr and Mrs Wittner were the first to arrive. Pera remembered this very clearly, because until that first car came up the driveway, the girls were free. He drove the car himself, right up to the front door, almost up the step. He left his keys in the ignition, one of those people who assumed others would sort such things out for them. Men like him forgot about all the people in the war, forgot that many households, wealthy or not, had to park their own cars, bring their own luggage in these days. They had three children, all of whom sat in the back and refused to get out until Justine told them there was hot chocolate inside.

Mr Wittner dug deep into his pockets and tossed money about; he seemed to think it was funny. Mr Wittner was a very tall man with a deep, affecting smile. He was handsome and had dimples, which lent him a boyishness that made him look friendly.

Pera liked him in spite of his arrogance; he gave great whirlies, picking her up and spinning her wildly.

'Lawrence!' his wife said. She was one of the mousy ones. Even her fur wrap looked like mouse fur rather than anything else, and the girls had little time for her.

1993

Pera had many regrets about the loss of her sisters, and amongst them was that she had no one to remember those painfully annoying meals with. No one to understand. She still had two of her mother's lipsticks – Alizarine Crimson and Rose Madder – long since gone rancid and lost all their colour.

'Are there any ghosts in this room?' the daughter asked.

'Do you hear anything? Sometimes people hear the buzz of conversation, like the background noise in a movie restaurant scene. Sometimes I can remember the taste of Cook's pea soup, because that was my favourite and I'll never eat it again. Does anyone else have a food like that? A food that you love and is gone?'

Lucky put up his hand. 'My grandmother's chicken sandwiches. I don't know what she did but no one's ever been able to copy it.'

'When I worked in the city, before the kids, this one corner shop had a beef curry I've never tasted anywhere else,' the mother said. 'It was so good! I couldn't eat it now, I don't think.'

'That's because you used to have lunch every day with Jeremy Whatsit,' her husband said. 'So of course it tasted better.' But he kissed her cheek, and Pera could see how much he loved her.

'What about you?' she asked him.

'I'm not very gourmet,' he said. 'I like everything. What about you, kids? What's your favourite thing to eat?'

It wasn't the question, but Pera didn't mind. The daughter said, 'Nana's cheese on toast.' One son didn't answer, the other said, 'Chips.'

'You're all making me hungry!' Pera said. 'Let's move on.' She guided them upstairs to the first floor.

7

THE MINT (THE SAFE ROOM)

The room was papered with currency notes from around the world. Money people left behind, or sent her. Money she'd found. The carpet was a gentle mint green, and the furniture too. She used this as the spur to collect the ticket fee from her visitors.

'Look!' the daughter said. 'There's one from Nepal, one from China, one from something I can't even say.'

'Some say this room is haunted by the god of the love of money. My parents called it the safe room, because this is where the safe was kept, believe it or not! It didn't really have a name otherwise. But only the greedy are affected by the ghosts in here. If you feel your fingertips getting itchy, might be time to take a good hard look at yourself!' Pera laughed to show she was joking, but all of them rubbed their fingertips together. This happened every tour.

She dinged open the cash register she'd found in an antique shop in Canberra, making them all jump. 'Sorry! I need to collect the ticket money here. If you don't mind.'

They didn't.

On the way out of the Mint, Lucky tripped over a loose bit of carpet. 'Need to get that fixed,' Pera said. Under the carpet were old newspapers, postcards, letters. Her school reports – she remembered how kind the teachers had been, how much they knew what had happened to her. 'Pera does well under the circumstances,' they often said.

Stories from the past, flattened by hundreds of feet.

8

FACE VALUE (ART GALLERY 1)

Pera led them to the wide corridor she called Face Value. She said, 'I have little art galleries scattered all over the house. This is the first. My father's job during the First World War was drawing how faces should look when they were reconstructed. A map for the damaged. It was part of a process you can see on display here. Watercolour paintings show the appearance of the wounds. The casts show the way the limb was lost or deformed. Then artists like Dad would do the drawings. The surgeons used these as a guide to fix noses, jaws, chins. They'd use bits of the hip, shin or rib. Better a repaired face than a perfect gait. It's a bit gruesome in here, so stay outside if you have a queasy stomach. You'll see the befores and afters. It's really about how we are judged; at face value.'

They all crowded in.

'I learned the hard way the importance of keeping a record, and this is a part of what I'm trying to do.'

The tour group murmured about cleverness as they pressed against the walls, looking closely at the drawings. This would keep them occupied for a while; Pera could spend the time with her thoughts. It was one of her favourite places in the house, dedicated to the lady who called herself Princess Mary, although she wasn't. Her father never created a piece of art again, and naming this gallery after one of the silliest women he'd ever known was a way of pretending all of it was meaningless.

20 JUNE 1941

The one they adored arrived next. Lady Langhorne worked for a newspaper, something almost unimaginable, and she was so glamorous, so confident, she made the sisters breathless with admiration. Her husband Lord Langhorne was quiet and adoring, given to delivering the most delightfully rude *bon mots*, after which he'd say, 'I didn't, did I?' as if shocked by himself. Pera and her sisters loved him, too.

'Look at us, showing up out of the blue!' Lady Langhorne said.

'Out of the blue! When you've been helping me plan this ridiculous event for months!' Pera's mother said. Lady Langhorne was so funny.

'Look at you girls,' Lady Langhorne said. 'I can't wait till my two are your age. They're like little blobs at the moment, aren't they, Charles? They wouldn't care if we're there or not. They are perfectly happy at home with Nanny.'

'At least before long they will grow out of their blobbishness. If only one could say the same about our dear nanny,' Charles said, and the girls all squealed with delight. 'I didn't, did I?' he said.

Pera and her sisters were slightly horrified that Lady Langhorne would speak about her children in this way (and having never met them, somehow doubted they even existed) but at the same time adored her independence. Their mother wouldn't leave them in the care of a nanny, not in a pink fit. Their mother was big-bosomed and lively. But even she wilted in the presence of the lady journalist.

Lady Langhorne brought along her paid companion, the foolish 'Princess Mary', who loved to say, 'I'm not just a pretty face,' to which the party would chorus, 'Yes, you are!' to squeals of laughter.

Pera's father didn't hesitate to name his gallery after her.

1993

When choosing her clothes, Pera sometimes thought, 'Would Lady Langhorne wear this? Or Mrs Wittner? Or Princess Mary?' And that would help her decide.

Pera was desperate to be like Lady Langhorne. But she didn't feel snappy or smart these days. She felt old and helpless.

'Those poor people,' the older son said, standing before a drawing of a man missing half his jaw. His mother leaned up against the wall, eyes closed.

'Visitors often feel a lot of sympathy, like you do, young man,' Pera said. She was impressed with the children; most would be fidgeting and bored by now.

9

MING'S PALACE (THE GOLDEN ROOM)

'This room is the Golden Room, an exact replica of the original. We called it Ming's Palace, because all the so-called important people slept here. They all thought they were very important! More than one prime minister slept here.' It really was one of the most beautiful rooms in the house and Pera had spared nothing to make sure it felt luxurious and opulent. A high double bed, always made ready although no one had slept there for years. Thick-pile golden-yellow carpet, replaced every couple of years. An over-the-top bathroom, all fittings golden. The walls were papered in a gold thread print, the curtains gold brocade.

'I LOVE this room!' the daughter said. 'I want to live here when I grow up!'

'You could be one of my tour guides. A live-in tour guide,' Pera said. The girl squealed.

'We'd put the most important people in Ming's Palace so they wouldn't have to wee where anybody else did. I've dedicated this one to the prime minister and his wife, because they were the last important people to stay in the Golden Room.'

20 JUNE 1941

The prime minister and his wife arrived on time. They had a small entourage with them, including a secretary, a driver, and a handsome young man her sister Justine quite liked. They were on a tour of Australia even though the war was on, because the prime minister thought it worthwhile, to remind himself what they were fighting for: home, hearth and family. His young man collected small items on their travels; a pebble from the path, small coins left behind by international visitors, a beautiful leaf. He said it was the best way to maintain the memories, that these things would evoke remembrances long after the words had faded. Pera thought this was wonderful and she would do the same as life passed; collect a pebble here, a book there, small items that would make her remember moments. The young man was painfully shy, and blushed bright red whenever anything risqué was said. Lord Langhorne in particular rendered him almost speechless with embarrassment.

'Happy birthday for tomorrow, old man! Who ever thought we'd reach fifty!' The prime minister handed Pera's father a beautifully wrapped gift: a wallet made of crocodile skin. He was an old friend of her father's; they had been at school together. He and his wife were kind. The wife in particular looked right at Pera, as if she really existed.

Pera climbed to her room on the third floor. It had a small balcony, like *Romeo and Juliet*, a play her sisters loved to act out after they saw it on a school trip. She could climb out the window (no one could explain why no door was built) and stand, looking out. Above her was a light stone turret, so she could pretend she lived in a castle. Way, way in the distance she could see the town, and there were the neighbours who kept horses, and there were the neighbours who kept bees, but mostly, if she wanted to, she could pretend she was alone in the world.

From her bedroom window she saw movement in the old sheep shed. It was the people they didn't talk about. Her parents knew they were there and let them stay so long as they didn't cause any fuss.

Her sister Hope said they were all escaped murderers – although there were children as well – and that they'd slit your throat like they were cutting into an apple, and care as much.

Justine said they were ghosts, every last one of them.

Pera knew they weren't. They were simply people with nowhere else to go.

1993

Even now, years later, Pera could remember the colours, the smells. The ultramarine of the prime minister's wife's coat and what a stir that caused in the press. The burnt umber of Cook's chocolate cake, and the warmth of it, and the way the smell filled half the house. The house itself, every room with a different scent, so that she could tell where she was even with her eyes closed.

'Most people feel a sense of calm in the Golden Room,' Pera said to the tour group.

'It feels very decadent. I think I feel more jealousy than anything else!' the dad said. Every item in the room was worn but clearly valuable.

'The prime minister really loved this room. He was not the type to show off his wealth, but everyone loves a bit of gold! Let's move on.' She led them up the stairs to the third floor.

10

THE STRANGERS' ROOM (THE WELCOME ROOM)

'We were supposed to call this the Welcome Room,' Pera said. 'But my sisters and I called it the Strangers' Room. It's where we put the people we don't know. My sister Justine always said, "We don't have anything valuable in there in case you pinch it," to put people off! She was a funny one.'

Justine was the one most likely to succeed. She was the one who got to usher in the young man from the prime minister's entourage. There was a bit of a battle amongst the sisters; they all rather liked him. If they hadn't died, Pera was sure he would have married Justine.

The Strangers' Room was the most private in the house, up the back stairs, down a narrow corridor, around a corner and up another small set of stairs. Her sisters used to talk about the things that went on there. Pera understood none of it, although she would remember later and chuckle at how cheeky her sisters had been, then cry at their memory.

She wished she'd enjoyed them more. Mostly she'd envied them, or resented them, or misunderstood them.

'From the Strangers' Room you can hear things downstairs. Sometimes you'll hear things that happened long ago. Sometimes, every member of the group will hear something different.'

It was a comfortable room, with the best chairs and couches, soft rugs for laps and paintings of dogs on the walls. Figurines of cats. She asked them all to sit and be quiet for a few minutes. 'Listen,' she said.

20 JUNE 1941

Pera, Hope, Charity, and a friend of Charity's who called herself Barrette, sat in the Strangers' Room. Pera could hear glasses clinking and high laughter. They were having cocktails; Pera would go on the hunt to steal swizzle sticks when they weren't looking. Then the quiet but clear voice of Lord Langhorne. 'Virile old chap, aren't you, Douglas! Five daughters! Not many could muster up the stamina.'

The girls looked at each other, horrified, and Pera supposed the prime minister's young man blushed bright red. He was, apparently, Barrette's cousin, but you never knew with her if she was making things up.

Their dad laughed. He didn't mention that there was once another daughter; they rarely mentioned her.

People didn't talk about murdered daughters. They didn't count them anymore.

The adults sang 'For He's a Jolly Good Fellow' in an exaggerated way that made the girls roll their eyes at each other.

Pera heard the young man say, 'Oh, goodness! My watch seems to have stopped!'

'That's Pera. She always stops clocks and watches,' Pera's mother said.

She did, too.

1993

'So,' she asked the tour group, 'what did you hear?'

'Doors slamming,' the father said.

'Footsteps,' one of the boys said.

'Snoring? It sounded like snoring,' the mother said.

'The low hum of conversation. I couldn't hear any words, though,' Lucky said.

'I heard Dad's tummy rumbling,' the little girl said. That got a laugh.

'Down to the ground floor we go!' Pera said. She was pleased; they were responding well. She liked to think of it as casting a spell, drawing people in until they followed her without question.

11

SCHOOL OF OSTEOLOGY (THE LIBRARY)

'I don't get it,' Lucky said. 'Osteology?'

'You won't see more spines than in a library!' Pera said. 'This library is dedicated to my story-telling sister, Hope. She doesn't haunt it though; only my murdered sister haunts the house.'

There were walls of books, the oldest four hundred years old.

'It's a shame about all the fittings, isn't it? I suppose it's too hard to maintain them,' the father said, running his hands over the wood panelling, which was lifting in places, split in others, and Pera knew needed repair.

His wife hit him on the arm. 'Don't listen to him. He's one of those home-renovator types who talks about it but never does it.' She took a deep breath. 'Oh, I love that old book smell.'

'This was a favourite place to escape to when I was a child. I had a grand collection of postcards and I could lay them all out on the floor here, sorting them into different categories or looking at the pictures.'

The little girl tugged her mother's arm. 'I don't like it here, Mum. Stinky old books.'

'Did you see a ghost?' Pera asked. 'A stinky ghost?'

21 JUNE 1941

The adults had all been up late the night before and were only now emerging for breakfast, even though the day was half over. Justine and the prime minister's young man were being boring, talking quietly out by the chapel. Pera couldn't hear what they were saying, so she took herself to the library with her box of postcards. She was known for greeting everyone with, 'Send me a postcard! I've got the world's biggest collection.'

She spread the postcards out on the floor. Her favourites were from her father. He wrote so beautifully and kindly and he always remembered little things, such as the name of her teacher, or her best friend, or the book she was reading when he'd left for his business trip. He was in business. None of the sisters were exactly sure what that meant. He was gone a lot, and when he was home there were lots of parties and phone calls and serious discussions.

The best postcard of all was the one from Fairyland, Jinnistan, which was pure golden magic. She felt as if every time she looked at it something new appeared. There were crayon scribbles on some of the postcards, from when she was three or four trying to write a message back, thinking they were a magical form of communication and that simply writing on them, her father would get the message. The later ones had little pencil marks, Pera keeping track of what order they arrived in so she could tell herself a story if she wanted to.

Another one she loved was Italian, from Chiesa del Sacro Cuore del Suffragio, words she tried to say over and over again. He had written on the back, 'If you ever come here, look for my message to you!' The postcard showed the church itself, something she never forgot.

'Pack up now,' her mother said, coming into the library. She was dressed in a pale mauve dress, and her hair was wispier and messier than usual. She'd stayed up far too late; Pera had heard her say in a high-pitched, overexcited voice, *You lot are a terrible influence! My head is in a state!* 'Our guests may want to come in, and we don't want them slipping on your collection.'

Pera sighed but put the postcards back in their box. She found her drawing pad and her coloured pencils and set to, sitting in the large bay window. A heavy curtain concealed it, so it was another of her favourite places to hide. There was a smaller window at the side she could open to let the breeze in. It was almost perfect. She'd been there for twenty minutes or so, working on a picture of their front gates and the colourful flowers along their base, when the adults walked past outside and waved to her. She waved back, partly annoyed they'd found her spot. The prime minister's wife gestured for Pera to hold her drawing up.

'So clever! You've got a natural feel for colour,' she said, poking her head through the open window.

'Shape, too. Clever indeed. A name to watch in the future,' the prime minister said. He was a tall man and broad, but when he spoke in a low voice, he seemed kind. 'Here,' he said, fishing a soft-covered notebook from his pocket. 'You might like this. My little scribbles. Scribble wherever you go, young one. Always be observing.'

In the notebook were pencil sketches. Lots of turrets and stars, small animals, tiny buildings. She tucked it into her box of postcards, so it burnt to ashes, along with everything else.

Pera joined her sisters, who were lounging on the steps outside watching two of the Wittner children running through a great pile of autumn leaves, swept up a month earlier and saved for a bonfire. Pera would have loved to join them but her sisters sneered and laughed behind their hands so she didn't think she should.

The oldest Wittner boy was very handsome, all her sisters said so. Tall, with black hair, and so lively with his words. Justine said she thought their parents were bringing in potential husbands, to save the girls going out looking.

At dinner, the ladies were all in furs and pearls, dressed up for Pera's father's fiftieth birthday party. Her father took photos, and the prime minister had a movie camera he insisted on using. Looking at the photographs years later, Pera thought how thin, bright and neurotic they all looked. At the time, Pera found them all quite terrifyingly gorgeous, the most glamorous creatures she had seen. Her own mother was beautiful, bright-cheeked and full of conversation.

The women posed by the statue the girls called Mister Man. He was a nude.

'Doesn't he have a good figure?' Lady Langhorne said. The ladies all giggled.

'A fine figure of a man indeed,' the prime minister's wife said. They'd all had quite a few glasses of wine and were now looking slightly less glamorous.

Lady Langhorne spotted Pera lurking. 'Don't you think so, dear? Already dreaming of your husband?'

'Lady Langhorne!' Pera's mother said, but she laughed with the rest of them.

Pera blushed. She felt shy, awkward and slow. She wanted to be quick, witty and sharp, like Lady Langhorne. 'I might not get married,' she said, and blushed further.

'Good for you,' Mrs Wittner whispered loudly. Her breath smelt like brandy, sweet and fruity.

'Sleepy-bye time,' her mother said. 'You've got friends coming in the morning so you'll need to be up nice and early.'

'Who's coming?' Pera asked. Sometimes her mother's idea of 'friend' differed from her own.

'Good friends! George and Harry Ashly!'

'Goody!' Pera said. The horse-loving brothers who lived nearby. They *were* her best friends. They hadn't come that day because they were getting over the measles but maybe in the morning they'd be better.

Pera's mother took her up to bed and they lay there together for a while with the hum of the house in their ears before her mother went downstairs again. Pera couldn't sleep, so took her pillow and blanket to the Strangers' Room, where the couch was old and comfortable and the acoustics such that she could hear most of the goings-on.

She fell asleep to the sound of laughter.

12
THE RACECOURSE (ART GALLERY 2)

1993

The brothers George and Harry Ashly had been her friends her whole life and the Racecourse was their favourite room. They were cross with her at the moment because she stabled her horses elsewhere rather than with them, but she didn't like to be an imposition. Neither of them were as young as they used to be and she hated to feel like a burden, as if they were doing her favours because of friendship.

This was where racehorse portraits hung, including one of Phar Lap, who some said had been killed rather than died of natural causes. It was a copy; the original painting had only arrived a day or two before the accident. Pera was obsessed with Phar Lap, as many were. That horse was powerful and proud, ready to race. He looked so alive in the portrait, and yet he was dead. George and Harry never got to see the original painting, which made her sad. She was the only person who remembered it. She didn't know how it got into her father's possession; things had a tendency to show up.

'This place is so huge. Very easy to get lost in,' the mother said. 'And you're leading us up and down and round and round!'

'That's why a tour guide comes with you! Mind you, sometimes I almost feel like I'm lost myself. Some days it feels as if the house has grown. Or shrunk. It feels as if it changes shape. I know that sounds like nonsense but some days, it feels that way.'

'It doesn't sound like nonsense at all,' the mother said. She was about the age of the child Pera could have had. One of her miscarried pregnancies could have been this kind woman, and Pera could have had these lovely grandchildren. She gazed at them wistfully.

'Do you manage all of this on your own? What about your kids?' the mother asked as if reading Pera's mind.

'I don't have any . . . things didn't work out that way.' She smiled at the three children. There were times when she wished she did have a family. But other times she knew she didn't want to bring children into the world. To take on her family name. 'How old are yours?' The two women had drawn away from the others.

'Twelve, eleven and eight. And they say you can't get pregnant breastfeeding!'

'Do they now?' Pera said. 'You're lucky to be so fertile, and healthy. I was the former but not the latter. Never could hold onto one.'

'I'm so sorry.'

'Not sure how many I lost,' Pera said. She smiled, a sad smile that almost hurt, but she didn't want this dear woman to worry. 'But it wasn't meant to be.'

'It happens to so many of us. I lost two. Can you imagine? I'd have five children!' The woman shook her head. Blinked. Tears formed. She turned away to find her family and Pera wondered what it was. Was she sick or was it one of the others?

22 JUNE 1941

The adults were once again subdued at breakfast the next morning. 'The morning after the night before after the morning after the night before,' the prime minister said, and they all laughed. It was one of those adult jokes that are not really funny.

It was a wonderful meal, with Melba toast, kumquat marmalade, crispy bacon and pots and pots of tea. Pera kept sneaking back for seconds; toast and marmalade was about her favourite food in the world but usually she was called greedy if she had more than two pieces. Today, she ate until she almost burst.

None of them knew, how could they know? That this would be the last meal at that dining table.

When the breakfast things were cleared away, Pera ran down the stone steps to the iron gates, thinking to swing on them while she waited for George and Harry to arrive. The gates were solid and had a satisfying heft and squeak. Sometimes a squeal, after the rain.

There were vans and cars parked there and people milling about. Her father had said, 'You can wait by the gate but don't talk to anyone. That's the newspaper mob, after something about the prime minister.'

'The press are the vultures of the living,' the prime minister had said, smiling. 'You know there's a dead body close by if you see vultures, and you know the prime minister is close by if you see newsmen. Pretend they aren't there. They'll call out to you but you stay firm.'

She climbed onto the gate and stretched over it, looking out for George and Harry Ashly. The journalists immediately starting yelling questions at her.

'What's he like, then? Our PM?'

'What's a PM?' she said, forgetting she wasn't supposed to speak.

'What do you think PM stands for?' one of them asked.

She didn't know what PM stood for but knew who they were talking about. She told them Pretty Marvellous, because he was. They laughed, thinking she was joking. She liked that.

'Nasty, is he?'

'No, he's lovely,' Pera said. 'He's a funny, lovely man.'

They'd quote her on that, in headlines. 'Funny, lovely man dies.'

She waited for an hour and then Justine came down to fetch her, all dolled up, hair done, make-up, the works. The press took lots of snaps of her. 'Dad says you're to come in. The Ashly boys still aren't well enough and won't be coming after all.'

Pera was bitterly disappointed and cross, and she made sure everyone knew it back at the house. Lady Langhorne made a face and said, 'Pera is unhappy? Pera not be sad!' in a baby voice. Pera suddenly hated her. She would never talk to a child that way. Princess Mary was sick in her room. Lord Langhorne told anyone who'd listen she'd been sick in all the pot plants and they all enjoyed that.

'Photo time!' her father called. He'd brought back a camera from one of his earliest trips away and always insisted on lining up Pera and her four sisters as the seasons changed or for any other occasion at all, always by the big flame tree, with the house behind them. Sometimes he gave them ice cream in an attempt to draw a smile, because mostly they resented the interruption. He'd had photos taken here since he was a boy, with his brother Michael and their parents, then with his wife Winnie. Then with the girls as they appeared, Hazel, Justine, Faith, Hope, Charity and Temperance.

The vicar appeared amongst them like a blowfly and followed along. In the footage Pera watched later, he looked confident, a welcome part of the group, with Lord and Lady Langhorne on either side of him, surely having a joke at his expense. Pera saw him trip and fall, tugging on the prime minister's wife's coat, pulling her back a bit, and all the men tutting, as if they thought very little of him. He had fluffy white hair, even more unkempt when the wind blew, and carried a handkerchief in his pocket, as if that made him a gentleman.

They said his cross was found melted into his chest. Embedded. She didn't see it, only heard it. The lesson to her was that his arrogance, his wanting to be a part of a famous group, led to his death. Meanwhile, a sick parishioner waited in vain for his visit. And it was a Sunday, which made it even worse. The news headlines had a field day with that one.

The servants, even the religious ones, were unimpressed by the vicar. 'How did he get through the gate?' Pera heard one of them say. He came uninvited, grass seeds on his trousers. You could always tell an uninvited guest, because they had to walk through the long grass and they had seeds around their ankles and mud on their shoes.

Charity drew Pera and Hope aside. 'Don't stand near the vicar. He's revolting.'

They saw the man laughing, his hand on the prime minister's shoulder. His other hand played with the cross around his neck; it was gold, and he was overly proud of it. 'I can't tell you what I heard about him.'

'What?' Pera and Hope said together.

Charity said, 'Barrette told me. You can't tell anyone.' Barrette had finished off some of the adults' wine the night before and was sick in bed. She was Charity's best friend but she was more like Hope; a dreadful storyteller herself. She'd been caught lying and for punishment had to help out with Sunday School. She was skipping it today, it seemed. Perhaps the vicar would pretend he was there to collect her?

'Barrette says she saw him. Naked from the waist down. Washing HIMSELF in the holy water!'

'Ewwwww!' Pera and Hope said. Pera wrinkled her nose. They looked at him, his skinny long legs, his hunched shoulders, his fluffy hair flopping into his eyes.

The adults gathered under the flame tree. 'Come on, Temperance! Don't dawdle!' her father said. There was to be no bribery today to convince them to stand still. Another photo, another another another, and she could see the prime minister holding up his movie camera as if it was a great treat for everyone. She still felt cross that the horsey brothers hadn't shown up and that no one seemed to care. Her sisters stood in place, wanting it over, their hair done, make-up on. Pera had a short bob, clipped back behind the ears. A pink vest with red edging. Grey pleated skirt. Long dark grey socks, black shoes. Her best home clothes.

An aeroplane buzzed overhead. 'Buzz buzz,' the vicar joked, 'the vultures on the move,' tossing his head slightly to show how confident he was. He knew this was something the prime minister said.

The tree was stark now, not beautiful as it was in spring. Her father thought there was beauty always, which was why he took photos. He said, 'There are so many variations of beauty.' Birds' nests sat clumped in the bare branches, like dry fruit. The tree was older than the house, family history said.

'Smile, Temperance!' her father said. She scowled. Why couldn't they call her Pera, like she asked and asked and asked?

Whenever Pera looked at those photographs now, she wished she had smiled for him, because it was the last photo he took, and the last one of her and her sisters. Much later, she had the photo printed over and over again, enlarging it, until she thought she could see the aeroplane reflected in their eyes. Charity in particular had lovely brown eyes.

'The thing with photographs,' her father said, 'is that they capture both the absolute present and the immediate past. Nothing else can do that.'

The prime minister asked her to step out from behind the large tree and walk through the sea of yellow and white jonquils the gardener had planted. She walked carefully, her hands behind her back. Again instructed, she looked at the camera. She liked that bit; it was fun. Then her father wanted another photo but she wanted more movie-making and he said, 'Stand STILL will you, Temperance?' in such a harsh voice. Mr Wittner stood behind her and held her chin, forcing her to lift her head and smile. He thought this was very funny.

The prime minister's wife Patty gave her a look of sympathy at having to perform for the camera. 'I understand how you're feeling. Sometimes I feel like a puppet. A marionette,' Patty said, and she lifted her arms comically, pretending to be on strings. Pera giggled. 'Do this, go there. But these things are important, dear. The men understand that things need to be seen to be done. Certain faces must be kept on, if you know what I mean.'

'Now, pick a flower and spin around,' the oldest Wittner boy said jauntily. 'Spin and spin like a lovely little top,' and all the grown-ups laughed, even Mother and Father, even the prime minister's wife laughed, and she'd seemed so kind. Even Lady Langhorne laughed.

Her father felt bad so he let her hold the camera, telling her to capture something beautiful. He had the knack of making her feel better. The prime minister gave her his movie camera to hold too but he didn't say she could use it.

So she had both around her neck, and that's why both survived.

'Go on, spin!' the Wittner boy said.

'No!' Pera said, and she ran off, fast as she could, knowing no one would chase her. None of her sisters better marry that boy. He was awful.

Her mother's last words to her were, 'Lunch in fifteen minutes, you silly thing,' and they all laughed. Her mother was the silly one. Didn't she remember Pera's watch didn't work? Watches stopped on her wrist and sometimes clocks, too, depending on how close she stood to them. She couldn't have an alarm clock on her bedside table because, while the gentle ticking helped her go to sleep, at some time in the night it would inevitably stop and she would awaken with a fright, thinking someone had stopped breathing.

When they went inside the house, not one of them looked back to see if she was coming.

13

THE HANGING ROCK

By the time Pera reached the pond, which was quite large and full of fish, she was puffed out.

She climbed onto the great overhanging rock which, the story went, had stood since the beginning of time. It was flat on top, and still warm from the winter sun. A rope swing hung off the jutting corner edge and she climbed down into it. Hope told her their father's brother Michael hanged himself there when he was twenty-one. Justine said he haunted the rock making people feel bad. Making them feel like dying. Pera didn't believe in ghosts so that didn't bother her, but she did feel sad for their uncle, if the story was true.

Her father's camera banged against her chest and she stopped, wound the film on and took a photo of the rock. Then she turned around and took one of the house, too. No people were visible; they'd all forgotten about her. From that distance she could capture most of the house itself and the caretaker's hut, too.

Faith was sent to get her. Too lazy to walk to the pond, Faith called out. 'Time for lunch! Hurry up, Pera.' But Pera thought,

If they don't come to get me, I'm staying here. They don't even care.

She swung from the rope, even though chill air came off the pond and she really was hungry.

She loved to watch the water. The fish poked their noses up now and again, snuffling for whatever it was they ate. She felt like she was their god; only last week one had flopped onto the dirt and almost died, until she picked it up and threw it back.

Pera jumped off the rock and sat on a warm flat stone on the pond's edge, dangling her feet in. The water was warm only at the surface, but chilly below that. Sometimes the fish would nudge at her toes, which made her squeal with delight.

She felt a shadow across her and pulled her feet out, thinking it was probably her mother, which would be fine, or one of her sisters, who would tell her to grow up or stop being a boy or something. Or maybe her friend, the migrant boy, who lived in the sheep shed.

He was about her age and spoke odd words that sounded wildly romantic to her. She taught him English words like 'water' and 'fish' and it made him laugh. He had curly hair that always seemed to have twigs in it, and he smelt like the food they cooked in the sheep shed where they all lived, but they had fun together. They sang and played music, creating instruments out of anything. He was a fast runner and they raced. She was yet to beat him but she would. The only time Pera heard her mother be down on them was about the horrible kerosene stove they cooked on back there, how dangerous it was. How they could all die from a fire. Her mother loved their music, though, sighing, 'Puccini!'

Later, Pera wondered if her mother had seen the future.

She didn't know his real name. She called him Phar Lap because he was so fast. The only way she could beat him was to run into the pet graveyard that surrounded the family chapel, and he'd stop short and cross himself. All her fish were buried there and the various cats and dogs. Her mother drew the line at horses, though. Pera's favourite was the one with her dad's carefully painted sign: 'For Tibbles. A beloved pet who shouldn't of died.' She sometimes saw a glimpse of that little boy in her father.

She gave Phar Lap a stopwatch she'd found in a drawer in a room they called Purgatory (her dad said she could) so he could time himself. He taught her the word *Purgatorio* and they played an odd game in the Underhistory, pretending to be trapped and escaping. There were tunnels in the Underhistory and running out from the house, and Phar Lap seemed to know them all. He and Cousin Frankie were around the same age but Frankie was tedious, whiny and weak but also cruel to animals and was a sly pincher. Phar Lap tried to give her a small metal truck made out of scraps, but she wouldn't take it. She knew he didn't have very much.

He wasn't casting the shadow, though. If she believed in ghosts she would have said it was her hanged uncle Michael. But she didn't, and it wasn't.

The high hum of an aeroplane came from above and she glanced up. That was the shadow. They didn't get many over this way and she wondered if it was the one that had passed over before. She wondered where those people were going. Somewhere wonderful, like Paris. Although people weren't travelling much; she'd heard Lady Langhorne complaining of having to stay 'onshore'. Pera practised saying 'onshore' because it sounded so sophisticated.

The hum grew louder, much louder, and the pond seemed disturbed, darker, and she looked up to see the aeroplane so close if she squinted, she could touch it. She scrabbled up onto Hanging Rock, craning her neck to see. The camera around her neck banged against her chest again and she lifted it to her eye. She'd seen her dad do this in order to look at something up close. She closed one eye and saw the aeroplane, large now, but it was lower, too, far lower, and she clicked her finger on the button again and again as the plane veered down and into the roof of her house.

Time . . . stopped.

She watched through the camera, thinking at first that Daddy had made some brilliant thing, a tiny movie in the camera. She dropped it as the flames grew and she could hear screaming.

She slid down from the rock, scraping both legs from thigh to knee. Later she would see her blood there and think: *Justine would say the ghosts will get me now.*

The aeroplane was nose first in the house. It was big enough that three-quarters of it stuck out the top. It sat at an angle, not like a straight stick in the ground but like one that was bent sideways, like when the tomatoes got too heavy for their stake.

The roaring deafened her, the flames and a cracking noise, and screaming, like of a thousand people. She ran. She was fast, not as fast as Phar Lap, boy or horse, but she was quick enough to be there in less than a minute.

'Stop!' she heard, but she didn't. The flames covered the front of her house and every step was someone else she had to save. Mum Dad Justine Faith Hope Charity, fish cats dogs so many.

The prime minister and Patty and their young man who helped and would marry one of her sisters and the Wittners because one of them would marry a sister too and her friend in the sheep shed and the caretaker and the cook. Lord and Lady Langhorne, and Princess Mary.

'You have to stop!' and this time a strong arm grabbed her. She wriggled to get away. She thought she'd seen him at the front gate. One of the newsmen. A reporter, they called them. The driveway was full of them.

'My mate's gone for help. We can't do anything. We can't get in there.' He didn't sound as if he was sure. 'How many in the house?'

She was the only one who had any idea, but she said, 'I don't know.' She knew enough to be careful of newspapermen.

The reporter took out a notepad. 'Think, sweetie. Forget that' – waving at the house. 'We need names. Numbers.' Other reporters – how many? A dozen? – were trying to break windows, trying to get in, but it was this man's work that would be remembered because they would save no one.

She told him everyone she could remember. She hoped she hadn't forgotten anyone.

She was only nine. This was too much. She was too young to think about the victims beyond her family but she did, and she would. She'd be haunted by the lives she didn't save.

She didn't save anyone.

Once the reporter had the names, he said, 'Stay safe,' and he ran off with his notebook to the police, the ambulance people, the firemen, who were now swarming around the house.

No one would notice Pera again for a while.

So much noise and heat, and the names she'd given, to him they were just names. But to her each one had a person attached.

She tried to get into the house but the heat was too great. And the men in uniform annoyed at her IN THE WAY, a nuisance. She ran around the side because that door, guarded by the well-made man statue, was always open, and there were tiles on the floor and no curtains so she thought it might not be on fire.

The statue's head was sheared off and he was tipped sideways, onto his elbow. She tried to lift him but couldn't shift him even a bit, and he blocked the door so she couldn't open it. She peered in, saw nothing.

She heard more sirens and thought *the men will move him* so she ran to them and made it clear, in a voice she'd never heard before, that there was only one way in.

Everything was burning.

She ran around the back. The sheep shed where her friend Phar Lap lived was ablaze. The heat was so intense she felt her cheeks burn, but she ran anyway.

All the grown-ups were around the main house. Pera went from one to another, desperately seeking help for the people in the shed.

'There's no one in there,' one fireman said.

She ran back towards the shed but it was so hot she had to stop. She couldn't hear anything. No moans or cries. Nothing.

'Are you there?' she called, and then, remembering, she said, '*Bon journo? Bon journo?*'

She heard an awful high-pitched screaming. It was the horses in the stables, trapped with their wrangler. She had been banned from the horses. 'You're too absent-minded. You'll wander behind one and he'll kick you to Kingdom Come,' the wrangler had told her. At the time she had no idea what that meant.

The caretaker's shed didn't burn. Pera thought it was because he had it piled up with greenwood, from a tree knocked down in a recent storm. 'Wait long enough it'll come good,' he said most mornings.

It didn't come good. He was inside the main house when it happened. He'd survived the war, only to die having his tea-break with Cook. She wished he had a different story, that she could give him more reason than that to haunt the place.

Noise, and so many men. Fifty, she thought, or sixty or a hundred in dozens of cars and vans and fire trucks and ambulances.

No one noticed one man in particular for a while, or they thought he was with the police, taking official photos. Pera could see, though, that he had grass seeds on his pants like the vicar had. Sneaking in around the side, not with the rest of them. Pera ran at him, pushed his knees in from the back.

'Watch where you're going, you little bitch,' he said, and he lunged at her, so she ran to her safe place, the pet graveyard. It wasn't safe, though; some of the plane had landed on the roof of the chapel and stuck up sideways. The chapel was almost flattened.

Smoke held her knee-deep. It billowed out of what was left of the tiny chapel (not that they ever used it) and over all the crosses in the pet graveyard. Something burnt in the graveyard, too. More of the aeroplane? She thought she could try to save the wooden crosses, 'For Tibbles. A beloved pet who shouldn't of died' at least, but firemen came and they wouldn't even let her do that. The walls of the chapel had collapsed and she hoped nobody had been inside.

A man picked her up and carried her a distance and she let him do it because her dad hadn't carried her for a long time and if she closed her eyes it could be him. Someone gave her a lollipop and she didn't want it but licked it anyway because she didn't know what else to do.

They watched the flames. It was pitch black now, the moon clouded, so all they could see was the bright red-orange of the fire and the dark shadows of the vehicles and the stick-like men up and down ladders, but none of it did any good.

The lady bee neighbour – they always called them the Bees but they were Mr and Mrs Bailey – arrived and called Pera's name, but she said Temperance, so Pera didn't realise. Finally, the man who'd carried her said, 'Is that you?'

Mrs Bee wrapped Pera in a blanket and led her down the driveway. It was like walking in Pitt Street Mall, it was that busy. In her own driveway. Mrs Bee started crying, whimpering, 'I'm sorry, I'm sorry,' until they started carrying stretchers out, then she quickly drove Pera to her own house.

Pera was hungry. She'd missed lunch. But thinking about food, with all that had happened, didn't feel right.

It felt bad to feel hungry.

Luckily there was a big pot of stew on, and fresh bread with honey. Pera ate without speaking. Mrs Bee chattered away, thinking she needed to fill the silence, until her husband said kindly, 'It's okay to be quiet for a bit.' They didn't have any children yet; Pera had heard her mother talking about them 'trying' and 'the tragedy' but she didn't know what that meant.

'Come out and see the bees, love,' Mr Bee said. They were wonderous things; twenty hives lined up, and she had to look from afar. Mr Bee set her up inside the glasshouse as he worked and she would watch him as often as she could from that day. He seemed so brave, and the honey so sweet.

They had crumpets and honey inside, with fresh butter.

Pera swallowed. 'Do you think I will be on the news?' Her dad loved the news.

'Do you think you should hear about it?' Mrs Bee said.

'She was there, love.'

'Yes, but . . .'

Pera felt suddenly queasy and dizzy. Mrs Bee got on the phone to the doctor's office but he was at the hospital, so instead she bundled Pera up and tucked her into bed. There was a hot-water bottle, and Mrs Bee covered the bed with soft toys and brought in the cat, a gentle black and white girl, for comfort.

She left the door ajar so light crept in.

Lying there, Pera felt almost numb. It was only hours ago she'd been cross with her family. Not hating them, never that, but irritated and ignored. She thought of her mother's last words, *Lunch in fifteen minutes, you silly thing*, and her father's hand on her shoulder, and her sister calling her in, and she cried, soft at first but then great heaving sobs that shuddered painfully through her.

She thought she saw shadows in the doorway and was grateful Mr and Mrs Bee didn't come in. Later she would think about how insightful that was, leaving her alone.

She slept for an hour or two, exhausted, but she woke suddenly and alertly, sure she could save her family, save something.

She pulled on the big jacket Mrs Bee had laid out for her and went to the kitchen for water. She had no clothes but the ones she wore that day. She should go and get some from home.

She would go.

She was a fast runner and she reached home in thirty minutes or so. From the gate she could see the house smouldering and shadowy figures here and there. She would figure out later they were looters, but they looked like ghosts. She liked it better when they were shadows, before she knew they were thieves.

She walked the long driveway alone. She'd done this many times, but in the past she'd known her family were ahead. Anxious, she ran. She wanted her clothes, and her postcard collection.

Oh, her house. Great piles of rubble. She'd seen newsreel footage of air-raid bombings and this looked no different: stone, brick, mortar. Two corners of the building crumbled, as if an enormous mouth had taken a big hungry bite.

The aeroplane looked ridiculous, still smoking, like a child's toy thrust into a pile of bricks.

There was a young policeman on duty, smoking as if he didn't have a care in the world. Young Bobby, her father called him. Her father had nicknames for everyone; he said it helped him remember their actual names. Bobby was another one who wanted to marry her sisters but she didn't know which one. She watched him stub out his cigarette and put the butt in his pocket. He hadn't noticed her so she snuck around the back and started to climb the pile of rubble to get to her bedroom balcony window.

'Oi! Temperance Sinclair!'

She fell over in shock, slipped down the pile. Young Bobby

helped her down to the ground. She'd always had a crush on him. All the sisters did, and Justine told them he was a very good kisser.

Pera couldn't imagine wanting to kiss any boy but she sort of did.

Tattered curtains flapped in the windows. Her mother would be sad; that material came from Ireland and was soft to the touch, silky. She thought she saw faces in the window. She could hear rats or something larger, scratching under the house as if they were trapped in there. A tapping noise that must have been a loose window frame in the wind.

'You shouldn't be here. It's not safe,' Young Bobby said, and he gave her a pat, like a big brother would. 'It's not only all this' – and he waved his arms at the rubble – 'but it won't be long and the place'll be overrun with nasty little shits coming round pinching stuff. They are not the type to be nice to a little girl.'

She loved that he swore in front of her, but then he had to call her a little girl.

'I'm not that little,' she said, but being there, the absolute understanding that she was the only one left, made her burst into tears. The scratching grew louder and she covered her ears. How many rats had been trapped in there? Why had they lived while her family died?

He bundled her up and put her on the back of his pushbike. 'Don't tell anyone,' he said. 'Not supposed to have a passenger.'

The last thing she saw as they rode off to take her back to the neighbour's was the curtains flapping, and movement in the caretaker's shed, and the birds circling overhead.

Mr and Mrs Bee's house was quiet and dark, so they hadn't

noticed her going, and Young Bobby promised not to tell them.

He was back again the next day with his boss, a big old gruff man who predictably played Father Christmas in the yearly pageant. He had a copy of the day's newspaper, and, after checking with the Bees, he showed it to her. 'Thought you might be able to help us with this,' he said.

The news report said: 'There was one survivor of this freak accident, daughter of financial adviser to the prime minister, Douglas Sinclair.' Then lots about all the important people who'd died, and some of the plane's passengers. It was written by the reporter who'd asked her for names.

She was the only one who actually knew who was in the house. The police asked her to list them all, like she had for the newspaper man. She tried her best. 'Mum and Dad.'

'Names too, please. I know this is hard. But let's get the names if we can.'

'I don't know all their names.'

'You know Mum and Dad's.'

'We've got their names,' Young Bobby said.

'Let's run through it. Mum's name?'

'Winnie. Winnie Sinclair. And Dad is Douglas.'

She said the rest quickly, wanting this over, wanting to curl up in bed with the cat. 'Justine, Faith, Hope, Charity. And . . . and my sister Hope's friend Barrette but I don't know her real name, and the prime minister, and Patty, that's his wife. And his young man and they had a driver, too, and one other. Mr and Mrs Wittner. I think his name is Lawrence, and they have three children, John, James and Jeremy. They are awful boys. And Princess Mary, I don't know her real name. And Lady Langhorne and Lord Langhorne, his name is Charlie Boy. The vicar came. And the cook, Joan, and her helper, Jean, everyone always mixed their names up, the caretaker . . . Keith, and the man who looks after the horses, I think he is Smithy, and the people in the sheep shed.'

'The what?'

Too late she remembered they weren't supposed to talk about it. She put her hand over her mouth.

'No one's going to get into trouble. We need to know who was there,' Young Bobby said.

'We've got a heap of bodies and we need to name them all,' the old one said. Pera stared at him. Oddly, it was his face (florid, sweaty, red-eyed) she saw in her nightmares, not the heaps of dead bodies he helped her envisage.

So she told them about the families. They showed her the newspaper part that said, 'Unnamed victims were found in a flattened shed and in the collapsed chapel. Police believe up to five people were there but with no records they are difficult, if not impossible, to identify.'

'I can!' Pera said, but she realised she never knew her friend's name. And only five? Surely she hadn't imagined all the rest of them? There had been at least twenty. Or did some get away?

'No one was seen leaving,' Young Bobby said. 'And you know the reporters were watching the place like hawks. Taking photos and all.'

'I have photos too,' Pera said, and she ran to get them her father's camera and the prime minister's movie camera. She wished she had the prime minister's notebook but that must have burnt in the fire with all her postcards.

Byron drives too fast through the old gates. They all get tossed from their seats, especially Devon, in the corner, no seatbelt. They're changing out of their prison uniforms into the clothes he's brought them, Alex is whinging about the colours and the fit, but better than the alternative. Alex says, 'I mean, I look good in anything but this is a bit of a stretch.'

'Shut up, dickhead,' Ike says, looking sideways at Byron. He's been keeping the men quiet. 'You do not want to annoy my brother,' he mutters to Devon. 'He's the mean one in the family.' This with a rough grin.

The driveway is muddy, difficult to drive. The wheels spin but Byron gets them out of it and he says, 'Fuck youse, that's why I'm the driver.' He slides the van in to park, perfectly aligned, always showing off. 'Why are there other cars here?' he says. 'Place is supposed to be empty.'

'Should be,' Wayne said. 'My grandma said.'

Ike and Byron laugh at this, sneering laughter that makes Wayne cringe. Devon joins in, knowing whose side he wants to be on. 'I'll cut the phoneline before I go,' Byron says to Ike. 'Don't want any of these fuckwits calling people they shouldn't.' He gets out of the van. The others finish dressing and peer towards the house.

'Jeez, look at this place. Falling apart. Looks like a squat,' Ike says.

'Yeah, well, the lady's old so she probably can't even see it,' Wayne says.

'How old?' Chook asks, rubbing his hands together.

'Fulla rats, I bet,' Byron says, returning to the van. 'Right, phoneline's out. Go on, fuck off, the lot of youse.'

'Not coming in?' Ike says.

'No way. I hate rats. Money in me bank by Tuesday, right, or

people will be having their heads torn off.'

Ike laughs, but his shoulders twitch at the same time. Byron leans forward and punches him in the stomach, fake-gentle. 'Money in me bank.'

They stand on the steps to the house as he spins his wheels getting away.

The house is enormous and pretty much a wreck. The steps are cracked, the paint peeling. Dead pot plants line the base of the walls. A large wind chime hangs motionless; there is no breeze to make it sing. Devon used to have wind chimes at his place because his dad reckoned it made people think a good family lived inside. 'Evil arseholes don't hang wind chimes,' he'd say. Chook gives the wind chimes a flick; Ike says, 'Quiet, fuckwit.'

Wayne pushes the front door open slowly and peers his head around. 'No one here,' he says, lazy as ever. Alex pushes past him.

The foyer is quiet and smells of polish. Ike tries some of the doors; locked. He gives them a good kicking but they are solid as you'd expect. They'd need the keys.

'We fucken did it,' Wayne whispers. Something about this place makes him want to be quiet.

'You called anyone?' Ike says, just as quietly.

Wayne shifts his eyes. 'Nah.'

'Not having you fuck things up again.'

Wayne had been arrested once after he called his grandmother and gave shit away and that was something Ike never forgot.

'It almost felt like a dream. Like I was sleepwalking,' Devon says.

'That was your first one, wasn't it?' Chook says. 'It still happens to me. It's like I blank out and it's been done when I wake up again.'

Ike says nothing. They're losers. Anyone who isn't in control? Loser.

14

THROUGH THE LENS ROOM (ART GALLERY 3)

1993

The camera that once belonged to her father was now displayed in a room Pera called Through the Lens. The photos, too.

She led the tour group up to the second floor. They were all silent; most were at this stage in the tour. It was as if the weight of her history fell on them.

'I always like to start with these photos. The very last ones taken with my father's camera. They're of my house. If you look closely enough at the picture, you'll see people who aren't there,' she said. 'It changes day by day. Depends on who's looking. You'll see a lost relative, most likely. Or if you feel responsible for a death? In one way or another? You'll see them in these photos. Most often people will see things in these windows.' She pointed to an enlarged photo of the front of the house; so many windows, so many rooms. Much of the glass had flecks and reflections where they'd imagine their ghosts.

'One of my relatives had a connection to this place,' the father said.

'Did they, dear?' Pera said, barely listening. Almost everybody claimed a connection.

'Someone's here,' one of the boys said. 'They've got a big silver van.'

Lucky looked at his watch. 'They're very late. Are they on the next tour? We've only been here half an hour.'

'No, there isn't another one,' Pera said. She felt slightly panicked, at the end of her tolerance for people. 'Let's pretend we're not here and they'll go away! Who wants to see a movie?'

15

THE FLICKS (FILM CAMERA STORAGE AND VIEWING ROOM)

Pera led her tour group into the room she called the Flicks. 'We haven't got a large collection of cameras and films, but golly what we have are good,' she said. 'The prime minister's home movies, spy footage found on a dead body, Hollywood movies you won't see at the cinema anymore. Have a look around. If you wanted to watch some of the movies, that's another tour I'm afraid! We'll all have to watch together some time.' She heard a noise coming from downstairs. 'But for now, have a wander here and look at anything you like. We have movie snacks, if not the movies!' She scrabbled in a cupboard for a couple of packets of sweets. 'Help yourselves, I'll be back in a tick.'

She got them set up then walked to the top of the first-floor stairs, and peered down, listening.

Wayne Bailey? Pera thought. *He IS out of jail?* She knew Wayne Bailey, Mrs Bee's grandson. She'd met him a few times, when he was a sullen teenager with badly inked tattoos. Not a pleasant young man and she didn't imagine he'd improved with age. She hadn't seen him since 1981, when his grandmother had dragged him along to one of the crash anniversary parties. He'd been an awful little shit, she remembered, although his grandmother had dressed him neatly and even ironed and starched his shirt.

Wayne was always called 'a bad kid'. People said, 'Goes to show that shit can come from good families' because no one had a bad word to say about Mrs and Mr Bee. He'd disappear for months at a time, and Pera thought this brought the family some relief.

She recognised his whiny voice; his father had sounded the same. She froze on the steps, remembering what she'd heard in town, that Wayne had called his grandmother Mrs Bee to tell her that he was out of jail. She'd dismissed it as gossip at the time yet here he was. She'd call Mrs Bee again. That would clear things up. She walked quietly to a small cupboard where she kept a phone. There was no signal and she sighed. The phone was often out of action; she'd check the other handsets when she had the chance.

She paused. Mrs Robertson had said that Wayne *couldn't* have been getting out. Pera couldn't remember what he was in for this time; poor Mrs Bee could barely keep up.

She returned to the top of the stairs and peered over. She was an eavesdropper, always had been. As a child she'd hidden under tables and behind doors to listen. As an adult, she did it still. People loved to talk.

'. . . fucken place.'

'Keep your filthy . . . fuckwit.'

'Where's the fucken—'

'Sleep when you're dead—'

The words froze her. Not good men, then. Not ghost hunters but thieves, perhaps, or worse.

She wouldn't go down there. She'd call the police station. Get them to pop over. She wished Young Bobby was still there; he was a patient man, but he was long retired. She had friends who called more often than they should for every creak and shadow, always panicking; the police assumed all ladies of a certain age were the same.

Careful not to alert the men downstairs or the tour group in the Flicks, Pera made her way back down to the Mint to try the phone there. Nothing. She pushed at the cradle, which sometimes worked, then gently placed the receiver down.

For the first time she regretted not installing emergency call buttons around the house, as Young Bobby had recommended, but then realised they probably wouldn't work, anyway.

The last time they'd shared a meal was up by the pond; cold beer and prawns. It was a glorious clear day, every line sharp. Her house looking like a photograph.

'I don't know how you live here. Reminded every day.' It wasn't the first time he'd said this.

'Yes and no. Facing it has been good.'

'I'm haunted every day by the lives I couldn't save.'

'I know. Me, too.'

'You were only a kid.'

'You were young, too. And you were following orders. They forced you to stop trying. I was there, remember?'

And the last thing he'd done was wag his finger at her, telling her to get the alarm sorted.

She truly hoped she'd hear him say, *I told you so*.

She walked quietly back to the tour group. They were bored, wanting to move on to the next room; Pera wanted to keep them away from the men downstairs. She didn't trust Wayne as far as she could throw him, and his friends didn't seem any better.

'Who were they? Surely they can't expect to join the tour this late?' Lucky asked.

She debated lying and telling them it was a delivery van. Or telling them the truth. Telling them there were men downstairs who shouldn't be there, and that they should all leave as quietly as possible and send the police.

She could go with them. They could all slip away. Instead, she told them she'd go check it out, back soon.

She heard the front door bang and hoped the men had gone, but when she peered through the thin curtains at the end of the hallway on the second floor, she saw them milling around near the family's minivan. No escape that way. The men held their faces to the sun. *Maybe they're okay*, she thought, *if they love the sun*, but then one of them ran through her sea of flowers, kicking his boots until he'd uprooted dozens of colourful blooms.

The flowers would survive; they'd weathered far worse. But the action made her dislike the short man with his tight pants.

Another of them ran through a pile of leaves, kicking them up, and ran back again, his arms wild in the air like a child's. The others laughed at him, pointed, did not join in. He was one she could reach if she needed to.

Wayne looked much skinnier and much older than the last time she'd seen him. Mrs Bee, who for so long had thought she wouldn't have children, fell pregnant not long after Pera came to stay with them.

'I didn't even think about making a baby,' she told Pera many years later. 'The doctor kept telling us not to worry. "Keep trying without trying," he told us. But in my heart, I'd given up. Then my dear son came along, and of course he had Wayne young. You know his wife said to me, "I didn't want to be an old lady mother like you were."' Her son's wife never improved. Mrs Bee wondered if it was something they did wrong, that their son would marry such a woman, but Pera told her, 'You were lovely. It's her, not you.'

She moved to a window at the front of the house and watched as the men stood, smoking, on the front step. She could hear them talking; there was clearly one in charge (Ike, they called him), then there was Wayne. An older man they called Chook. A young one, couldn't be more than twenty, they called him Devon. And a grey-faced, powerful-looking man with scars on his cheeks and a face full of teeth, as her mother would have said. Alex.

Any hope of sending the tour group away quietly without the men spotting them ended when the boys started shouting, having a rolling fist fight that could be heard all over the house. The men looked up, looked at each other, headed for the house.

Pera ran into the first-floor bathroom. She looked at herself in the mirror, stared into her own eyes to the child she once was. Helpless to control the things that happened to her. As an adult, she made things happen, and she wouldn't stop now. She assessed herself. She wore a jacket bought those long-ago years on their honeymoon. It was a bit tight now, but still suited her, she thought. She looked smart.

Too smart. Too visible. She moved through the halls and upstairs to the room where she kept the lost and found. It was incredible what people left behind. She shrugged the jacket off, dragged her enamel necklace over her head, then pulled on a nylon spotted dress, stained and dowdy. She swapped her pink shoes for an ugly brown pair, slightly too big. There. No threat whatsoever. She gave a moment of thanks that she hadn't had her hair done in town, that Marcia had been such an awful cow. She brushed it down rather than up, knowing from past experience this aged her by years, and she dropped her shoulders. Then, keeping an ear out for their movements, she went quickly down to the kitchen, where she turned the oven on high, got out flour and milk and started on scones, her second batch of the day.

She felt ill, so terrified she thought she'd faint. She had been through a lot. But this . . . she didn't know what would happen next.

The scones were in the oven by the time she was discovered.

'Oh, Jesus.' It was the one they had called Devon. His voice was squeaky with nervousness.

She smiled. 'Oh! Hello! I wasn't sure if we had an extra tour today but I thought I'd make scones just in case.'

Devon was pale, his face drained of blood. 'Are you a ghost?' he said, a stupid question that helped her figure him out.

'Me? No! The ghosts are far more terrifying than me. I'm the owner. I've had a night away, forgot I had a tour, this silly old brain of mine.'

'Guys,' he called out. 'Someone's here. It's an old lady. Ike?'

She didn't mind being called old, for once. That was her plan.

The one she thought of as the boss came in next. Ike. He was what they used to call tall, dark and handsome, with his hair cut short, dark, piercing eyes, strong arms folded over his broad chest.

'Who the fuck are you?'

'I . . . live here.'

'You're supposed to be away. Wayne, you stupid cunt.' This drew Wayne into the kitchen. She glanced at their feet. All of them with the same shoes. Prison issue.

'Wayne Bailey! How is your grandmother? She never mentioned you were coming in her postcard a couple of weeks ago. You and your friends are most welcome here. I'd do anything for her. Such a wonderful woman, a dear friend of mine. She was so good to me when I was a child. When was the last time you saw her? I'm sure she'd be delighted with a visit. So much warmer there than it is here!' Sowing the seeds, hoping they might travel up to Queensland instead (and thinking she could warn Mrs Bee, perhaps) but at the same time not naive enough to think they'd go anywhere the police might be looking for them, nor that they would give her the chance to call anybody.

'You were supposed to be in New Zealand,' Wayne said.

'I decided to stay home. They'd invited me to a big party over there and I thought perhaps they'd be giving me an award. I hate that sort of thing.' This sounded ridiculous; she'd lost her knack for telling stories.

'Fuck,' Ike said.

'Sorry, Mrs Sinclair,' Wayne said. Most people made this mistake, calling her Sinclair rather than her married name. He'd been dead for thirty years, and anyway she preferred Sinclair.

'Mrs Bee was very kind to me when I was a girl. Very, very kind. I owe her and her family a debt. Now. Scones?'

'What the fuck?' It was the one called Alex, standing there holding the ceremonial sword one of her lovers had given her.

'I wasn't sure if we had another tour through today or not, but

I've put some scones in anyway.'

'Pumpkin scones, izzit?' Alex said, face twisted along the lines of his scars. Was he insulting her as an old lady or was there more to it? He snapped his teeth at her. 'Something we can get our teeth into, ay? They don't call me Al Dente for nothing.'

'Nobody calls you that. No one ever will. Faggot,' Ike said. As he turned, she saw the outline of a gun tucked into the back of his waistband.

'Means "to the tooth".' He tapped his front teeth with a fingernail. 'But Alex will do. Don't worry about it.'

'More like the Tooth Fairy,' Wayne said.

'Always give a lady a cuppa,' the older one, Chook, said. 'Puts her at ease and a lady at ease is the best kind of lady there is.' He was silver-haired and neat and she supposed older ladies, older than her, might find him charming.

'Such fatherly advice,' Alex said.

'Fuck you, I'm not your bloody father,' Chook said.

Pera pulled the scones out of the oven and tipped them into the tea-towel-lined basket. She set the table with jam and plates. 'Who wants to whip the cream, boys? Takes a good steady hand.'

She poured a bottle of cream into her favourite blue and white striped bowl and handed it, plus a hand beater she'd found in the rubble, to Wayne. 'Go on. Don't overwhip it. Light and fluffy.'

He did as he was told.

'Why don't you use an electrical beater? Seems stupid to do it by hand. My mum had all the mod cons,' Alex said. 'My second wife used the one I gave her. She didn't want to at first, fucken pissed off with me, can you believe it? Give her a present and she cracks the shits? She did use it, though.'

His eyes shifted slightly and Pera thought that, at least, perhaps, he felt guilty about his wife. Not proud.

She put the kettle on.

'We don't usually have tours in the off-season, but I'm happy to show you around though, as you're friends of Wayne. Have any of you been to Sinclair House before? You've probably come for the afternoon tea. I'm famous for it. And this lovely jam from a neighbour, which is heavenly.'

Talking talking talking so they couldn't ask her any questions about the children upstairs.

'You here alone? Just you and all your stuff?' Ike asked her, looking her direct in the eyes. 'No hubby? We heard kids shouting.'

She thought for a minute, wondering if she could fake a husband who'd be back soon. She didn't think so, and she didn't think they'd care anyway. 'Only me,' she said. 'Footloose and fancy-free.'

'You were supposed to be away. Grandma said,' Wayne said again.

'I was all set to go. But I'm old and tired, Wayne. You young people can't imagine such a thing. But I'm tired. And I do like being here, alone in my house. Looking at all my treasures. All my stuff, as you say.'

They exchanged glances and she knew she'd picked a good ploy to keep them interested.

'And those kids?' In the silence that followed Ike's question, they could hear footsteps.

'Ghosts,' she said. 'I've got a whole tour of ghosts going on upstairs.'

She fussed around at the sink while they whispered. She felt bolstered by the fact they didn't want her to hear; it meant they were seriously considering not killing her. She ran through their names in her head. She had to humanise the men. If she saw them as evil, she wouldn't be able to make the connections with them she knew she needed.

'Nice place you've got here,' Alex said, scratching at his side. He hadn't eaten much, only picked at a few crumbs.

'Except it's a pus hole. You should maintain your property,' Devon said. 'How the place is even still standing I don't know.'

'They built them well in the old days. After afternoon tea, I can show you around.' She jangled her large keychain. Each door in the house had a different key. She knew every one by sight, no need for labels. It was part of her performance.

'Jeezus,' Ike said. They couldn't smash the doors open; too solid. It was going to be easier with the keys.

'I know! People are surprised that I know which key matches which door, but I do, every one.'

'Got anything else to eat apart from scones?' Chook said. He was a stout man who clearly loved his food.

'I don't cook much. Too much else to do! But I have lots of frozen stuff in the freezer. And soup. Always a pot of soup on the go.'

She looked in the pot on the stove and added a few chopped vegetables from the fridge.

'Always be nice to old ladies,' Alex said. 'They know how to make soup.' He smiled, his teeth shining.

'Old ladies'll destroy you,' Chook said. 'They know everything, especially what you're doing wrong.'

Ike pointed at Pera's keys. 'How about that tour, ay? You can feed your fat face later, Chook.'

'How much is it for a group?' Chook said, patting his pockets as if he intended to pay.

'You're a group of lovely strong men, how about you help bring some firewood up from the Underhistory and then I'll give you a tour all your own?' As she said this, she wondered if she'd made a tactical error. For most people, paying for something meant they respected it more. She wasn't sure these men had any money, though. And she was hoping this would distract them from the others. If she sent them down to the Underhistory . . .

'The Underhistory?'

'The cellar. You'll find as we move around the house my family had a lot of sweet names for the rooms. I feel like I'm honouring their memory by keeping them.'

'Did they all die?' Devon said. He was the one who ran through the leaves. She wouldn't mention that, though. Wouldn't admit she'd been watching them.

'That's what I'm famous for!' Pera said. 'How my family died. I'll tell you the story as we take the tour. Are any of you scared of ghosts? We might see some along the way. I can't guarantee it, but . . .'

Ike told them to hang on; he needed to shit. They heard him in there, theatrically grunting and groaning. He called out, 'Hey, Devon, that was a massive shit. It'll be all right if your mother cooks it,' and she watched Devon shrink further and further into himself, the anger going inside. She wondered who he would unleash it on.

She couldn't let him. She said, 'I'm famous for my family dying.

I was drawn into tragedy. I'd be unknown otherwise. Fame has changed me, and it's changed my house. I think that every time a person comes in, it changes again.'

'We're not keen on fame. Not in our line of work,' Ike said, coming out of the bathroom.

'I loved it. Mostly. Fame is never what people expect. Still, it's got me plenty of free drinks over the years. I'm almost forgotten now, though. Like most people who have fleeting fame beyond their own control.'

At that moment, the sound of running footsteps. It was one of the boys from the tour, red-faced and excited.

'I found you!' he said. 'Mum asks can we keep going?'

'Is she feeling all right?'

The boy shrugged. 'She always feels sick so she says she's used to it.' Pera hadn't yet figured out what was wrong with the mother, but it was clear the family all worked around her illness.

The men tensed. Ike said, 'Who's this, then? Great-grandson?' He was trying to insult her but she wasn't sure why. She didn't mind, though; it meant he was still focused on her.

'Oh, didn't I say? There's a tour in progress. We can join them if you like.'

'That's their minivan out the front, is it?' Ike said. 'I thought you said you were alone.'

'I am! But they're part of a tour. If you'd been here on time you would have started with them,' she gently scolded. 'I don't usually take people who are late.'

'Yeah, you said,' Chook said.

16

THE NEWS ROOM (ARCHIVES)

The tour group had found their way to the News Room and was clustered outside the door. Ike and Alex watched them. Ike's head tilted, assessing, and Pera said, 'We're nearly done, then they're all going to the mother's surprise birthday party. She knows but she isn't letting on!' She paused, as if telling Ike this secret meant something. 'They'll need to be out of here soon or people will miss them,' she said. 'I've not told them all the stories of this place. Have I, Wayne? All the secret treasures.'

Wayne said, 'It'll be all right, Ike. It will.'

Pera hoped so. She let the tour group into the News Room, and Lucky began exploring every nook and cranny, peering at the walls, which were entirely covered with yellowing newspapers. The mother sat on one of Pera's brocade chairs, smiling. Pera would describe it as 'smiling bravely' if she were a writer. The dad stood by her, his hand on her shoulder, as if he could heal her simply by touch.

'Look who I found! Some strapping gentlemen to join our group!' Pera said. 'The more the merrier!'

Only the mother seemed to notice her change of clothing, and Pera said quietly, 'I felt the need for a bit of comfort. Can't look fancy all day long!' She cleared her throat. 'As I mentioned to the others, the ghosts of soldiers who were billeted here before the war go marching through the house sometimes. These are their names.' She pulled out a newspaper from a folder on the table and showed them an article that listed the ones who were posted to the original house. Some clever reporter trying to make her home the death house or something.

'So, wait, all of the soldiers who were billeted here died?' the dad said.

'Oh, no, there were maybe five who didn't. You can see there, on the next page. But a sadly high percentage.' She showed them a group photo hanging on the wall, the soldiers clustered by the flame tree.

The Men, as Pera thought of them, said nothing. They looked at each other, sussing things out. Then Ike said, 'Bullshit.'

1941

The funeral was two days after Pera's tenth birthday. Her first birthday without her family was almost unimaginable but she did imagine it, lying in the soft grass in the Bees' garden, dreaming of the most perfect birthday ever.

That evening the horsey brothers Harry and George came by with presents and cake. Mrs Bee said, 'Oh, I feel so awful I didn't know,' but Pera gave her a big hug and a kiss and said, 'I'm so lucky to have you.'

She woke up at all hours and wandered the house, using the bathroom, pouring herself a glass of milk drawn at dawn from the cows on the farm, nibbling the lovely honey-dipped biscuits that sat on the bench, covered only with a thin mesh to keep the flies off. The house felt small compared to hers and she rather liked it. She knew where everyone was all the time, could hear and identify footsteps. At home the kitchen was so far away she'd never go in the night-time, nor the toilet. She'd hold on till dawn broke.

The officials identified most of the dead, even those on the aeroplane, and they at least counted the dead people in the sheep shed and the chapel, even if they didn't name them. All the grown-ups tried to keep word of the Sinclair family funeral from her, as if that would make it not true. But she wanted to be there. She had to be there. This was her family. It was a massive affair, with hundreds of people she'd never met, all of them wanting a piece of her. She thought that Hazel should have been part of the funeral, too, even though she'd been gone half a decade. Hazel's funeral had been quiet, secretive, trying to avoid the press attention.

Everyone said, 'They are with Jesus now.' Pera kept a picture of Jesus by her bed. He looked kind. She hoped he liked roast beef and potatoes so her dad would be happy and that there were wide green fields for Hazel to run wildly with the dogs, and saucers of milk, and a huge kitchen for her mother to bake biscuits in.

That's what she hoped.

She had lots of people to keep her company at the funeral. The shopkeepers from town, the policemen, the neighbours, her friends Harry and George, who tried to make her laugh and did, when they pretended to be blind and kept bumping into things. Her only living relatives, Uncle Alan, Auntie Paula's widower, living overseas but back for the funeral, and his son Frankie who was two years older than Pera and horrible. He kept kicking her ankles, spitting on the floor, pointing at people and laughing. He called her stupid and ugly. Uncle Alan told him to stop but that made no difference.

'He misses his mother,' Uncle Alan said.

'I miss my whole family but it doesn't make me be awful,' Pera said loudly.

Auntie Paula was Pera's mum's sister, who died in 1939 of something – maybe pneumonia. Pera wasn't sure because it was one of those things you didn't talk about.

Uncle Alan had adored his wife. She was a tiny, lively woman, given to loud laughter.

Paula had left a gap in her mother, too. Pera remembered that. There was the Hazel gap, and the Aunt Paula gap.

Hope had told silly stories about Auntie Paula and Uncle Alan. She said Auntie Paula had died because of a failed murder–suicide. Well, not failed murder. She said Uncle Alan was evil. But he was a very sweet man, out of his depth as a sole parent. Pera's mother used to talk about Cousin Frankie and how awful he was when he was little, how glad she was she hadn't had boys. Always dirty, no matter how often his mother caught him with a wet face-towel. He wouldn't eat anything other than jam sandwiches, and refused to use cutlery. He wet the bed on purpose and in fact went to the toilet anywhere he felt like. He broke things any time he came to visit.

Pera wondered if in fact it was pure exhaustion that killed his mother.

The local newspaper published a special eight-page wrap-around for the funeral, listing the names of the dead with pictures and descriptions. Some of the pictures were from her dad's camera and they made a big deal out of that. The idea made her cry and wish she'd smiled for him. Mrs Bee didn't think Pera should see it but Mr Bee said no good hiding from the truth and at least they're making a big deal out of her. There was a half-page on Pera, 'daughter of financial adviser to the prime minister', and she hugged herself, feeling guilty pleasure at it.

The only bad thing was that they used an annoying old picture, before she had her hair cut, and they called her Temperance. There were also lots of photos of her beautiful sister Justine. The other sisters were described as 'strong-minded' and 'clever' but only Justine was called 'beautiful'.

There were photos of people hanging around the gates, wanting to get in, as if they could breathe in the trauma, suck up the death as it lay thick on the ground. They'd interviewed one man, a mean old thing Pera had never seen before. He had nothing to do with any of it, but he was furious the police wouldn't let him in. He thought it was his right. His right! To go into her house and look at it as if it was some kind of entertainment.

1993

Of course, she let people in now. But that was different. She was the one who decided.

'I'll give you a few minutes in the News Room,' she said to the tour group. 'People get lost in here! I've laid out the most relevant articles on the table, but feel free to look through any of the folders.'

The three children looked bored, and she showed them the corner where all the comics were kept. It wouldn't occupy them for long, but a short time was better than no time at all.

She never threw out that special edition. All those lives she couldn't save. She later bought dozens of copies, and used them to paper this room.

1941

The next time her photo was in the papers, it was one taken at the Bees'. A journalist wanted to know what she thought about the looters. Mr Bee said that was a daft question, but they kept at her. Finally she said, 'My dad always said that looters would be cursed.' He'd seen it during the war. 'So anyone who takes things from my house will be cursed.'

That got her the front page again.

The newspapers never stopped loving Pera. They never turned on her like they did on politicians or movie stars. The sole survivor of a terrible tragedy.

She was followed everywhere she went for a while by journalists wanting to know what she was doing. All sorts of people – from the local politician who came to school once to talk about the importance of loyalty, to a famous television actor – clustered around like gnats, trying to get their faces on screen.

For a fortnight at least, every news show opened with the footage of her walking through the jonquils. She hated watching it. Could still feel Mr Wittner's hand on her shoulders, forcing her into position, and on her cheeks, that awful joke of making her smile.

'Last footage taken by the PM,' the announcers said, over and over again, her dancing through the flowers, hiding behind the tree, poking her head out, wishing they would all go away, not wanting to be in the film, *I won't, I don't want to.*

And yet there she was, over and over again.

They hardly ever named her. She was 'witness to the tragedy, a young girl of nine' even though she was now ten.

Then they left her alone for a bit (except for 'Sole survivor returns to school' and 'Sole survivor goes horse riding') plus articles about her murdered sister. 'Were they all meant to die at the hands of the killer and had somehow cheated fate until now?'

1993

Wayne stood close to Pera while the rest of The Men explored the room. The tour group read the news clippings and looked at the photos; The Men opened cupboards and archive boxes. She wasn't sure what they were looking for; money, she assumed. Or her family jewels, which they perhaps imagined she had lying around.

Some of the photos on the walls showed famous arrests, others mugshots, others childhood pictures of criminals. One of the photos was of one of the young soldiers posted to her house, who'd survived the First World War and gone on to become an arsonist, finally killed when a house he set fire to collapsed on him.

17

POSTHUMOUS GALLERY (ART GALLERY 4)

From the News Room they moved to another portrait gallery.

'Ours was the first haunted house tour in Australia. I got the idea when I was in York; they do a marvellous tour there.'

The father said, 'Have you visited all the other haunted houses?'

She had visited other historical houses when she was deciding how to manage hers. Artists' colony? No, she decided. Too many creative egos. Too much fragility. She didn't want the drama.

'Unlike the National Gallery, which prefers only to display pictures of those painted while alive, this is a collection of posthumous portraits. There is a superstition amongst curators that a posthumous portrait carries the ghost with it. I'll let you decide that for yourselves. This room works best with the underglow of the floor lights, so we're going to turn down the main ones. Everyone all right with that? Take a seat if you want. Or lean up against a wall. Many people feel dizzy.'

She'd listen, see how The Men breathed. See if they would be affected by her stories, by the possibility of ghosts. See if she could share her nightmares with them, ones she'd been having for so long they no longer frightened her. Recurring nightmares like the one where she was chained to a gravestone, with ice-cold smoke (it didn't make any sense) rising from her ankle to her knees to her waist, her neck, her head ... she always woke up choking. The first time she'd had it was after her tenth birthday.

1941

Most nights in the Bees' house, nightmares woke her. Shadows, looters, ghosts, family still alive but damaged, someone trapped in the Underhistory.

Finally, Mrs Bee said – and like many, she didn't say anything until she was cross, rather than early on when it was a minor irritation – 'You can't go wandering around at any hour.'

'What hour can I wander around?'

Mrs Bee was a kind woman and this made her smile. 'From five o'clock in the morning at the earliest. We'll get you a little bedside clock.'

They did, and every day it stopped.

Finally, Mrs Bee said, 'Let's go to your house. You need to see it, I think. It will be beautiful again, it really will.'

Mrs Bee's car was bouncier than her father's had been. They rattled up the driveway, Mrs Bee chattering endlessly. Pera liked the sound of her voice. It was so ordinary. She didn't believe in ghosts but she believed in Jesus and that was comforting. Mrs Bee parked the car.

What was left of Pera's house was surrounded by piles of

rubble. In the grounds she saw men playing rugby. 'Men will always play sport,' Mrs Bee said. 'It makes them feel better. Good on them, I say.' They were there to clean up the mess.

There were floral tributes covering the surviving front steps, thousands of them, Pera thought. Most still had colour but all were beginning to decay and there was the thick smell of it in the air. A dark, rich perfume she never forgot.

She spent the whole afternoon laying out the dying flowers in rows on the lawn. She remembered what the caretaker had always told her, 'Wait long enough, it'll come good.'

Once she'd laid the flowers out, she and Mrs Bee walked around the house. It wasn't safe to enter; she'd have to come on her own, without adult supervision, if she wanted to go inside.

'Let's see if we can find a treasure. A memory. One special thing,' Mrs Bee said.

They found quite a few things, although Pera realised a lot had been stolen. How could anyone steal dead people's things? They would all be cursed; she had no doubt of that. Even the head of the local council took a 'souvenir', everyone knew. A battered cigarette case he said had belonged to the prime minister. He kept it on his desk as if he was the hero somehow.

There was no way of telling what part of the rubble had been her bedroom. If she could sneak inside, she might be able to figure it out, but for now, all she could do was turn over piles of stone and metal, looking for familiar things. She found a child's blanket, charred on the edges but intact. She didn't think it was hers, unless it was a keepsake her mother had stashed in a cupboard. There was a small battered suitcase as well, cracked open and empty, and she placed the blanket in the suitcase. They smelt of fire and felt greasy to the touch, but she couldn't bring herself to throw them away. She would find a place for them.

The building started to creak and Mrs Bee said, 'We better head off.'

Then Pera saw a goldfish tank Charity had received for Christmas. Split in half, dried up, all the fish shrivelled on the ground.

'The pond!' Pera shouted at Mrs Bee, and she ran her hardest, as fast as she had run to the fire, until she reached the water.

They floated, belly up. Bloated. Mrs Bee ran up, panting, and stood by her.

'Why did they die?' Pera asked.

'Ground vibrations, maybe, from the crash. Or fuel from the plane?'

'It's because I didn't feed them. I killed them all,' Pera said, although she had never fed these ones; somehow they fed themselves.

She stood up on the hanging rock, looking at her destroyed house. She felt certain she caused the accident, brought the plane down. She was so angry with them all for forcing her to be in the photo, and her mother calling her a 'silly thing' which was mean and horrible. She was so cross she must have wished it. She stopped the plane's clocks and made it crash.

After this visit the nightmares faded and eventually she slept through the night. Sometimes she'd wake with the faint echo of ghosts in her thoughts and she would take a trip back home, which seemed to quieten it all.

1993

'Lady?'

Pera opened her eyes. She must have dozed off for a minute. The chair she was sitting in was comfortable and she'd always been calmed by the sound of voices. One of the boys stood looking at her, concerned.

'Oh, my gosh. I am sorry! How long have we been in here?' It wasn't dark, although the lights were still down. 'How did you all go? What did you see?' She turned the lights on and saw that the mother and two of the children were no longer there. Her heart froze for a moment; surely nothing bad had happened while she slept?

'It was a bit scary!' the father said. 'The younger kids couldn't quite cope.'

Ike said, 'Yeah, mate, fucken terrifying.'

The father put his shoulders back. 'It's amazing what the imagination does, especially when there's a grain of belief.'

Lucky raised his eyebrows and grimaced at the father. He perhaps understood more quickly who they were in the room with.

His son said, 'Yeah, Dad.' Pera imagined they would have conflict in years to come, as all children and their parents do, but in this moment they were united.

Ike watched the exchange, his arms crossed over his chest, and Pera wondered if he wished he could have an ordinary interaction like that, a momentary connection between people who loved one another.

'Sometimes I wonder what it would be like to change places,' she said quietly to Ike. 'To live someone else's life.'

He looked at her in surprise. 'Fuck that,' he said. 'I don't want anyone else's life.'

'Sorry, Mrs Sinclair,' Wayne said. 'He can't help swearing.'

'I don't mind.'

The boy watched with a delighted horror. Clearly adults rarely swore in his presence.

The younger boy poked his head through the doorway. 'This room is boring, I want to go back to the money place.'

'You mean the Mint?'

'Yeah.'

'Yeah,' Ike said. 'Let's go to the money place.'

If she'd doubted before that The Men weren't quite right, despite their prison-issue shoes, she was certain now. They weren't saddened by sad things.

'We can go there again at the end if we have time, and everyone behaves themselves,' Pera said.

18

THE BOX ROOM (ART GALLERY 5)

Pera led them along another corridor. *This one needs a bit of a fix-up,* she thought every time she walked it. It was one of the darkest, and there was a dull smell of decay. She wasn't sure where it was coming from; she needed to find that out before too long. She unlocked the door to the Box Room.

'Now, this is another little gallery. In the old house, our box room was full of empty hat boxes, suitcases, valises, briefcases; all the things to contain an everyday existence. It all went in the fire. Burnt up.'

The room was full of boxes. Along one wall were neatly stacked, variously sized, cigar boxes. On benches and tables were displayed music boxes, lacquered boxes from Japan, carved sandalwood boxes from Indonesia, small wooden boxes from artists across the world, folded paper boxes, painted cardboard boxes, and more. On the floor, one removal box, with the words SITTING ROOM written in black.

'Such a collection!' the mother said. 'Where did they all come from?'

'Left behind. Given to me. One of those cigar boxes was my father's, I've been told. It was given to me by a friend of his but I don't remember which one. My grandmother owned a musical box that was stolen; perhaps one of those is hers. This one,' she held up a bright green lacquered box, 'was found in the arms of a young woman who died of a broken heart when her fiancé was hanged. An innocent man, it was proven. So many are innocent, aren't they?' She was worried this might be too obvious, but even Ike nodded. 'True love is a beautiful and tragic thing.'

Devon laughed. 'Love is just sex, babe, with nicer words.'

'Jeez you're a loser,' Wayne said. 'Ignore him, Mrs Sinclair. He thinks he's a big man.'

Ike flicked Devon's skull with his forefinger. 'Oww!' Devon sounded like a child.

'Was she someone you knew?' the mother asked. Her eyes widened at Pera. It was clear she knew something was not quite right but didn't want to worry her children.

'Not a close friend. Someone I was at school with.' She waved the lacquered box again. 'Don't open any of them! The superstition is that if you open a box, the ghost of the owner will attach itself to you.' Devon was about to open a box but he paused. 'That's what I think, anyway. The memories have somehow trapped the ghosts.'

There was usually at least one who opened a box, facing up to the dare. This time, most of them did, all these men not wanting to be the one to show fear.

The father opened a cigar box. The younger son said, 'No, Dad!' but he did it anyway. The older son said nothing. He was there reluctantly; you could see that. Dragged along by loving parents holding on to a time when family holidays were fun for all. Pera thought, *Wayne and his friends were already on the streets by this age. Committing crimes. They'd already made their choices in life.*

The younger son opened a musical box which played 'Pop Goes the Weasel', which made Devon and Wayne laugh.

Ike opened a small black lacquered box; inside it was velvet-lined, slightly torn, so he ran his fingers under it, plucking out a key. 'What's this for?'

'Oooh, that's a sign. It must be. It's for the booze cupboard!' Pera said. She was dry in the throat, and the thought of a drink, some nice clear vodka, lifted her spirits. She opened a concealed panel and unlocked the cabinet inside. 'Who wants?' she said. She handed out small hotel bottles of liquor to The Men, but the parents and Lucky declined.

Wayne opened a large chest. Moths fluttered out; inside was an old coat that should have been thrown away long ago. 'Someone died in there,' Pera said. She felt the usual sense of anticipation, of slightly sick delight, at the prospect of telling them a story that might upset them. 'It was a young girl, a relative of mine, but I've never been sure how she was connected. She hid in there to get away from her father, who was going to beat her for speaking back. But no one missed her; her father drank himself into a stupor. So no one looked, and she went to sleep. Even though there was some air in the trunk, the coat, they say, snuggled her so close she couldn't breathe, and so she didn't wake up. What do you think she dreamed of, as she died? Her beloved pony? Her mother's roast dinner? You should all think about that. Think about what you might dream of. Anyone want to hop in, give it a try?'

No one did, so she slowly closed the lid.

Devon opened up a fake book and found a small pipe inside. He pocketed it quietly; Pera said nothing. Better not shame him in front of people.

Chook lifted a heavy metal box. 'This looks interesting!' he said. It held papers; nothing of importance, clippings of deaths that Pera had collected over the years.

Alex opened a tin. 'I thought there might be biscuits,' he said. 'Hungry, I guess.'

She regarded them all. 'How do you all feel? Any different? You won't always notice it straight away. But there might be a weight on your shoulders. Or a sense of the wind in your hair, those of you who have hair.' Here she looked pointedly at Chook. Ike laughed. 'Bald old cunt,' he said. He didn't apologise for the swearing.

This room should have made her sad but these things weren't hers. She remembered none of them.

19

THE DEAD TOY ROOM (THE TOY ROOM)

This room did make her sad. It was full of children's items discovered in the debris: a small gold locket, a rattle, the sole of a shoe, and the blanket and suitcase she'd found that day with Mrs Bee. In the old house, this room had been their toy room. A place of joy and play.

'This room is dedicated to the pilot's daughters. They were with him, you know. A special treat, he'd told them. He'd fly them over the Blue Mountains.'

The mother and father put their arms around their children. Parents did this, without fail. The only time one hadn't, Pera talked to the kid, *Are you okay?* And he wasn't, so she'd called the authorities. It wasn't the first time she interfered, and it wasn't the last. She understood people, after all these years. She could pick a type most times.

'Why do you think he crashed his plane into your house?' Lucky asked. Someone always asked on every tour, even though it was a matter of public record.

She guessed they wanted a meaningful answer. 'I sometimes

still think it was my fault. My sisters and I believed there was a malevolent ghost in our cellar. In the Underhistory. A man who'd died violently and wasn't leaving until he'd had his revenge. He somehow confused the pilot, made him think he'd reached an airport. My fault because I'd been down there the week before, on a dare.

'For years, I destroyed myself, believing it was my fault. If it wasn't the ghost I'd angered, then it was because when the plane flew over, the clocks stopped, like they always do around me. The plane fell out of the sky. I'm still not sure that isn't it, no matter what we know now about the pilot. I'm still not convinced it wasn't my fault.' Her throat caught. This wasn't a performance; she rarely confessed this. 'No matter what anyone says,' she told them. 'Regardless of all I know. I am convinced I caused it.'

'It wasn't your fault!' the father said. 'Everyone knows that.' Lucky stood with his arms crossed, nodding his head.

'You're right. You are. It was deliberate. The pilot killed his wife, took his two daughters on the plane, and crashed it into my home. The girls weren't on the manifest, that's why it took so long to figure out, and with the mother dead no one missed them. He'd given them false names. That blanket belonged to one of them. A relative identified it. I'm still trying to find some reason for it. Why, what, how?'

'Would it help to have those answers?' Lucky asked her.

Once she would have said yes, but so many years had passed she was no longer sure.

There were many theories about the crash at first. One was that the pilot had an epileptic fit so somebody else took over the controls and they didn't know what they were doing. There was the idea that Pera's father had enemies, failed men, throwaway people who blamed him for not saving them from financial collapse when it was not his job to advise them at all. That the pilot was one of those men.

The truth was that the pilot had followed the press like a homing pigeon. He knew exactly where the prime minister was because of all the journalists' parked cars. The *Sun* newspaper published the last postcard he sent to them. Pera kept a copy of that issue, along with her other historical newspapers. The picture was of Parliament House in Canberra and on the back it read, 'We are the nameless ones whom the law ignores. We are the good fathers and we deserve more and so do our children.'

Pera described this to her listeners. 'Of course, he wasn't nameless at all, just a pathetic murderous twit.'

Ike laughed and the others followed. 'Strong language,' he said, which made her smile.

'It's always made me cross. "Nameless". Rubbish. There were several families living in our sheep shed. All killed. No one knew their names. That's what you call nameless. Nameless, he says!' She snorted. She wasn't sure why she was telling them all this, particularly The Men. 'I do feel an enormous amount of anger towards the pilot, who took everything from me.'

1941

Once the pilot's postcard was published, the press were after her for opinions. But she was only ten. What possible opinion could she have beyond sadness? How angry could a ten-year-old be?

They asked her what she thought of capital punishment, but she had to ask what that was.

'People like deserters, or murderers. Maybe they don't deserve to live, so we put them to death. People like the pilot who flew his plane into your house.'

It seemed absolutely horrifying, hearing it for the first time.

'Nobody should kill anyone,' she said, and that made the front page. They had a quote from Uncle Alan who said, 'If he wasn't dead I'd kill him.' This annoyed Mr and Mrs Bee because Uncle Alan hadn't even been to see Pera since the funeral – too busy with his company over in England, whatever it was, although he was looking after Pera's financial interests at least – and yet there he was being quoted. They were not impressed.

There was another wrap-around in the newspaper, once the inquest was complete and the apparent truth was known. 'Piecing together a Hideous Act'. They had new photos of her, and they quoted her as saying, 'Every morning I wake up and don't know where I am. The place I was is gone.'

1993

'There are ghosts of children in the Dead Toy Room. If you quieten down, tune out all other noise, you can hear the spirits talking. A word here and there. They'll make you sad, not scared. These are children who never got the chance to grow up. My sisters, the Wittner boys, and those poor children from the sheep shed. Just to mention a few.'

'Are you lonely?' the mother asked her quietly. Pera had been asked this before, usually out of pity. This woman asked her out of a desire to know.

Pera nodded. 'I do get lonely. There are times I enjoy being alone, others when I think this house should be full, with my five sisters, four kids to each of us. And some of those kids would be parents themselves by now, so more and more and more. Instead there's only me. I should have married again, I suppose. But like I told you, I couldn't carry a baby.' Pera couldn't stop the tears forming and the woman put her arm around her shoulders.

'I'm so sorry.'

Pera could have sobbed. She couldn't bear to think of this small and loving family being without their mother. If she could give something up, she would. She'd give a decade of her own life. She'd sacrifice . . . she'd sacrifice any one of the new arrivals, even Wayne, who she'd known since he was a baby.

1942

Mrs Bee fell pregnant with Wayne's father soon after they found out about the pilot, and that changed things as far as the living arrangements went. Pera was still welcome to stay with the Bees, but she felt a physical restlessness of spirit, in her legs and arms, propelling her to pack her bag and run. She left a note for Mr and Mrs Bee saying *Thank you*, and *It isn't your fault*, and *You are very kind*.

She only made it a few streets away before Mr Bee drove along beside her and gently suggested she come back home.

She ran time and time again over the next nine months, never making it more than a few miles. Finally Mrs Bee said she spent too long worrying and out of sight out of mind would work best. It was because she had a baby now and they needed all their energy for the little one.

Pera understood. She told them she could babysit if they wanted her to.

So Pera was sent to live with Uncle Alan, who had come back to live in Australia and was a perfectly fine person, and her cousin Frankie, who was not. She didn't want to live anywhere near him.

The newsmen followed her to Uncle Alan's house. 'Survivor on the move again'.

Her cousin Frankie was worse than he'd been at the funeral. He would push her, kick at her heels, throw something of hers out the window, snarl at her, snarl at anyone who entered the house in fact. There were always lots of people; Uncle Alan loved parties so their home was often full of laughing and dancing. Pera admired all the beautiful women who came, and the handsome men who seemed so charming and funny.

There were sometimes children at these parties. The adults liked to drink a lot of wine and beer, and they tended to forget there were children about. So Frankie made them play War Preparation, which mostly involved missiles, with the girls being the Germans.

It was never fun.

Frankie told her she was a drain. That she sucked up all the money. But the money was hers; the wills clearly gave it all to her. It was supposed to be divided amongst the five girls but she was the last one. Uncle Alan managed it all for her. He had plenty of money of his own and was a generous man. A good businessman, for all his gentleness and love of a good party. He liked to laugh, chuckling at Pera's long tales of her day. She embellished to entertain him. She loved to tell a story.

Eventually he broached the subject of clearing away her family's home. Pulling the whole thing down and maybe selling the land. But she was hysterical at the idea of any of it being thrown away.

'I'm not saying it's rubbish,' he said. 'We'll reuse it all. Sell it. It'll make you lots more money and then you could buy a nice place in Sydney or Melbourne when you're grown up,' and she had to agree it would be fun to live in the city. She didn't want to lose Sinclair House though, not with her being the last of them.

Frankie scared off any woman who came close to being a new mother. It was stupid of him; his life would be better if his dad had a lady friend. The ladies liked Uncle Alan but his dead wife was his one true love.

To be honest Pera found him a bit boring at times. She was often bored by people. No one was interesting enough to match her. Not that she made it obvious.

Frankie made her feel small, and he physically surrounded her most of the day so she felt she couldn't breathe. She complained bitterly to Uncle Alan, but all he said was, 'It's here or your grandparents.' There was no way she was staying with her grandparents, her mother's parents. They rarely spoke to her, certainly didn't comfort her. They lived in Mosman in a lovely little house that most people wouldn't complain about. Her grandfather had been a missionary in Fiji and it had changed him for the worse. Some people travel and the best of them emerges; his concept of himself as a superior being was instead increased. Whenever Pera stayed with them she was always in trouble for shoelaces untied, or leaving a scrap of food, or for not praying loud enough, hard enough, for not being the Virgin Mary who was pure and perfect. Grandfather spoke mostly in Bible verses, and her grandmother barely spoke at all.

There was no way she could live with them. But there was no way she could carry on living with Frankie either. Cousin Frankie liked to tell her she was taken by the fairies as a baby, that her family hadn't really been her family. 'The fairies like to swap babies round so no one belongs to anyone,' he said. He would cut out news clippings about dead families, saying, 'Maybe this one is yours.'

It was her own fault. She'd tried to convince *him* that he was a changeling, placed into this human family weak and sickly and soon to die, but he wasn't having any of it. It sounded so much more convincing when he said a twisted version back to her. He was better at lying than she was.

The worst thing was something she was too scared to tell Uncle Alan about, something Frankie hid under the house. He wouldn't tell her where he got it. Did he steal it from the ruins of her house, the day of the funeral? She wondered this, sometimes. If her father had brought the thing back from his travels. It wasn't the sort of thing a father would show a daughter. It was the worst thing she'd ever seen or ever would see, apart from the crash.

It was a rat king. Fifteen or more rodents, it was hard to tell, their tails locked together. They couldn't even reach around to eat each other so they were all complete. Rictus faces. Dried out like mummies. It was a tangled mess like the accident was. They had starved to death because they'd struggled against each other, all wanting to go this way, no that, tugging and pulling and fighting until they died.

1993

'Is it freezing in this bloody house or is it just me?' Wayne said.

'It gets colder every time someone dies,' Pera said. She raided the lost property for warm jumpers and it was hilarious, all of them actually laughing, as The Men dressed in pink cardigans, teenagers' hoodies, big fluffy handknitted jumpers.

She liked it cold. Mostly she left the rooms unheated. They'd built the walls triple thick, and all the windows were double glazed. The builders had joked, 'You could easily gas someone in here, it's so airtight.' She remembered that now.

Her bedroom, the kitchen and sitting room were all heated with electric fires. As for the rest of the house? If people shivered on the tour, all the better. 'Shivering and goosebumps make you more alert,' she told them. 'The ghosts like cold people. No one knows why.'

The mother shook, and the father took off his jacket and gave it to her.

'You'll be off soon,' Ike said. 'Don't want to be late.'

The mother said, 'We won't,' then, 'Oops!' as she realised she'd given away that she knew about the surprise party. 'I mean, late to what?' she said.

'Nothing!' the father said.

'Something!' the daughter said.

'You should go soon,' Ike said. The father almost responded but the mother begged him with her eyes.

'We will, we will,' she said.

20

OFF TO SEE OATES (THE BREAKFAST ROOM)

Pera said to Ike, 'I'll move them on as soon as I can. Okay? Then you and your friends and I can explore better. But I don't want to rush them or they'll complain. I've had people do that, you know. They like to be scared in a haunted house, but not really scared, if you know what I mean?'

'I know what you mean,' Ike said. 'And I think you know what we mean.'

She nodded.

Pera led them all upstairs to the Breakfast Room. They passed a tall mannequin dressed in a bloodied butcher's apron. Distracted by that, none of them noticed the outline of a door behind it, and that was its purpose.

A small dining table sat in the corner. It was overcast at the minute but often the sun would pour in. She kept this table set with beautiful china and glassware, although she never used it.

'This was the place my father liked to eat in the mornings. It's a nook, really, but he'd come here, with the sun streaming in, and he'd read the morning papers. We didn't disturb him when he was in here. He always said, "I'm off to see Oates." Visitors would think he meant he'd be having oats for breakfast but no!' Pera couldn't help laughing. 'He took so long at breakfast, he said it was like Captain Oates, you know. Antarctic explorer, "I may be some time"?' The father got it and laughed. Chook seemed to understand but was not the type to laugh at someone else's clever joke.

It was a gorgeous little corner of the house. She remembered it well and her builders had replicated it perfectly. Servants' stairs led to the kitchen below, where breakfast had been made every morning they lived here.

The mother smiled, and the youngest boy said his favourite breakfast was Froot Loops, and for a moment, Pera felt a sense of joy.

Then Ike swept the table clean of crockery, causing a crash that made them all jump, and the parents grab their children close.

'Sorry,' he said, looking directly at Pera.

The parents hustled the children out into the hallway, leaving Pera with The Men and Lucky. 'My father sometimes entertained in here. Had business meetings. Should we have a business meeting, gentlemen?'

Pera pulled out bottles of wine, of whisky, she found glasses, and The Men cheered. Wayne said, 'To business, right?'

She smiled but knew that she had no power beyond the illusion she'd drawn over them all, the pretence that this was ordinary, normal, that all of them were the same kind of people. She opened another secret cupboard, pulled out bags of beer nuts, and more small bottles of liquor.

'Do you have booze stacked in every room?' Ike asked.

'Pretty much!' Pera said. She didn't make the joke about Temperance and lack thereof; she didn't think any of them would understand it and didn't want to insult them by explaining. She'd heard enough of the joke over the years, anyway, and seen the headlines: 'Will Temperance Take the Oath?'

1946

The press would drift away, but then something new would happen and they'd be back, looking for further comment on the pilot or the prime minister, every time anything relevant happened. She was twelve, then thirteen, then fourteen, then fifteen.

She ran away again when Frankie put the rat king in her bed, jealous of all the attention she got; she wasn't sure she deserved it herself.

She hadn't run for a while, but this time she was serious. She was fifteen; she could look after herself. She'd go back home, sort out a few rooms that were still standing. Get a job in the town so she'd have food, but there was so much land she could grow anything she wanted. Perhaps her horsey friends the Ashly brothers would bring her a box or two of fruit and veg after they'd been to the market, some nice cheese, and she would get along fine. She put layers of clothing on, ending with a big green woollen coat Uncle Alan had bought her in Sydney, and she packed a few books and as many clothes as she could squeeze into a suitcase. Kind women had given her make-up – lipsticks and foundation and powder – and she took that, because it was hard to get. She wouldn't be able to afford it herself, not until she figured out her finances.

It took much longer to get back to the house from Uncle Alan's than it did from the Bees' years earlier. She hadn't quite thought of that. It was dark when she arrived, and she tripped and fell twice before realising she couldn't explore until morning. She'd wanted to find a good hiding place, because she knew they'd come looking for her. If she could find a wall cavity, or a space in the roof or floor, she could set up an alarm system so she knew when someone was coming. A bell on a piece of string, that kind of thing. Then she remembered that the caretaker's shed had been untouched by the crash, by the fire, because of all that green wood. She made her way in the dark by memory, and pushed open the door. She felt her way to the corner where she hoped the bed still stood.

It was there, and she curled up sleepily. There was no pillow so she bundled up her big coat and used that. The night was very warm so she needed no blanket. The sandwiches she'd made before dawn were slightly dry but tasted good. Once she'd had dinner at a friend's house who had a scary mother who made them eat late, because she said that an appetite made all food taste good. She said that the poor children never wanted fancy food, they were happy with what they got and Pera didn't realise she wasn't joking and laughed her head off.

She wasn't invited back to that girl's house.

That mother was right, though. Pera was starving hungry and the stale sandwiches were delicious.

She woke up early but it was already too late. A policeman's bike was against the shed; when Pera peered out she could see the policeman her dad had called Young Bobby staring towards the pond. She joined him.

'Are the fish back, do you think?'

'I haven't looked yet,' she said. They walked down there; she could hear frogs croaking, and there were gnats flying overhead, but there were no fish.

'We'd better head back to your Uncle Alan's. Everyone's worried about you,' Young Bobby said. His shoes were old but shiny and she wished he had enough money to buy himself new ones.

'I hate it there. My cousin Frankie is the worst person.'

'It won't be long before you'll be finding your own way. Getting a job, finding a nice boy to marry, settling down.'

It sounded horrifyingly ordinary.

'But in the meantime, we'll get you back where you belong. I can have a word with Frankie, if you like. Put the fear of police into him. Tell him I'll throw him in jail.'

She could imagine how that would be received.

'I have to do something first.'

They walked to the big flame tree, standing amongst the descendants of the memorial flowers she had laid out, and which now grew in neat lines. Pera paced it out again and again. Picking flowers. Smelling them. Standing still for a photograph. Amusing the adults. Keeping the people outside for longer.

'What are you doing?'

'I'm seeing how I could have kept them outside. If I hadn't been so stubborn.'

'The timing wasn't that fine,' he said. 'Even if you'd done as you were told, they would have been inside. But you would have been dead too.'

She said, 'Clocks can't be trusted. Neither can time.' So she paced it out anyway, again and again.

'I'll give you a dink back on my bike. Let me do a quick circuit. We're always rousing out swaggies and squatters. Well, not always. I found one once. But we owe it to you and your family to keep the place clear for when you can come back.'

He told her to go wait by the bike. It was a nice one, shiny and big. She sat on the seat; her feet could reach the pedals at a stretch and she tested it around the forecourt, and up the driveway, through the gate, along the road.

She kept riding.

They didn't catch her for a couple of days, because she kept changing direction. By then she was tired and hungry and it was almost a relief to be arrested for the theft of a police vehicle. She went quietly, not wanting to cause any fuss.

Young Bobby and Uncle Alan tried to keep her out of trouble, but there was the bike and the food she'd had to pinch on the way.

The best they could arrange – and there was plenty of help, her dad had been well connected and she still had people looking out for her – was entry into the Dillon School for Domestic Science, better known as Jail for Young Ladies, or, as her cousin put it, Borstal.

'You're gonna get beat up every day. And worse. But at least you'll be amongst your own kind.'

'Borstal isn't that. And this isn't Borstal,' Uncle Alan said, but he really didn't know. Pera didn't care. She was glad to be getting away from her cousin, and looked forward to the company of other girls. Uncle Alan said, 'Too many men around here, you won't learn a dot from us except how to be filthy.'

Days before her departure, Frankie was uncharacteristically nice to her. This would be a lesson going into the future; don't trust a person who is suddenly nice.

'Let's go for a ride out to your house,' he said. 'I have a picnic!'

The picnic was a bottle of beer and a pork pie he'd wrapped in a tea towel.

21

PURGATORY (THE WAITING ROOM)

1993

Pera led them to the waiting room, a rectangular, heavily wallpapered room on the ground floor, lined with two old church pews she'd picked up from an antiques' dealer. Her father used to make business associates wait here before a meeting, in what Pera and her sisters had nicknamed Purgatory. There were no chairs at all, back then, part of the ploy to 'put them on the back foot', as her father would say.

In Purgatory there was more booze, all of it in tiny hotel bottles. She bought cases and cases whenever a hotel closed down.

She said, 'You can never be sure who is real, who is a ghost. I might be one, for all that. I've certainly got enough spirit in me!' They all laughed at that, even The Men, and she felt warm, flushed, able to take on the world.

The family – and Lucky too, after his earlier misgivings – were enjoying themselves; Pera wondered if they thought this was part of the show.

'There's a poet called Yeats, who wrote a play called *Purgatory*. It's marvellous, it really is. About a man who killed his father, and now must kill his son, to save his mother from purgatory.'

'Plays aren't about cool shit like that,' Wayne said.

'Some are! Each of us has a dead one in purgatory who needs rescuing.'

They all knew it. They all had someone.

She'd first read the play in English class and sat there, entranced. The teacher told her off for daydreaming, which to this day annoyed her. If you can't daydream about a play, what's the point of it? Pera had said this to the teacher at the time and it didn't go down well.

From then on, though, she had the idea that she had to replace her loved ones in order for them to escape purgatory. She could say, *You replace my mother, you replace my father.*

The father kissed the mother on the forehead. 'That's quite beautiful, isn't it?'

'Who you going to kill for me?' she whispered, and he kissed her forehead again.

'Plays can be about cool shit, anyway,' Devon said.

'You're smart for a young fella. An old soul. Tell me. Who would you save from purgatory?'

'Oh, I dunno. My sister?' and they all started muttering, all of them with someone they actually cared about.

'I'm the lucky one, got no one,' Alex said. He rolled back and forward on his heels. There was a rattling sound coming from his pockets.

'That's so sad, Alex,' Pera said.

Lucky said, 'Some say ghosts are the souls in purgatory,

begging for help and release.'

'Fold back the rug there,' Pera said to the oldest son, ignoring Lucky. The son peeled back one corner, revealing a trapdoor.

'No one knows why this is here. It's part of the original house. It leads down to a self-contained storage space my sisters called the Great Nothingness, though there's a hatchway that connects to the rest of the cellar: what we called the Underhistory. My dad thought it was for hiding alcohol or the family jewels! But no one is really sure.'

The trapdoor was a favourite part of the tour. She sometimes paid people to hide underneath and pop up to terrify tour-goers, that kind of thing. She'd done it herself; appeared in clothes from fifty years earlier, calling 'I never did, I never. I never had a baby or went on a boat or in a car. I never did those things.'

It terrified people for some reason. She wondered if she could pull it off with The Men, scare them into leaving, but she'd had no chance to prepare.

1947

Frankie and Pera rode his motorbike to her house. He parked it at the base of the front steps, letting it drop to the ground as if he didn't have a care in the world. 'Come on, cuz! Show me how the rich people lived.'

'We weren't rich,' Pera said, although she knew perfectly well they were.

'Show me where your dad kept all his war stuff. That's what I remember the most. Maybe there'll be a souvenir for me. A shrunken head or something. A dried-up toe he took off a native.'

'He never did anything like that, he painted,' Pera said, although there had been locked cabinets she wasn't supposed to look at. One of her regrets was never knowing what was inside them. 'His war stuff used to be in Purgatory. That's because he felt bad about everything he'd seen,' she said, feeling tongue-tied and stupid.

'Show me that,' he said. It had been a room on the ground floor, so not completely destroyed. The trapdoor was covered with debris and he cleared it off. 'What's down there?'

'We used to say the Great Nothingness. It's a storeroom, separate from the rest of the cellar. My dad said they used to hide booze in it, when his relatives came to visit. Otherwise they'd drink him out of house and home.'

Frankie lifted her effortlessly and dropped her down into the space, slamming the trapdoor shut. She heard him dragging something over it. She could reach the trapdoor with her fingertips but no way could she get enough power to push it open.

'Frankie! Let me out!'

'You're gonna die in there, Pera. I'm saving you from a life of misery. And if you survive, you'll thank me. I'm preparing you for imprisonment at Borstal.'

Pera stood in the darkness. Cracks of light shone through from above, but around her there was nothing but black. Making her way along a wall, she felt around for the hatchway she thought was there, and she found it. Using a rock she found at her feet, she levered the hatch open, slowly and quietly. 'Let me out, Frankie,' she called. 'You bastard. Let me out.' She didn't know if he was up there enjoying himself at her expense, or if he was trawling her house. She wasn't frightened at all; she and Phar Lap had played a game he called Purgatorio, where they would hide down here, in the darkness, then find their way out. She never knew what he meant by it; not until she was older did she understand the word itself, but she still didn't know what was going on in his mind.

She crawled through the tunnel she and Phar Lap had discovered. Along the way was a vent, thick with rust, and loose. Through it she saw the main cellar, the Underhistory, almost glowing with light compared to the tunnel. The tunnel ahead narrowed and was unpleasant to consider, so she rattled the vent until it lifted, and squeezed her way through.

Standing in the Underhistory, covered with dirt, she felt more powerful, more capable, than she'd ever felt in her life.

1993

'Sometimes I have nightmares about that trapdoor and the Great Nothingness underneath,' Pera said. 'I don't really know why. I was locked down there once and I suppose I keep wondering what would have happened if he'd left me down there. If I never got out.'

'Who? Not your husband, surely?' the mother asked.

'No, no. My nasty cousin Frankie.'

Ike sent Devon down through the trapdoor. 'It's dark,' Devon called up. 'Just a room, doesn't go anywhere.'

'Anything down there?' Ike said, squatting and peering down.

'Just dirt and shit.' He climbed back out.

1947

Pera loved the Dillon School from the moment she stepped through the gates. She had her own little space – bed, cupboard, set of drawers – that no one invaded, and anonymity. They didn't seem to care about her past; she was just Pera, the new girl, then Pera, friend.

She learned domestic stuff; cooking, sewing, knitting, ironing and cleaning. She learned basic farm skills and how to arrange flowers. She knew how to bake a sponge and make her own apron. She could produce a batch of award-winning scones. She told them about Mr Bee's honey and how good it was and all the girls wanted to go there. The Bees would send a parcel every now and then – more than her uncle did – and inside would be jars of honey, wrapped in crocheted blankets. *My little boy is running me ragged,* Mrs Bee wrote, *but oh my goodness he is a treasure!*

She could type and take shorthand and knew how to set a meeting agenda. She could roast any cut of meat you cared to provide. They did a lot of first aid. She learned how to dance and they played competitive sports as well. Netball, basketball and athletics. They went to the cinema every week, and during the 1948 London Olympics they went daily for the updates.

Most of the girls had lost their mothers in one way or another, which bonded them. They all became like sisters or replacement mothers to one another. These were her friends for life. In particular there were two sisters, Claudia, who became her best friend and who shared all her classes, and Isabel, a couple of years older but preferred their company to most others. They met within the first few days, and Pera was drawn to Claudia because her shoelaces didn't match. One was bright yellow and the other black. They called her an adopted sister. She spent a lot of Christmas holidays with their family.

Pera, Claudia, Isabel and their friends were the fun group, who always had wine hidden in their rooms, or vodka if they could get it, and who could be relied upon to fall into peals of laughter at the slightest provocation. They held seances, sitting together in the dark, touching knees. They almost always failed because the girls ended up laughing too much, but they kept trying. Only once it worked, in a way they didn't expect.

They were deep in meditation, trying to focus on the spirits in the room, when Isabel started to cry. Deep heaving sobs that set the others off. Four or five girls sobbing so hard their shoulders hurt.

'I'm sorry,' Isabel said later. 'It was the pain of other people. I saw what happened to them, and it hurt. I saw your sister,' she told Pera.

'Which one?'

'The murdered one. The others died so quickly they didn't have time to leave a trace.'

Pera felt the most incredible comfort in the latter. 'But you saw Hazel? You're saying she *did* suffer?'

Isabel took her in a bear hug and sobbed quietly. 'I'm so sorry. I'm so sorry.'

'You weren't there,' Pera said. 'You can't know.' Up until then Pera had thought it all a joke, a fun prank. But why would Isabel be cruel like this? There didn't seem any purpose. 'What about my awful cousin, can you see him? Why is he so bad? Does something haunt him?'

'Do you want to try to find out now?' Isabel said. 'Have another seance? Or was that too awful? There is something nagging away at me. Something about him.' So they tried again, deadly serious this time, but she couldn't find anything. 'There's something,' was all Isabel would say. 'Not to excuse him. But to explain him, maybe.'

Uncle Alan visited her a few times but Frankie never did. Her horsey friends George and Harry did – although before long it was Claudia Harry wanted to see – and every visit lifted both her spirits and her status, because the boys were handsome and charming and made everyone laugh.

1949

They released her on her eighteenth birthday. The girls had a lovely party for her to celebrate both her release and her coming of age. They all cried and promised to stay in touch forever and they did, with monthly and then annual get-togethers and frequent letters. Isabel would travel for the next twenty years, never wanting to settle, while Claudia would marry Harry and have six children.

Pera was old enough that she didn't have to go back to Uncle Alan, but he was there to pick her up and Frankie had left to join the army, so she thought she might as well spend a week with him while she got herself acclimatised.

Uncle Alan's house was quiet and peaceful compared to the school. Her bedroom was silent; no night-time noises to disturb her.

He gave her money to buy clothes and when the time was

right, she packed up her things and they left for Sinclair House. She did ask if he would like to share the house with her; it was huge, and he was home alone, but he gave her a look of absolute horror at the idea.

'I'm planning on shifting into somewhere so tiny I can clean it with one swipe!' he said.

They reached the outskirts of the town.

'The caretaker shed's fixed up enough for you to live here, but I don't know how comfy you'll be, Pera. You can always stay with me of course,' he said, but she didn't want that. 'Just until it's all done,' he said.

She laughed. 'You can manage without me, Uncle!'

He was the administrator of her money until she was twenty-one. He'd received a generous amount – very generous, town gossip said, given he wasn't her father's blood brother – but Pera didn't begrudge him a penny and he had no greed for the rest of it. He set up a generous bank account for her.

They bought groceries, and he drove her home, with a new bike strapped to the roof.

She felt awful, but she really wanted to experience her home-coming alone. She didn't want to talk, or hear comments, or explain anything. She wanted simply to feel. Absorb. So she had him drop her at the end of the driveway.

She pushed through the gates, rusty now and off their hinges. She'd have them fixed or remove them altogether; she never quite saw the point of them. Someone had dumped a pile of mirrors there; she wondered if they'd tried to steal them but found them too heavy.

Her long driveway was both welcoming and daunting. She

stopped on the side of the road, bereft again. So many lives were lost in the war but she had lost everyone and that hadn't happened to anyone else.

She felt as if there were blank spaces inside her. Her mother had had the same thing. As if grief blocked something, or physically took something away.

She lay down beside the driveway. The grass was lush and cool. Dandelions grew all around, and native frangipani, and the scent of those made her drowsy.

There was no rush. She could rest. She was an adult. No one was looking for her. No one wanted her elsewhere.

Birds squawking overhead spoiled the peace and she sat up. The house loomed in the distance, still blackened, a shell. She'd long ago forgotten anything they might have owned, but now it came back to her. Her postcards, her sisters' beautiful shoes, her mother's inherited cutlery. The plates. The paintings and sculptures. Her father's photography and his diaries and all the books in the library.

The lawn was awash with flowers and she was glad she'd spent the time with the bouquets all those years earlier, allowing their seeds to settle. Every bloom was hers.

Piles of debris sat covered by tarpaulins as they had for years now. The aeroplane had been removed, but the safety rope, tied by the police, was still wrapped around the house. Mottled now, faded, it sagged against the ground. The first thing she did was to bundle it up and put it on the rubbish heap.

There were piles of rubble and shattered glass, metal pieces. Looking at it sparked her imagination. She could do something with this.

Walking around the outside of the house, she could see that

much of the inside was burnt. Black, ashy, almost shiny. The floor was littered with shards of things no longer recognisable. She could see what were perhaps the remnants of picture frames, and there was the skeleton of their dining table, and there were the legs of some chairs.

The front door was off its hinges, affording enough space to squeeze through. Debris blocked her path in every direction, but she thought she could bunk down and sleep in the foyer, at least, if she got tired of the caretaker's shed.

The kitchen was gone, but she had brought a camp stove with her. It reminded her both of the caretaker, and of those families who were never named, not even her friend who she'd called Phar Lap. No one really tried to name them; they vanished. She thought sometimes she'd imagined them but she was sure she hadn't. They had existed. If they had survived, they'd be dozens by now. Her friend would be working somewhere, making a living, and perhaps he would have children already. She wished she hadn't called her friend Phar Lap. She wished she'd asked him his actual name. But at least it was something to make him real.

She settled into the caretaker's shed. She'd brought bedding and food and a good torch and she was exhausted, so she nestled into sleep.

She heard noises and her imagination ran wild. It was a comfort, though. If there were ghosts, they were her ghosts, at least. Not that she believed they existed; they were simply her memories, and her nightmares, wrought living.

The next day she visited her neighbours, the Bees, and stayed for dinner.

'You should stay the night at least. Stay as long as you like until you get your place sorted. At least until next week, and even then. You won't take up much room!' Their son was seven and quite cute, a chubby little thing, lazy as all get out, who loved nothing more than to eat and eat and eat. He liked Pera because his mum made cake to welcome her, and he kept whispering, 'Tell her to make more cake.'

22

HOME OF THE RANGE (THE KITCHEN)

1993

She could see his father in Wayne; the slightly petulant face, the tendency to scrawniness in later life. 'I've got some cake in the pantry,' she said. 'Who needs a snack?'

Should she separate the groups? Leave them on their own? She was torn. In no way deluded that she was keeping The Men from doing anything, still she wanted to be present.

'I could put on the deep fryer, make everyone some dim sim or something. I've got so much in the freezer.'

'That'd be bloody good,' the father said. There was a momentary silence at that; he hadn't sworn before. He was showing off for The Men, so at least he'd understood that much about them. Pera wondered when the rest would click.

She thought about who she could throw the boiling oil at. What would be the most effective use of it? And would this give her the upper hand, or make them turn on her?

She wished there was something she could put in the food that would make them docile. If she could make it upstairs, maybe some of the sleeping tablets her doctor gave her?

'Go on then,' Ike said. 'Wayne, go help your grandma's friend.' He said it with a smile, more like a grimace, and Pera's heart beat faster as she and Wayne walked to the kitchen. Was there a message in that smile? Had they already decided to kill her?

1949

First thing was to clean out the shell of the house. She paid squads of children from the local high school to help on weekends to clear debris. She made sure nothing was thrown away. She had them stack things in piles; books, clothing, metals.

Uncle Alan got her a job with someone in the building industry he knew from England. She started off as a typist but she wanted to know everything about materials, how to reuse them. When to throw away, when to keep. She wanted as much involvement in the recreation of her home as possible.

Most in the village thought her house was haunted, even the cynics amongst them, and they didn't go there much anymore.

Isabel had started using the shell of Sinclair House to run seances, trying to make sense of the voices she heard sometimes. The participants would eat a lavish meal first on the front lawn, with lots of cheese variations to induce visions. Lots of wine. Claudia and Isabel would listen carefully to their conversations, taking mental notes. They'd ask unobtrusive questions. They'd listen as people talked and they gathered information without them realising. Pera would always use this to her advantage. It was better to know than not to know.

Part of her worried she'd see her parents or her sisters but she never did.

Most of the participants were relatives of the dead who came to her looking for answers she knew they wouldn't find. She'd let herself be convinced that trying to contact the dead would help but she saw time and time again it didn't. 'The answer isn't always the one you want,' Isabel liked to tell them at the outset, but this didn't really help either.

They were all so hopeful, Pera found a tiny glimpse of it herself. She wondered what her mother's last words would have been if she'd known? And would her father have made her be in the photo?

'There is no such thing as ghosts,' Pera would say to Isabel.

'They don't know that. They want hope. They want to believe that spirits exist, that their loved ones live on in another plane. I'm the most cynical person on Earth so if I say I feel something, it's genuine.'

Pera put a stop to the seances soon after. There was a presence, definitely a change in the atmosphere, and a fist fight broke out amongst the relatives over whose ghost it was.

23

HALL OF REFLECTION (FIRST FLOOR BACK PASSAGE)

1993

Pera shook herself. The tour group had spread out beyond her reach; she called them all back to her. She wasn't sure where The Men were; for a moment she wondered if she had imagined them. Then she heard a door slam and she said, 'Those ghosts are out and about! Come on, upstairs we go.'

'Upstairs, downstairs, upstairs, downstairs. We're going all over the place! Why don't you show us the place in order?' Chook said.

Pera restrained herself from saying, 'Stupid old man.' Instead, she said, 'I follow the way the stories go, not where our feet lead us.' And of course it wouldn't hurt to have The Men a bit disoriented.

'This room I call the Hall of Reflection. I know I said before we never see the ghosts of my sisters, apart from the murdered one, but here, sometimes. Just a glimpse. A reflection but no person. I actually found these mirrors stacked at the gate, soon after I moved back in. No one knows where they came from, and no one confessed to dumping them. They absolutely, definitely did not come from my house. So strange.'

She left the mirrors dusty, to catch the light, make people jump. She'd left a message on one written in dust for a previous tour and no one had yet wiped it off: *Look close*. On another, she wrote: *You are not yourself.* Sometimes messages appeared that she hadn't written, which was fun. Rude words, mostly, but sometimes sweet ones. She knew that one of the visitors had done it, but maybe they were channelling her father, her mother, or one of her sisters. That's what automatic writing was.

1950

Pera bought herself a small run-around, a tiny Morris Minor that got her from here to there but wouldn't impress anyone very much.

It came in useful when she was called away because her grandmother was ill and, while there was no love between them, Pera knew it was her duty to be there. Her grandfather had died while she was at school, so it wasn't such a scary visit, but she was glad when it was over. Her grandmother had moved into a retirement village and was no longer very interested in anything much.

Pera stopped in town for supplies on the way home. Her uncle Alan had hired a company called 'Deniston's Digger' that employed returned soldiers to come to the house to work as labourers; the children were a great help on the small things, but there were heavy materials they couldn't budge.

She wanted to be at home when they arrived. She'd learned not to trust anyone when it came to her belongings. She raced through her shopping, remembering beer for the men. Beer always made a difference. In the end she ran into friends, and her car blew a tyre, and she was there an hour after the men were due to arrive.

As she pulled into her driveway, a middle-aged man came to greet her, saying, 'Hello, ma'am. I'm Deniston. Steve Deniston. I've got a couple of carloads of blokes coming to make sense of this lot.' He waved both arms to encompass all he saw.

'Call me Pera. Sorry I'm late! I meant to be here to greet you but you know how things are.'

'I do indeed, ma'am. I'm sure you have a bigger load than most, given your family story.'

'They're all dead,' she blurted out, then instantly covered her mouth.

In the awkward silence that followed she thought she could hear her sister calling.

People treated her with kid gloves and that was almost worse than doing or saying nothing at all. They exchanged glances of pity if there were more than one of them, and got a down-mouthed sad look, a shininess in the eyes. She was old enough to know pity when she saw it. She saw it from this man but he offered it with such kindness it didn't bother her as much as usual. Also, he was flushed in the cheeks so perhaps he admired her. She'd been shopping in Melbourne the week before and was proud of her new clothes; a pale mauve skirt set, above the knee, cut so well she barely felt she was wearing anything at all.

The labourers lined up to meet her. She saw them twitch and

blink in the heat and didn't want them to have to stay there long, so called out, 'First person to get me a cold beer wins the afternoon off.'

They laughed and cheered. Deniston dispersed them back to work.

'I hope they don't mind being here. It must seem very dull.'

'It gives them work to do. It's a bit of a halfway house for a lot of them, to be honest. A lay-by until they figure out what they're going to do with themselves next.'

She walked into the caretaker's hut but saw that they had already set up card tables there. *It's their place now*, she thought, and she backed out, embarrassed.

'Sorry, ma'am. The boys thought they might venture out there in the evenings. I can have them move? It won't be long before we knock up a couple of good rooms inside to go on with.'

'That will be fine,' she said. She could smell burning wood and she said, 'Can I ask that they leave that woodpile? There's plenty else to burn. It's a silly superstition of mine. Our dear caretaker always collected green wood, saying "one day it'll be ready" and it rather breaks my heart to burn it. Is that the silliest thing you've heard?'

'Not at all. Many of us are more superstitious now than we were.'

'You're very kind.' She'd been sleeping in the remains of the dining room, on a mattress on the floor, but they brought in a camp bed for her and hitched up some feed sacks for curtains, and that was her space.

The men worked on repairs in return for a place to stay and three good meals a day. They restored the kitchen first, hooked up the gas, so she could make them cakes and scones. She hired a cook for the rest of the meals, though. She had some of the older women in the village come over, too, to help the cook and look after the cleaning. Some of them had been there when soldiers were posted at Sinclair House before the last war, and this made them feel young again.

She found little stacks of pebbles and thought of the prime minister's young man and his collections. She made them now herself, without being sure why. She liked the idea of memory, but she had little memory of him.

She had the labourers pile the remaining aeroplane parts together, but she knew the children and even the soldiers all took mementos. She didn't blame them, but she also knew they'd all carry a curse.

She loved having them there. They enjoyed a drink, and there was her father's cellar, somehow unscathed. Brandies and rums, whiskies; all for them to enjoy. She'd never had so much fun, and had her friends join her for small parties some nights. Some of the locals were scandalised, the rest were happy to see some life in the place.

The men worked in their own time to rebuild the chapel. The flooring was undamaged but needed cleaning, and the bricks could mostly be reused. She had mixed feelings about going near the chapel; there had been bodies found in there, unidentified. More of the migrants, perhaps, running to the chapel for sanctuary. The men prayed in the chapel, looking for comfort, and she was happy for them to have it as their own.

The caretaker's hut was well maintained; that's why they played cards there at night. It had barely been damaged in the disaster and she thought again how if the man hadn't been doing his job, if he'd been slacking off, having a lie-down, he wouldn't have been killed.

Before the ruins of the sheep shed were dealt with, Pera looked through the rubble. She hadn't thought to do this before. She found a few small items, which she kept and labelled: one damaged silver earring; one cooking pot; the small truck made of scrap metal her friend had played with. She wished she'd taken it when he'd offered it. Looking back as an adult she understood that he wanted to give her something, even though he had very little to give, and that she should have taken it in order not to appear superior. She'd hoped to find the stopwatch she'd given him but that never showed up.

The rest of the sheep shed clean-up was assigned to two of Deniston's men who found it difficult to work indoors. 'The war, you know,' Deniston said. It was something Pera heard often and never questioned. She understood enough to know there was trauma the men couldn't always manage.

A week or so later Deniston came to her with exciting news. 'They've found something, Pera!' He called her that now, although she loved calling him Deniston. It had a dashing ring to it.

They joined the two labourers in the shed, who were standing over a hole in the floor.

'Most of it is totally fucked . . . er, ruined,' one of the men said, 'so we were lifting the floorboards for firewood. But we found this.' He pointed at the hole. 'It was a tunnel!'

'What's at the other end?' Deniston asked.

'I said it *was* a tunnel, mate. No longer. Full of dirt down there now, probably after this thing collapsed. No way anyone's getting through there now. We found this though and I wondered if I could have it for me mum.' He showed them a small, tarnished pendant of the Madonna and Child.

'Under no circumstances,' Deniston said. He and Pera had agreed they shouldn't set a precedent of the men taking items. Later, she would give them all gifts.

In the kitchen, Deniston poured them a shot each of rum as Pera turned the pendant over in her palm. Tears pricked her eyes; she was sure this had belonged to her friend Phar Lap's mother.

'Anything I can do?' Deniston asked. 'Beyond provide rum, of course.'

He blinked at her with his sweet, brown eyes, and she kissed him. It took him by surprise but he kissed her back, tasting of rum, the sweetness of his mouth making her teeth ache.

Once the clean-up was almost complete, she had the big naked man statue moved back where he belonged, to the conservatory. The statue had been repaired and cleaned but you could see the line around his neck where his head had been severed. He was scarred and stoic. She thought of him as a testament to war, like the statues being unveiled all over the country, proud men standing tall or slumped, with a friend, a cobber, comforting arm tight across their shoulders.

The soldiers did a good job of the basics; the house no longer felt dangerous, as if it could collapse on itself at any minute. There was only one floor, and the rooms were temporary, and in fact if she didn't know where she was, she would have not known it was her own home.

24

THE POST OFFICE (ARTEFACT DISPLAY ROOM)

1993

Pera led the tour group into the Post Office. 'This room is dedicated to all those who wait patiently at home for a loved one to return, and are instead rewarded with a telegram or a letter.'

The youngest boy was making a low-pitched whining noise. He was bored. The rest of The Men had wandered off, but Alex clung to the tour group as if he belonged. He stepped closer to the boy, fingers clenching, and Pera raised her cane and laid it on Alex's chest. 'Ooh, sorry!' she said. 'It's this toothache. I got a sudden twinge of pain.' That attracted the full glare of his attention. Ike called his name and he left the room reluctantly.

She needed to get the family away. Why didn't they leave? Why didn't the idiot father see what these men were? She found herself being irritated with him. He'd jollied along, tried to be blokey with The Men. She'd seen this before, men who were usually gentle and kind acting up around tougher men. As if dropping letters, throwing in a swear word or two, would make them mates.

The mother leaned heavily on the oldest son. Her face was drawn and she was very pale. 'We can cut the tour short,' Pera said. She hated to use illness as an excuse but also didn't want to give these people the danger of knowledge. She didn't want things to escalate.

'We should,' the father said.

'No!' It was as forceful as the mother had been. 'You've been wanting to do this for as long as I've known you. You're not missing out because of me.'

The father looked helpless. Then he said, 'How about you all go wait outside? Get some fresh air?'

'That's a good idea.' They'd be out of harm's way. A raised voice came down the stairs but The Men had forgotten them for now. Pera hoped it would stay that way.

This room had two layers to it; on the surface it was simply a testament to those who fought in the wars; photos, and medals, and letters home. A small inscribed Bible.

But in the concealed cupboards behind the walls she kept the letters her lovers had sent her over the years, and the pictures. It was the place she remembered being desirable.

1950

It was here she took Deniston, whom she teasingly called her war hero, after the labourers had all gone home for the day. The door had a lock, and there was a large comfy couch Uncle Alan had delivered to her when he closed down his house and moved into a small flat in the city.

It was awful, but she was soon bored with her war hero. He was a gentle but unimaginative lover and she found herself falling asleep while they were making love. She watched the big brawny labourers, so unworried by anything at all, and wished she could play with them as well. Could she? How much hurt would there be?

Her war hero was like a puppy dog. Very sweet and kind and he made a serviceable egg and toast. He was a clever man, with plenty to say and a good ear. He was good with his hands, too, and creative.

He suggested making clocks out of the aeroplane parts that remained. 'I've got a watch made from the plane my father was killed in. We've got nothing else left of him.'

She collected up some of the smaller fragments and the next time she was in the big city, took them to a watchmaker who created the most beautiful timepieces. 'It doesn't matter if they work,' she said, knowing they'd stop anyway. She wondered if one day she could control her effect on time. If she would no longer stop the clocks.

25

THE HEAD ROOM (THE MEN'S DRAWING ROOM)

1993

'You won't find a room like this in any modern house,' Pera said to the father and Lucky. 'Well, I guess you could say that about every room here.' She heard shouting, scuffling, and talked over it. The more The Men fought amongst themselves the less they'd be concerned about the others. She'd seen this in men over and over again.

She'd never been in here as a child; it was a place for gentlemen. Now, one wall was almost taken up by a painting, completed by her cousin Frank before he died; his memory of how the room was, once upon a time, when it was the men's drawing room and women were not allowed.

She'd decorated the room to stay true to how Frank remembered it from a single visit: dark walls, leather chairs, animal heads. Dusty paintings. Thick curtains. He'd walked in and been so clear, so definite, about how the room had looked before. He'd said, 'I never forgot it because they said I was a man that day. For a long time I had the wrong idea of what being a man meant.'

It was the first time he apologised for being a bully. She didn't know if his memory was correct but had no reason to doubt him and no other ideas for the room. As a child she'd imagined easels and art pencils, the men drawing vases of flowers, or a pile of books.

1950

The men's drawing room was the soldiers' favourite room once it had been cleaned up. They dragged chairs in – really building crates with some hessian thrown over – and made it as their place. They'd found magazines hidden under loose floorboards, surprisingly intact. Pieces of them, at least, enough to see skin and lady bits and other things that seemed to make them happy.

She drank here with them most afternoons.

Then the soldiers packed up and left, back to their lives. Renovations stalled for a while, and Pera travelled Australia for six months, place to place, city to city, friend to friend. She felt thirsty for new experiences, finishing with a three-week visit to New Zealand, but at the same time she ached for her home.

1993

'Nothing lasts forever, though,' Pera told Lucky and the father. 'I had a wonderful time with the men rebuilding my house, hearing all their terrible stories of war, but all their hilarious jokes, too.'

'Do they haunt this room?'

'No, not them. They were too happy. They had too much life in them. I was slightly in love with one of them, if truth be known. It's my cousin who haunts here. A frustrated genius, by his own account. He's very jealous; any artists amongst us?'

There were none. 'That's actually good. He hates artists. He's been known to scratch anybody creative. To make people slip and fall. He's never done any lasting damage, though.' She liked to believe Frank would have loved this; not only her pretending he was a ghost, but also pretending he was a frustrated genius. She imagined him laughing his head off at that.

1951

She was home from her overseas adventure. Man's shirt on – she wasn't sure which man, it had appeared in her luggage and she wasn't sure which of them had left it behind – rolled up to the elbows. A pair of old pants. Her hair tied back and all of her dotted with orange paint.

The door chime rang downstairs. The old one didn't survive the crash and she'd hated it anyway. It rang dark and low like a falling tree. This one tinkled, and she sheathed her paintbrush in a tin, glad of the excuse to escape the fumes for a bit. Whoever it was, she'd offer them tea on the lawn.

It was a damaged man.

He stood, arms straight down, eyes closed.

One eye squinted shut and surrounded by shiny scar tissue. Shoulder hitched up, left hand splayed as if out of control. Cheek scarred. Neck bright red. Mouth askew.

'Hello, Temperance.'

'Frankie?' Her cousin.

'Frank,' he said. 'I'm just Frank now.'

'And I'm Pera. As ever and always. What . . .' she started, but then, his face . . . he closed his eyes so he didn't have to see her reaction to his damaged face. 'They've tried to do a facial reconstruction but not the best of jobs. But I'm still the same man.'

'Of course you are,' she said. 'Come in. Come on. I'll make us a cuppa.'

He shuddered. 'I really don't like the indoors. Can't abide a roof. Can't stand confinement.'

'And yet you locked me up like that!' She tried to keep her tone light.

'I know! I'm a terrible person, Pera. I always have been.'

'Hey, I got out! It's okay.'

But she could see he'd carry the guilt with him no matter what she said.

They sat outside on the veranda and he told her how war had been for him. She'd heard many such stories, but his was different because she'd known him as a child. It was hard to connect the brave man who went back over and over to the battlefront, sustaining twenty-eight injuries, with the boy who used to stab her with his geometry compass.

'How did they let you in? You were only sixteen when the whole thing was done!'

His eyes shifted and she understood that the war he was talking about was not the one the other young men had fought. He'd had battles all his own.

'I was in Korea,' he said. He lifted the corners of his eyes to make them appear slanted, and she saw a glimpse of his old awful self.

'You poor thing,' she said. 'How dreadful.'

He needed a place to stay and the best she had for him that wasn't too enclosed was the temporary shed the soldiers had made to keep sand and tools in. There was no roof on it now – a great wind had blown it off and into the pet graveyard – but it offered some protection.

'You're welcome to stay here if it suits.'

'You always were the best of us,' he said.

She took him meals out, and they would sit quietly together. He walked into the town once a week and always returned with a gift for her. Something small and sweet that she could not reconcile with the boy he had been.

He was quiet, once his story was told. Almost silent. She couldn't get a word out of him then. When he was a boy he couldn't shut up for a minute.

This was a lesson for her: people can change.

He came back with house paints. Mr Thomas, the hardware man, would ask about him next time she was in. 'Polite chap,' he said. 'Troubled.' He began a massive painting on a board he made out of loose planks. It was a room he said he remembered from the old house, the one he called the Head Room and she knew as the men's drawing room.

'I always pictured men doing drawings in there,' she said, and he laughed for the first time since he'd arrived.

'Mostly they looked at pictures of women,' he said. 'I found it very awkward. I didn't want to look at any of it, so I had a lot of time to study the room. All these animal heads! I don't know what happened to them all.'

'All burnt or wrecked or pinched.'

He added the animal heads to his painting, but also other treasures, things he knew she'd lost. There was evidence he'd always listened to her, even when she was a child.

This was his gift to her. His apology. He told her it was his one and only piece of art, just for her.

'Thank goodness you went away,' he said. 'I was so awful to you.'

'I was sent to Borstal!' she said, but laughed. She offered to get him a job with the building company she worked for but the idea set him shaking so hard she said, 'Don't worry, don't worry. You stay as long as you like. But don't you want to see your dad?'

'Not like this. And I don't want him in trouble, if the army come looking for me.'

'All right for me to be in trouble, then?' Pera teased him.

'You can cope with anything, Pera. You have to swear not to say anything to him.'

She promised.

She took Frank a cup of tea and a scone most afternoons. Usually he'd be lying on his camp bed, in a pair of shorts and nothing more. Not sleeping; his eyes wide open, staring up.

He was covered in scars.

Usually he sat up when she called 'ooroo', gave her a smile. This day, he didn't even have the energy for that. He'd finished his painting and seemed to lack motivation for anything at all.

She put the cup and plate next to his bed, on the square rock he'd found and used for a bedside table.

'Look at you,' she said. 'Lying around. There's plenty to be done.'

He turned his head to her.

'You do it. I'll rest for a while.'

He always had been lazy but she didn't say this. He needed to feel he was welcome, and that she wouldn't give him a hard time.

His voice slurred and he didn't even lift his hand to swat away a fly.

His eyes slid closed. His lips were dry and he breathed in and out, weak, erratic. It wasn't right.

She searched frantically around him. 'Did you get bitten? Snake or spider?'

He managed to lever himself sideways to reveal an empty bottle of pain medication. She'd always been suspicious of his pills; he said he had a friend who was in medicine.

She ran inside to telephone the doctor. An ambulance would take an hour or more.

'Sit him up if you can,' the doctor said. 'Give him black coffee, see if you can get him vomiting. Try to keep him moving till I get there.'

But there was no movement left in him.

After the undertaker took Frank away, she found a note, addressed to her.

You made my last days happy and comfortable. I've never felt safer than I did under your non-roof. I'm sorry for being a shit. Anything I have is yours.

He had very little. A couple of books, some photographs of a swimming pool she didn't recognise, and his rat king in a glass box, the terrifying thing she'd had nightmares about as a child. She didn't know where it came from, but it was always kept a secret from Uncle Alan.

And now it was hers.

Her cousin Frank may have died feeling a failure, or as if the world had failed him. That he couldn't live with his nightmares. But he would be buried a hero. He'd been injured twenty-eight times defending his country, and that made him worthy. She wanted them to know that one of theirs was dead. She wanted him given a hero's burial.

She made phone calls to the authorities and discovered that her cousin was a deserter. There was no official record of injuries sustained in battle. She spoke to one of his company, who, while trying to be polite because she was a relative, could still not hide his contempt.

'Some of it came from fights he never had a hope of winning. That was him in a nutshell. But did he not tell you what he did to himself?'

He hadn't.

'Set fire to hisself, love. Worst thing any of us ever saw and we saw it all. Poured petrol over himself, lit his Zippo. Did it behind the shed where he thought no one would see; I'll give him that. But they saw, and put him out soon enough. It was the infirmary he got away from.'

They buried Frank quietly, she and her uncle Alan. It was so good to see him she cried. He didn't blame her for a minute for

Frank's death, although he did scold her gently for not telling him where he was. There were no other mourners.

'He was a man of violence,' Uncle Alan said.

1993

A man of violence. Like The Men in her home.

'Mrs Sinclair? Are you all right?' the father said. Tour members always called her that, although her married name was different. She was never sure what to go by; none of it seemed to fit. Her husband had been dead a long time, but then so had her family.

She started. 'My apologies. You caught me daydreaming into the past. Time doesn't mean much in Sinclair House. Don't mind me if I drift off. Old ladies like me have a lot of memories.' Sometimes it was useful to be perceived as elderly. They walked to a large window and gazed out. The mother was sitting peacefully on a bench, her head tilted to the winter sun. The children were running in circles, collecting things off the ground. Flowers and rocks, Pera guessed.

'Where are youse?' Devon called out. 'Oi! Ike wants the keys.'

Pera shook herself. 'Let's move on,' she said to Lucky and the father. 'Let's move on quickly. The ghosts are on the move.'

26

THE STONE ROOM (ART GALLERY 6)

'There you are!' Devon said, finding them as they climbed stairs to the second floor, heading for the Stone Room. 'Where's everyone?'

The father started to answer, presumably to tell Devon where his wife and children were. Pera 'accidentally' hit his shins with her cane.

'The boys are all about! You should try to find them and we'll meet up,' Pera said. But it was too late. Alex found them, jumping down the stairs three at a time, stomping and whooping. He carried a walking stick that she knew concealed a knife and the menace in his smile chilled her. Wayne shouted, 'Where are you? Wheeeree arreee youuuuu?'

'Here, mate!' Devon called, but his voice was weak, a kid's voice, so Alex stood with his mouth cupped and called for them. Ike, Wayne and Chook appeared.

Pera sorted through the keys and unlocked the door. 'The Stone Room is one of the most beautiful rooms in Sinclair House. My husband's life's work is kept there. He only had a short life but you will see that he was a brilliant sculptor. It is one of life's great tragedies – as well as a very personal one – that he was taken from me, and from art lovers as well.'

It was a beautiful room, a testament to a very talented man. His small sculptures, his larger works, his hand studies arrayed around the room. Stone, but also wood and metal. An antique grandfather clock sat in the corner. Its tick always sounded slow, but it was the only clock that kept time.

'Oh my God, this is incredible,' the father said. 'He must have been an amazing man. So you married that Deniston fellow? The one you fell in love with?'

'Oh! No. Not him. I met my husband not long after that, though. I always say he fell in love with the shape of my hands before anything else. I fell in love with . . . well. His talent, perhaps, but he was a wonderful man as well.' She often shared her life story on the tours but some things she kept to herself.

'So what, anything worth shit in here?' Ike said. He lit a cigarette. Pera didn't want him burning her beautiful room, or spreading ash, but was anxious about asking him not to. She thought about the gun hidden under the man's shirt.

She said, 'One piece has been valued at close to a quarter of a million dollars. But of course you'd have to find a buyer.' She found a saucer from under a pot plant and gave it to Ike. She was surprised that he took it and used it as an ashtray.

Devon prowled the room, poking at things. Chook watched Pera, his fingers flexing.

'You like telling people what to do? Like knowing more than other people?' She couldn't help laughing at him. What a ridiculous man. His shoulders flinched and she understood just how weak a man he was.

Lucky and the father walked around admiring the work, much of it found pieces of masonry that had been reimagined or changed. The Men tilted the art, made jokes about dropping things.

'A lot of these are sculptures of you!' Lucky said. 'He must have really adored you.'

'I think he did, rather. He was very focused on his work, but he often said I kept him alive. He had some very dark days, as many artists do.'

Ike stood too close to Lucky. 'He *adored* her, mate. No chance for you.'

Lucky blushed. 'I wasn't.'

None of them asked how she met him. Pera wished people weren't so predictable; it was always a woman who asked this question. A man had asked only once in all these years. She said, 'How did I meet him, do you ask?' She loved to tell the story.

1951

The night she met her husband Pera had arrived home from work past eleven. It was so dark the headlights of her car seemed to push it forward, like a blanket, only to have it fold in behind again. When the night was black like this, even the nocturnal creatures stayed put, but still she watched for rabbits and kangaroos.

She should have left the office earlier but there was so much work to be done and she was keen to spend the next day at home rather than go back in to finish it off. Plus she'd been late for work, as ever. Much as she loved her job it didn't mean she could make time behave for her.

As she neared the house, she saw a small glow. Thinking it was the reflection of her car headlights in an animal's eyes, she slowed down. It could be a cow wandered over from another property, or a fox.

It wasn't an animal, she saw as she pulled in, but the glow of a cigarette. She pulled her car around so that the person was highlighted and she saw him, sitting on the front steps. A broad man, she thought. No hat. He stood as she parked the car. Later, she would reflect on the number of times she arrived home to find a man waiting. Almost as if she summoned them up.

The man waiting for her was very tall, with the bearing of a soldier: shoulders back, head held high. For a moment she considered driving back to town. Young Bobby had told her many times that she was too trusting. He said that not everyone had good intentions. She told him, 'I'll manage that when it happens. Most people will listen to reason.' Besides, she thought she'd had all the early death God would dole out to one person.

He leaned up against an enormous flowerpot that stood at the base at the steps. He stubbed out his cigarette, putting the dead butt in his pocket.

'Hello, miss,' he said. His voice deep and gentle. 'I'm so sorry to appear on your doorstep like this. Almost literally.' She smiled at him, welcoming him as her parents had always welcomed guests, expected or unexpected.

'How can I help you?'

'Ah—' He sneezed.

'Let's go inside. We'll have a cuppa. Or some soup. Would you like soup? I have a lovely big pot of mulligatawny. I'm quite good at that.'

'Soup would be marvellous. I've been on the road for a while and I don't fancy the food at the hotel in town.'

'You'll have to excuse the house, the state it's in. Almost liveable, is what I call it! Ground floor sorted, at least, and my kitchen.' She didn't mention bedrooms. 'We'll get to the top floors before too long. I have visions!'

She stumbled at the front steps and he reached out to steady her. She had a small entrance light that should be brighter but was good enough for joining key and lock.

Pushing open the heavy front door she stepped inside and turned on the foyer light. 'Come on in,' she said, as she put her handbag and keys on the hall stand. The door nibbed quietly shut. She turned.

He was not handsome but very nice-looking, with pale brown hair cut close to his head, pinkish cheeks, a gentle smile she hadn't noticed outside.

He smelt of bonfires and, strangely, of pond water. Her nose wrinkled; he noticed.

'I took a bath in your pond. Terribly rude and I am sorry. But I wanted to freshen up. I didn't want to show up looking grubby, smelling worse.'

'Did the fish have a nibble?' she said, and he blushed to his hair roots.

'My clothes are full of smoke. I sit by fires outdoors a lot and I don't really have a change of clothes.'

'I don't have any men's clothes here,' she said, realising belatedly she should have pretended she had a husband, that there was a man in the house. But there was nothing aggressive about this man.

'Please don't worry about me!' They stood in awkward silence for a moment. She didn't like to ask him directly why he was there. It was possible he was a relative of one of those who died in the plane. Usually the relatives arrived with gifts, flowers and chocolates, and they begged to be allowed in. He showed a confidence of place, a sense of belonging, that threw her.

'I'm sorry,' he said. 'My name is Joseph Sheely. I have been meaning to come for a long time but things . . . intervened.'

The name was familiar.

'My brother Simon . . . went out with your sister Hazel.'

In the silence that followed, the clocks around the house ticked. Every one was on a different time.

'But he was the one . . . he was her last boyfriend. He was the one.'

It was Simon Sheely who'd murdered her sister. And, she sometimes thought, caused the deaths of the others. Justine and Hope were old enough to leave but they stayed at home because of Hazel, close to their mother to stop her worrying. If not? They might have been scattered throughout the country when the plane crashed. Safe.

'Yes. That's him. That's me. I've been wanting to come. I've lost everyone, too. I've been wanting to meet you. In this place. But everything has been so messed up. The war . . .'

'Did you see active duty? In Europe? Or Korea? My cousin did,' she said, unsure why she lied about Frank.

'No . . . no. My eyesight isn't good and there are other issues.' He tapped his temple. 'Not bad ones. Not like my brother had. But they are there.'

One thing Pera's life had given her was the ability to absorb the astonishing. To react calmly when the bizarre occurred.

'I'm going to have a brandy. Would you like one?' she said.

She led him into the conservatory via the kitchen, where she collected ice cubes in a bowl. She had a drinks table set up, and loved sitting there in the evening, looking out, thinking about parties she'd have once the house was fixed. Her best friend Claudia had been there a week before and they had planned the most ridiculous things. Pera laughed to think of it. A glass elevator that travelled up and down outside the building, big enough that she could have a chaise longue and a small cocktail table in it. A rooftop bedroom, glass-ceilinged, to sleep under the stars. A dozen bedrooms for people to stay over, with beds that pulled out from the walls. A room for every person who'd died there. Wonderful things.

The big naked man statue stood with his arse towards them. She gave it a quick pat for luck as she often did, and Joseph laughed.

'He's rather magnificent. How long have you had him?'

'He survived the crash. You could say he's my last family member,' she said. His eyes opened wide until she smiled and then he smiled back. 'You have to laugh,' she said.

'I'm actually a sculptor. An artist. It's what I do.'

'Really? Where have you been shown?'

'Ah, if only. I wish! But they aren't really looking for people working with stone in the way that I do. I want to prove that sculpture can capture truth as well as any art form.'

'You'll have to meet the people I work with. The architect loves stone. I think I'm going to get him to work on this house.

Some men came and sorted out the ground floor well enough, but I want it to be something like what it used to be.'

They drank in silence. Pera felt a pleasant warmth, and had another, then she said, 'I didn't meet your brother. I was only five or something when . . . when Hazel died.'

'I was ten. He was eight years older than me. But I think . . . I always think . . . I could have stopped it if I'd timed it better. I could have asked him to take me to the shops, or to listen to the footy on the wireless. It was Carlton versus Collingwood that day. Big match. I could have stopped him walking out the door.' He was on his feet now, acting out the motions. Turning on an imaginary radio, putting his arm around an imaginary brother.

'It's the same with me. Not about her, but the rest of them. If I'd been quicker, having a photo taken. Or slower. Or I'd made them all come out to have a look at my fish.'

'I saw in the paper that's what you think. That you act it out sometimes. The paper said it and it made me think, *I have to go. I have to see her*.'

'I'm glad you're here.' She thought that she would never be able to tell anyone who he actually was. Even to have spent this small amount of time with the brother of her sister's killer would have people looking at her sidelong for the rest of her life.

1993

Only the father, Lucky, and Wayne remained. The others were gone. She felt for her keys. She'd been lost in her memories again, but they hadn't taken the keys, thank goodness.

'Sorry to bore the others so much!' she said. She gave a slightly hysterical laugh; could she bore The Men away? Would that work?

'Wait, hang on. Hang on,' Lucky said. 'Are you saying you married the bloke whose brother killed your sister?'

'She fucken did,' Wayne said gleefully.

'Yes. I married the brother of my sister's killer. But I was so young. I didn't understand anything beyond the fact he seemed to adore me.'

'You poor thing,' the father said, and she wanted to put her head on his shoulder and cry.

27

THE TIME ZONE

In the next room, Pera waited for a minute or two, letting them take in the sight of over a hundred clocks; on the walls, the floor, hanging from the ceiling.

'I can't hear any ticking,' the father said. He looked at his watch, and at Wayne. 'Have we really only been going for an hour?'

'We can finish up, if you like,' Pera said. 'Get you out that door.'

'I can't. Honestly. If you're tired, we can just sit a bit. But she wants to know I've done this. She wants to know I got to the end. We've talked about it and she's got it in her head this is my last chance.'

'Might well be,' Ike said. The rest of The Men all squeezed into the room. Wayne had stepped out into the hallway and shouted for them. 'What's this shit in here, clocks that don't work?'

'The clocks worked better when my husband was around. I used to wind them all every day or two but I don't bother very often these days. Look at them! Every one tells a different time. It proves the untrustworthiness of time. The pretence of it, the artifice. How about we all wind them up? I used to set them all to the same time but now each clock is on the time zone of where one of the people who died in the house is from. Many of the rooms have a ghost, and the clocks are tied to the ghosts. Clocks can't be trusted. Neither can time.'

'Yeah, well,' Ike said. He picked up one of the clocks and smashed it to the ground. 'These are shit. You can't tell me they're worth anything. There must be stuff hidden inside.'

'You can smash as many as you like, you won't find anything. The value is themselves. They *are* the value.'

'These clocks are works of art, anyone can see that. If you don't know art you can't be expected to know that,' Lucky said. He sounded snarky, indulgent, and Ike jerked his head sideways, a message to Alex, who led Lucky away, whispering in his ear. Ike said, 'Is that so?' before smashing another clock to the ground.

'Come on,' the father said, but he made no move to stop the destruction.

Devon tried to push a large grandfather clock over, quite a comical sight even given the tension in the room, and Pera laughed. Devon let go of the clock and stood face to face with her.

'Something funny?' he said.

'Well, I was picturing you trying to walk out the door with that, walking into a pawn shop saying, "Wanna buy a clock?"'

Ike snorted, then the others laughed, and even Devon smiled. Still, something had shifted even further. Things could turn at any minute. She couldn't stall them much longer. She'd made them laugh, though. That was something.

The father watched them but looked away when Devon

stared back. 'What's with all these little piles of pebbles here and there?' he said, looking at a pile of grey stones she had stacked by a Micky Mouse table clock. 'Is there a reason for that?'

Pera smiled. 'Me being silly, really. Remember I told you about the prime minister's assistant?'

They looked blank. She couldn't remember if she'd told them or just remembered it, thought it. 'Anyway, he was a great collector of small pebbles. He said it helped him remember where he'd been, and to leave a small mark, a small absence behind. He was quite the poet!'

'It looks messy,' Wayne said. 'And what about the wallpaper? It's coming off in strips. It all makes the place look like a wreck. You should keep it beautiful.' The others leaned forward; they'd all probably wondered the same thing. Everybody did.

Pera picked up one of the broken clocks and cradled it in her hands. Tears pricked her eyes.

'Do you need help with repairs, because I can help. I'm quite good at odd jobs,' Ike said. 'I am a very handy man.'

'The house is fine,' she said. She closed her eyes to their stares of disbelief.

Have I really been renovating for forty years? she thought.

1951

Frank's death brought public scrutiny again, and she was struck by the photographs and by the commentary of how awful her house was. It was taking so long! They'd managed half the second floor, but she didn't want them to rush things for the sake of it. She wanted every room to be just right. It was only when someone new saw it that she realised quite how much work was needed. She had built a good friendship with the chief architect at her office; he was often throwing ideas at her. With the financial approval of Uncle Alan, she hired the company to complete the restoration. They were well respected, with a reputation for creativity and an understanding of history. The chief architect was a man of great vision who loved a challenge; he couldn't wait to get started.

Was it Joseph who had been the final spark in getting things going? Certainly he loved the house, as much as he grew to love her.

Pera had Claudia, Isabel, Harry and George for lunch to meet him. Harry and George were a dab hand at meals so they cooked the whole thing; she loved them for it. Isabel was as glamorous as ever, regaling them with marvellous stories of her adventures in the spirit and in the real world. Claudia and Harry were clearly falling in love with each other; George was defiantly single. Lunch went swimmingly; they were into the fourth hour of it when the architect arrived. She'd invited him, too, but he was horribly late. She wanted him and Joseph to talk about stone and sculptures. She rode her bike up to meet him at the gate, leaving her friends behind to pour more drinks and gather ice from the kitchen.

The architect's car was shiny, silver, as stylish as he was. He said to Pera, 'Want a lift back to the house? Leave that pile-of-junk bike in the ditch,' and she shook her head.

She offered him a dink on her bike and he laughed explosively, the loudest laugh she'd ever heard, and then she pedalled madly away. He drove past her, racing, then slowed carefully. She figured out she could grab his side mirror and coast along that way.

He shook his head, mouthing, 'No! Dangerous!' but she held on so he slowed the pace and, laughing, drove to the head of the driveway. It was rocky and grassy; not maintained over the decades.

'We need to sort this,' he said. 'Needs better access.'

'The builders won't mind.'

'The builders drive rattle-traps with no suspension. They're used to it.' He climbed out of the car and she was impressed to see he had canvas slip-ons, far more appropriate footwear than the expensive leather shoes he usually wore.

He shone the hood of his Mercedes with a coat-sleeve, grinning at her. In his office at the Paris end of Collins Street, he was stiff and serious, with a perfect suit and tie, his hair well groomed, his voice modulated, and he talked about cornices and mouldings while his staff nodded.

Pera had never been intimidated by anyone, however, and a man like him, no matter how brilliant, wouldn't do it either. And she discovered, once he was on site, his pure love of structure was infectious and lent him a certain childishness.

At thirty-eight he was eighteen years her senior, happily married with three children, and it was nice not to worry about anything with him. His oldest was seventeen. Around the age Hope was when she died.

'So, your famous boyfriend is here? The artist?'

'He's a genius! But he isn't famous yet.'

'If he's a genius, you have to watch out. A lot of geniuses are pretty rotten to the people around them. If he thinks he's a genius but he isn't, run a mile. If he just wants to be an artist, if he gets joy out of observing shape and movement, give it a go.'

'He's a man who honestly seems to think I'm beautiful.' When she looked in the mirror, she could only think about what her father used to say: 'There are so many variations of beauty.'

'Here they are!' she said. Her dear friends were all in the conservatory, lolling around; everyone smiled broadly as they entered. Joseph looked the best of the men; they'd been shopping and he was well dressed, his face shaved, his hair clean. He was as handsome a man as she had ever met. Meanwhile the horsey boys were dressed as they always were: loose pants, flannel shirts, boots they had at least cleaned for the occasion. Claudia wore a very stylish twin set that was a bit smudged (she could never keep herself entirely clean) and Isabel wore pants and a man's shirt, looking every bit the Melbourne Bohemian.

The architect didn't judge her for having Joseph there; he'd lived in Europe, where moral choices were often different. Joseph, meanwhile, behaved like a gentleman. He'd made it clear that he didn't take 'casual girlfriends', was how he put it. That were she to commit to him, that would be it.

'Which one is he?' the architect said and they all laughed. Joseph blushed deep though, and his smile was so broad she thought he'd split his face.

They gathered at the dining-room table looking over old plans of the house the architect had brought, and she thought champagne was called for. After the second bottle, the architect and the sculptor were like brothers. What made her happiest was they both loved the house as much as she did.

They walked the grounds. The architect tripped over, his foot caught in a small hole. 'Bloody rabbits,' he said. 'We're going to need to dig them out.'

They walked around the back where the sheep shed had been. The soldiers had bulldozed it so all that remained was a clear area, untouched by grass.

'This is a great space,' the architect said. 'You could put in a greenhouse here. Or a gallery, to exhibit.'

'You could make it a gallery with some place for the artists to stay,' Joseph said. 'Like they can come in for a month or two. Three months. And they look after themselves but they get that beautiful space.'

'It could be a memorial to the people who lived there,' she said. She hoped that such a thing would absolve her of further action.

'Do you mean everybody, or just that migrant family you told us about?'

'This one for the family. But I guess another one for everyone else? People like to have somewhere to come to. But whatever I do, people will complain.'

'I say do exactly what you want to do,' Joseph said. 'We'll help you.' He really was marvellous. She was very attracted to him, and he seemed to be absorbed by her, although he didn't want to take any physical steps with her. Religion ran deep in him and it didn't feel right, he said.

They discussed fixing the chapel beyond the simple repair job the labourers had done. Given that Pera wasn't greatly religious, it would be a place for quiet contemplation rather than worship. It was low on priorities, though, because it was serviceable as it was. The men had wanted a place to pray and, to be honest, take some of the young local women for private times.

They stopped for drinks. Pera felt light-headed, excited. She wore men's shoes (well, boys') because they were so comfortable, and stockings and shorts. Her style. And a man's shirt tied about the waist, almost wrapped around. She felt as if she was one of them. She loved that they listened to her.

'So how did you two meet?' the architect asked.

Joseph and Pera exchanged glances. She hadn't told anyone the whole story, simply that Joseph had shown up on her doorstep. It was too strange, too . . . awful, that she was spending time with the brother of the man who killed her sister.

The architect listened when Pera told him her idea of having a room for every person who died.

He came to her with a blueprint all folded together, like a fan, because each room related to the ones next to and above and below. It was the most beautiful thing Pera had ever seen.

They spent many days finalising the design. Many nights they stayed back at the office, and the architect's glamorous wife would join them. She made Pera laugh with her jokes; she was the wittiest woman Pera had met since Lady Langhorne, long, long ago.

They talked about how many bathrooms and bedrooms. About secret hallways. About whether to preserve the remaining walls or start again.

'We're doing lots of rooms,' Pera told her. 'One room for each person who died. And some extras, so I can add to them as I hear people's stories.'

The architect wrote, 'In my father's mansion there are many rooms', at the top of the blueprint and she could have kissed him.

He said, 'What about the library?'

'Not interested in a library. Dusty, and no one touches the books anyway. What's the point?' but she knew she'd have one. There had been one; there would be one again. In the end there were two, one large and one small, plus bookcases around the house. She filled those shelves with trinkets rather than books.

The architect touched her shoulder and gave what she thought of as the Pity Look. Most people gave it to her when they heard what happened, or when they suddenly *remembered* what had happened to her.

They talked about what the feel of the place would be; old or new. Memory or activity. He helped her engage a master builder, a man who understood that some buildings will survive long beyond their original owners and that they needed therefore to have a character of their own.

28

THE BANNED ROOM (THE SECOND LIBRARY)

'Well, looky, looky,' Alex said. 'The loving family returns.'

Despairingly, Pera saw that they had. 'You need to go,' she hissed at the father.

'Have you told her yet?' the mother said.

'I haven't seen a ghost at all,' the daughter said, her mouth downturned. 'Except where all those stinky old books were.'

'The library? There's another tiny one up here. About the size of a closet, really. My parents used to keep all sorts of things in here us girls weren't allowed to look at. And things they took off us if we were naughty. It's where I keep all the banned books. All the ones children aren't supposed to read, nor grown-ups, really!'

'Can we look?' Chook said. 'Might be ghosts there.' She hated the idea of this creep touching anything of hers at all.

'Might be money hidden in the pages. That's where people usually hide money,' Wayne said.

'The books in here are worth a lot of money. Please be careful. And please be careful about looking at the pictures, kids!' Maybe the parents would be so offended, they'd give up and leave.

No such luck.

The parents chivvied the children away once they realised Pera hadn't been joking about the adult content of the books. Chook stood with one close to his face, looking at details.

The other Men all started taking book after book from the shelves and shaking them, looking for money. They left the books in a pile, face down, pages creased, covers bent.

'Careful!' she said. 'Please don't treat my things like that.'

'Ownership is . . .' Ike said. He paused, as if seeing a classic quote before his eyes. 'Bullshit,' he finished.

'Well, I own all this. Inside and out,' Pera said. 'Even the rock out there, and the pond. All mine.'

1951

She stood on the hanging rock facing the house with Joseph, the architect, and the master builder. It remained one of the best moments of her life; a moment of vision, of all possibilities.

'It's happening,' she said.

'Out of any rich, dark nothing the whole gazebo could be built up again,' the architect said. 'Says he, butchering another quote!' Pera knew him well enough by now not to say, 'But there isn't a gazebo!'

'Yeats,' he said. 'The master of all things odd and beyond.'

They had walked the perimeter of the building. The builder and the architect talked about some of the difficulties ahead, with supplies and labour and all the rest of it. Joseph talked about colours, and vision; hers, not his. He was helping her to make it real.

Every night she put herself to sleep doing this walk in her head; the halls, the stairs, the rooms, each one with a different name, remembering.

And work began.

She supervised the building of a stable. She thought she'd quite like to have horses again and knew that George and Harry would help her with them. In the back of her mind she thought maybe racehorses, but soon realised that would take a lot more dedication than she was willing to give.

Joseph supervised the build of his art studio where the sheep shed had been; lots of light, lots of space. Walking in there, Pera thought even she might be able to create within those walls. She thought of it as a place to remember the Italians who had lived and died in there, and allowed the townspeople to use the art studio space if they wanted to. She invited the local primary school for an art day, and invited them all to paint 'Italian Things' on the wall. She wanted that innocence, that simplicity, and she got it. Awkwardly painted bowls of spaghetti and meatballs adorned the walls, and Italian flags. She loved it.

She was mostly welcome wherever she went in town. Lots of the young people were moving away so they were glad to have her, bright and lively, with her dark past and her house that would draw the tourists in, make them all richer.

And yet there were some who didn't approve of her plans, who thought she was being disrespectful. There was a new spate of interest in the house, and her, and the studio-memorial, and the dead, for the ten-year anniversary of the accident. She was interviewed about new streets going up in town, what she thought they should be called, as if she was the one to know. They showed the prime minister's camera footage again and again, in newsreels at the cinema, and the papers dug up all they could about 'where are they now' (where is she now), which meant all the questions, all over again.

The mayor arranged the naming of new streets after some of those who'd died in the plane as it crashed, such as the pilot's daughters Mimi and Josie, although not the pilot himself of course. It was a nice thought but it did seem to remind people often. Journalists asked Pera about it, and she said that anyone was entitled to have a street named after them. That she was happy all were considered. 'We are all equal,' she said. 'Everyone deserves a street.'

1993

The family still hadn't returned to the Banned Room. Pera couldn't hear them. Perhaps she'd underestimated the mother. Perhaps they had run to their minivan and were already miles away. Although they seemed motivated by something, and she wished they'd get it over and done with.

She didn't know where Lucky had got to, or Alex, who scared her more than the rest of them. His eyes. His intensity . . . she hoped Lucky was okay.

Ike said, 'Because we're getting nowhere fast, here.'

Devon had found a fifty-dollar note in one of the books and they were hoping to find more. Pera had no memory of the money at all. She must have tucked it in there years ago. Chook stood out in the hallway and bellowed, 'Kids! Mummy! Daddy!

Your presence is required!'

He turned to look at his companions, a grin on his face as if delighted with his joke. The Men stared at him. Ike shook his head. 'Fuckwit,' he said.

The youngest boy appeared, running in front of his family waving a plastic sword he'd found somewhere.

'King fucken Arthur,' Ike muttered, showing more education than Pera had thought him capable of.

29

THE FIRST-FLOOR FOYER AND THE FRONT STEPS

'Where is everybody?' It was Alex, on the third floor, calling down.

'Here, mate,' Chook called up, although he was no one's mate. 'First floor.'

Alex slung his arm around Lucky and effectively dragged him down the stairs. 'Me and my buddy here have been having a chat.'

The group stood at the large window on the first floor which looked out over the rock and the pond. 'Oh, it looks gorgeous out there. So mysterious,' the wife said.

'I can tell you about mysteries,' Alex said, grabbing at his crotch. She didn't see him, and neither did her husband, but Lucky did. A small frown creased his face, but he said nothing. He had a cut on his cheek and he nursed one hand in the other.

'We'll get there soon,' Pera said. 'We'll see my veggie garden, too. I'm very proud of it. I know lots of you might not be interested in veggie gardens. You might prefer to stay in the house and explore the nooks and crannies. Find more to drink, boys!' she said, hoping to jolly The Men along, keep them inside.

'I reckon we should stick together,' Ike said. 'Don't you?'

'That's what they all say,' Alex said.

Pera nodded. 'Let's head outside, then. We came in the back way, the servants' entrance, so we'll go out the fancy way. Via the front door. Then I'll take you to a room that can only be accessed through a concealed door on the outside.'

She led them down the wide steps to the ground floor then out the front door. She was pleased to see them all follow; even The Men had fallen into the spell of storytelling and the house. She waited until Chook placed his foot on the first step before calling out, 'Stop! Careful where you walk. One of the angriest ghosts in the house haunts these steps. A man who did a job once common, now rare. A chauffeur.' She waved her walking cane at the thick red stain that dripped over the five stairs. 'Doesn't matter how many times we clean it, the stain returns. The poor man, all he was doing was dropping off a lady for dinner here. He could have been home by his fire, with a nice mug of tea.' She gave a shudder. 'So very ugly.'

'He died here? On this spot?' the older boy said.

'Right here.' She pointed to the top step with her toe. 'And his blood dripped all the way to there,' pointing to the bottom step. 'This was eight or ten years before my parents got married. They didn't even know each other then. My grandparents still ran the house. I think they had even more parties than my parents did! The chauffeur was leaning against his boss's car, which was parked exactly where your minivan is. It's a memorable minivan, that one, isn't it! Colourful and so large. My car is so boring no one would ever notice it or pick it out of a line-up, so to speak. But plenty of legroom nonetheless.' Pera didn't pause to see if the hint had struck home. *Take my car if you want to. You don't need their van.*

'Anyway, the chauffeur was leaning against his car, chatting to the horse wrangler, when he heard a scream. A man of duty, he ran towards the front door. He tripped, somehow. Cracked his chin on the corner of the step, split it open like a peach. But that wasn't what killed him.'

'What did kill him?' Devon asked.

'The horse wrangler hadn't heard the scream. He always said that, if you asked. He saw the chauffeur run, and trip, and ran to help. In his statement to the police, he swore he saw a child's roller skate at the base of the steps, although no child lived in the house then. And there was no roller skate to be found.'

Pera paused here.

'As the horse wrangler reached him, a chunk of stone broke off the eaves.' Pera pointed up. 'Smashed the chauffeur's head in. That's what killed him. His bloodstain comes back anytime we wash it away. Some don't see it, strangely enough. Does everyone here see it? Be careful. If you get any of your own blood on those steps, you'll come back here when you die. You'll become one of the ghosts.'

They all gathered around, looking closely, whispering, 'I see it. I see it.'

'Who screamed?' Devon asked. He shuddered. He was the most easily scared, Pera noted.

'No one ever found out. Poor Mr Chauffeur,' she said. 'I think ghosts are like chameleons, merging with the background. Out here there is so much distance they fade into it. They're still there. Only we can't often see them. He's here; trying to stop his fall. But we can't see him.'

She let that sit, as she always did.

For a while she'd told the truth about how the paint first appeared. The vilification she'd received. But it was too real. Ordinary. It didn't scare people; it made them feel pity and she didn't want that. So now she told a ghost story about the blood that wouldn't go away.

Sometimes tour groups figured out it was paint, not blood. Once she'd even been caught with some of it dripped onto her shoes after she'd refreshed it; that had caused great hilarity. She bought the tins from the hardware shop in town every six months or so, had been doing for decades. This batch was nice and fresh; she'd had the joy of pouring out the whole tin a week earlier. Every time she did it she felt strong; no one would bully her. No one would judge her, call her a scarlet woman. It was a constant reminder to herself, and to others, that she didn't care. That they could call her what they liked.

1952

It was dear Mr Thomas, who used to own a tiny hardware store where the video shop was now, who had helped her figure out who threw the paint, and how to clean it off.

The township was high on a slope, a steep ride. She had a Vauxhall she'd bought for cheap from the architect, who thought that might get her to work in a timelier fashion than her Morris Minor, which she sold. She often got stuck behind a struggling old bus; you could hear it puffing from one end of town to the other. She'd get infuriated but would wait and pass only when she got the wave from the driver.

Mr Thomas's shop was dark and cool. Lots of containers with nuts, bolts. He knew the size of a thing by looking at it. He'd been working there since he was fourteen, and he was a man in his seventies with a wild white head of hair he tried to keep neatly tamed. Pera and her sisters used to hide amongst the shelves whenever they went to town, because the shop was dark and perfect for hide and seek.

Mr Thomas always breathed quite heavily. You knew when he was coming.

Pera chose a large tin of industrial cleaner and carried it to the counter.

'Find what you need there? Going to wash out your stables or something?'

'Someone threw red paint all over the front steps,' she said. She'd come downstairs after a good night's sleep to find it. At first she thought it was blood and was greatly relieved to realise it was otherwise.

His mouth drooped and his eyes, too. She knew the look: pity. Such great pity they never knew what to say, which was good, because she preferred not to say anything back.

'Hmm.' He tapped his pen on his front teeth. 'Let me think back. Who bought that red paint? That'll give us a clue.'

'They probably didn't buy it here, Mr Thomas. They probably got it from the city.'

'The city!' He was offended.

'Not me. You know I buy only from you.'

She insisted her builders did, too, even if it cost more. Mr Thomas was a kind man who always had a cheery word.

There was plenty of opposition to the rebuilding of Sinclair

House, beyond the superstitions. Some thought it should remain derelict, a monument to the men and women who died, although mostly they meant the prime minister, whenever it was talked about officially.

The superstitious thought the place was haunted, riddled with ghosts.

Any of those people could have thrown red paint on her steps. And there were many in town who thought her liaison with Joseph was disgusting. Little did they know, he insisted on marriage before anything physical happened between them. She had to laugh at the disapproval she didn't deserve. And they didn't even know the full truth of it. They didn't even know who he was.

Mr Thomas said, 'You pop off and finish your messages and I'll have a look back at the ledger. See if we can't track this down for you.' He lifted a great heavy book onto the counter, flipped it open, and noted her purchase. Mr Thomas never forgot anything. He figured out all his sums on butcher's paper; never had a cash register or a calculator.

So Pera went and had her hair done and a good chat with her dear friend Claudia, working in the salon for money but also for all the latest town news. They gossiped about the red paint and Claudia said, 'You should have a party and invite everyone. People love a party and no one would throw paint on your steps again.'

It had been a long time since there was a party at Sinclair House.

*

Between them, she and Mr Thomas figured out who did it. They had a great time investigating; looking at the ledger was all it really took, and for Pera to innocently make a comment in the presence of the guilty party. It was a young mother, six years older than Pera, not a local, who'd married Kev Taylor, the butcher. She was deeply unhappy; everyone knew that. And she was very much against anything considered communist, and with Pera reported in the news as saying, 'We are all equal. Everyone deserves a street,' she was incensed.

Dear Mr Thomas arrived on her doorstep with even more solvents and his son, to scrub the paint away.

'Good enough to eat off!' Pera said once they were done.

'You're doing a marvellous job on the place,' Mr Thomas said. It was true; she had. And it was time to show it off.

The party started with afternoon tea, because some of the older locals didn't like being out late, with the clear indication that it would segue into an evening party. 'Party dress optional,' she said on the invitations, although she planned to dress up for the later guests. Parts of the house were presentable: the kitchen, the dining room, the men's drawing room. The foyer looked lovely, too, and the front steps were shiny, no red paint splashing them. She put up barriers across some of the doors but knew that people wouldn't be able to resist sticky-beaking. Hopefully no one would be hurt.

She asked all the town along, and she paid the Country Women's Association to bake. It wasn't just to win the town over; she really was grateful to them all, and she did understand that they had been affected by the accident as well. They were famous; the town was synonymous with the aeroplane crash. The population had grown again in the last year or two, and it was livelier than it ever had been, with two small restaurants competing with the local pub for evening entertainment.

New houses were being built, and old ones renovated, bringing a housing prosperity to the town. People forgot sometimes the crash-site was her home; they thought it belonged to them.

Mrs Robertson, who was very glamorous and wore diamonds to the opening of a paper bag, helped Pera set the party up. She said, 'Pera's got an announcement, hasn't she! That's what this party is about. Do tell! You're getting married, aren't you? You won't want to leave it too late, dear. Better to have your children sooner rather than later. I had my first at eighteen and never regretted it. My life is almost my own again already!' Mrs Robertson was only just old enough to remember when the soldiers had been billeted in Pera's house before the war. 'Oh, the stories I could tell you!' she said, blushing and giggling like the eighteen-year-old she'd been.

Gwennie, who at thirty-five was considered a great wag (meaning she'd never marry), said, 'Oh, Pat! Leave the girl alone! Don't embarrass her!'

'Oh, you can talk, our Gwennie! You nearly married half of them, don't think we don't remember!' Mrs Bee, as always there in the background doing all she could, threw her head back and laughed.

Joseph hovered nearby, looking tall and bronzed because he'd spent some time in Queensland getting ideas from the rainforests.

He was glad to come back to her and not to his family, he said. His family business was cabinetmaking, with no room for creativity. He was glad for the practical knowledge he'd gained, but wanted nothing to do with the business.

'I haven't got an announcement. I wanted to say thank you to everybody. You've looked after me so well, stepped in for my family when I lost them. There's not one of you who didn't do so,' Pera said.

The butcher and his wife arrived. People called him the New Butcher, because he'd been apprenticed to the Old Butcher, even though the Old Butcher had retired six years earlier. The New Butcher was always kind; in fact Pera got the impression he rather liked her. This could be the reason his wife threw the paint, not politics at all. Pera tried to win her over, would try for decades, without much success. Envy was a terrible thing.

Also, there was Young Bobby whose bicycle she had stolen, and his wife. There were other policemen, too, standing around awkwardly with their delicate cups of tea.

There were slices of many types: lemon, vanilla, caramel, peppermint and date. There were Anzac biscuits, chocolate biscuits and yoyos. There were sponges. Sandwiches. Tiny quiches. Enough food to feed an army, they all said. Joseph hated every minute of it, cowering in the corner, hoping no one would talk to him. No one did; they found him a bit intimidating, with his apparent brilliance.

'He painted the invitation and the posters!' Pera kept telling people, and they'd say, 'Oh, did he? Isn't he clever?' which only made him cower further. He was terrified people would ask him about his family, about his brother.

Her best friends from school arrived, dressed to the nines, hair lacquered and fabulous. Claudia wore high shoes that skittered across the floor, and her high-pitched squeal was enough to trigger the departure of some of the afternoon-tea guests. Isabel farewelled them all as they left because she was like that; always friendly. Harry spent his time trying to stop children eating all the cakes, and jollied Joseph along. He'd already proposed to Claudia and perhaps he had in his head that they would be a power quartet, that the four of them would have family holidays on the beach and the children would grow up together. Harry always was one for thinking into the future. George also tried to jolly Joseph along to give a rendition of 'Along the Road to Gundagai', which they'd done drunkenly the first time they met and which George thought made them friends ever since.

The architect and his wife were there as well, enjoying the country cooking. She was a career woman so there was little baking done in the home.

Some of the police left but the others finally relaxed and took a drink.

Mr and Mrs Bee seemed tempted to stay, but he said, 'It's only for the young ones.'

'We're all young at heart, Mr Bee!' Pera said, pouring him an ice-cold glass of beer. 'Take a sip of that and see how old you feel.'

Pera slipped upstairs to change into a slinky gown. Trying to pretend to be an adult, and she'd sit at the table this time, not underneath.

'Look at you! A vision!' Joseph said, and truly he did not take his eyes off her all night. She was never sure if he already loved her by then, or if he fell in love with her image, the sophisticated party girl face she put on.

Word got out that Harry and Claudia were engaged and that meant more champagne and singing and celebration. Pera drank too much and it made her sleepy. She went and curled up in a window nook upstairs. She could hear everything up there ('Dirty little eavesdropper' her sisters would call her) without having to have any input, and that was nice for a while. She was grateful none of them knew yet who Joseph was; who his brother was.

It wasn't long before they noticed she was missing which was gratifying, so she fixed her hair and went back downstairs.

Later, Joseph commented that she was like a chameleon. Different skin for different people.

30

KINGDOM COME (THE STABLES)

1993

She walked them to the stables, over which hung a carefully painted sign, 'Kingdom Come'. She liked her private joke, the wrangler long ago telling her the horses would kick her to Kingdom Come. If anyone ever asked about the name (they rarely did) she'd tell them she found the sign at a trash and treasure market. The story itself wasn't interesting enough to share.

'Where's Alex?' Chook said.

'Having a wank. You know he can't go more than ten minutes without it,' Devon said, mimicking the act. He looked at the mother, and at the daughter. Pera stood between them. She felt ill. She needed to get these two away at the very least. They were so caught up in their own world, their 'look at our perfect family' world, they were oblivious to those around them. For a moment Pera wanted to leave them to it, let them see they weren't so perfect, they weren't better than everyone else.

But of course they *didn't* think that, or act like that. They were perfectly nice, good people. Pera just felt a moment of pure jealousy that she didn't have this simple family unit to nestle into.

Lucky said, 'I didn't know your family kept horses.'

'Yes,' Pera said. 'But sometimes I don't know why *I* do. So much heartache. For some reason animal stories make me sadder than people stories.'

The parents murmured agreement. 'I only have two now because I don't want to care for them. I pay a local teenager to come twice a day to tend them. They're off at the local stables at the moment, though. Having a little holiday! And their annual check-up.' She was relieved that the teenager wouldn't be coming face to face with The Men.

'Some early mornings, you can hear a gentle whicker of a dozen horses. It'd be comforting, if it wasn't that they were ghosts. I keep the living horses to scare away the ghostly ones. These are happy horses. They get ridden every now and then, but mostly they are here for company. Well . . .' She paused. 'They're here to keep the horse spirits away. When the stables are empty, you can hear neighing. Hooves stamping. Horses screaming . . . that's a terrible noise. It was awful. Horses trust you; they don't know any better. Once they trust you, they always will. So for my family's horses to be trapped, burnt to death . . .'

She sniffed. The mother dabbed her eyes. 'Can you smell smoke?'

She gave them a minute. Lucky shook his head. Wayne and Devon nodded; Ike and Chook didn't respond. She periodically set fire to stacks of hay in the stable, so the smell of burning was there.

'All ghosts are about guilt,' Pera said. 'Regret, yes. But isn't regret guilt, too?' She knew all the tricks how to scare people. It was mostly about the story. Without the story, the bangs and whispers meant nothing. 'Is this place haunted by a young boy who ran away from home and hid with the horses, and they didn't find him for a week, suffocated by the straw?'

In the silence that followed, she heard deep breathing, like the horses after a morning run. The daughter started to cry, so she led them out of the stables.

'It gets worse. I'm sorry. But it gets worse. Perhaps we should cut our tour short here?'

'I'd say we should stick together,' Ike said.

She led them past the sheep shed she'd rebuilt into an art studio and memorial. It was dilapidated now, to her great shame.

'What's in there?' Lucky said.

'This used to be the sheep shed. A place of refuge, a home for some.'

'Who are you talking about? A long-lost relative or something?' the father asked. Something in his tone made her stop and look at him.

'I feel so bad thinking about it. But in a way, they had a better life. Until they died,' she said. 'They were interned Italians. So-called "enemy aliens". The men were let out of the camp to work on farms, and some families escaped. I like to think they had the freedom here. And I love that my father let them stay. Now come along. I have something terrible to show you.'

She led them around the side of the house to the door of the Douglas Room.

31

THE DOUGLAS ROOM

She pushed open the door. Breathed deeply. '*Pseudotsuga genus*. Douglas fir. Can you smell it? Heaviest wood in construction,' she said. 'And you'll notice there is no inside door. I had it sealed off.'

She flinched slightly as she always did at the memory of what had happened there. 'This is the room we call the Douglas Room, after my father. He loved his privacy, much as he was a genial man and a good father. I had this room built into the outside wall. Like a shed, but built in.'

'My dad had a room like this,' Chook said. 'It was where he used to beat the shit out of us. Makes my bum itchy just thinking of it.' He gave a shudder.

'That's terrible!' the mother said. 'You poor, poor man.'

'Don't waste your sympathy on him,' Ike said. 'He's an out-and-out liar.'

The Douglas Room had a sense of luxury about it, with its hardwood floors and gold trimmings.

The father asked, 'How did you afford all of it? This must have cost a fortune.'

'Well, I inherited everything when I was twenty-one. There would have been enough for all of us, all the sisters, but I ended up with it all. My uncle Alan managed it well. He was good at that sort of thing.' She didn't say a lot of it was money made during the Great War. People seemed to find that distressing. 'You might say this house is literally made of money,' she said. She looked directly at Ike as she said this, hoping her meaning was clear: *Be nice. Stick with me. And I'll tell you where the money is.*

'Tell me more,' Ike said. He took hold of her arm, so tight it felt like a tourniquet.

'You catch more flies with honey than vinegar,' she whispered to him. 'Something I've learned to my detriment over the years.' She gave him a brilliant smile and he let her go. 'Everybody has a room they think is the most haunted. You wait until you're on your way home. You won't be arguing over politics or religion. You'll be arguing about ghosts. This is the room I argue for, mostly because I saw a man die here. I knew his name. I held his hand as life was extinguished.'

Lucky said, 'So many more people have died in this house than lived in it.'

'That's true. There have been a lot of deaths in this house,' she said. 'As opposed to the opposite house.' No one ever got the Emily Dickinson reference. 'I could tell you about a death in my life every night,' she says. None of them have a response to that. She'd already told them so many stories.

Devon said, 'It must have been cursed from the start. What was it made out of? What's it built on?'

Ike said, 'Nothing's cursed. You have a shit life or you don't. That's all there is to it.'

'In Lancashire they used to believe that to build a house was fatal to the designer if they intended to live in it,' Pera said. 'Once a man started on the building, his life would cease when it was finished. There was one man who believed so fervently he hired men to build a massive wall around his house, going on for years. But during a heavy frost no work was done and he died, they say. I'm not superstitious but at the same time it doesn't hurt to leave some things undone.'

They had done a good job of covering up the death; certainly there was no visible bloodstain and she could see no gouges in the wood from his fingernails and from where the wood fell. Still, she remembered the feel of his hand, its weak pulse fluttering like a butterfly's wings. And his eyes on her, as if she could do anything beyond give him comfort. The least she could do was listen to his last words.

1952

The repairs had been going well before the accident. She stood watching from Hanging Rock as she liked to do, because she was away from the action, not causing a nuisance, but she could see everything. The bricks glowed in the afternoon heat, almost buzzed, and Pera felt a buzz of excitement to match it. Joseph wanted her to travel to Europe with him, see the world, he said. 'Come with me on this adventure. London, Italy, France.'

So far, she had resisted; she felt as if her adventure was here, watching her house grow.

Three cars filled the driveway. Two were utes, covered with

mud, cement, dust. The other was a Holden, shiny blue, new, belonging to the architect.

The hum of men working rose as she walked towards the house. Hammering, shouting, laughter. She loved it. There was something very sexy about men at work.

She met the architect on the steps.

'Oh,' he said.

'Nice welcome!'

'No, sorry, we're expecting another carload of blokes. Shifting some wood slabs into place but need more muscle.' Each slab weighed close to 150 kg; it took four men to shift them.

She'd helped choose all the wood, a different grain in every room. Today they were laying the Douglas Room, named for her father.

They moved through the house. 'It's looking good!'

She headed up to the highest room, which she'd chosen as her residence because she loved to be at the top of the house. They built in a tiny kitchen and a bathroom for her, and she would sometimes sit up there and watch all day as the workers came and went. It seemed highly organised; everyone knew where they were going and when. They were strong men and she didn't mind that at all, watching them stripped to singlets carrying in the great slabs of wood, the bags of cement, the loads of brick.

The Douglas Room was going to be beautiful. The wood was hard and glorious in colour. No art would ever hang on those walls; the wood was the art.

The slabs were heavy; the men struggled with them. She heard them calling out to each other and thought she'd better keep out of the way, but then the shouting rose, sounded panicked, and she ran to the Douglas Room.

Inside, a slab had fallen on one of the workers, and two men were working to lift the wood off him.

1993

'The man screamed, high-pitched, animal-like, his eyes rolling in his head. One arm was loose and he grabbed at the men trying to help. He gouged scratches in the wood. They stood around the slab, one two three lift one two three lift one two three lift as the man's voice faded, his arm stopped waving. Around the slab I could see the thinnest edging of blood. I sat by him. "It'll be all right," I told him, as if I knew. "We'll save you."

'He shook his head. His tongue was swollen, white, and I didn't know why.

'I bent close, willing to hear his last words. It was a sad attempt at his life story. I wrote parts of it down but there was little of interest and he both repeated himself and contradicted himself, so I wasn't sure what to believe.

'I knew it was my fault, that somehow time . . . that men had been late for work that day. One had slept in and missed his ride to the site. If he'd been here things would have been different. Accidents of time are always my fault.'

During the plane crash there was a moment when she felt absolutely and completely alone. This had felt the same.

'Ever since then, whenever I come into this room I feel my hand being squeezed, and a flutter in my ear as if he is still trying to get me to write his story down properly. Does anyone else feel that?'

Devon and the father nodded. The mother had tears in her eyes. 'That's so sad.'

'It is sad. I wish I'd listened better.'

'It's not your fault!' the mother said.

1952

After the accident, the architect told her she should go on that trip to Europe. 'We'll sand back the floor. Varnish it all. You won't be able to see where it happened and then you'll be able to forget.' He told her it was all going to take two years. Three, even, if they were to get it right.

'I would rather like to go offshore again,' she said. No one else spoke that way, but she remembered the glamorous Lady Langhorne using the term and loved to mimic her. Her last trip had been to New Zealand; she wanted to really travel this time.

Joseph was delighted at the prospect of an overseas trip, and even, after some argument, allowed her to pay the costs. 'You are an artist,' she said, 'I am your patron.' Her full inheritance had come through and she had more money than she could possibly spend in a lifetime.

She was terrified of flying but had no interest in taking a boat. Too slow, too dull. She wanted to be moving, seeing, experiencing, she wanted to throw herself into this new world.

She said, 'I shouldn't fly. I'm too worried I'll shut the clocks down.'

'That's not possible. It's not going to happen.'

'It's what happened with the plane. Flying over me was enough.'

'You know that's not true. So tell me; where have you dreamed of going?'

She told him about her postcard of the Roman church Chiesa del Sacro Cuore del Suffragio, and how her father said he'd left her a message there.

'Should we go, do you think?'

'Let's make that our goal.'

1993

The Men circled the Douglas Room, opening drawers, lifting clocks and cigar boxes, moving curtains aside as if looking for a hidden cupboard.

It annoyed her; she couldn't stop herself saying, 'Can I help you, boys?'

'We heard there's a shitload – sorry – lots of treasure here,' Devon said.

'Ah, you never know, do you? Under the carpet, in the walls, in cupboards; there is treasure everywhere. I'm the only one who knows where it is, how to find it, and which key to use!'

To demonstrate, she reached behind her father's heavy oak desk, one of the only pieces of furniture to survive the fire and only just; it was burnt and damaged, but she still loved it. She fiddled around until a small drawer popped out; inside, four rolls of sweets, which she handed to the children.

'You see? I loved this desk and all its secret compartments so much as a child. There are more around the room, see if you can find them!'

The daughter squealed with delight, and all three of the children joined The Men in finding buttons around the room in smaller desks, in armrests, in the wall, and in a small carved cupboard. Everybody laughed. There was no awkwardness, for the first time. These men were not comfortable with children or with women, or with men who didn't use violence as a way to communicate. She was relieved that Alex was wherever he was; something in him terrified her more than the others did.

She found bottles of whisky; how old she didn't know. That made The Men happy.

32

THE REMNANTS ROOM (LOST AND FOUND)

Pera led them up to the third floor. 'I call this room the Remnants Room because I haven't thought of a better name. It's the place for things left behind here. Some deliberately, some accidentally.'

There was a large collection of umbrellas in one corner, and shelves of books, knick-knacks, purses, shoes.

There was a sheaf of letters on a side table.

'Some of it I found during my trip to Europe. I didn't steal anything, don't worry! But anything I saw left behind I rescued. I've dedicated this room to the young man who was part of the prime minister's entourage, who would have married one of my sisters. He was obsessed with keeping souvenirs.

'Things ... appear in this room. I didn't place them all here. Like this riding crop. Where the heck did it come from? And this silver cup. I didn't put them here.'

'Maybe visitors do,' Wayne said. His voice quavered slightly.

'It's possible. But sometimes they are there in the morning when I've been in the house alone overnight.'

1952

The brother of the PM's young man helped her get the Europe trip sorted. He knew people who knew people and made sure she had letters of introduction and all she needed. She planned to be away for six months or more; the architect assured her the renovations would proceed, now all the plans were in place. One thing that presented itself as necessary to easier travel: Joseph and she should marry.

They married in the registrar's office in Sydney, going through the motions with the promise they would have a proper wedding once they were settled. Pera looked at Joseph, staid in his borrowed suit but with plaster dust streaked across his cheek and thought, *This will work! I can love, I DO LOVE this man.*

For their wedding night, they booked into the Savoy. It seemed more private than a small hotel; they were two of many, with less scrutiny from the other patrons.

They had dinner in their room; lobster, champagne. He had whisky, too much, she thought, because he couldn't handle it. He wasn't a drinker really, couldn't keep up with her, that's for sure. They had crêpes Suzette and squealed at the flames as people did, then the waiter departed, taking the food trolley with him.

Joseph was flushed. More nervous than she was. She wondered if his experience was less than hers? She had taken her chances during school, and later. Taken lovers. She knew that life could be short and decisions should never be made out of fear of disapproval.

She dressed in her new nightgown, which was lacy, a golden brass colour. It felt soft on her skin and she loved walking in it, the way it clung to her legs, her creases, the way it made her feel.

He watched her sidelong.

'You're allowed to look! We're married!' she said, and she moved towards him and sat in his lap. He flinched. She was sure he flinched. He was so nervous!

Then he kissed her, and held her with his strong, artistic hands, and there was such a stirring in her. She had never felt anything like it before. He moaned softly, from deep in his chest. His eyes were closed; his temples throbbed.

'Come on,' she said, and she led him to the bed.

She was not wildly experienced but more so than he was. She didn't want to terrify him and she was in no hurry. Like most men, he was ready for love with simple bodily contact; simply the sight of a woman. The gentle touch.

He ran his fingers over her skin, his eyes intent. It made her laugh. 'I'm not a piece of stone!' she said, which made *him* laugh, and he played then, pretending she was stone and he was the artist, and that eased all the awkwardness from him.

He was a beautiful artist.

He was the most beautiful lover she would ever have.

Joseph had travelled overseas very little, and Pera only to New Zealand, so they eased themselves into the experience by beginning in London. They could understand the language, and the faces were familiar, and the places they knew from the history books. Pera knew them also from postcards her father had sent and that was how they developed their travel plan, ticking off each site proudly.

33

THE FLEA MARKET (ART GALLERY 7)

1993

'I do love the art in this room. It's named after a flea market in London where I found this amazing piece. It's another rendition of a famous painting called *An Australian*, can you believe it? I loved it on sight then found it was by Hilda Rix Nicholas.'

Not one of them knew who that was. 'A brilliant artist with a tragic life,' Pera said. She loved this painting; the toss of the young woman's head, the red of her scarf and hat, the glorious black coat.

'How much is it worth?' Chook said. 'On resale, I mean. Actual value.'

'Hard to say. Amongst all of this, a lot.'

'You should have security in place,' Lucky said. 'You have so many people through.'

Ike smiled. Pera felt relief; it was better when he smiled. Lucky was an idiot, though.

She used to name the paintings and boast about their worth,

until someone stole one. Usually she told people they were reproductions. Many were, but some were originals. She had two John Glovers, four William Ashtons, a Streeton and a number of Namatjiras. Some she had acquired privately, and she wouldn't ever show them in public. Flinck's *Landscape with Obelisk*, Lucas Sithole's *Groping their way home in the dark*, Carlo Maratta's *David and Bathsheba*.

There was a series of paintings picked up from a deceased estate, all of them cared for badly in the intervening years. There was Richard Redgrave's *The Sempstress*, and Konrad Cramer's *Summer Afternoon* and what could only be a forgery of Millais's *Ophelia*.

She showed them a simple picture; a cat in a window, gazing out.

'The thing that drew me in was this.' She pointed to the artist's shadow. 'Not many artists do this, but I love to see it. It gives them a powerful presence.'

She could remember clearly the shadow the aeroplane had cast. Watching it move across the ground. At least she thought she could remember it; there were no photographs of the shadow itself.

'While this room doesn't have a ghost, the spirits of all these artists are clear, aren't they?' She liked to commission pieces from artists who had suffered a tragedy. Even without telling them she wanted shadows, they had painted them.

There were some wonderful cartoons as well, although not like the funny ones in the newspapers. They were tragic, with ghostly soldiers, and long rows of crosses, and the saddest faces she had ever seen.

34

THE HALL OF DAMAGE (ART GALLERY 8)

Pera led them down the hallway where she displayed paintings that had been deliberately damaged, mostly for political reasons. There was one of the man she considered *her* PM, the one who liked her drawings. He'd been slashed from corner to corner, and 'Destroyer' written on the exposed canvas beneath.

There was a big armchair in this room, faced towards a portrait of Winston Churchill (defaced with purple paint). This was her preferred snoozing spot in the day, because it was tucked out of the way and the chair was very comfortable.

There was an ornate mirror hanging there. Months ago she'd written something in candlewax. It showed up when light was reflected off the mirror's surface; it couldn't be seen otherwise.

As soon as one of them flicked the floor lamp on (and they'd have to; the ceiling light didn't work) they'd see the message. She hoped it would upset them.

1952

Pera and Joseph walked hand in hand. His grip was firm and dry, his hand large, surrounding hers. She felt in a stupor of physical love for him; each night was sweeter than the last, and some days she wished they could stay in bed and not bother with going out at all.

They ate in an underground restaurant, which was candlelit and wildly romantic. There was a small barred window; through it they could see the feet of the passers-by. She entertained him by telling him the story behind each pair. He laughed at her invention, and he said he'd paint a picture of her as she sat there, in the dim light, with her eyes bright with storytelling.

Then he was silent, gazing at her.

'What is it?'

'We did the right thing, getting married. I feel as if we could complete what they started.'

She shook her head, lost.

'My brother. Your sister. They must have loved each other once, if only at first. If we have a good marriage we can perhaps bring them back to life.'

He kissed the palm of her hand, sending a thrill running through her body. 'What I'm saying is, I think this is going to stick. Don't you?'

When she recovered herself, and agreed, she said, 'I'm going to have to send a telegram to the architect and tell him to add a "Wives' Room" to the house.' He stared blankly and really it was at that moment she realised he knew very little about her.

The Wives' Room was her mother's joke. When the men had

business, especially financial stuff which they seemed to talk about in tongues to keep it more mysterious, she would gather the women to go to the Wives' Room. In there her mother kept . . . what? The day's newspapers, perhaps. Books of philosophy. She said, 'We can discuss the problems of our own lives.'

Mostly, they'd be gossiping within minutes. 'Problems of the world are solved at ground level,' her mother said. 'If only more people would understand that, we wouldn't be knee-deep in a war.'

Before the war she used to say, 'We wouldn't be hearing about war.' Once the war began she tried to avoid saying 'I told you so' more than once a day.

Joseph and Pera walked back to their hotel, hand in hand for a while, until he started to pick up bits of stone. Even years after the war, piles of debris and rubble littered street corners in London, daily reminders of the bombings. Every piece a work of art in the making, he said.

He wanted to capture the war. The destruction of buildings, the nature of collapse.

She considered it her job to send postcards; she sent them to friends from school, to Claudia, Isabel, Harry, George, Uncle Alan, Young Bobby. She sent them to herself. She sent them to anybody she'd ever known. She followed in her father's footsteps in this way. She replaced what was lost, although what was lost could never really be replaced. She was only glad she'd read his postcards so many times, so she remembered the words on many of them. She found she stood out less in Europe for having lost her whole family. Many families lost all their sons, their daughters, their father.

'It's not a competition,' Joseph said when she mentioned it. She didn't speak to him for a day after that. How dare he misunderstand her so badly? To recover themselves they had a wonderful picnic on an old bridge on a day trip out of London. Bottles of wine, sandwiches in a packet, with a sleepy dog for company.

The second to last stop of their tour was Rome. Being there reminded her of Phar Lap and his family, and the rest of the migrants; overheard words, and the smell of garlic. For a short while she thought she might be able to track their relatives down but of course that was foolish. Beyond the language barrier, she had no information about them apart from the secret that they lived in her sheep shed. Had died there.

They went to Chiesa del Sacro Cuore del Suffragio, the beautiful church in the centre of Rome. While Joseph investigated the statuary, Pera became obsessed with the Museum of the Souls of Purgatory. Pera looked for a message from her father but could find none; she wondered if he'd been serious at all. When she saw the artefacts dedicated to the notion of purgatory, the burnt books, the photographs of singed clothing, she wondered if he had seen the future, if he was telling her to save him and the rest of the family, that they would sit in purgatory until she helped them out. Was this the message from her father? To understand this? Or was he simply having fun with a child? Pera couldn't leave this place. This was *her family*, she thought, singed and burnt and lost.

*

Pera never did find a record of the Italian family, not in Italy or Australia. She felt sure she'd find them here, given her friend's obsession with purgatory, but there was nothing. If they were ever there, they'd been forgotten.

35

THE ROAMIN' ROOM (CORRESPONDENCE)

1993

'I call this the Roamin' Room. It's full of postcards! It's about my favourite room in the house, I think. So many happy memories. On my trips away I always send hundreds of the things. Lots to myself as well! It's nice to come back to find a great mound of them on the kitchen table. My houseminders and helpers pile them up for me. I bet they read them, too. Sometimes I'll write something cheeky, just to shock them!' The postcards were displayed in albums, in glass cases, and in file boxes.

The room was decorated like ancient Rome. Once the tour group realised this, they all chuckled, even The Men. It was always nice to hear. She didn't expect guffaws; she knew her room names weren't that funny. But she did like a response.

'There are so many postcards!' the youngest boy said.

'Lots of the locals sent me postcards when I travelled. Funny lot! I collected them at various post offices over Europe. It was partly a joke, sending me postcards when I was the one travelling, but I loved them. They took a long time to reach me so sometimes the news was old. They all sent one for my twenty-first. Wasn't that kind of them? They knew I had no family to celebrate with so they made sure to take care of me. I suppose they thought of me as their responsibility. But I've never been one to sit back and feel sorry for myself.'

1952

Then it was back to London, another stop on their adventure. Joseph became infuriated by her inability to be on time. For her there was Now, Soon or Later. She didn't deal in anything more certain than that. She told him, as she told many people, 'Clocks can't be trusted and neither can time,' and certainly he'd given up wearing his wristwatch because it seemed incapable of keeping time in her vicinity, although even the watchmaker he consulted could find nothing wrong with it.

For an artist he was very particular.

'It's my fault. I could even slow down Big Ben!' she said, and they went there to prove it but he refused to look.

They took a day trip out to another church featured on one of her father's postcards. Pera wondered if her father had left her a message in this church instead of the other, but she made a search and found nothing. Whatever it may have been was long gone, she thought, unless it was some symbolic item she didn't understand. There were some scratches on the walls, some old books in the corner, but nothing that sang out to her.

While Joseph wandered around taking sketches, touching stone, carefully choosing small loose pieces to put into his pocket, Pera placed a jumper on the floor in the aisle and sat there, imagining herself centuries ago, a young girl, hands calloused from farm work, entranced by a handsome priest who was powerful in his words.

She could almost feel the weight of a respectful veil on her head, so clear was this daydream. She blinked, but the pressure didn't lessen. She stood up, brushing at her hair, and what she found was a veil of spiderwebs, a great sheet of it dropped from somewhere above.

She drew breath, the wrong thing to do because she sucked in a lungful of dust and web, sending her into a long coughing fit.

She staggered up the aisle, hoping for fresh air outside and a friendly thump on the back. As she moved to the double doors she heard a hissing noise and a sigh, and wondered why that person didn't come to her aid.

Outside, she coughed herself double, bent at the waist, her whole body in pain. She heard the hissing again, and another sigh, but there was nobody close by. Peering into the church she saw it was echoingly empty.

Joseph had wandered off into the church grounds and she didn't have the lung power to call him, so she sat instead and waited until her breath returned.

Anytime she faltered or felt frightened, she thought of her sisters. She knew her sisters weren't there but still they helped her to be who she was.

Joseph sat on an old stone bench under an oak tree in the far corner of the church grounds, and seeing him calmed her instantly. It was magnificent and she wanted one for home. She coughed; her chest hurt.

'I'm sorry, it's my lungs. They always tell me I have weak lungs.'

'I have exceptionally strong ones,' he said, and to prove it he sang '*Che gelida manina*' from *La Bohème*, making her choke with laughter.

'I can tell you a story of lovers,' she said, and she did, spinning a kindly tale of a couple married for decades who couldn't bear to be apart, even after death.

She loved the feeling, the chill, of imagining that ghostly couple, bound for eternity.

1993

None of the postcards from around the world recaptured the magic of her father's postcards and mostly made her sad because of this.

'We should stick some of Byron's postcards up here. Works of bloody art they are, mate. Seriously,' Ike said, touching one hanging on the wall. To and from, to and from, every one a memory.

'Is he an artist?' Pera asked but Ike ignored her. She wondered about Byron; who was he?

'Some of those were written by the pilot, the man who died killing my family, postcards he'd sent home to his mother, full of love. You wouldn't know he was a murderer by reading them.' The postcards were simple platitudes and tiny drawings of love hearts and flowers.

'These postcards arrived wrapped in Christmas paper. Must have been around 1975; somewhere around then. They were all addressed to his mother. There was no accompanying note with them but I wondered if the mother had sent them to me, wanting to tell me *He wasn't all bad. He loved his mother.* I found out later the woman had died a hoarder and her body hadn't been found for weeks. The postcards were in a box with my name and address on them. Somebody had found them and sent them on. You can smell her on the postcards,' Pera said, 'if you hold them close to your nose. The molecules as she ... wasted away.'

Only Chook was game to take a sniff. 'I love the way a woman smells,' he said. Pera had to swallow hard to stop herself from vomiting.

'He sent others, hundreds, to the prime minister's office but never got an answer. They haven't got time to answer lunatics. He blamed the PM's policies. But why did he have to take so many with him?'

There was a story at the time in one of the less reputable newspapers that detailed 'an imagination' of his children's last moments, inspired by the 'work' of a self-described 'eminent' psychic. Much of the focus was on the prime minister, with the other victims rendered secondary. Pera found the story of the children too harrowing to read, imagined or not.

'Some of these postcards are the only ones of their kind. Rare as hen's teeth and worth twice as much. Some of them are heart-breaking. Last words from a dying mother, or a joyful message from a friend never heard from again.'

The father said, 'That is so sad.' He gathered his arms around his family and Pera felt her heart break to see them grieving someone who wasn't yet lost. The mother's shoulders slumped and her eyes filled with tears. Pera recognised the look on her face; it was one of guilt. Of guilt at causing a fuss, at being a nuisance, at making people sad. Pera thought, *This is a loss yet to come.*

She saw a lot of grieving people. Many of them came to the house thinking it would give them closure. Not only for those whose loved ones had died in her house, but others; somehow they felt that coming would fix things.

She could pick a spouse recently bereaved. She offered small comfort, saying broadly, as she did now, 'It does give me hope to know there may be spirits, because it means there is a life beyond. There is something next. Ghosts might be someone we loved.'

'So the ghosts aren't always scary?' the youngest son said.

'Oh, they are always scary. Let me tell you; if anyone offers you a million dollars to stay in this room overnight, don't do it. Somehow, I think, the postcards absorbed the pain of generations. Can't you feel it now? A twinge in the ankle? The heart? A harder ache in the eyes? I know two people who have stayed here overnight. You can visit them if you like. But you'll have to go to the dementia ward to do it.'

It was one of the largest rooms in the house but with so many big men, it felt confined. There was a rank, leathery odour and Pera realised it came from Chook.

'What's all this worth, then?' Devon asked. 'All these postcards?'

'Some are worth a dollar. Some are worth fifty. There are a few that are worth thousands.' Ike ran his fingers over one of the glass cases and rapped gently with his knuckles. 'Not too sturdy.'

'No,' Pera said. 'But I don't usually bring people in here because of the ghosts. These ones are cruel. They look for your weaknesses and cling on. They'll jump on board if you let them and won't let go.'

'How do you stop them?' Devon said.

'I wish I knew how they chose people. Hopefully none are here today. If things start to fall apart, we need to get out of here quick sticks.' She said quietly to Ike, 'Whatever you can take, from anywhere in the house, you can divide amongst yourselves.'

1952

They spent their last fortnight in Paris, eating out every night. Perfect bowls of onion soup that made them both fart all the way back to their hotel.

Joseph savoured every bite. 'Back to steak and potatoes next month, Princess.' She wasn't comfortable with the nickname, wondering if he was being sarcastic. She started calling him Bluebeard, after a painting session where he'd worked on shades of sky, and rubbed his chin repeatedly with paint-stained fingers, a mannerism he thought made him look masculine, and she teased him that he must have a dozen wives or more. 'Man your age,' she'd say. He had a boyish face and didn't even look the five years older that he was.

They ate well, from the best restaurants to tiny hole-in-the-wall spots run by two people standing in dirty aprons. He chose the wines until she proved more adept, or at least gained more understanding of local vintages.

Pera handed out postcards with her name and address on them to anyone who looked interesting.

'Send me a postcard or come along in person. I have hundreds of rooms,' she told people.

'Don't say that,' Joseph said, his face so hard against hers his beard pressed into her cheek, leaving a mark. 'You're too trusting. They'll take advantage,' but really, she thought, he didn't want to share her.

'I love a house full of visitors,' she said. 'Takes me back to my boarding school days when I always had someone to talk to. And to my house, before.'

'Not always good to talk when you have little to say. Speaking for myself, not you, Princess. You have lots to say.'

If he didn't call her Princess he called her his muse, his amusing musing muse who is not very musical, making people laugh.

Somehow that week the newspapers got wind of her. A half dozen or more reporters appeared, wanting photographs and quotes, life moves on, survivor still surviving. Joseph spoke to them about his own work, and let the reporters follow them to the places that were to have been their honeymoon spots, their memories. He winked at the reporters as he closed the front door of their tiny hotel room, as if to say, 'Ah-ha! We're about to make love!'

The headlines were both coy and suggestive. He laid each newspaper out on the bed, hopping on his toes like a tiny fieldmouse.

That was her first inkling that he was keen on the attention. That he wanted to latch on to her celebrity. He thought it would give him fame. She was known as 'Survivor of the Sinclair house tragedy', and usually 'in which the Australian Prime Minister was killed.'

He whooped with joy to see 'Her new husband, Joseph Sheely, a well-known artist'.

He began to behave outrageously when he could, when he thought people were watching.

'Be careful. The press are always on the lookout to destroy reputations,' she told him, but he didn't stop.

He did do beautiful work. She loved him for that. She would forgive much for that, and for how much he loved her.

The press loved his antics and called him a bon vivant. Pera was often quietly drunk while he put on a performance, when he danced on tables and talked them into bars that were supposedly closed but that hummed with locals.

The press did turn. Someone figured out who he was, and then the headlines changed: 'Woman Marries Brother of Man who Murdered her Sister'.

They raked over all the dark and nasty details of Hazel's death, of his brother's, and that was all the press wanted to know about for a while. Joseph had framed the front page of a newspaper with the headline 'Temperance Sinclair, sole survivor of the Sinclair House Disaster, drives her new husband to drink'. There was a photo of her husband with a champagne glass, raising it to the unknown photographer. She kept this by the door. She lost count of how many copies people had sent her back then. Some with his name underlined. Some with older clippings about her sister's murder. Some with notes telling her she always had a place to run to.

Once people met Joseph they thought he was gentle, but they still worried about her. 'What if it runs in the family?' people asked.

Joseph was miffed because she was the more famous one even though he was the talented artist. He thought she got the easy, undeserved fame whereas he had to fight for it. She did wonder if perhaps he had leaked their connection to the press, that he wanted the notoriety.

She was her husband's sharpest critic, if only because he'd asked her to be. 'You do make me better, even if I hate you for it sometimes,' he told her once, as he painted over a canvas he'd thought finished.

'You don't hate me.'

He smiled but didn't answer. It was the first hint that things could go wrong. Would go wrong.

1993

'I'm tired,' Pera said. 'We've been going close to ninety minutes!' She was keen to stop. 'We could cut the tour short if you don't mind. I can give you a refund.'

The family fussed over her. Ike gave her a look.

Wayne helped her out into the hallway to a comfortable chair. He said, 'Ike says to tell you that it's good if we stay for a bit. And that no one else comes, know what I mean? He says they're a nice family and no one wants to make dead ducks out of them.'

Pera laughed. It was such a ridiculous thing to say.

'Quack quack,' Wayne said.

1953

Europe had been a wonderful adventure, and Joseph found it hard to adapt back home, to the ordinary life where they didn't eat out every night, no bottles of old wine, no fancy cheeses or heavy breads. Joseph found the life flat and lacking in inspiration. 'There is always you though, my muse,' he said to her.

He would have stayed in Europe forever but the air was bad in London at that time and Pera began to crave the clean fresh air of Australia.

She loved to be home, began the joy of filling the house with treasures. She had already allocated most of the rooms.

She tried to keep their meals interesting, using cookbooks she'd bought overseas. No oranges; they agreed there were to be no oranges in the house because of the association with his brother.

They had to shop at the further town for a while because word had got out who he was and people couldn't believe she had married him. They were horrified. Isabel and Claudia were furious she hadn't told them the truth, and it caused a rift in their friendship that lasted many months. Still, gifts started to arrive. Crystal glasses in sets of six, three pressure cookers, four toasters, a crystal ice bucket (that wasn't, actually) and a baby book, with pages for photos and hair clippings, and spaces for dates to be filled in.

Life seemed very ordinary. Pera wore the beautiful designer clothes she'd purchased in Paris every day because, she said, she'd be too old for them before long. Joseph kissed her and said, 'You'll be beautiful even at ninety.'

36

BLACK AND WHITE AND RED ALL OVER (ART GALLERY 9)

1993

'In here I have a collection of photos of what you might call "my" air disaster. I don't go in very often. It's too hard. But you can see it if you like. It's a bit dusty in there.'

'That pilot was a bit of a mongrel, aye. Doesn't get any worse than that,' Ike said.

'Makes you wish they kept hanging,' Chook said. 'He woulda hung, I reckon. If he hadn't died a fiery death.'

'Oh, I agree absolutely. I am a believer in capital punishment for the irredeemable. If he hadn't died, I would have been out there calling for his hanging. Or I would have killed him myself.'

Ike laughed at that. Good. Best they thought her incapable.

'What do you mean by irredeemable?'

Her ears buzzed. 'Someone like him. A child killer.' She didn't think any of them had killed a child but she wasn't sure. 'You know? One of those men all other men despise.'

None of them would want to be that man, she thought, which

meant it would be good to identify one of them as such. They would want to be better than that man.

'Although sometimes I think it was all my fault. Because I stop clocks. You might have noticed.' She knew they had. 'And when the plane flew over, I stopped the clocks and that's what made the plane fall down.'

'Yeah, I doubt that,' Ike said. 'Fucken idiotic, seriously.'

'It was the pilot. He woulda had his if he'd been locked up,' Chook said. She found it interesting that these men, like every person she told the story to, wanted to be clear it wasn't her fault. Chook slurred his words and she wondered how drunk he was. She was surprised her own words weren't slurred.

'The co-pilot should have stepped in. Everyone said so. But there's this thing about people following orders, even if the boss is making a bad decision. The boss isn't always right. Just because they have the power. The arrogance. Doesn't mean they are always right.'

She was sowing a seed here. 'Sometimes a leader makes a wrong decision. Weak men who are army-trained will never disobey an order and can do terrible things. Strong men can stand up to it.'

'Yeah,' Wayne said. 'I hate that weak shit.'

Pera nodded agreement. 'This room is my least favourite, I think. Not least because it almost glorifies one of the worst people I have ever met.'

The room was full of photographs taken by the man who had snapped pictures of human remains after the accident. At the time, people had assumed he was police, or at the very least a journalist. But no. He was a man out to make maximum profit from death. He even took advantage of her uncle Alan's death.

1953

Not long after Pera and Joseph returned from Europe, Uncle Alan died simply. Faded away. It didn't seem real, because everyone she knew had died suddenly. Shockingly. This kind of natural death didn't seem right. It was as if, once Pera seemed settled, he could let go. He knew she would be all right.

The photographer was an old alcoholic. He thought he could take advantage of her now, with the so-called 'elder' of the family gone. As if Uncle Alan had done any more than be a good man to her, a kind man. She had done it all. She'd kept herself alive, restored her home. Made a life.

He tried to sell her his photographs, all taken within hours of the plane crash. People and things. Her house destroyed. He'd taken close-ups, far too close. She said, 'I'll call the police if you don't leave my property.' His shoes were messy-looking, dirty, scuffed. They probably weren't even leather.

'Not my fault it happened.'

'It's your fault you're trying to profit from it.' She didn't want them. Why would she want them?

He eventually sold them to a dodgy 'news' magazine. She didn't buy the issue, although someone still sent her a copy. His ploy was telling the 'other stories'. Not her family and their friends, but all those who might be forgotten. The servants, the minor visitors, the animals.

Anything to stretch out the story for longer.

One of the photos was of the piles of dead animals. Pera had thought she'd imagined that; it seemed too horrific. The dogs. The goat. The cats on top. How long had they stayed there? Who had cleaned them away?

Pera could never think of them without feeling ill. Now she had no pets at all. She missed pets terribly. But thank goodness there were none for the men to play with.

One of the photos was of the vicar, and proved the rumours true. His cross was embedded into his chest from the heat.

1993

She explained each picture to the tour, using her cane to point. Her ankle was barely giving her trouble now but she liked the artifice of the cane. 'I refused to buy these photos at the time, but one day the man who took them sent them to me for free. One of those interesting little twists in life, isn't it?'

Devon was entranced. 'No good ones happen to me.'

'Is this room haunted? Who is here?' the father said.

'I think it might be him, actually. The photographer. He disappeared a few years ago and I've always had a weird feeling that he was watching me, taking photos. I do sometimes wonder if he got stuck in a wall cavity and died. If his ghost haunts me. Still watches me.'

'Wouldn't you smell it, though? Sorry to be gross,' the father said.

'You would. But a lot of things die in these walls. You rather get used to it. One day, the house will be knocked down and there he'll be.'

1953

For nine years after they returned from Europe, Joseph filled the front yard with sculptures. Many were inspired by those they had seen in Rome, including one of St Cecilia, whose head in death was turned to a difficult angle, as he described it. 'I do love a difficult angle,' he said. These grew increasingly precise, with little room for error. He worked to exact timings, and grew infuriated with Pera when the clocks failed to be accurate.

She modelled her hands for him and he made many versions, as great an act of love as any she had known.

It was hard to remember that young woman. She was lost in time, absorbed by Joseph and his genius, in his shadow and convinced that she was lesser although he treated her like a goddess.

There was always a dark side to him. He could shift at any minute. He'd put on a show for the locals, or for her oldest friends, or the architect, then he'd pour poisonous words over her that she learned to ignore. He threatened to kill himself (never her) time and time again. The world was against him. No one believed in him. He should have died in the war, he shouldn't be alive.

But physically she couldn't resist him; he was the complete lover, something she hadn't known before. Intellectually he was fascinating and he had such a true talent. But most of all he didn't bore her. And he loved her small odd ways: her towers of pebbles; her collections; her delight in found objects.

1993

On cue, a faint baby's cry could be heard.

'What's that?' the mother said. They always did, without fail. Chook leaned over and sniffed the woman but only Pera noticed.

'We hear it cry sometimes,' Pera said. The tape she'd set would play for three minutes then stop. 'There's no baby in this house, I assure you.'

A baby's cry evoked something in her. A kindness, a desire to nurture, perhaps. She believed there was nothing personal about the response; there was no desire to *have* children, but this didn't mean she didn't *like* children. She loved Claudia and Harry's children and grandchildren, and sometimes had them to stay. Claudia was away at the moment, visiting her son in Goulburn. Isabel was off on some wild adventure, some dangerous place that she'd tell them about when she got back. George and Harry were annoyed at her because she stabled her horses elsewhere but that wasn't serious. Of course they'd come if they knew she needed help.

All of them were getting on, but if she could call them they'd come to the rescue. The three of them together had always been formidable.

1962

The first official miscarriage happened in 1962 and once she'd had that one she realised there had been more, not only to her husband but to previous lovers as well. It was the pain, and the bleeding. She'd thought it was normal; she had no mother to ask, no sisters. She and her friends had shared everything at school; they knew each other's cycles to a day. But it didn't occur to Pera to tell them about it.

This one stayed in the womb for four months, and looked so beautifully formed. So . . . ready.

She made a special room for him but she didn't take people there. It was more like an alcove with a door, a tiny place in the chapel that was hers alone. She called it the Prayerful Place, because there she would meditate on what might come after and on where her tiny baby might be. In purgatory, she thought.

Waiting to be replaced.

37

BLUEBEARD'S CHAMBER (ART GALLERY 10)

1993

'I've told you my husband was an artist. You saw his sculptures in the Stone Room. This room contains ... different works. I wasn't allowed in here while he was alive. This was his place to express his true feelings.'

They crowded in. Pera stood in the doorway. It was dark inside. She wouldn't turn on the light just yet.

'Smells like an old furniture shop,' Devon said.

Pera took great pleasure in the smell of linseed oil. She loved to polish, loved the absolute difference the work made. If it wasn't done, the furniture would degenerate.

'When have you been in one of those?' Chook said. 'All your furniture is made out of old cardboard boxes.' They all snickered. Devon, too. Pera realised that not one of The Men really laughed properly. They snickered. Was it something you had to learn in childhood? If you didn't laugh as a kid you never figured out how to do it right?

But Pera could tell Devon was hurt.

'I keep the furniture polished in here, even though I don't come in much. I find it pretty upsetting. But it's an insight. I wanted to see how my husband's mind worked.

'Every tour takes me back. I remember everything, the good and the bad. Please excuse an old lady if her mind wanders. We tend to live in the past, don't you know.' She rubbed her eyes. 'I say that I never had a child. We almost did. We almost did and we lost him.'

She and the mother exchanged glances, a secret shared between women who were now friends.

'Not meant to be and never was. Women's issues,' she whispered, patting her abdomen. 'And soon after that my husband died, and I never met another man who I wanted to be the father of my children.'

This was where a tour group would make sympathetic noises. And they were always curious. They always wanted to know.

'He died of a brain haemorrhage. Nothing we could have done. It happened here in this room. I call it Bluebeard's Chamber, because while we shared most things, he didn't like me to come in here. You'll see why in a minute.'

She told different tours different causes of death. Sometimes a brain haemorrhage. Sometimes a heart attack. Sometimes she said Joseph committed suicide, other times she said it was an intruder.

He didn't die of a brain haemorrhage, and anyone who cared to could discover that.

'I've only recently had this room repainted. The walls seem to peel so easily and I don't know why. I can't abide the smell of paint. I won't join you inside. I feel him very strongly in this room and that's too sad for me. He's keen for me to join him on the other side, I think. I've had things fall on my head in this room. I've tripped. The door has slammed shut, locking me in. If that happens, I'll let you out, don't worry. Keep very quiet. If you feel pressure on your shoulder, it might be him. He chooses people who remind him of me in one way or another.'

She told them more of the truth than she told most tours. 'I think he was possessed by his brother, or at least the memory of his brother. Because he changed, once we came home after our honeymoon. He remained a loving man, but he became so riven with jealousy, so desperately sure that he would lose me, he kept me in a tight grip.'

She put her own hands around her neck. 'He spent days in Melbourne, amongst odd men with strange tastes, who drew him into a world I was not interested in joining. I still loved him but nothing could convince him I loved him enough.'

She flicked a light switch just inside the doorway and the dark room was illuminated. Now the tour could see the truth of Bluebeard's Chamber.

They stood, shocked, staring at the paintings that covered the walls. Dozens of images of a young Pera. A young Pera dying, over and over and over again. Dying painfully, dying on a sick bed, in a heap at the bottom of a flight of stairs.

She hadn't received the pity look from any of The Men until now. That was something. Surely she could talk to them, reach them at a human level? If they all pretended they were normal and proceeded from there, she should make it out alive.

1963

He could have died in many ways. Week after week he threatened suicide, and she'd pay for a holiday or some treat or other to pull him out of his doldrums. He sold some of his art, but somehow that money never made it to their shared account. She never saw the spending of it.

Being in her house seemed to make him angry. He didn't like the ghosts, he said. The air of suffering and the blame he felt rained down on his shoulders. 'It was my brother, not me,' he said. 'I'm not the one. And yet everywhere I step I feel guilty.'

'There are no ghosts here. And I don't blame you. I really don't, Joseph. I don't even know if I blame your brother. I wasn't there. I don't know what happened. How it happened.'

'He'd be alive today if it hadn't happened,' he said, and the logic of this, the crazy backward defensive logic of him saying that if his brother hadn't murdered her sister he'd be alive, made her angry with him, made her stand up and walk away from him.

His mother wrote to him constantly. And to Joseph's dead brother, too. 'Please give him my regards and tell him that no matter what anyone says you can go home again. He is always welcome. A mother doesn't mind what her son does. She loves him regardless.'

'Doesn't she know he's dead?'

'I've told her many times but it never sinks in. She can't even remember what he did, or refuses to believe it. Mind you—' he said, then closed his mouth as if physically trying to restrain the words.

'Mind you what?' Pera asked.

'Are we sure it was him? That it wasn't someone else trying to make it look like it was him?'

Joseph visited Melbourne many times. Each time he came back worse, more obsessed with the murder, more lost in that moment in the past.

On his return he painted and repainted her sister's murder obsessively. He wouldn't let Pera see anything he produced, after the early stages. Never after that.

'Too disturbing for you,' he said. 'We don't want you having nightmares.'

He painted in the conservatory, wearing only his underpants. He cared little for paint spatters, so the floor and the walls became multicoloured. The Perfect Man statue looked like he had chickenpox.

He chose a room on the ground floor to store them. The room had a lock, and he kept the key in his pocket. 'Whatever you do, don't go into that room. You don't need to and I don't want you to.'

'All right, Bluebeard,' she said, but he failed to see the joke anymore.

He spent most of his waking hours painting. He slept five hours a night, restless, turning constantly, so that she had no rest either. She could only get some sleep when he got out of bed, often with the sunrise, so her habit was to stay in bed until eleven or twelve in the morning. She took a lot of drives to get away, visiting friends. She told the sisters what was going on, that things had escalated.

'That's a very long way from normal. Even further from normal than last time we spoke.'

'I don't know what's changed. Why he's different. He never used to look right through me as if I was a ghost.'

'Does he believe in ghosts?' Isabel said.

'There is no such thing as ghosts,' Pera said. 'I'm not sure what he thinks about it all. He certainly believes in atmosphere. He's an artist and all that. He's going to Melbourne again next weekend. You and Claudia should come visit. It'll be like we're back in school. Come and we'll pretend we're schoolgirls again and everything is simple.'

The girls arrived together in a dusty Holden, and made a great fuss as they dragged suitcases out of the boot.

'We've brought marvellous things,' Claudia said. 'I found the most delicious gin, you won't believe it. And cheese and chocolate and some wonderful grapes.'

'I've brought different wonderful things,' Isabel said. 'We are going to track down all the ghosts in your house and figure out which one is haunting Joseph.'

They settled in with champagne and cheese. 'How is married life after more than ten years? Is it the bliss we always imagined?' They all laughed; they had never been under any illusion about the nature of marriage.

'I don't know. I'm not sure how it should be, so I don't know if this is okay. I know he doesn't know me at all. I'm a set of fingers to sculpt. I'm the owner of this house. I'm the sister of his brother's dead girlfriend. I'm his wild lover. Am I anything else?'

'It's still good in the bedroom department?'

'The bedroom department!' Pera said. 'Fourth floor, bedroom

department, menswear, toiletries.' And they couldn't be serious for a while after that, but later, when they'd had more champagne, and cocktails, and whisky, she found herself telling them some of the details of her married life. How she felt that he still loved her, but obsessively, as if she were a statue to be worshipped, rather than husbandly, like a partner.

'That's not normal,' Claudia said. 'He's obsessed with your fingers, and your sister. He doesn't let you talk. He might not be a basher, but he's not all that good a man.'

'I think he is a good man. But he's a haunted one,' Isabel said. 'Come on. Let's see if we can find out by whom.'

Claudia and Pera exchanged glances. They didn't really believe in Isabel's seances; they didn't believe *she* believed in them.

They moved around the house, closing curtains. Isabel said they had to try to keep all the natural light out, that seances worked better that way. 'You want even the memory of natural light to seep away,' she said.

They walked up to the room Pera kept for Hazel. It was cold in there, and dark. They didn't turn the lights on.

A small white table sat in the centre, and three small stools, where Pera had set them up earlier. Isabel laid out a lace tablecloth and asked Pera to place an object that had belonged to Hazel in the centre. She chose a cigarette lighter.

'Do we have anything of His?'

Pera knew she meant the killer. She shook her head.

'Let's try a selection of things, then. Items left behind by those who've died here.'

Claudia snorted. 'That's the whole house, Isabel. What are we doing? This is making me cold and sad. Let's go drink some of that gin, open the windows, get the fires going. What do you say?'

Pera shivered. 'It *is* very cold, Isabel.'

'Find me a couple of things. Let the house lead you to them. Go on.'

Pera wandered out. She'd had a lot of brandy and was feeling emotional, missing Joseph and wishing he was there. She picked up a vase and a fountain pen, taking them back to Hazel's room.

'Will these do?'

Isabel snorted. 'They'll have to, but you are not taking this seriously.'

Claudia and Pera exchanged glances and got the giggles.

'Shhh!' Isabel said. 'If they think we're laughing at them they either won't come or they'll be angry. We don't want them angry. Close your eyes. Hold hands.'

They did this, Claudia squeezing. Making Pera laugh again.

'Ghosts often manifest around the throat. It's a vulnerable place, carrier of both blood and air. The soft skin is sensitive, isn't it? Can you feel it?' Isabel said.

Pera imagined a fluttering at her own throat.

Isabel cocked her head, listening.

'I can hear someone. Not words, though. Breathing. Slow. Like . . .' Isabel drew in deep, shuddering breaths. 'Painful. It hurts. This person . . .' She opened her eyes and looked at Pera. 'It's Hazel, I think. I'm so sorry, Pera. I wanted to see him. The other. But all I'm seeing is her.' She closed her eyes again. 'Wait. Wait. There's a man's voice. Young man. Strangled-sounding, like . . .' She spoke as if hands were around her throat. 'Off with the fairies. Off with the fairies.'

'That sounds like my cousin Frank.'

'Ooh, he was such a shit!' Claudia said, breaking the mood, and all three of them laughed then, pausing for a drink.

The front door slammed, causing all of them to jump. Claudia dropped her glass, spilling gin everywhere.

'I didn't think I was spooked, but crikey,' Pera said.

'Who's there?' Isabel said, her eyes closed again. 'Who are you?'

'What's going on, ladies?'

It was Joseph, standing in the doorway, arms stretched up, hands holding the door lintel.

'Joseph!' Pera leapt to her feet. He hugged her, kissed her briefly. He tasted of beer and cigarettes.

'What are you crazy ladies up to? Lucky my flight was cancelled. You've got a fire roaring down there in the drawing room and not a soul keeping an eye on it.'

They moved down to the drawing room where the heat was a relief. Isabel had the shakes, was very pale.

Joseph whispered to Pera, 'What are they doing here?'

'They didn't get to see your work last time they were here and they are so keen. Isabel has a lot of questions, you know. She's a bit of an amateur artist and is so admiring of you and your success.'

All of it lies.

Claudia and Isabel brought out more brandy and they drank a lot, pouring Joseph glass after glass until he began to slump and a foolish grin sat on his face.

'So, Joseph, we were talking to the ghosts in the house. We want to know who's haunting you,' Claudia said.

'I don't really believe in ghosts,' Joseph said. 'The only ghost I might see is my brother saying "Save me. Save me." I should have proved his innocence.'

'But he wasn't innocent. He killed Pera's sister. No one has ever said otherwise,' Claudia said.

'But was it him? Do you know how many girls died in Melbourne around that time? Hazel was only one of them.'

Isabel said, 'If his ghost comes he'll tell you soon enough. Ghosts can't lie.'

'No such thing as ghosts,' he said, but his voice cracked and he looked at Pera as if expecting her to call a halt. He shook his head. 'Not interested, ladies.'

'Who feels the most haunted? The most weighed down with guilt and grief?' Isabel asked.

'Me?' Pera said, though she wasn't sure. It had been some time since she'd felt literally weighed down with grief.

'No. Me,' Joseph said. 'You couldn't have saved anyone. I could. I could have told my brother to stay home. I could have not . . .' He choked. 'I'm dry,' he said. 'I'm that dry.' Pera reached for the gin and poured him a glass. One for herself, too.

She reached over, took his hand and pressed the glass into his palm.

'Gin?' he said.

'You know my feelings about water,' she said, and he half-laughed, and she felt sure in that moment he did love her.

'You can stay here,' Isabel said, her voice quiet and calm. 'My friend, there is a place for you here. You can leave that body that has so kindly brought you here. You can leave him alone now. In peace. And you can live in this room, or another, and you can be at peace.'

Joseph covered his face with his hands.

'I'm sorry,' Isabel said. 'But with both of you here this is very powerful. You are here and they are there.'

'Is it my brother?' Joseph whispered. 'Does he have a message?'

'He says let it be. Love and be loved and let the past go. Paint things of beauty, not of sorrow.'

Joseph rolled his head, twisting it from side to side as if riding out a kink. 'I paint what I paint,' he said. 'I see stuff you don't see. I see truth you silly cows can't even imagine.'

He took the bottle of gin, kissed Pera and left the room.

'What did you see about cousin Frank?'

'Do you want to keep going with the seance?' Isabel said. 'Or was that too awful? There is something nagging away at me. Something about him.' So they tried again, deadly serious this time, but she couldn't find anything. 'There's something,' was all Isabel would say. 'Not to excuse him. But to explain him, maybe.'

Later, Joseph said, 'Do I look different?'

'No. I don't think so.'

'Look into my eyes. I am different. I left Joseph behind and now I am my brother. Do you see? Joseph is somewhere about, slumped on the floor like a jellyfish.'

'Stop it, Joseph. You're being horrible.'

He poured her a glass of wine and he had some too and there was beer and sherry and there was brandy, too, she thought, and he said, 'I feel as if we could have saved them both. Him and her. Brother and sister.'

She shook her head. 'Of all the things that are my fault, that wasn't one of them. I was only five.'

'But what if we act it out? And you stop me. To show it was possible. Maybe we're proving that she actually wanted to die. She chose it. And if she chose it, then my brother wasn't really a murderer. He was selfless, giving her what she wanted.'

'She didn't want it.'

He caressed her face. The touch of his fingers always softened her. The gentleness, the insistence. She could never resist him, even if she was angry with him. Even on their worst days, their lovemaking was sweet.

'So beautiful,' he said, and he kissed her. Then his hands were around her throat, squeezing.

She choked.

'Fight! Fight me!' but she couldn't. She flapped her arms as if she was trying to fly, trying to hit him, but he twisted out of her way.

He squeezed until she fainted. She came to with him sweeping a warm cloth across her brow. He'd made tea.

He did this often after that. She never knew when it was coming; she was never prepared. She hoped he'd stop before too long.

'You want it,' he said. 'You do.' She managed to hit him sometimes but it was weak, useless, and served only to annoy him.

She grew stronger. Angrier. But he did, too, and her body was bruised after each re-enactment. Bruises on her back where his knees pressed in.

Every night they drank, sometimes four bottles of wine. They played loud music on the record player, arguing over classical versus Trini Lopez.

'Fuck the adagios!' he would say, and they'd fall about laughing at that.

She didn't tell her friends what was happening and she hated herself for it. It made sense when he spoke; a kind of sense. And he made her feel as if she was a hateful sister if she didn't comply. Maybe she could have done something. Maybe it was her fault. Maybe this was retribution.

1993

She learned that things can escalate. That a belief in ghosts could change the way a man behaved. If a good man could change to a bad one, perhaps a bad man could change to a good one.

The Men left the room. Pera turned to the family and Lucky. 'My husband died of fear. He bellowed like a cow. Bellowed himself to death at the bottom of the stairs. Bellowing for me.'

She waited until their exclamations died down. 'I found something else in the room, besides the portraits. It was a glass ashtray that he must have stolen the first time he ever came to visit me. Can you believe it? All those years he was a thief after all.'

'I don't blame you for never coming in here,' the father said.

'I did go in once. To leave him a message. Pull that curtain back.'

They did so. She'd painted on the wall, 'I Do Not Want to Die'.

'Good on you,' the father said.

'These paintings are horrible,' the mother said. The little girl was shaking; none of them were smiling.

The father said, 'I hate that he used your face. Why would he do that? Why would he make you a victim over and over again?'

'Thank you for asking that, and for feeling that way. He thought I looked like my sister. He was projecting, I suppose. Artists do that.'

'There are many victims,' Lucky said. 'He was a victim in a way. Your husband. And everyone else who walks through this house.'

The mother watched Pera with tears in her eyes. 'How can I leave them?' she said. 'How is that a possible thing?'

1964

There was a period of time, six months or so, that was lost to Pera after her husband died. She lost herself in wine and brandy and the sedatives her doctor prescribed. She couldn't remember a single thing, no matter how hard she tried. There was the inquest and the coroner's decision. There were the newspapers, dozens of them, digging up the past, revelling in the fact that Pera, again, was the last survivor.

Isabel bought her a flight to Greece. 'Get some sun,' she said. 'Be somewhere entirely different.' That holiday, the time with the girls (and then alone, when Pera decided to stay a bit longer) was exactly what Pera needed.

Greece was wonderful in many ways but also difficult and in the end shocking. She had no end of possible lovers; it was gratifying, really, to have so many men adoring her. She knew that none of it was real, but nonetheless it helped. They were all on the hunt for a rich wife. She didn't tell any of them how rich she was because all she wanted was a fling, with no hint of anything more. In the end she settled on a slightly older man, who seemed happy with her apparent lack of wealth. He made her laugh with his attempts at English – she knew he was doing it deliberately and found that endearing – and they spent the days eating and drinking. He took her to a beautiful beach on Corfu (to this day she didn't know the name of it). That's when things went bad.

Her lover insisted on swimming, although he was wobbly on his feet and red in the face from all the champagne. 'Come into the water!' he called. 'Swim with me!' She shook her head. 'I'll be back soon to make love to you,' he said, then turned and dived under the surface.

Five strokes out and he'd forgotten her existence. Another ten and he went under, quick and final, like a stone in her pond at home, or a fly taken by one of the frogs.

She stepped into the shallows but there were a dozen men going in after him, shouting to each other, so she turned and walked to her small pile of belongings, which she bundled into her arms. She didn't look back as she walked to the road and caught a bus back to the hotel. That night, as she washed the sand from her hair, she thought of him one more time. He'd left a T-shirt in her room and she gave that to a boy on a street corner. He was surprised by the gift but not displeased, giving her an enormous, innocent smile of pure thanks.

She considered cutting her holiday short but, in the end, didn't want to miss out on the last few days. Home beckoned, and wouldn't change. It would be there whenever she returned.

38

THE THRONE ROOM (FIRST FLOOR TOILET)

1993

She found Ike standing on the first-floor landing, staring down. 'This place is huge,' he said.

'It is a bit ridiculous,' Pera said. 'The one that burnt down was even bigger.' She felt a momentary affinity with him. He was cold-hearted and so was she; thinking about that holiday in Greece, leaving her lover drowning, not caring, really and truly not caring . . . was she any better than Ike?

'I had some marvellous parties here, back in the day,' she said.

'Anyone need to pay a quick visit?' She led them to the bathroom. 'My father used to say this was the best room in the house for thinking. I've dedicated the toilet to my sister Faith, who was one of the great thinkers of her generation, it's been said.' This never failed to raise a laugh.

Some nights, alone in the house, Pera thought the voices would deafen her. The wailing. She knew it was only the wind outside battering her windows, but if she fell asleep in her armchair, the wailing would become the voice of a banshee, and some believed you carried your banshees with you. Some people came to Sinclair House to unburden themselves. This was all very well for them. They felt better afterwards, and were suitably grateful to her, but there she was with the left behind, the dregs, the debris of it in her house.

1965

Pera loved parties, loved her house to be full of people having fun. She loved misbehaviour, finding underpants under couches, bottles all over. She threw one on her return from Greece, inviting everybody she knew. 'A Celebration of a Life', she called it.

Young Bobby had always taken an interest, in her house and in her. Even once he married, things didn't change. His wife was very understanding. At the party she said to Pera, 'If you and he were meant to be together it would have happened long ago. So I'm not bothered. You be my friend as well as his.'

'I'd love you as a friend, too.'

'And we'll find you a fabulous new husband. Look at you. You're a gorgeous thing, aren't you? Lovely shiny hair.' They smiled at each other. 'And anyway,' the woman said, leaning forward confidentially. 'Anyway, it's for the best. Isn't it? Given who he was. No one liked him.'

'Beverley!' Young Bobby said. 'Stop gossiping.'

'It's not gossip if everyone thinks it!'

Pera told no one about what happened in Greece.

39

THE FREE SPIRIT ROOM (THE BAR)

1993

'This room is another of my family's great jokes. We called it the Free Spirit Room. It's where artefacts of booze-making are kept. Mostly from Prohibition when it existed in Canberra. I always did like a party. The room is dedicated to one of my sister's friends, Barrette, she called herself, here visiting out of the blue. Spur of the moment. I think she was related to the PM's personal assistant so wanted to come see him. These things happen. I adored her. She wore ridiculous clothes and told us outrageous things.'

The father cleared his throat. 'They were cousins. He was my Uncle Colin. It was very hard for my father, losing a brother like that. She was my cousin once removed or something. We're the only ones who remember her these days.' This explained why this family was taking the tour. Pera had wondered what had brought them here.

'She was such wonderful fun!' Pera said. 'She's lucky she has you to remember her.' Pera didn't add that she had no family member to remember her. This wasn't the time to complain about that. She had to remind herself of this often; it wasn't always about her.

'Your family stories include my family home, because of what happened. What was lost. What could have been,' she told the father.

He nodded. 'It's true. We all talked about the place. I've heard about it all my life. Though I think after the next death, they decided it was cursed.'

'Who was that?' Pera said, horrified.

'My father never came to visit because he thought it would bring bad luck. But his other brother, my last uncle, used to come quite often,' the father said. He looked embarrassed. 'A long time ago. He visited you quite often. I think he turned into a friend of yours.' He blushed quite red.

'What was his name? I've had lots of friends. Lots of *friends*, too.' She winked then. There was something delightful about a young man's embarrassment.

'I bet you have,' Chook said. 'I like lady friends myself.'

'You've never had a lady friend you didn't pay,' Ike said. 'Whereas Devon here is still waiting to get hairy enough for lady friends.'

'Today might be the day,' Alex said. Pera moved to stand in front of the young girl so he couldn't look directly at her. She had no idea where he had been in her house but it made her skin crawl.

'Mervyn Pritchard,' the father said.

1971

Mervyn had been one of the dozens of people who showed up to the open house she'd put on for the thirtieth anniversary of the accident. The press loved these things; one of the national newspapers offered to pay for catering if she'd let them invite all-comers but she thought that was a bridge too far. She didn't mind the relatives coming, and the locals, but she didn't want any old pervert showing up.

The relatives of those who'd died in the accident all seemed to feel a deep connection to her. Just by meeting her they thought they knew her. No one blamed her and she was grateful for that.

Some came to the anniversary open house for the ghosts. Some came for the history, because it was the last place the prime minister was alive. Many came for a relative or a friend.

Her kitchen was full of chattering people getting stuck into the tea and scones. Their voices would linger, and she would relive the jokes and the stories later, when she was alone. Mervyn Pritchard stood in the corner, with the deep stoop of a lonely person. He had a certain glow about him, though, and he was very handsome; a sharp jawline, but soft eyes. He smiled at her as she showed the visitors around, and when their hands brushed, she felt a buzz.

'I wanted to give you this, if that's okay.' He handed her an envelope full of money. 'For upkeep, or whatever.'

'Oh, no, seriously. I can't take this.'

'No, you must. I've got no one to give it to, and you are doing a wonderful thing for us, keeping this place up and running. My brother would have wanted this, I know it.'

'Your brother? Did he know us?'

'My brother worked for the prime minister. Loved the job. I think even now, if he had a choice somehow, he'd still choose to have worked for that man and die by his side.'

'I remember him. He was lovely! My sisters fancied him like mad. He was the good-looking one. Barrette's cousin, I think.'

'Yes, Barrette. She was always plain old Doris to the family. My cousin, too.'

When they were alone, she took Mervyn back to the Free Spirit Room. Lots to sample there, and they got good and drunk. He said, 'I saw the life sucked out of my mother from the grief. She could never take a proper breath again, it was like this,' and he sucked in three short, ugly breaths. 'Barrette's mother, too, the two of them sitting there together like grey lumps of clay.'

She gave him a memento, as she gave all of them. Sometimes a flower seed from the blooms grown from the floral tributes. Sometimes a piece of masonry. She gave Mervyn one of the emptied bottles, which they filled, over time, with a pebble every time he came to visit. It made her think of his brother and how he'd collected pebbles, too. It made her think, *Is this fate? Instead of one of my sisters marrying the PM's young man, I will marry Mervyn?*

She wasn't keen to marry again, though. And he wasn't interested in her that way, a point he made politely but clearly by flipping through her *Cosmo* magazines, murmuring admiration for the male models.

He came back many times. She loved his company, and the fact he could compliment her without wanting anything in return. 'You're so fit! Look at your calf muscles!' she remembered him saying. He was still so clear in her mind; his curly dark hair, bright eyes, a bouncing step that spoke of great energy.

'All those stairs,' she said, but it was genetic, too. Her mother had a fabulous figure and never did a minute of exercise.

She offered to rename a room for his brother. 'I can at least put his name in brackets,' she said. 'And you come back any time.'

He did come often, always leaving money. Then he didn't, and eventually she found out he'd died alone, in his flat.

1993

'Your uncle died alone,' Pera said to the father. 'That seems a shame, when he had family.'

The father didn't speak for a moment, glancing around the room as if looking for answers.

'Nobody likes to die alone,' Pera said.

'Maybe he was a fag. Nobody likes fags,' Alex said.

The father said, 'Look, I'm sorry, but could you please watch your language around the kids?' It was either remarkably brave or remarkably stupid.

'Yes,' Lucky said. 'There's no need for it.'

'Your uncle Mervyn was a good man,' she told the father.

Every room in the house had an answer for somebody who needed it; it was a matter of figuring out which room.

She said to Wayne, 'Oh, while you're here! Remind me. I have some things of your grandma's that I've been storing for her. All I have of hers is yours now. Wait till after the tour and I'll give them to you.' Mrs Bee was fit as a fiddle at eighty-seven. Pera was glad Wayne hadn't gone to her; she couldn't have coped, seeing him in his true light. She still idealised him, no matter what his jail term.

'What sort of shit is there?' Ike said. 'Any good shit, or the shit shit like this stuff?' He lifted up a somewhat damaged, cloth-bound book and waved it.

'That one is actually a Dickens first edition, believe it or not. Worth a few hundred, at least.'

'Dickens!' Devon sniggered.

Ike put the book down near the door. They'd been making piles like this in every room, she realised.

'I do envy your grandmother, Wayne. I have no one. I'm like Willie Wonka; always on the lookout for who I can leave everything too. I have no one to outlive me,' she told them. 'No one to remember me. That's why I tell stories. And listen to others.'

Even though she'd said this to give these men pause, at the same time it rang true to her.

'Bullshit. Old lady like you, you've got six kids at least.' Chook shook his head, his face creased with disgust.

'She hasn't, she told me,' the mother said. 'Why would she lie about that?'

'Old women lie about everything,' Chook said. 'Young women, too. Women lie.' He sniffed, too close to Pera for comfort.

'Now, now,' Pera said. 'You can't use your own bad experiences to judge everybody. Imagine if I did that! I'd hate every pilot on the planet!'

She laughed, and the father joined in.

'Let me show you Mervyn's favourite room,' she said.

40

THE WIVES' ROOM

'Your uncle Mervyn loved it here. He said it reminded him of his own home. He said that even when he was alone, his thoughts of how loved he was gave him solace.' He hadn't ever said this, but Pera knew it was true. She didn't like to lie to people, but she did like to help.

'That's so good to hear,' the father said.

The Wives' Room was built for both comfort and femininity. Soft cushions, rugs, snacks, recipe books. All the stereotypical things a wife should be. She'd never been that kind of wife, although she'd play-acted one long weekend, long after her husband had died, soon after she realised Mervyn Pritchard wasn't interested in that kind of thing.

1971

It was the week of her fortieth birthday. She'd been out with the sisters and some of their other school friends, causing a great ruckus and stir. She felt sexy and interesting, bright and gorgeous. She met a charming man, no youngster himself, far from home on a business trip. He swore he wasn't married and there was no ring mark. So she let herself enjoy his snide humour and his seeming entrancement with her.

The first night they spent in his hotel, then he said, 'I want to see where you live.'

He'd loved the Wives' Room. Actually, he'd loved all the rooms. He said, 'Let's stay together forever and we can make love in every room.'

She thought he didn't know who she was, but he found out, from files in the library and old news cuttings. He said, 'And every room is dedicated to a dead person?'

No look of pity, but sick curiosity. That she could live with.

'Is it haunted?' He didn't wait for her to answer. 'You should do tours. Like the ones in York. I did one of those last time I was there. Lots of fun! People are dying to see ghosts. Why not show them and charge them for it?'

He had a point, one that was proven over and over again, in many ways. If people paid for something, they respected it more. Conversely, anything paid for in a relationship was not considered real, nor was it respected. This delightful lover gave her a ceremonial sword that he said could do battle with demons.

He was difficult to get rid of once she tired of him. She didn't really like having lovers in her house. She was a different person there. Quieter. Less exciting. Some were easy to budge; all she had to do was demand they left their wife and marry her. This one, she had to break his heart, having him find her with another lover in a fancy hotel. Dramatic but effective.

She couldn't even remember his name, now.

41

THE GREEN ROOM

1993

The Green Room, besides containing green furniture, had photos of actors, movie posters, scripts and film reels.

'This room is dedicated to an actress. She was in the plane, flying to an audition or was "with" a film producer who said he could get her a role. People say she was the next Jean Harlow. Her brother came to visit me a long time ago, when his father died. I'd just started doing tours of the house. Must be fifteen years ago now. No, twenty! Oh, my, I am getting old. He brought his father's obituary with him, as if that connected the two. As if it proved something. He was a nice fella, though, that brother.'

The father's obituary said, 'Survived by a son and wife but not a daughter.'

1972

The son stayed after the tour, sitting there on her emerald-coloured couch, saying, 'Dad pretended he never cared about Sophie dying. But that meant he had to pretend not to care about me and Mum, too.' He was a small, very neat man who smelt of Fabulon, and his clothes did indeed look well starched.

'Some people don't care,' Pera told him. 'Some come here purely out of curiosity. Others are like you, feeling it deeply.'

'I always wished it was me who'd died in that plane.'

He gave her a gift: a framed picture of his sister's acting debut, a movie Pera had never heard of, and they fussed about where to hang it. 'I had a premonition of danger. I have them quite often. I'll show up in places right before something happens. Or if nothing happens, I wonder if me showing up *stopped* it from happening.'

'Good on you,' she said.

'My father called it being off my tree. And not in a good way! He would stop me acting on my premonitions. That's the kind of man he was.'

There was always at least one man who caught her eye in every tour group. It was the way he moved, or smelt, or the way he spoke. It wasn't always about confidence. Sometimes she took a lover because they wanted her badly. They wanted to adore her. At forty-one she looked and felt a decade younger; certainly she never had any complaints. She slept with this neat, clean-smelling man and he was sweet but so sad she didn't think she could be with him again.

She gave him a small piece of the aeroplane to take with him.

'This is her,' Pera said, showing them an old framed movie poster. 'In the background. Dressed as a nun. Who knows if she would have been a star or not? She might have had nothing but sorrow. Who knows?'

She heard a sob. Lucky snuffled, wiped his eyes. Not even the mother or the daughter had such a strong reaction, although she had seen men do this before. Something about the vulnerability of the young woman got to them.

'What did he look like? The brother,' Lucky said.

Pera laughed. 'I can't remember, to be honest. I'm not good with names or faces at all and do you know how many hundreds and hundreds come through here? People feel a strong connection to me and my house, as if we are all tied up together. Tangled. You, too, Wayne. Your family stories are tied up with mine. Your grandparents were so kind to me after the accident. I didn't think until later, but they would have been mourning, too. They were good friends with my parents, in a way.'

'Except your parents were too good for anyone else around here,' Wayne said. 'That's what my grandma said.'

'She would never have said that!' Pera said. 'Goodness, Wayne. You do live in a fantasy world, sometimes.' She sighed. 'I'm feeling my age, dear friends. How would it be if we cut this short by the tiniest bit?'

'I don't think so,' Lucky said. 'I think we should see it through. We're here now.'

Ike said, 'Men like you sometimes bite off more than they can chew, you know.'

'Men like him don't know who's a friend and who's an enemy,' Alex said.

Devon punched Lucky's arm. 'He's one of us, aren't you, mate? He'll fight in the trenches for us.'

Lucky flinched at his touch.

42

LITTLE SHOP OF HORRORS

'You still haven't shown us shit,' Ike said. 'You need to show us shit that's worth something.'

'I do have some items of value for sale, in a little shop I've set up on the ground floor, at the back of the house. I only sell things if the curse seems to be lifted, but I can't guarantee! It's good to share things around, don't you think? Rather than let them sit.'

She had gathered so many boxes of things left behind and things rediscovered they threatened to take over the back landing, so Pera set up the shop. Every item had a memory tied to it. Teacups, books, decorated plates, vases, clocks. She collected items from the plane crash; many had been stolen but she bought them back and sold them. She sold the clocks made from aeroplane parts. Those were very expensive but people loved them. She sold jewellery made of the same.

She usually managed to sell at least a few items every tour. Some people loved the shop; others found it awful and told her so.

The Men looked at the items, not impressed. 'So how much

for these?' Ike said, holding up a set of napkin holders, and she opened her mouth to answer, to tell their story and give the price, but he snickered. As if. As if they were going to pay.

A gold watch and necklace, a lion-crested ring, diamond earrings; these they took, but they wanted more.

She told unverifiable stories about some of the items. You never wanted to make a customer feel ripped off. You wanted them to come back. That's why she gave them little treats and surprises, so they'd forget that they didn't actually see any ghosts. She had a roller skate, priced outrageously. One of these days someone would buy it, she knew that. Dear, gullible creatures. Not this lot, though.

'Is that the roller skate the chauffeur tripped over when he died on the front steps?' the older boy said. 'I thought you said it wasn't found?'

'I didn't tell you the story of *this* roller skate,' she said.

'Bullshit,' Wayne said. 'This stuff is mostly crap.'

'Didn't realise you were an expert,' Pera said. The Men began to talk quietly about how to transport it all. They'd dropped the pretence they weren't going to rob her penniless and she didn't care. She was tired. She needed to think.

Devon found a football, left behind by a boy whose parents were in such a hurry to get away that Pera was sure they'd stolen something, and Chook picked up a fishing rod. She didn't know where that came from.

'Kick to kick, boys?' Wayne said, snatching the footy.

'There's a lovely green area out the front,' she said. Ike picked up a croquet mallet and swung it over his shoulder.

'Who wants a kick?' Ike said. He lifted the footy at the father and the boys. The boys nodded, hopping about, but the father shook his head quickly. The older boy had taken on a swagger, mimicking Ike.

Lucky said, 'I'm not very sporty, I'll wander around by myself.'

'I think we should stick together. Men against the world, know what I mean?' Alex said. He bent over to kiss Lucky on the head, one of the oddest gestures Pera had ever seen.

Pera's ankle ached and she leaned heavily on her cane.

'Are you all right?' the father said. 'Can we call a doctor?'

She glanced at Ike, and the look in his eyes . . .

'No, no, that's okay. Honestly, I'll be fine.' If only, though, if only she'd gone to the hospital when she'd fallen over in town. If she'd gone to hospital, all of them would be safe. The tour group would have given up and left, and The Men would be in the house on their own.

There was much she would change in her life. She wished she could change that one thing.

Her fault again.

Life was so simple then, a few hours ago. All she had to do was worry about Marcia the nasty hairdresser.

So much of her wished she had taken their advice; she'd be safe in a hospital bed by now, eating the evening meal of stale sandwiches and listening to the news on the television because the picture would be bad.

'Are you okay?' the mother said. Pera realised she had tears in her eyes and wiped them away. 'Are you sad about your family? Remembering is hard.'

Her husband choked.

Pera said, 'It is. Of course it is. But at the same time, those memories are so important. Every happy day. Every good meal. Every small gesture of love is important.'

Ike whispered in the older boy's ear. The boy's face was stony, showing no emotion, then he nodded briefly, a small smile on his face. While the adults were distracted, the boy pocketed a small item. Pera couldn't see what it was, but she thought, *This needs to end.*

The tour group spent half an hour or more in the shop, all of them making a purchase. She gave the daughter a small Ned Kelly souvenir, supposedly a piece of his armour.

It was time to show them the rat king.

43

THE UNDERHISTORY (THE CELLAR)

'Are we ready for the Underhistory?' she said. 'As I told you before, it was the place I was most frightened of as a child, because of the stories my sisters and I told each other about it.'

'You had such a scary childhood!' the mother said. Chook stood close by her and Pera saw him stroking his hands together. From him, it was a disgusting gesture.

'I really didn't! I had a wonderful childhood. Before. Full of adventure. For my eighth birthday, every child I knew arrived dressed as animals, and my parents arranged for the circus to come! We had actual tigers, here, on the lawn! It was even in the newspaper.'

'Sad,' the mother said.

'In what way?' Pera asked, but the mother didn't say.

'You were lucky to have such a wonderful family,' the father said.

'I did have a lovely family but you never know what lies beneath. Take that photograph I showed you, for example. The last photo of my house, with us all beneath the tree. You wouldn't know that I didn't want to be there, and that all of them would be dead within the hour.'

Lucky looked over her shoulder.

'Is that a face peering through the lattice? Is that the cellar?'

'The Underhistory,' she corrected. 'Show me.'

The photo had been blown up, investigated, printed front page; almost everybody in the country must have seen it a dozen times.

'Who is it?' Lucky said. There was a face there; there definitely was.

'That's my freak brother they kept locked in the basement,' she said, on impulse. 'He was blind, deaf and dumb and only had one arm. He had the fattest stomach even though my parents never fed him. I think he ate the rats.'

Cold silence until she laughed, head back. 'I'm sorry. It is a story my sisters told me, though. They said he was my twin, that I'd eaten half of him while we were in the womb and that's what happens to the brothers of greedy girls.'

'They didn't!' the mother said, and Pera had to agree that was true. She looked at the photo again. *Who was it?*

'Can we go down to the cellar now?' the youngest son said. 'I want to see it.'

'I shouldn't really. That's where the bodies are buried.'

Ike laughed. 'Six feet under or shallow grave?'

'Who's buried down here?' the oldest son said.

'No one buried. But there was one death, to my knowledge. A man who killed himself. He was the one whose sister was an upcoming actress who died in the plane crash. Remember I told you about him in the Green Room? So sad. He never really recovered. This was the first time he'd come to visit for years, though.'

'I remember that!' Wayne said. 'That was cool.'

He'd hanged himself down in the Underhistory. Left her a note:

> I'm sorry for you to be the one to find me, but I didn't want it to be Mum. I didn't want her to be the only one left. And it felt right to do it here. I can't save everyone and I'm tired of trying. The people I haven't helped haunt me. I want those voices to stop.

'Do you know what I found in his pocket? Remember how I said I gave him the piece of the aeroplane? That. That. He'd kept it all those years.' She shook her head. 'I blamed myself for his death, too.'

She didn't find him immediately. He'd left, and it wasn't for a day or two she realised his car was still there. Keys in the ignition. Some weeks were like that; she didn't venture outside at all. Or only to the horses, and his car was parked around the side where she didn't see it.

His note said *I didn't want her to be the only one left.*

'Such a thoughtful man,' people said, until they discovered he had killed his mother before coming to visit Pera.

Lucky seemed to shrink into himself, almost vanish into the wall. 'You might not like it down there,' she said to him. 'It's a bit grubby. And there are probably rats. Rats will live on anything. When I first came back here as a child, the night of the plane crash, all I could hear was rats scratching under the ruins of the house. Sometimes I think I still hear them when I come down here.'

The strains of Puccini's '*O mio babbino caro*' started, although she couldn't remember setting that tape playing. The music was so sad it brought prickly tears to her eyes every time.

'I want to see,' Lucky said.

'In no way was that your fault!' the mother said. 'You should stop blaming yourself for so many things.'

Pera had a news article that appeared at the time: 'Dead Actress's Brother in Bizarre Murder–Suicide', alongside a photo of the piece of smooth metal, itself captioned, 'Cursed artefact?'

'If you have an intense feeling of guilt as we get closer, that could be why. His ghost is so full of guilt he infects people. I shouldn't let you down there; it really isn't a safe place anymore. Even I don't venture down often.'

'You have to let us go down!' the older boy said.

They followed her to the foyer, and Pera unlocked the cellar door under the main stairs. She led the tour down the rickety steps into the dark of the Underhistory.

There were remnants of the old house in the cellar that had fallen through and been built over. Part of a wall. Tiles from the guest bathroom. Part of the wooden dining-room floor. Pera shone a torch so they could see the bloodstains.

'We've tried a hundred ways to remove those stains. They disappear but by the next day they are back again, as if those souls are saying, "Don't forget me!" As if they think by cleaning their blood, we are cleaning away our memory of them.' Pera smiled to herself, thinking of how often she'd had to repaint these bloodstains. Remnants of old rope still hung from one of the rafters.

'Oh yeah, this is where he did it. I remember now,' Wayne said.

'Even if the bloodstains did fade, and you cut off that last piece of rope, you could never forget. How could you?' one tour member could be reliably expected to say. This time it was the father.

'People forget very easily. They move on,' Lucky said.

'There was a lot of blood. The plane came in at an angle, and crashed through three floors. It was the wing that caused most of the damage here. Bodies were crushed together as if they were in a food processor. And somehow a kind of . . . channel was formed, and so much blood poured down here, the emergency people were up to their ankles in it. It dried into a solid, thick scum you could slice.'

'Ewwwwww!' the daughter said, and Ike laughed.

Pera had tried to explore to the very edges of the cellar but no matter what she was wearing she'd be chilled to the bone. It was larger in area than the new house, so in places there was nothing above but grass, or the outer buildings. It was like a warren, room after room connected by doors, many hidden. And there were the tunnels, of course.

'The story goes that it was a criminal who financed the construction of the original building in around 1860. It was always intended to be a hideout. A safe haven. Supposedly there are escape tunnels running out from the cellar, in case the police came. And places to bury stolen goods. It's a rumour, though, an El Dorado amongst criminals.'

'Was the criminal one of your relatives?' Wayne asked. 'I don't remember Grandma ever saying that. Although I do reckon she used to say you were a pack of crooks.'

'I'm not sure. I think it was my great-grandfather but I've got no one to ask. No one who knows. They say he had a great fear of the hangman's noose.'

Lucky backed away, his hand to his throat. 'It's very dusty down here,' Pera said.

One corner ended flat and low. You had to crawl on your stomach to get there. On the other side she thought there was a room almost intact. She could see it through a crack in the floorboards above. But she had never ventured far enough to find it.

'Where's that trapdoor go? The one you showed us in the waiting room?' the daughter asked. 'That was cool.'

'You can't see where it leads from here. You'd have to go through one of these doors, and through a tunnel or two, and a hatchway. It's almost cut off from the rest of the Underhistory. I think that sound is absorbed there, so you could scream as loud as you want and no one would ever hear you. And time stops in there so you're screaming and screaming and no one comes. Forever.'

A rough laugh from the father, intakes of breath from the daughter and the mother. The Men silent. Alex with his mouth hung open, his bottom row of teeth small, neat and white.

'But if you're brave, it might be worth exploring the Underhistory. It's where they say the treasure is. The gold, the diamonds. Anything my family ever stole got hidden down there. And my father's wine cellar. Gosh knows how much those bottles would be worth, if you could get to them.'

There was a dull glow in one corner. One pale globe providing light; it shone directly over the small table she'd set up. On the table was a large dome, covering a glass case.

'Over there is something you don't want to see. Oh my God, that'll give you nightmares all right.'

Ike laughed. 'We've seen it all.'

'This is something my cousin left behind,' she said, lifting the dome to reveal the rat king.

'Oh, Jesus,' Devon said. 'That is disgusting.'

'They die, one by one, but the others can't get away. They have to drag the corpses around for as long as they survive themselves. They fight for food, all dragging in different directions, none of them giving in, until one by one they die of starvation.'

'Why the fuck would you show us that?' Devon said.

'Maybe because it reminds me of you,' Pera said quietly. 'All tangled up together until you die.'

It was the father who had the strongest reaction, something approaching a panic attack. That didn't happen often and when it did, she thought something had been triggered. A memory of some kind, a trauma that the sight of the rat king stirred. Sometimes fright got them, or tiredness, or the closeness of the air in the Underhistory, their last stop.

She wondered what his memory was. The children stared, gape-mouthed, at their father. It wasn't the way they usually saw him.

'It's okay,' she said. 'You're a sensitive man and there's nothing wrong with that. The world could do with more of you.'

'That's terrible, that's . . .' the father said. Why the rat king disturbed him so much she didn't know. That was for his family to sort out.

The father recovered and made a joke that made no sense but

that his family laughed at out of kindness. He was weakened though, she could see that, damaged somehow.

'I am sorry. I don't like people to be upset.' Pera hoped her ploy would work, that they would be disturbed enough to leave now.

'No, no, it's fine,' the father said. 'We got our money's worth, that's for sure.'

'It might be time to head off though,' the mother said. The youngest boy had his face buried in her side and his arms around her. The girl stood staring at her father. The oldest boy was obsessed with the rat king.

'I don't want to go,' he said.

'You'll have to come back for another visit,' Pera said. 'Most people come at least twice.'

He nodded.

They all clambered up the stairs to the foyer, The Men included. Ike stood with his arms crossed under his underarms, his thumbs sticking out.

'Drove here, did you?'

'Yeah, got ourselves one of those big family vans. Slow, but fits us all in. Of course I'd rather have something a bit more zippy,' the father said, then cringed as if aware of how pathetic he sounded.

'I hiked,' Lucky said. 'Best way to see the country.'

'We can fit you in the van, at least into town,' the father said.

'I've got a big car,' Pera said quietly. 'Comfortably seats five. I barely use it. I've been thinking about getting rid of it, actually. That's what I've been thinking.'

Ike watched her.

'You could get me some things from town. Do some shopping for me. Take my car. I won't miss it. And I have something to show you. Once they're gone.' She didn't, of course, but she'd worry about that once the family were safely away.

Ike waved his hand at the other men, mouthed, 'Let them go.' Alex was edgy, flexing his fingers, his facial scars livid as the blood rushed to his cheeks, and a terrible part of Pera thought that Lucky would have been an okay sacrifice. That he could be the one they took if they needed an outlet.

Pera packaged up some scones in a commemorative tea towel for the family and walked them and Lucky to the front door. Ike followed.

'Why do they get to stay?' the older son said.

'They've paid for a sleepover. You can next time.'

'How much is it?' the father asked.

Pera named an outrageous amount.

'Wow,' the father said. It was the closest he'd come to rudeness. 'Maybe next time.'

Ike handed the father his wallet after flipping it open to see inside. 'You dropped this, mate. Hey, now we know where you live. Maybe we'll come visit. Or if we're caught up, we'll send someone else to see you. Right? We'll come visit. Or we'll send a friend. You know. If we need to.' His tone friendly and light. His words would have meaning to the family later; *Don't tell, or we'll kill you.*

Pera said, 'I forgot to get you all to sign the contract of silence!' Her tone bright, excited. 'Because of the ghosts and things. I don't like people to give away my secrets. So everything you've seen and heard, everyone you met. Don't tell a soul. Not a soul. The ghosts don't like their secrets told.'

The older son nodded, watching The Men. He'd cottoned on, Pera thought, more than the rest of his family had.

'We won't tell a soul,' he said.

Pera wished she could squeeze into their minivan and go with them.

They watched from the front steps as the family drove away, Lucky sitting with the children.

'And now,' Ike said, once they were gone, 'now we can get to it. You've done the right thing and so have we. Right?'

She nodded.

'I'll kill them if you make a wrong move,' he said. 'Just for fun. I'll walk out of here and fucken kill them in a bad way. I love walking.'

'He does,' Wayne said. 'We escaped because he wore a path all the way through his cell floor by walking.'

'That's actually quite funny,' Ike said. 'If we see anyone coming up that driveway we shoot on sight. Don't care who it is. Anyone on their way, far as you know?'

She shook her head. 'They all think I'm abroad. No one will come by.'

'What about your policeman friend?'

'No, he won't bother coming round till he thinks I'm home again. Anyway, he's seventy-three! An old bastard, you might say. Long since out of the force, long since past caring.'

Pera felt an incredible sense of relief. The family were safe. She wondered how long it would be before they reached a television set or listened to the radio. Would they heed the warnings, realising after the fact what they meant?

As if reading her thoughts Ike said, 'We've got a while. I don't expect it'll be long before they hear the news. I wrecked their car radio, though. And, you know. The dad is gutless.'

'He loves his family, that's all. Can I show you my pond before we go back inside? And Hanging Rock. Standing on it helps you get a sense of the house, you know. You can get an idea of how big it actually is, and how much is in there.'

She had Wayne come with her to the kitchen to help her put together a picnic basket.

As they packed it, she said, 'Wayne, listen. All of this can be yours, not just the things I've been storing for your dear grandmother. You're the closest I've got to a relative! I've said that to your grandmother more than once. But you'll need to be a good boy. You'll need to help me stay healthy. Stay in the house with me, fix it up. It will be fun!'

Wayne smiled at her. 'Nah. You wouldn't.'

'Seriously, Wayne! Who else?'

'Need a hand?' Alex said, standing in the kitchen doorway. Of all of them, he was the one she trusted the least, the one she feared the most.

'Always the gentleman,' she said.

'Oh, I am. I am.' He hefted up the picnic basket, leaving Wayne to carry the cold beer.

Wayne whispered to her, 'You watch him. Don't let him touch you, okay? He's a nightmare.'

44

THE POND

Hanging Rock had long been a place of calm for Pera and she wondered if it would affect The Men that way. For a moment she thought she had, at last, seen the ghost of her long-dead, sad uncle. But no, they were real men out there. Devon, Ike and Chook. Devon started scratching at the rock with a sharp stone. Chook relieved himself against her rock, *her* rock, and she knew that she could slit his throat if she had the chance.

'If you get a sense of despair as we head to the pond, walk away quickly. It can overwhelm you before you know it.'

She liked to take small groups for a picnic there. Only the people she connected with. The ones who made her laugh, or had interesting stories, or a kindness to them. She liked being amongst people who got along well and had an openness about them.

Those people she'd invite to stay after a tour, and she'd raid the freezer for snacks to picnic on. The large freezer contained much frozen finger food. If she felt like a treat, she'd cook herself a tray of tiny quiches, pies, fish cakes and spring rolls.

She was never at a loss to feed visitors.

*

She showed The Men the blood on the rock. Long ago the blood had been real, from when she'd scraped herself sliding down its rough surface when the plane crashed. The skin on her knees and thighs was rougher because of it. Now the blood was painted on regularly and she liked to say someone was murdered there. She loved the deception.

'So here,' she said. 'It's a beautiful spot, isn't it? Peaceful and quiet. You can't always tell, can you? What's happened in a place. Sometimes there is no atmosphere. Nothing left behind. Yet still the thing happened.'

'What thing?' people would reliably ask. She could usually pick which one would ask. It wasn't always the loudest one; usually it was the curious one, the one who'd lag behind to read the plaques. That kind of thing.

Today, it was Alex. He stood too close to her and she could smell him, a weird chemical scent she couldn't identify but that made her feel sick.

'For a while, the house was rented out to a group of chefs. They thought they'd run a restaurant here. Actually, a pretty good idea, if you had the skills. This was in the mid-seventies. People were discovering vegetarian food and all sorts of hippy stuff, but these people wanted it to be meat, from the farm straight to the table. You could watch your calf being slaughtered, if you wanted to. Your fish being caught. That kind of thing.'

'Fucken vegetarians. Hate them,' Alex said.

'You could do a restaurant here,' Chook said. 'People would flock to it. Meat pies made from scratch. I'll be your head chef.'

He thumped his chest proudly; she wasn't sure if he was joking or not.

'Maybe!' she said. 'These chefs were headed by a man called Claude. No one knows what his real name was, but it wasn't that. They were isolated out here, and all they did was cook and argue.'

Pera hoped none of them had noticed how crappy the kitchen was, how unlikely the story was.

'And they became a bit cultish with Claude as the guru. He said he'd studied at Le Cordon Bleu and wanted them all to do as they were told. He wanted the women to be more than sous-chefs to him. All of the young women, at once. As you can imagine, this didn't go down well with the women, or the men. Apart from one young girl, who can't be named because she was only sixteen at the time. So young, but the acknowledged master of the knives.' In her mind's eye, Pera pictured her sister Hazel, who was wild, tempestuous, glorious. 'She was the jealous type. So when she found Claude in a clinch with the pastry chef, a woman who specialised in millefeuille—'

'Whatever the fuck that is,' Wayne said.

'She killed her?' Devon asked.

Pera held up a finger. 'Not straight away. First, she terrorised her, and the others, pretending the house was haunted, and that a ghost had promised to slaughter one of them.'

'*I'll gut you like a pig, just to hear you squeal.*'

The voice came out of nowhere. Pera stopped, her heart thumping. Alex laughed. 'Whooooo the rock is haunted by a cunt with a knife. Whooooooo.'

The Men laughed.

'She convinced the pastry chef to come out here one night,

putting on a panic – "I need to get out of the house, he's coming" – and the two of them ran to the rock. No one said the pastry chef was bright. Not stupid, but naive and kind and always wanting to help.

'At the rock, the knife expert slit her throat. This stain is her blood; it will not wash away. No matter how much it rains, the stain remains.'

One by one they touched it.

'But of course those women don't haunt the rock, my uncle does.'

Alex snorted. 'What, another one? You've seen more dead bodies than I have.' There was a pause. 'Than I have had hot dinners.'

Pera didn't want to think about that.

For all their joking around, she could see she'd got to them.

'Stand up on the rock,' she said. 'I can't get up there anymore but I used to spend half my life up there.'

Chook was too creaky to climb up but Ike, Wayne, Devon and Alex did.

'Kings of all you survey,' she said. 'You'll see a face up in a window. It's in every photo taken of the house, but there's no one inside. I don't know who it is but he's watching me. He's watched me for years, although I don't think he was in the early photos. I don't know if he's watching *over* me, or just watching.'

'That's a big difference,' Ike said.

'Can I tell you another story?' Pera said. 'This is one my awful cousin Frank told me. He was another family suicide! He was a terrible man, terrible.'

'Go on, then,' Wayne said. 'I love a good story. I kinda

remember your cousin. I think he gave me cigarettes once. He wasn't so bad.'

'Whoever that was it wasn't my cousin, Wayne. He was long dead before you were born. Might have been his ghost, perhaps? Think about that.'

Wayne lit a cigarette, his hands shaking.

'So there was a stable full of horses owned by a lazy woman who never looked after them. She took them out riding one after the other then set them loose in the stable with their reins still attached. She was too lazy to wash them down, too lazy to take the reins off.

'One day she left the door of the stables open and all the horses got out, running together, all tangled up with the reins and the more they ran, the more they got tangled until they were a terrible great mess. Not one of them could see and they fell over a cliff, every last one of them crushed to death by the other and no one going to bring them up. If you could find that cliff you'd see at the bottom the reins and the bones of those poor horses.'

'Jesus,' Ike said.

'Yep. Frank called the story "The Horse King". You know. Cos of the rat king.' She shivered. 'Time to go inside, I think. Or if you want I can give you my car keys. It's a good car, you know. It's a '66 Mustang!'

'No way,' Chook said.

'It is! It was a gift from an admirer. I've barely driven it. I only ever go into town.'

'We don't want to leave,' Ike said. 'Not quite yet.' But he still put his hand out for the keys.

'Well, you can help me inside, then. I'm feeling stiff as a plank.'

*

She moved through the house, making sure dust covers were over everything. 'Let me get this fiddly stuff done, otherwise I'll forget. I like to reset the moment people leave.'

She ensured the public entrances were locked up and checked the car park was empty. Nobody had left their car behind to kill themselves in the cellar.

She tidied up the foyer table, restacked the pamphlets and headed upstairs. Wayne said, 'Where are you going?'

'I need a quick shower. A freshen up. Is that okay? I'll be back down soon.' She held up the keys. 'I need to remember which key goes in which door and where I put things. Money. I've got so much loose money stashed away but my brain is tired, Wayne. I'm tired. I need to freshen up.'

He let her up the stairs.

It was the first time she'd been alone in many hours.

Pera dreamed of being back at boarding school. Nights were disturbed, there; girls fighting, or waking with nightmares, or sneaking in after being out with a boyfriend and wanting to share all the details. Pera's dreams were always invaded by those voices, and that's why now, even deeply asleep, she started to awaken. There should not be voices and yet there were. The tour had gone, hadn't it? She was alone, starting her holiday. In her half-awake state Pera thought the noise was a visitor returning. It wasn't unheard of for guests to return in the night looking for ghosts. They seemed to think because they'd been invited in once, they could come in any time, even if the gates were padlocked shut, with clear, large signs saying CLOSED and Do Not Enter, and Beware, Work Site. As if the hour or two spent in her home, exploring all the nooks and crannies, made them think it was theirs. She always said she'd take down the gates because they were pointless, not really keeping anyone out except the cars and looking worse as each year passed, but she never did.

Her room was bright with late afternoon sunlight from a high window. She'd fallen asleep in a chair. She took a moment, she always did, to enjoy the fabrics as they played off each other. She'd done well at school with this stuff; if she'd had the impetus, she really could have made something of herself. Become something other than 'the survivor'.

But those voices. She knew who it was; sleepiness dropped from her now, all thoughts of childhood and school and friends gone.

The Men.

There was only The Men's voices and the knowledge they would soon be looking for her. There was an air vent near her bathroom, which funnelled noise from below unless she blocked it off. She dragged a stool close by and listened in.

'Fucken starving,' she heard, and footsteps; they were going into the kitchen.

She listened as they threw open the lid of her freezer and helped themselves. She smiled at that; she'd been meaning to clean out the freezer for ages, but she'd reach in, clear out the first layer and find it too hard to reach in further. The hinge was broken and while you could prop it open, more than once she'd taken a hard hit to the back of the skull. Some of the food at the bottom was a decade old; she wondered if they'd be stupid enough to eat it. Her fridge was full of the treats she'd gathered for her stay-at-home holiday. She didn't want to share that food with The Men. She'd eat it when they were gone.

She could smell them cooking downstairs. It was disgusting. What were they using to cook the spring rolls and pies or whatever they'd dredged up? Were they deep frying?

She thought about climbing out through a window and across the roof, something she'd never done but kept in the back of her mind in case there was a fire. But the tiles were loose and slippery with moss.

Turning on the TV, hoping to catch the news (hoping to hear that the police were on the trail), sound down, she cut herself a slice of bread and spread it with some of the lovely plum preserves Harry had brought over after Christmas. He'd taken over most of the cooking at home, pleasing Claudia no end. Looking at the jar irritated her, because they'd had a conversation that annoyed her, one they'd had time and time again. Harry saying: we would have been there, inside when the plane crashed, and you would be too, if we hadn't had the measles. Measles saved our lives.

She didn't dare make toast; she didn't want the smell to waft downstairs.

She was a ghost.

The Men were quiet, then. Sleeping, perhaps, but she wasn't about to go looking.

The news came on, with the five escapees pictured using their mugshots, and she thought, *Why don't they show us normal pictures so we can actually recognise them?*

She scribbled the names and descriptions of The Men, not worrying about those who'd died, on some blank postcards. She always had a pile of postcards handy.

Ike was really John Hubble, aged thirty-three. He was charged with the violent murder of a young woman, and other killings since being incarcerated. He was sentenced to life.

Wayne ... well, she knew who Wayne was. His real name was Thomas, which she'd forgotten. They'd called him Wayne, or John Wayne, since he was a kid, because he walked like a cowboy with his big nappy. She couldn't believe he was thirty-one, though. She was so old. He was charged with the same violent murder as Ike, with a sideline in theft and the bashing of gay men. His sentence was for life but with parole, because they didn't consider him the primary motivator in the murder.

Devon was Devon Burns, aged twenty. He was charged with multiple cases of rape, all of which he denied. He was in jail for thirty years, with a parole period of twenty-five.

Alex Bryce was aged twenty-nine. He was charged with the torture and murder of eight women, with more under his name that couldn't be proved. He was also charged with the torture and murder of six gay men. He was sentenced to life without parole.

Chook was really Mick Masters, aged sixty. He had killed nine elderly women and was sentenced to life without parole.

Pera wished she didn't know the truth about them. She had guessed; that wasn't hard. But to know these details, to see the names of their victims? She felt ill to think of the family, and teary with relief at their release.

Through the vent, she heard footsteps and took mental notes, trying to match footfall to man. Every man walked differently, no matter the footwear. Heavy boot, heavy walk. Heavy boot, light walk. Slight limp. There was one with a strange gait; that could be Wayne. He'd fallen out of a moving car as a teenager and the leg never set properly.

She heard a loud call, a hooray, and pulled her chair close to the vent to hear.

They were back in the Free Spirit Room. Usually she locked it but she'd had more to drink on this tour than she usually did, so maybe she forgot.

She could hear them, shouts rising up through the walls and oozing out like ghosts.

There was a lot of swearing, conversation that she couldn't hear properly, then she heard 'Fucken bitch,' and a chair falling and she jumped up, knocking over a small table. She froze. Now they'd come for her. She looked for a weapon, knowing how stupid that was but thinking that at least she could put them off, frighten them if she looked like a crazy old woman . . .

'What the fuck was that?' she heard.

'Ghosts,' one of them said, and they laughed.

She didn't think they would frighten easily but it was worth a try. She'd done it to tourists for years. She set a long play tape going, checked her watch, then she went back downstairs, her keys held before her like an offering.

'Boys! I want to show you something I don't usually show people. I call it the Bloody Mongrel.' This is what kept her safe; she knew the secrets of the house.

PART II

THE MEN

What Ike loved about the guys inside was they didn't ask why. Why did you beat the shit out of that girl? Force your dick in her mouth? They got it; they did it themselves. It was about being in control.

In jail, you get by by being sociable. Not in a 'how are you today?' way, but in the figuring out where you stand way.

He chose Old Chook because he knew how to manipulate people who listened to men in their sixties. He could pass as normal, as a guy who hadn't killed half a dozen old women. They had to keep him out of the action a bit because of his age. He was too slow. And he had to work up a rage to be effective. They'd seen it; he was stone-cold when he was blind with fury. Bloody terrifying. He had a thing about shoes.

He was the oldest but it didn't make him the boss. Fat old white loser they called him. FOWL, then Chook. That was Ike; a genius at nicknames. Chook even started to walk a bit like a chook. He ran the prison laundry and that's the way they'd get out. They gave him shit about where he worked, because he stank, always, even after a shower, even with fresh clothes, he reeked like a rat or a guinea pig.

Alex asked himself along. He was one of those guys who overstepped the mark. Even amongst people who liked what he liked, who mixed sex and violence, he went too far. But he heard about the plan and wouldn't take payment to shut up, so he was in.

Wayne Bailey was in because he had a lead on a hideout, a rich one too. His parents hated his guts but his grandmother loved him. She sent him letters full of pathetic gossip about the town he'd grown up in, who was who and who was going on holiday. So good on Wayne's grandma. Wayne backed up everything Ike said by repeating it. 'Right?' he said, and the person had to nod or be thumped.

The two they called 'the kids' were in, partly out of pity. Ike reckoned they were too young to be locked up for life and the bitches had asked for it. Davo was unpredictable, but had that flair for violence Ike knew would be useful, at least at first. Devon on the other hand could have been something. You could see it, the way he laid out his cell. Artistic, you looked in and it almost felt like home. More importantly, his family was rich. He'd got his dad to send him enough money to fund the escape, including bribing one guard and smokes for all the men inside who knew but wouldn't tell anyway.

Planning out the escape was like a game of chess, except Ike had never played chess so it was more like Chinese chequers. Thinking of Chinese checkers made him think of his dad, the time his dad put Ike's marbles in a sock and beat the crap out of some guy. Ike put his marbles back in the box after, wiping blood off some of them. He never forgot that.

Ike wrote initials on pieces of toilet paper, moved them around on his bed, making sure every area was covered. He used smaller pieces for weapons. He flushed the pieces down the dunny when he was done.

He'd chosen well. Every one of them was an evil bastard, though not at his level, he didn't reckon. Mind you, Chook and Alex were sick as fuck.

He put himself in the first group because he'd have to start it all. The second group was Alex, Devon, Wayne and Davo. They needed to get to the laundry, and the best way was via the visitors' waiting room. That needed to be cleared. Ike didn't know how many deaths there'd be but he didn't want any man who'd baulk at it. They'd do it during visiting hours for more panic. More bodies to pile up. Ike told them, 'For the kids, you can knock 'em out. People will drop anything to save them. The others, though . . . any problems?'

No one had a problem.

The third group was Chook in the laundry, which he was happy with.

'Way I see it,' Chook said, 'is we can escape smart or escape crazy. Crazier is easier but people get hurt.'

Ike said, 'Well, we're sure as shit not smart.'

It was Mother's Day. Soon the visitors' waiting room would be packed, but it was early. Better to do it before there were too many for them to handle.

Ike went first. Waiting behind him round the corner were Alex, Devon, Wayne and Davo.

Ike approached the guard standing at the gate. 'What's up, Ike? You don't have any reason to be here,' the guard said. They put the nicest guards here because of the families. The family waiting room beyond the gate led to the garden they called Serenity. You were a lucky bastard to get a visit out there. You had to have a family, for one (wife, kids), who gave a shit. You had to have a good record, because there was only one guard out there, and you got to eat food from outside. Men would come back smelling of it; pasta sauce, garlic bread, sweet cakes, and sniffing could make you wish you were them.

Ike never did; he hated even having brothers to worry about. Life would be easier if there was only himself to worry about.

'My wife's in the waiting room.'

'Yeah, I don't think so, Ike. Nice dream but I'm pretty sure . . .'

Ike slit the man's throat with a shiv and had the keys off him before he fell to the ground.

As Ike opened the gate, he whistled low and deep. The others came around the corner and in a hard mass they pushed open the door to the visitors' waiting room. Only one family in there so far. Good.

One guard at the door; Devon took him with a home-made cosh to the head. Then all of them set to.

They made no noise, so at first no one understood what was happening. Another guard, flirting with a pretty wife, stood up, stunned, as Alex slit his throat, whispering, 'I'd beat you to death if I had time.'

Davo took an older woman, perhaps the grandmother, wrapping a sock he'd brought along tight around her neck and squeezing.

Alex took the young wife, strangling her like Davo did to his but using his bare hands. He knew when to stop but there was something so incredibly sexual about not stopping. He thought he never would again. He was hard; has never been harder. If he came in his pants they'd laugh at him, never let him forget it but he didn't care.

The children hadn't figured out what's happening. This was far beyond anything in their experience. The oldest was nine or so – all of them too young for violent video games or movies. These kids, though, had seen more than other kids their age.

Devon elbowed one kid in the nose, knocking it to the floor. Then he used a fist on the side of the head. They'd all practised this, how to knock someone out. They'd used the guy everyone called Dumbo. Big ears and stupid as fuck. He barely noticed the blows.

Wayne muttered as he hit another kid in the face. Said sorry to his grandmother like he usually did when he committed a crime. He hit pretty soft, though. If he could have coaxed his kid to close his eyes and pretend to be unconscious he would have.

Ike knocked out a little girl with brown curls who gave him a cute smile. He hesitated, hoping no one saw him because he'd have to kick the shit out of them if they did. All too busy though. The kid was cute and he felt weak as piss but he was glad he didn't have to kill her. That face would have haunted him.

The floor was sticky with blood. Davo picked up a chair and went for the youngest kid, maybe two years old. He really didn't care; all of it was meaningless. He went too far.

Ike saw and thought they should've put him away somewhere, somewhere other than prison. He was like a baby, the craziest shit-head Ike'd ever met.

They dragged out the guards and the two women, laid them across the hallway, then the kids, all of them bloodied. They put the dead little kid on top because it might stop the guards, give them pause.

It even gave Ike pause.

Chook felt at home in the laundry. He only wished they washed lady things, too. Men things were coarse, rough. Lady things were silky. Lovely.

He had a sharpened fork in the back of his pants, the tines wrapped in toilet paper to stop them digging into him. He set out the irons, handle up for easy access.

One of the guards said, 'What are you doing?'

'Cleaning the irons.' Chook's voice shook. He hoped the guard wouldn't notice. The guards wouldn't survive, but the two other inmates might, depending on how they behaved.

He heard a shout and knew it was time to do his part.

The first guard was easy. They always put the lazy ones in the laundry, because only the well-behaved inmates worked there, and it was hot and tiring.

The female guard came out of the storage closet (lazy bitch) and Chook whacked her hard over the head with an iron, then pounded her face.

One of the other inmates tried to stop him. Chook stabbed his left eye and couldn't remove the fork, so pushed him hard between a dryer and the wall, out of the way. 'Fuck off,' Chook said to the other inmate, who backed away.

The others ran through the laundry door, wild and bloody. Chook had done a good job of the guards; the woman sat twitching in the corner, the man was slumped over the ironing board. They piled the bodies in the doorway as a barrier.

Then shouts and the sound of the gate being opened.

This was the moment Ike had been concerned about. Would the van be there, and who would be driving it?

They ran through the back door, Chook holding it open for all of them, and the laundry van was there.

It was Ike's brother Byron in the driving seat. The van was too small but Ike didn't point that out, wouldn't have fucking dared.

'Youse are all fucken cunts,' Byron said. He'd shown up but he wasn't happy. He was doing it for the money; Wayne reckoned the place they were going was like an unguarded museum. There'd be a huge payout ripping off the old woman.

Byron had brought a couple of guns which would make life easier.

'Oi!' It was the remaining laundry inmate, a sleazy little shit whose name they didn't even know. 'Take me! Go on!'

'Come on then,' Ike said, holding the door open. 'Hurry.' Byron handed Ike a gun and when the sleazy little shit was close enough, Ike shot him through the head.

Davo freaked out, his hands shaking, pounding up and down in the dirt like a jumping bean, so Ike shot him through the head as well, clean and neat.

That had always been Ike's plan, to be honest; Davo was not easily controlled. And there wasn't enough room in the van.

'Jeez,' Devon said, but mostly he was relieved. No one had trusted Davo. And he had killed a kid. They weren't supposed to do that.

The others were silent, none of them even looking at Davo's body leaking into the dirt.

They all piled into the van, Ike up front, Chook grabbing the seat behind him, leaning forward, face red, full of something. Alex was in, and Wayne, and Devon.

Byron said, 'How was it?'

'Over too quick,' Chook said, and they snickered, even Devon, who missed out on a seat so squatted in the corner, making himself as small as possible.

'How the fuck areya?' Byron said to Ike, then without waiting, 'Youse fucken owe me. The missus'd kill me if she knew.'

'Mate, that woman doesn't appreciate you.' Ike clapped Byron on the back. Byron gave him what Ike called privately 'the look'. 'Sorry, mate,' he said quietly so the others couldn't hear. Byron had done plenty of time but was trying to go straight. He had a kid.

They drove for half an hour then swapped into a silver Toyota Hiace.

'Mate, would you look at this shit box.' Byron hated Toyotas. He was a Holden man. Ike relinquished the passenger seat next to Byron and Wayne took it, wriggling in his seat, excited like a kid. He got to sit there because he was the only one who knew where they were going.

45

THE BLOODY MONGREL

'May I present the Bloody Mongrel. Or the Curse Room!' That one always got a laugh.

'It's full of things that were stolen from the house over the years and were eventually returned, for one reason or another.' Jewellery and furniture. Pieces of the plane. Things taken in the years since, by visitors and thieves. She'd replaced many of the missing things that had been taken. She'd tracked down others, and some had come back to her of their own accord, either from relatives or friends of the thief, or the thief themselves feeling guilty. 'There are plenty more cursed items still out there. In here, it's the echo of the curse that frightens.' She let them look for a minute or two, then, 'This room is a testament to human nature, is what I say. Everything in this room was stolen from my house. They call them looters but that seems too gentle a word to me. It's taken years to bring it all back. Most of the items did indeed curse the thief, or their loved ones. '

'What's in here? More curse shit?' Devon said, pointing at a cupboard. Pera opened it to reveal a collection of necklaces and brooches. Devon pulled back. He clearly believed in curses.

Wayne picked up an item that had belonged to one of her lovers, a book of erotic photography. She'd never been keen on it; the visions of perfection made her uncomfortable. The lover had inscribed the book, 'For Pera, the most beautiful of all'.

Pera laughed. 'He stole it from the Banned Room and then sent it back, written in! What a bloody mongrel, ay!'

'Used to fuck you, did he?' Alex said.

'You're disgusting. Like the shit-smeared toilets at the crappy nightclubs you go to,' said Ike. Pera was surprised to hear him come to her defence.

'You never got into any of the clubs I go to.'

Pera watched Ike rising. Not physically, but his whole self seemed to lift.

'You're saying I'm not good enough?'

'I'm saying they have dress codes.' Alex said.

'You mean dressing like a wog? Yeah, probably right. I did go to one of your shitty clubs, though. After a wedding. We were fucken blind, mate. Ber-lind. I even danced.' And Ike stood up, shaking his hips.

Pera laughed. He turned to her, smiling, waving his arms. 'You woulda danced with me before you got old, wouldn't you?'

'I would have. I always did go for the naughty boys.'

He snickered. 'I haven't been called naughty since I was about three. What about you, Devon?'

Devon shook his shoulders, faking laughter.

They'd found bags somewhere and started filling them with the more valuable objects, no longer making neat piles at the door.

Pera said, 'I don't usually bring people in here. It's not the nicest of places and most don't want to take the risk. Especially if they have children. I tend to recommend not bringing children in.'

'Fuck that,' Ike said.

'This room is particularly haunted. It's not only the debris from the plane, but the other items I've rescued over the years, or that have been returned to me. Each of these carries . . . something. If you're quiet, you can hear a hum of voices.'

She watched them looking through drawers, in cupboards, wanting things of value. Gold chains, diamond rings, wristwatches; all of it they gathered.

Chook stepped outside, unwilling to touch anything. He clearly wasn't the brightest spark and very suggestible. 'I'm not risking it,' he said. 'You guys are idiots.' Still, he stood at the doorway and watched them.

'Well, you've been in the room,' Pera said, her voice gentle, caring. 'But you didn't stay long so you should be okay.' She winked at Alex, the most cynical of them. The sickest too, from what she'd gathered; he was the only one of them who killed for pure pleasure. He was the one who pulled teeth out.

'Whatever curse you put on me, there's far worse in my head,' he said, and she didn't doubt that.

'No such thing as a curse, mate. But I was born under an unlucky star, and that's why I have such shit luck with women,' Chook said.

Pera knew about men like him. On the one hand trying to act tough and cynical, on the other looking for an excuse to justify weakness. 'Well, I don't know. Some of the rescuers took pieces of the plane, and belongings. They came back years later, saying they'd been cursed ever since.'

'Are you warning us not to thieve anything?' Ike said.

'I already said what's mine is yours. But did you notice the door knocker?' She gestured to where it lay on a side table. 'The girl who took that died a horrible death.'

'Like how?' Alex said.

She held up the solid brass lion's head door knocker. 'This hung on our front door. I would have reattached it but sadly it's too damaged.'

'Is that what that girl stole? That's it? What a fucken loser.'

'It's a sad story. She was the granddaughter of a local shop-keeper, a wonderful man called Mr Thomas. She stole it when she was about fifteen and hid it in his shop. He never knew it was there. He was a fit man and his family all lived long lives, so when she was killed in a road accident, it seemed random. Nobody made the connection. And still Mr Thomas didn't know the knocker was there.

'He died in 1961, aged eighty-three. Not a bad age, you might say, but he looked awful. He suffered a lot in the end. Before that, he was fit as a fiddle. Should have lasted another twenty years.' She laughed; it was the sort of thing you said about a much younger person, but she liked to think of him at 103, still fit.

'He had something they called leontiasis ossea, which made his face look like a lion's; flat nose, broad lips. You won't find a soul in town who thinks it was anything but the curse.'

She took a small folder out of a wooden desk. 'In here, if you're game, are photos of him. They are post-mortem, so I warn you they are disturbing. You'll see why we think the way we do.'

There was always someone who'd look.

'Mate, someone should have put him out of his misery,' Ike said. 'That is ugly.'

Alex stole a set of false teeth, gold inlaid, but no way was Pera going to mention that.

Devon picked up a broken hand mirror, cutting his hand. He stared at the blood welling out.

'I guess you're cursed, mate. You're gonna have a shit life from now on,' Ike said, slapping him on the back.

'That is definitely one of the cursed things. I thought the curse might be lifted when I brought the mirror back to where it belongs, but it seems not. If you try to take that mirror out of the house, you'll see my sister Hazel reflected in it. Or the man who killed her.'

'Who killed her?' Ike asked.

'You'll think less of me when I tell you.'

'Tell.'

'It was my husband's brother,' she said, and that made Ike laugh so hard he cried.

'You've had a lot of dead people in your life,' Devon said. 'How come you're still so nice?' Pera knew she'd tapped into something in him in that moment. He felt safe with her. She offered no threat.

'I don't know . . . I never thought about being anything else. I was pretty rebellious as a teenager, though. And after my husband died well . . . you wouldn't want to know what I got up to!'

'You must have been a spunk back then,' Ike said. He bounced on the balls of his feet, agitated.

'Aren't you scared of death?' Devon asked.

'That is a very big question,' Pera said. 'I guess that's one reason I stay here. I'm looking for my family, hoping to see them. Even my husband.'

Chook snorted from the doorway. 'Typical man-hating woman.'

'Did you *see* my husband's work?' she asked. 'Yes, of course you did. But we can look again. And if you're nice, I'll show you something most people don't see. There is a literal hidden door in there. Behind it, I keep the paintings that are really worth something. You'd be able to sell them legitimately. I have the papers. Only . . .'

'Only what?' Devon asked.

'Let me show you.'

46

BLUEBEARD'S CHAMBER

She watched them search the room for valuables. She opened a hidden wall cabinet where she kept whisky and glasses.

'You little beauty!' Alex said. He clicked his teeth together. Kissed his fingers to his lips. '*Bellissimo!*'

'You are such a fucken wog,' Ike said.

'I'm not a wog.'

'Bloody look like it.'

'It's called a tan. You should try it some time. Chicks love it.' Alex clicked his teeth together and rolled his hands in his pockets. Pera swore she heard more teeth rattling.

She wasn't sure it was smart, encouraging them to drink more, but it did make them think she was a friend. These men were filled with venom, and alcohol wouldn't help that. But it might make them happier, at least for a while.

She got The Men to shift a tallboy and revealed a hidden doorway. This was a smallish room beyond, about the size of a suburban bathroom. Inside were racks upon racks of paintings, most of them ones she'd bought in London.

'Are these paintings worth anything much?' Ike said. 'Cos they look like shit to me.'

'It's what's underneath that's important, if you strip them back to the original canvas. Of course they're worth a lot to me as they are. Proof of my husband's love. That's what sustained me, after he died.' She sighed. 'I guess I should tell you how he really died. Do you want to hear it? We'll need a drink. Lots of drinks.'

They sat on chairs and stools in the main room and filled their glasses.

'There are a number of versions of how my husband died. The official one is that it was a household accident. But the truth? I was blind drunk at the time. I don't usually tell tours that. I heard someone shouting, bellowing. I thought it was my father, furious with me for being weak, saying, "Stop him! Fight him!" about my husband. About Joseph. But it was Joseph himself, roaring for me.

'"I've been calling for you," Joseph said. He'd had plenty to drink, too; I could see it spilled all down his shirt. Small spots of vomit as well. "I want to try again. We're going to try again." He was talking about strangling me. Replicating Hazel's murder, again and again and again.

'I told him no. That I didn't want to do it anymore. That we should sit and have another drink. I held a wine bottle, a good vintage, that I'd already polished off. "Let's get another," I said. But he came at me, got his fingers around my throat. I pounded his head so hard the bottle broke, and I used the sharp edges to slash at him. I swung at his head with this ice bucket' – she raised it to show them – 'and oh, my, the clunk it made. And down the stairs he rolled.

'"See! You fought back," he said, blood gurgling in his throat. "You didn't want to die so you fought back. Your sister wanted to die. My brother wasn't a murderer. He gave her what she wanted." That was what he was always trying to prove.

'I lay beside my brilliant husband's body for ten minutes, maybe more. Certainly until the blood stopped flowing. I began to feel chilled. I also wanted another drink, and food. I was suddenly starving.

'I didn't have a drink, though. My husband was dead, and I'd have to explain it, make them understand, and I couldn't do that if I slurred my words. So I had coffee, then I called the police. They were there within thirty minutes, and the ambulance, too. These were men I'd been at primary school with, they were family friends. They were men I'd always known. All men in those days. The paramedics carried the body off and the police did a search of the house, checking for . . . I don't know what. An intruder? But I convinced them it was an accident. That Joseph had fallen down the stairs holding an empty bottle and two wine glasses. That I had been resting in one of the galleries and heard his calls.

'If that bastard hadn't tried to kill me, night after night, he would be alive. We would be growing old together, seen the world, improved the house. He might be famous in his own right.'

'Shit!' Devon said.

'It was so odd. Like time stopped. I've heard people say that and it is absolutely true. It was as if I took a photo, and that frozen moment is the reality. I've never told anyone this.'

It was a forgetfulness that only drinking could replicate.

'Some people reckon that someone else steps in when you kill.

It might be a part of yourself, or maybe it's a ghost, hitching a ride,' she said.

Wayne said, 'Lotta people say they blank out. I don't know how many it actually happens to. Most people are full of shit.'

'Time is weird, though. I do feel as if it stops, sometimes. Not just the representation of it, but the actual thing. The weirdest thing is this clock. It's the only one that keeps time.'

There was a grandfather clock in the corner of the room. It carried a thin layer of dust and she could see small fingerprints in that dust.

'Little shits,' she said, as she used her apron to wipe the dust off. 'Always getting where they don't belong.'

'You could always push them downstairs,' Alex said, and she threw her head back and laughed, and The Men snickered, and for a moment she almost felt happy.

The clock ticked. Chook checked his watch. They were attuned to precise times after being in jail, used to things happening on schedule.

There was a freedom in not knowing the time.

'Could you do it again? Second time is easier,' Wayne said.

'Never,' she said, but she could. If her life depended on it, she could.

Devon said, 'I can't believe you murdered your husband.'

'And got away with it. Don't forget that part!'

'I call bullshit,' Chook said. He'd been getting steadily angrier the more she spoke. 'Who do you think you are, telling a bullshit story like that?'

'So many ghosts clinging to you, Chook. So, so many.' She turned away from him but she heard him wiping at himself as if he could brush off those ghosts.

'What about me?' Devon said. 'Do I have ghosts hanging around?'

'Not one,' she said. From what she's seen, he'd had no real impact on anyone in his life apart from his victims. 'No one except the people you've befriended. People you've helped.' She was pretty sure he'd never helped anyone, but the flattery wouldn't hurt. Planting the seed that helping was good. 'In this house they're waiting to jump on board. They are everywhere. Like dust motes. Think about how many people have died here. It's safer outside.'

'Why do you stay, then?'

'I'm used to it. And I don't have anywhere else to go.'

'Who've I got?' Ike said. 'What ghosts d'ya reckon I've got?'

'Aborted babies,' Alex said. That brought a laugh, which horrified Pera more than anything she'd seen or heard from The Men.

'No fucken way do I use a condom. That shit is up to the girl. Not my shit. Then they come to me wanting me to be daddy. I gave some of them money. Others – yeah, well. I don't hit women.' Wayne snickered. 'But I could give 'em one punch and they'd lose the whatever it was.'

'Bullshit,' Chook said. 'You can't abort with a punch. You do it with pills.'

'Thanks, Dr Cock,' Wayne said. He lifted his shirt. 'I gotta rash, can you check it out for me?' He mimed pulling his jeans off, then shook his head. 'Wanker,' he said.

'So?' Ike said to Pera. 'Ya reckon I've got ghosts?'

'No ghost would dare haunt you, Ike.'

'This stuff must be worth a shitload,' Ike said. 'You should have some sort of security set up.'

Pera's mind raced over the best possible answer. Lie, and say an alarm was easily triggered? Or tell the truth, that she had nothing.

'My friend is always telling me that. You sound exactly like him. Are you a policeman, too?'

Ike coughed; he clearly had them all tight under control. He was telling them *Keep quiet. Say nothing.*

'You got cameras and shit?' he said. 'Like security ones?'

'My policeman friend watches out for me. He patrols most days.'

That one popped out and she wasn't sure how they'd take it.

'Except you're supposed to be away so he won't, right?'

Except he would. He'd never forgotten the looters. He'd check from the end of the driveway in his car. If she could manage to hang something out the windows. Make sure the lights were on. It made her nervous, though, because he was old now, Young Bobby. Seventy-three and retired. He did some shifts as a nightwatchman but he'd be no match for Ike and his friends. The ladies' auxiliary might stop by for a sticky beak, and George and Harry sometimes checked in if she wasn't there. She also wondered about the teenager who helped her with the horses; she knew he brought friends here sometimes, when she was away. She hoped that wouldn't happen.

47

THE FREE SPIRIT ROOM

Pera led them downstairs to the Free Spirit Room again. Then she went to the kitchen and filled the bucket with ice. She loved this faux crystal bucket they'd received as a wedding present. Such a durable item. It hadn't even broken when she'd hit her husband over the head with it and pushed him down the stairs.

She gave it a swing. Old Faithful, she called it.

'Drinks, boys?' she said. 'Who'd like another whisky?' She produced snacks, then tried to be as unobtrusive as possible as she observed them. They were drunker than she'd seen men in a long time. She could lock them in this room and walk to town, or try to ride her bike. Or she could get her car keys from Ike. They were in his pocket but she thought she'd rather walk than risk trying to get them.

Alex sat himself by the door. Drunk or not, he was not taking his eyes off her. He raised his glass. 'Here's to all of us. After all we've been through.'

'What the fuck you been through?' Ike said.

'I've had a shitty life. Better than the rest of you, yeah. But it's tough being God's gift to women.'

Pera restrained a laugh but couldn't help rolling her eyes.

'Yeah, even the old lady calls bullshit on that one,' Ike said.

'Bitch, I've been married three times. First one lasted a week. She couldn't handle it. Second one lasted a few months but she pissed off when she woke up with my teeth in her shoulder. I wasn't biting. Just letting 'em rest,' and he picked up Pera's arm to demonstrate.

'Fuck off, you creep,' Wayne said.

'There's a lot of lonely ladies out there. They all want it.'

'True,' Devon said, and Chook nodded.

'They'll put up with a lot,' Alex said. 'My third wife did before she died.' He made a strange movement with his mouth, running his tongue over his teeth, back and forth. His teeth were very small, as if his baby teeth had never fallen out. 'Mostly I want head. You know? But I hate the teeth. So I tell 'em, take them out. You won't have to worry about them anymore. Doing you a favour. Half these chicks are druggies anyway, so rotten teeth. They ask for it.'

'They're always changing their minds,' Devon said. 'Bitches.'

The ashtrays filled quickly, then they used empty bottles. They had plenty of smokes; Ike's brother Byron had got them in. Wouldn't be free, though; he'd add it to what they owed him.

Chook said, 'You're right about the desperate ones. I tell ya. No one ever taught them to watch out. Ya know? When you're like us, you're on your toes from early on. My dad kicked me out the day I turned sixteen. All I had was a bag of clothes, nothing else.'

A moaning sound rolled over them. Pera's tape playing.

'Who the fuck is that?' Ike said.

'No one,' Pera said, regretting letting the tape run. 'It's the way the house sounds.'

'Go check it out, Dev.'

'Why me?' In that moment Devon really looked like the child he was.

'Because you're a fucken idiot so I don't care if someone shivs you,' Ike said.

Devon left, and made a search of the nearby rooms. He found nothing. As he headed back to the others, he heard stilettos behind him. He knew that sound; he loved women in high heels. They couldn't run. They could barely walk. Here, though? He turned slowly, putting on his grin just in case, but no one was there.

'Fucken freezing in here!' he said, as he returned to the others.

'It has gone a bit chilly,' Pera said.

They were used to the cold, though, in prison.

They were all quiet for a bit. Then they heard a baby crying.

'What the fuck is that?' Devon said.

It was coming from far away.

'Is it in the house?' Devon spoke quietly, his shoulders hunched as if trying not to hear.

The crying faded and they looked at each other as if to say *Did we hear that*?

None of them cared about the baby itself. All of them clearly thought, *Shut that thing up*. Pera had never seen this before. People always wanted to save the baby.

The lights went off.

'Excuse me!' Pera said. She'd had the best part of a bottle of brandy and felt warm from the heart out. 'It's an old house. These things happen. Wait for a bit, it'll sort itself. Otherwise one of you dear gentlemen will have to go to the fuse box and fix it for me.'

The lights came back on again.

'This place is a fucken dump!' Ike said.

Wayne said, 'How long are you staying, anyway?' Pera noted he said 'you', not 'we', meaning he was planning to stay for a while. The others didn't notice this slip.

'Byron'll let us know. He'll head back when he reckons it's died down a bit.' Ike's voice wavered very slightly between the sentences and Pera wondered why. Anxiety? She could use that to sow the seeds.

Ike said, 'Let's go to that money room. The one that kid was talking about.'

'You mean the Mint?'

'That'll do for starters.'

48

THE MINT

They behaved like many others before them when they saw the money on the walls.

'Jesus, look at this!' Devon said.

'Can you get 'em off or what? What a waste,' from Wayne.

It was one of the jobs Pera had enjoyed, papering the walls. Many had tried to prise off the dollar bills. Visitors had also added to the collection, had signed and stuck Australian dollar bills on the walls until they were phased out in 1984. Others stuck foreign currency, or sometimes five-dollar bills. There were no tens.

'Mate, it stinks in here. Like dead fish,' Devon said. They could all smell it. Pera had brought a piece of salmon downstairs with her and hidden it. It was amazing how disconcerting a smell was when you couldn't find the source.

'It's your own cunt,' Ike said. 'Cos we know you're a girl. Look atcha. Mate, don't worry, Simpson told me all about you.'

The name Simpson made Devon shudder. *No matter where he was in life, it was better than a cell with that man.* 'I'm going to get us more booze,' he said, his voice soft.

Pera said, 'Do you want me to come with you? Might be dark out there,' and for a moment he appeared to consider it, the comfort of having her with him.

'She's staying with us,' Ike said. The Men worked their way through the room as they had done in every room. They looked in the small desk in the corner, pulling out notebooks and a ledger.

Pera pointed to the small locked box hidden behind a couch. 'That's the week's takings. I'm so slack about getting to the bank.'

She fumbled for the key and opened the box. There were a few hundred dollars inside. Ike pocketed the notes. 'You're not making much, are you?'

'I don't need much.'

Devon trotted along the hallway. He didn't know where the light switch was, if there was one, and he wasn't going to be feeling around in the dark for it. He hated the dark. He liked the bright lights, the clubs, the flashing and the streetlights and all the rest of it. He liked the women who came through, the ones recently turned eighteen and the ones who pretended they were. All new to the club scene. Easily impressed. In court, one of the bitches who'd stood up against him said, 'He looked more impressive sitting on a barstool. Not as short, you know? He ordered drinks for all of us. He told us he owned the nightclub.'

This was true. His father thought of it as a tax write-off because he was sure that under Devon's management the club would fail. Devon didn't know this until it came out in court during the character references.

Defence: Clearly you believe your son to be trustworthy and sensible. Why else would you give him a nightclub?

His father said nothing to that.

Prosecution: How is the nightclub doing? Well? Or are women staying away because of the way they are treated there? There are multiple reports of rape in the bathrooms and of constant harassment.

His father said, 'Have you ever been to a nightclub? No, don't answer that. I can see by looking at you that you have not.'

Laughter from the gallery, and from Devon. No way would Devon let the prosecutor into his club. You need the spunks, the best-looking guys, to lure the ladies in.

None of it did Devon any good. His father's charisma had no effect.

Devon walked quickly, humming loudly, but still he heard, 'Careful you don't trip and bite off your tongue. Careful you don't choke and bleed to death drowning in your own blood.'

'Who's there?' he said, but quietly; he didn't want to know.

The others were still trying to peel off the dollar bills, with Alex going, 'You fucken faggots. Look at you. Scrabbling.'

All his male victims were gay men except for one mistaken identity, a plumber or something who he thought was gay. That's how he was caught. Finally killed someone with a family who gave a shit. He's done a lot more than the cops know about. A lot more than he'd ever let on to anybody. He never had sex with men, though. He only liked women that way.

Funny how many of them got sucked in because of his facial scars, the story they told.

'Leave him,' his dad had said when his mum tried to help him. 'Leave him right there.' Lying amongst the shards of the plate-glass window he'd been thrown through. His dad flying into a fury when his mum took him to hospital anyway and she paid the price.

The baby was still crying somewhere, they could all hear it, and Wayne was sick of the lot of them, bloody children, letting it get to them, freaking out over noises, making him freak out. The old lady passed him a bottle of vodka. Faggots drank vodka but it did the job.

When he picked up the bottle he could see his own face in there and more; it looked like it was full of ghosts. He heard *Baby, oh baby, oh dear baby, don't cut your guts up, baby* and he threw the bottle down and swore he'd give up the booze.

Then they told her the story of their escape.

She thought, *They won't let me live after telling me this.*

She sat quietly in a corner as they talked. They went over old ground, she could tell by the language, by the flow of it and the way they didn't have to pause for words. She listened as they crowed about the things they'd done, using the sort of voices other people used to describe a trip overseas, or a good party, or how big the queue was at the supermarket.

They were wrong, these men. She'd known it, of course. But this casual acceptance, this easy relaying of awful acts, made her want to curl up and disappear.

She was the one, though. She was the one between them and the outside world.

In the past, no matter what was happening, no matter how awful, she knew it would end. There was no such knowledge here.

It would only end if she stopped it.

How were these men alive and all her good people dead? Mother, father, sisters, the prime minister and his wife, her parents' friends, those on the plane.

Devon said, 'The only thing in my whole life I'm grateful for is not killing those kids.' He paused, then said, 'Bloody Davo did one. But I didn't.'

'Yeah, but they're fucked for life. Seeing their mother murdered? Piled up with them? Fucked,' Ike said.

Pera said, 'Wayne, should we go and look at your grandmother's things? I keep them in a storeroom. I call it the Bee Hive. My little joke.'

Ike said, 'We'll all go. How the fuck do even you find your way around? This place is so huge, so many rooms. Like a rabbit warren.' He reached round and scratched his shoulders, hard, and Pera resisted the temptation to offer to scratch his back. Walking through the house with other people gave her a sense of how easy it would be to get lost. She could lose these men in her house.

'Humans are adaptable. We familiarise ourselves very quickly, no matter where we are. Even in that Other Place, you must have made a home for yourselves.' It was the first time she'd acknowledged she knew where they'd come from. After what they'd told her it seemed foolish to pretend otherwise.

Devon nodded. 'I kinda laid stuff out that looked good. I could pretend that way.'

'I had pictures but you wouldn't wanna see them,' Chook said. She wasn't sure which of The Men she found the creepiest but he was close to the top of the list.

The house was big, yes, but compared to the vastness of outside? Of the adventures she'd been on, the places she'd explored?

It was tiny. Contained.

49

THE BEE HIVE

The Bee Hive was on the third floor; Chook complained about every step.

'Isn't this stuff of your grandma's wonderful?' Pera said to Wayne. 'It must bring back good memories.' She hoped it would also scare him, help him to expose himself to the others, because he'd be amongst things from his childhood and maybe that would stir emotions.

Ike, Chook, Devon and Alex moved around the room, looking behind pictures and opening drawers as they'd done in almost every room.

'Hey, you fuckers, leave my shit alone,' Wayne said. He held his shoulders back, as if he had something to be proud of. As if the contents of this room was something he had earned.

'You'll recognise some of the things in here, Wayne. Your grandmother didn't want to take them with her when she moved to Brissie and your parents didn't want them either, but I couldn't bear to see them thrown out or given away. Anything you want you should take. Really, these things are yours. There wasn't a lot left after her house burnt down.'

He met her eye.

There was glassware, silver candlesticks, a tea set over 150 years old, bone-handled knives, old cake tins.

'I remember some of this shit,' Wayne said. He picked up one of the tins. 'Grandma used to make fruitcake. I hated it.'

Pera remembered Mrs Bee describing the time Wayne had hidden fruitcake all over the house, in corners and under furniture.

There was a bookshelf with a dozen or so cookbooks, run through with pieces of paper marking favourite recipes. Wayne flipped one open at random; an Irish stew recipe his grandmother had notated with 'Use cheaper cuts'. The recipe itself was scribbled over in dark ink, the words 'Animal killer'.

'That was your mum, I think, on one of the first visits to meet your grandparents. Not long after she met your dad.'

'She's one of those pissed-off people. Dad always said she needed to eat more meat, but that pissed her off more than anything.'

'Eat more meat, ay? Wasn't she getting enough from your dad? Shoulda sent her to see me,' Ike said, making an obscene gesture. Wayne winced.

'Like I said, Wayne, it's your stuff. You can take whatever you like.'

'Isn't this stuff cursed?'

'I guess we'll find out.'

He pocketed a cigarette lighter she'd never noticed before, and other small items he found about the place.

'You don't need to steal, Wayne. It's yours. This whole room can be dedicated to you.'

'Can I bring one of those comfy chairs in here? These chairs are shit.'

She shook her head. 'Every room is carefully designed, every item perfectly placed. Mostly dedicated to someone who died. It seemed to be the right thing to do. Some rooms I've given nicknames because I can't always remember which room belongs to which person. No one could! I do remember which key with which lock, though. So many people.'

'What about us? Do we get a room too?' Devon said. 'Wayne got one.'

'You want me to dedicate a room to you when you die?'

'No, we want them now. Give us a room each and we can have whatever's inside,' he said.

'You want me to remember more rooms?' she said, then she nodded. 'You can all pick a room that's yours alone.'

'We don't need your permission,' Ike said, but she thought he was pleased she'd given it.

'What's given freely is sweeter than what's taken,' she said.

Wayne disagreed. 'People only give you stuff they don't want. It's much more fun to take what someone doesn't want to give you.'

50

THE BLUE ROOM (CHARITY'S ROOM)

'I think you should take the Blue Room, Devon,' Pera said.

As they walked towards it, Devon said, 'I thought I heard footsteps before. Like a drunk chick in high heels.'

'Sometimes people appear. They are just there. Like you lot. This might sound crazy but I don't always know if they're real or not. I tend to pretend they are until I'm sure. I still haven't decided if you're all real, or you're ghosts.'

'That's crazy,' Ike said.

Devon said quietly, 'I heard the footsteps but no one was there.'

As quietly, Pera said, 'We're followed by those we've hurt. Sometimes I think my husband is ten steps behind me.'

Wayne snickered.

The other men would choose big, open rooms with windows. Freedom. But Devon loved the Blue Room. In jail he'd decorated his cell and so this room was the one for him; well-decorated, with simple furnishings. Gentle blue tones for Charity. Prussian blue, cobalt, teal, ultramarine.

'It's beautiful in here,' Devon said.

'One of my sisters studied design for a while. I followed in her footsteps until I realised what a tough world it was.' After Joseph's death she had tried to get away from the house through studying, trying to find a different life. But she felt the drag back in a physical way.

Chook said, 'I knew an old woman who had fabrics all over the place. She thought she was pretty good.'

'These are all designed by me. They aren't very good. In my younger days I thought I'd be famous. People would pay thousands of dollars for a tiny square.' She lifted her fingers, making a square of them. She turned to Devon. 'You'll have to share this one with my sister Charity. She was the gentle one. The delicate one. The quietest. It took her ages each day to look perfect, although she pretended it didn't. You couldn't see the effort, but you knew she was perfect. This room is a bit like that. It looks very simple but took a lot of work. As the best things do. She wanted to be a teacher.'

'I like kindy teachers.' Alex, rubbing at his crotch.

'They don't like you,' Devon said. He'd liked his teachers, Pera guessed. All those who thought he could have been something. Who saw him wasting his life.

'I always had good teachers,' Chook said. 'They never bothered me.'

'Teachers are cunts,' Ike said. 'You're telling me you actually passed school?'

Chook shrugged; school was over a long time ago for him.

'I passed Year Ten!' Devon said. 'Dad reckoned he needed me to help out after that. I coulda got Year Twelve, easy.'

'Yeah?' Ike said, but looked suddenly weary, as if this target was too easy to even consider.

Ike'd had no education beyond primary school. No one could make the Hubble boys go to school. They were smart enough to get ticked off as present then not attend classes and no one was ever game to call them on it.

'Teachers? Fucken hate teachers. The women ones. Mate, the number of times they tried to have a fiddle with me,' Ike said.

'Bullshit,' Chook said. 'That's me. Don't steal my story.'

'Is that why you go for old women? Cos you lost your cherry to one? And anyone under the age of fifty thinks you're gross?' Wayne said. He always knew where Ike was going with things.

'Bullshit,' Chook said again, but they had him with that one.

'Whatdya reckon? Is he hot?' Wayne asked Pera.

'Oh, I haven't thought about things like that for a long time. But . . .' She looked Chook up and down, exaggerating. 'No.' She wasn't about to tell any of them about her sex life. Better they think her a dried-up old lady.

The Men hooted at this. 'We like her,' Wayne said. 'Don't we? Chook REALLY likes her, don't you, Chook? Ay?'

'We'd manage something, wouldn't we?' Chook said, winking at Pera. Not wanting any of them offside at this point, she winked back.

'Wild one,' Ike said.

'Come on,' Pera said. 'Let's go down to the conservatory. We haven't had a drink there yet.'

51

THE CONSERVATORY

They gathered in the light-filled room, where Pera made gin and tonics, although Ike preferred vodka and drank it straight out of the bottle. Pera said, 'Prime ministers got pissed in here, and famous artists and writers and movie stars, so why not us?'

'And who fucked who after?' Alex said. 'I know people. They're always fucking each other.'

'There was a bit of that. But not so much here. My sister had to leave to find that sort of thing. She was very keen. She left home when she was fifteen.'

In some light and from a distance the curtains in the room look like girls in white dresses. Not quite dancing but light on their feet.

The Men had fun posing with the well-made man, her wonderfully large and hard naked statue, draping things onto him, posing lewdly. There was usually at least one in each group who did it. The homophobic ones would be aggressive. Others would fake a sex act, if there were no children around. Or there were giggles and exchanged glances and at least one sarcastic, 'Art!'

'So does that mean that one of your sisters wasn't killed in the plane crash?' Devon said.

'She was already dead by then. She was murdered in St Kilda. Left in an alleyway. Nobody even looked at her for three or four days, they think. People thought she was a drunk. Or a pile of rubbish. I never saw the body. I was only five.'

They settled around the table. The Men were more relaxed now that she'd 'given' some of them a room. She'd proved she would share.

Pera said to The Men, 'I'm glad you're here. I'm lonely. You can be my sons. I never had sons. Never had a child. I need an heir. This place needs a future owner.' Her eyes were bleary, her vision blurred. Her doctor had told her to take it easy on the alcohol; it affected her far more than it used to. The Men were staggering, too. This had been a long session.

'You've got a lot of unhappy women clinging to you. Who do you see when you close your eyes?' Pera asked Chook.

'Old women,' he said, lop-sided-grinning, eyes squeezed shut. 'All carrying their shoes as if they want me to buy them more.'

Not quite sobered by this, still it resonated with Pera. She'd noted on his postcard that he placed his victims' shoes neatly beside them.

'People bring ghosts with them, I think. We had one man; he came to visit because he thought he was the reincarnation of someone who died in the crash. He was covered in ghosts, but they dropped off like bloated leeches, once we got down to the Underhistory. I think they liked the dark and cold down there. He was arrested not long after for the murders of a dozen young women. I've called to them by name but they never answer.'

Devon said, 'I know who's gonna be with me. All those girls – once they're dead. They love me, ya know? No matter what the fuck they might say. They wanted it. They're only shitty because I'm not like calling them every day. I hate clingy bitches,' and he shivered, as if feeling them all over him.

'Fuck these ghosts,' Alex said.

They all drank drank drank and Pera was happy, it was company and she wondered who she was, what she was anymore.

Everything was different, but from the outside nothing had changed.

Wayne said, 'How long are you staying, anyway?' That 'you' a slip again.

'I told you, it's up to Byron.' That waver in his voice again. Pera wondered if Ike was scared of his brother. The thought terrified her.

'So where's your room?' Ike asked Pera. 'Where do you sleep?'

'All over,' Pera said. But that didn't make sense. She knew he knew that she'd have a refuge in the big house.

Devon said, 'It feels like this place goes on forever.'

'Nah, I seen it built. It's not as big as it seems,' Wayne said. 'She keeps so much shit in here. Like my grandma used to till her house burnt down,' and he shucked his shoulders, silently laughing, and Pera understood he had done it. He had burnt down Mrs Bee's beautiful home that had sheltered Pera after the storm. And he hadn't seen the house built, of course. He was lying about that.

She felt utterly exhausted. She wanted to sleep in her bed but she couldn't, not with Ike wanting to know where it was.

'I need a bit of a rest, boys. Wonderful company as you are.

But a little snooze. Then we can keep touring. I'm an old lady.' She shrank herself down, looked smaller, weaker.

'Give us the keys,' Ike said. He held his hand out. The other hand held his gun.

'Let's all have a rest then I'll keep showing you around.' Pera slumped further. Devon helped her to a comfy chair.

Ike wrested the keys from her fingers and she didn't have the strength to stop him.

'Youse stay here,' he said to Chook and Alex and the two men sat quite happily, watching over Pera.

She dozed. Her body so very tired, her brain wanting to be alert, but she knew she needed some rest if she was to get through this.

Chook and Alex muttered to each other. She had good hearing though; she hadn't lost that.

'Old ladies have harder heads. Harder to crack but once you do they split right open,' Chook said.

'You do the same as me, but—' and Pera couldn't hear the rest, but Chook made some kind of movement.

'You could tie that scarf tight around her neck,' Chook said.

'Wait for a while. They'll bloody murder us if we knock her off too soon.'

Pera sat, eyes closed, fury rising up in her that these two pathetic men would discuss her like this, as if her life was in their hands.

She would figure something out.

Then she slept.

*

Ike poked her. 'Come on. Let's go watch the sunset. I haven't seen one in fucken years.'

'Oh my, the sunset,' she said. She'd been thinking of hauntings, of the ghosts she could call to her service if she needed to. 'I was having an awful dream, Ike. Thank you for waking me. Do you have dreams that come back over and over again? This one my house was on fire and I couldn't get out. Oh, my. I can't quite breathe. Do you think it's true, what some people say? That your nightmares are ghosts coming to visit?'

At the front door, the wind chimes tinkled. If she closed her eyes, she could imagine herself alone, with the gentle breeze, the scent of her flowers.

Then Alex pulled the wind chimes down. 'Hate that noise. My mother had 'em hanging all around the house as if we were some kinda hippies. Dad'd say, "Faggot shit," and Mum'd say "At least visitors know we're good people. Only good people have such things." She seriously fucken said that.' He slurred his words so Pera couldn't catch all of them.

'Wish I'd thought of that,' Chook said.

'You call it a dreamcatcher but what it really catches is ghosts. Otherwise I'd have them in every room.'

The sunset was beautiful.

'Ike hasn't chosen a room yet,' Devon said.

'Maybe he doesn't want to stay,' Wayne said. 'He might want to piss off at a moment's notice.'

'I can piss off whenever I like,' Ike said. 'What did you say about your father's wine cellar? That'll do me. The wine cellar.'

'It's down in the Underhistory,' Pera said.

He nodded. 'That'll do me,' he said again.

Devon ran down the front steps and started kicking at her flowers. 'They grew from all the bouquets,' she said. 'Hundreds of them people sent when my family died. I laid them all out, neat and lined up like graves in a military cemetery.'

'Oi! Fuckwit! Stop kicking the fucken flowers,' Ike called out. Devon stopped, looking at him like a naughty boy caught by a terrifying father.

Wayne picked up the football Ike had laid down on the steps many hours earlier, and he, Devon, Ike and Alex set to with a rough game of rugby league.

Chook found the fishing pole near the front door and said, 'I'll go catch us our dinner in the pond!'

Pera laughed, assuming he was joking, but the look on his face told her he was serious. She said, 'Watch out for my uncle's ghost. He likes to talk to people. He wasn't a very nice man, though. You shouldn't listen to him.' None of them would be scared of a nice man, she knew that.

The Men kicked the ball around, laughing. In that moment, they almost seemed ordinary. Pera thought back to long ago, the workers there to clean up her house. Playing rugby during their break, and there was a bit of give and take, some bloody noses.

But nothing like this. These men were different. The game was rougher, far rougher. Devon was soon covered in blood, and they eventually forgot about the ball and started in on him. He copped a pounding. They tried to see if they could make him cry.

They could.

Pera wondered if she could call a halt but there was nothing in her that wanted to. Then they got bored, and tired. Devon limped away from the house down the drive.

'Oi!' Ike said. Wayne and Alex trotted after Devon, catching him easily, and they dragged him back by his hair.

'You don't go till we say you can go. We see fucken everything, mate,' Wayne said.

Ike nodded, and Alex and Wayne kicked Devon until he curled into a ball, shivering. They dragged him inside, leaving him in the hallway. Pera went to him and searched his pockets until she found the pipe he'd stolen from the Box Room.

Chook joined them, holding up a fish the size of his hand. 'Dinner!' he said.

'You are a fuckwit, aren't you? Like the actual definition of what a fuckwit is,' Ike said.

'That is not an edible fish,' Pera said. She felt more sorrow for the dying fish than she did for Devon, bleeding on her hall carpet.

'All fish are edible,' Chook said.

'Come on, then,' Pera said. 'Let's have a fry-up.' She hoped they'd eat it; the fish really wasn't edible, and it could make them sick.

'Anything tastes good fried,' Devon said, his voice whistling through broken teeth. 'It was alive so you can eat it. That's what my mum says.'

52

HOME OF THE RANGE (THE KITCHEN)

A radio sat on the kitchen bench and Ike turned it on. Pera had it tuned to the classical station but he shifted it to a national commercial station. The DJ's voices set Pera's teeth on edge with their inane chatter but she let it play. She kept an eye on the time, though; she wanted to be out of the room when the news came on. She didn't want to see their reactions. She said, 'Who wants chips with the fish?' and they all nodded, so she went into the kitchen storage room where her big freezer stood. She carefully propped open the heavy freezer door and reached in, wary of it slamming down and whacking her on the skull. Last time this happened, a hospital visit had been in order. One of her workers, helping her prepare an evening meal for the team.

She was out of sight but not out of hearing; they were at the top of the news bulletin, although no new information had been released. 'Use extreme caution,' the reporter said, 'whereabouts unknown'.

'Fucken famous,' Alex said. 'We need a TV. See what they've got on us.'

They'd seen one in the Mint and Ike sent Devon limping off to bring it to the kitchen.

They laughed at the news report, joking about the awful photos used. 'Need to get a pro in. Get some good-looking shots,' Ike said. Pera told him he was handsome, no matter what the shot, and he gave her a wink.

The TV played while they ate, joked, ate more. Pera gave them bottles of beer and they drank those and more until the next news report came on. This one mentioned the two prisoners who'd died.

'Fucken Davo. What a dickhead,' Ike said.

'He was all right,' Devon said.

'He was not all right. Don't you remember what he did?'

Devon shrugged, hunched down on himself. 'He woulda been good here. He's good fun, you know?'

'Whole life ahead of him,' Pera said. She turned her back on the TV and brought out more beer, pretending she wasn't scared of them.

The news report was grudgingly thankful they didn't kill the other kids and they all congratulated themselves as good guys.

'We're basically innocent. That's why we're here. Do you think God would have let us escape if we weren't?' Chook said.

'You're a fucken idiot,' Alex said, spinning his finger near his temple. 'My lawyer reckons—'

'Your lawyer! Your lawyer!' Chook snorted. 'He hasn't even returned a call from you for months.'

'My lawyer is like a brother to me,' Alex said.

'You treat that arsehole better than you treat your own mum,' Chook said. Pera had muttered this into Chook's ear not an hour before. He liked to take credit for things and was so used to doing it he didn't even realise he was stealing anymore.

Pera said to Ike, 'You remind me of a friend of my father's. Way back. Oh, he was a charmer! The funniest story about him was when he got caught sleeping with the housemaid in the boarding house he was staying in. He hid under the bed but his feet were sticking out! He was caught by the lady of the house. Ha, you know how my parents and their friends described it? That she was outraged until he "extended service to her". They used to wet themselves laughing over all that. I do remember he was a very handsome man. He had a certain glow about him. Like you.' Ike was better at acting normal than the others. But there was movement in his eyes. Dark grey ghosts; something not right.

He gave her a kiss on the cheek and she honestly, for a moment, wished that she was a bit younger. She'd always loved men and wasn't ashamed to admit it. 'Let's have something else to eat. That fish is not really enough, is it?' she said. She ached all over, tension more than anything else, but the chance to make herself useful couldn't be missed.

She creaked her way out of the chair. 'Feel like anything in particular?' she asked.

'Cordon bleu caviar pâté lobster fucken Melba toast.' *It's all the fancy foods Ike has ever heard of,* she thought, *but he's never eaten any of it.*

'I can do a good steak sandwich if you don't mind toasted. Bread's a bit stale. And I have some lovely tomatoes if you'd like those with it. And onions.'

'That'll be fine. More chips?'

'If the others haven't eaten them all.'

'They fucken better not.'

There *were* more and she was relieved. She wasn't keen on saying no to this one.

She put a bowl of chips on the table, and like a teenage boy Wayne reached for them as if they'd disappear if he didn't get them all in his mouth. He knocked over the salt, and Ike backhanded him so hard he fell sideways.

'Wayne,' Ike said. 'What you do puts us all in the shit. You get bad luck, we all get bad luck.'

He was superstitious. Pera found that at odds with the rest of him but she wasn't going to call him on it.

'Hey,' Wayne said, trying to recover himself. 'Remember when Alex got the guard?'

Pera had heard them talk about their escape a number of times now, and each time it became more heroic. They were mythologising themselves as she watched.

'They'll be calling you the Kelly Gang before long,' she said. She went through a Ned Kelly stage as a young girl. 'But I hope you don't end up like that.' She pointed at a large reproduction of the killing of Joe Byrne that hung on the kitchen wall, something she'd picked up in Sydney.

She brought out some cake but didn't eat it herself.

'Poison, is it?' Chook said.

'No, I don't like sweets much.'

There was a famous photograph of her as a child, with a massive lollipop someone gave to her immediately after the accident. It showed her happily licking the lollipop while the house burnt. It put her off sweets, apart from the occasional piece of chocolate. She told The Men about it, and they joked around, pretending to be on a photo shoot. At that moment you wouldn't pick any one of them as a killer. Photos were the greatest liars of all, Pera thought. Ike asked if she had a camera and she did, a Polaroid she kept to take a snap of 'surviving the tour'.

Every photo Ike took had Pera at the centre of it. It was oddly inspiring. Pera felt she'd been an observer all her life. Sometimes a muse. Watching things happen without having any effect on events – she didn't set them off, she didn't complete them. Now she was at the centre of things. She had drawn them here with her letter to Mrs Bee. She was keeping herself alive. And she would defeat them, stop them killing anyone else.

She hadn't taken a lover home in a long while. She didn't want any of them to impress themselves in the house. She didn't want them thinking they belonged. And yet now she had a house full of men thinking they owned the place, changing it by their very presence.

Would she have to burn it down? Start again?

Devon was slumped at the table. He was still bleeding from the face, his fingers were bruised and, she thought, bent. His shirt was bloodied, his eyes dark. She poured whisky for him; for all of them. She took more beer out of the fridge.

Ike looked at Devon, said, 'That's what happens to a person who tries to leave.'

They drank, then Chook knocked over a glass and they all thought that was funny, so they started pouring drinks out onto the table. Pera imagined the giant man statue in the conservatory tipping over, trapping them under his penis, his long arms, his legs, keeping them still so she could walk away and let them all starve to death.

That was pure fantasy, though. He couldn't be budged.

The Men were now blind drunk and frightening. They started smashing bottles, throwing them against the kitchen walls. Pera felt something shift in the air. It was time to begin or she'd be dead before she'd taken her chance.

They were drunk. Horribly, dangerously drunk. Devon was the drunkest, she thought, because he was small. Weak. Start with the weak one.

'I'm pretty sure I'm drinking you under the table,' she said to him.

Ike threw back his head and laughed.

'Fuck you, old lady,' Devon said, and he skulled the rest of a bottle and walked about, tugging at his crotch.

'Need a piss,' he said, but he was so drunk that he opened a cupboard door and pissed in there.

'You repulsive animal.' Pera felt ill. The smell of it filled the room. 'Clean that up now, you filthy little worm.'

'Go, Nana!' Wayne said. 'Clean it up, shithead.'

'With what?'

'Take your fucken clothes off and use them,' Ike said, and they watched as Devon stripped to his prison undies.

'He really is pathetically scrawny, isn't he?' Pera said. 'Money can't buy muscles.'

Devon shivered. Scrabbled on the floor, pushing his clothes back and forth.

Ike stood in front of the portrait of her family. It was one of the only pieces of art to survive the fire. She loved it, because she was painted front and centre. Her father called it 'Near Perfect'. It was why she kept it in the kitchen, where she could see it often.

He said, 'Enough of this bullshit. Show us where the good shit is or we'll beat the fuck out of all this crap.' And he took a knife and slashed the portrait corner to corner.

The sight broke her.

'That can't be repaired.'

She started crying; she hated to show it but what could she do?

'My fucken life can't be repaired,' he said, and he took down the painting and destroyed it in a frenzy. She shook, her nerves gone, and backed away from him. He swept off a small collection of glass animals from a high shelf, each of them worth hundreds of dollars.

Ike said, 'Show us the fucken treasure or we're doing this to your whole house.' He threw a crystal glass across the room.

Wayne stood close to her. She could hear his heartbeat. 'We know there's good shit around here somewhere. Not just all this crap we won't be able to sell. We know you've got a money stash. My grandma always said.' Wayne's rank, old-sweat smell made her feel nauseous.

'I don't know why she'd say that. All my money is tied up in this house. In all my things.'

'We need shit we can carry,' Ike said.

'Ah, then let's go to the waiting room; there's something there that is more valuable than everything else put together.'

53

PURGATORY

Pera rested her cane against a brocade chair and placed her hand on a shiny, redwood box. 'In this box, completely airless, is something rather amazing.' She lifted the lid. There was a layer of glass that shouldn't be removed.

Beneath the glass was a greenish naked woman, beautifully rendered.

'This was marble. One of my father's priceless possessions. Priceless, really.'

'Doesn't look like marble,' Alex said.

'It doesn't, does it? The astonishing thing with marble is that it turns into lime with great heat. I found this under the plane's fuselage. Still perfect, but now made of lime. Even more priceless, I imagine. Don't lift the lid, though.'

Chook lifted the glass lid. Once air hit the lime, it crumbled to dust.

'Run,' she said. 'RUN.'

In the hallway, she made a show of counting everyone. 'That was terrifying. I've never seen a ghost be that destructive before.'

'I feel ill,' Devon said.

'Stop bleeding everywhere, you pathetic little man,' Pera said, and Ike threw back his head and laughed.

'What is he even doing with you all? He's nothing, a slimy little worm. He doesn't suit.'

'She's right,' Ike said. He smiled, a huge smile, the first Pera had seen from him. 'He's dead weight. Always was.'

'We should throw him into the Great Nothingness,' Pera said. She went back into Purgatory and opened the trapdoor. Ike nodded.

They threw Devon into the hole. She heard bones break as he fell. They wouldn't let him back up, kicking at him when he tried. Then they closed the trapdoor.

'Jeez, it stinks down there. It's like off meat,' Wayne said.

'Or your girlfriend's cunt,' Ike said. Devon wailed and called out, battering his hands on the trapdoor.

Pera was reminded of the terrible cries of the trapped man in the Douglas Room. At least people tried to help *him*. Devon whined down there like a dog, but Pera felt no compunction to save him. Devon wouldn't get any help. She felt a lifting of her spirits. She'd work on the others next. She'd found her way out of the dark space down there; she doubted Devon would.

'Come on,' she said. She gathered her cane and led them away.

54

SCHOOL OF OSTEOLOGY

It was cold, maybe eleven degrees. As cold or colder than outside. Sometimes Pera would turn the heat way down, if she wanted to move a tour on, or subtly convince guests to leave. She had good control of heat in each room; she'd spent a fortune on the system.

She led them to the library and brought out more wine. Tequila. She found packets of chips for them to eat. They drank. They dozed. Devon didn't reappear.

She thought of escaping then, while The Men were drunk, not noticing, and she eyed the door. She walked towards it quietly, thinking no one was watching. But she was wrong; Ike saw all.

'If you get free, we'll kill one person for every one of us. That's five. Hopefully we'll get it done on the outside but inside will do and I tell ya, we won't pick the arseholes. No one you reckon might deserve it. We'll pick the guys who are actually innocent, right? They do exist. The ones with wife and kids, lotsa kids. Or a feeble one; they feel pain more, you should see them. Or one of the young ones who came in, like Devon. You know Devon was eighteen when they locked him up? Dead set. So that's it, and we'll make sure it hits the news so you know you killed another one. And we'll let people know about that family. I know where they live. You'll be killing them, too.'

He found a rope to tie her to Chook.

'Two oldies together,' Wayne said.

'Oi!' Chook said.

'He's not so old compared to me,' Pera said, hoping to raise a smile, get them sympathetic.

'You've got great teeth for an old lady,' Alex said, and that shut her smile down.

'We can have sex if you like,' Chook said quietly. 'It's probably been a while between drinks for you.'

She shook her head, not capable of talking, then curled up in an armchair. Books surrounding her, left behind over the years.

She woke early. Chook untied the rope.

They found Devon curled up in the Great Nothingness. He was stiff. Still. Not breathing.

'I can't believe he just lay down and died,' Pera said. 'Pathetic.' She knew if he'd looked he could have found the way out. The hatchway that led to the tunnel and the Underhistory, that she'd escaped through all those years ago.

It smelt terrible; Pera covered her nose and mouth with her cardigan. She took a Polaroid picture of him and his watch, a cheap thing he'd probably stolen.

'He really was fucken stupid,' Ike said. 'I couldn't cope with the whining. I've done it with dogs before. Take them out of their misery. Kindest thing. Otherwise you're being a gutless wonder.'

He lit a cigarette with shaking hands.

'At least you have the courage for it. Most don't.' She wanted him to know she understood why he did it.

'There's no time for doctors and we couldn't let him suffer, could we?' Ike said. 'Plus he was giving me the shits.'

'That's what I'm saying,' Pera said. 'And you don't even know what a favour you did him. He wasn't letting on, but that boy was sick. Very, very ill. He wouldn't say what it was but I'm guessing diabetes, given his symptoms.'

Pera wasn't even sure why she said this and hoped he wouldn't ask about symptoms.

'Yeah?' Ike said. She could feel him tensing. He wasn't used to this, someone being kind to him.

'You did the right thing,' she said quietly, knowing he hadn't, knowing he knew he hadn't, that this young kid should have been protected, not killed. She considered telling Ike about her belief in purgatory, and that her family, and her tiny dead babies, waited there for someone to take their place. This dead boy would release Hazel, perhaps. She'd told people about this before and been given the pity look. She didn't want Ike to know how little she cared if he died.

They all stood around, silent for a moment. Then Pera said, her voice so quiet even she wondered if she'd spoken, 'He looks so young.'

'You seem to be coping pretty well,' Ike said. 'Most old ladies would be freaking out.'

'Well I've seen a lot of death.' This was the moment she could shift, be the other one. No longer grandma-like. The actual person. Would it help? Or would it make them see her as a threat? 'Do you think we could take Devon outside? I don't really want him in the house. He'll make it stink. I don't like to be around people who've just died. They're at their strongest. Their neediest. Their ghosts will jump on anyone. Can you feel it? If he's trying to cling on you'll have a headache. Or aching bones, as if you've been exercising. You need to get him buried quick. Get the ghost in the dirt.'

Three of them carried the body outside.

'We can bury him in the pet graveyard,' Wayne said.

They buried Devon with no ceremony. Alex wanted to strip him naked, pose him in an exposed way, but the others turned him down.

They had moved into another zone; an area where she could no longer pretend they were okay people. *She* was not an okay person.

She lost track of The Men. She didn't know who was where.

She sat still at her kitchen table for a long time, so long that she winced when she stood up.

'Toothache?'

Alex.

She shook her head. She hated the dentist – who didn't? – and hated even talking about teeth.

'Let me have a look. I was training as a dental assistant before they locked me up. Cruel, I know. Taking my skills away.'

She backed away from him. He blocked the door, casually, as if he didn't mean it, leaning against the door frame, picking his teeth.

'Plenty of time,' he said.

'Your skills are wasted here,' she said. 'I'm too old for you. There are some lovely ladies in town, though. Oh, my goodness yes. You could ride in there. You've got such strong thigh muscles; you'd be there in a flash. Those ladies are used to their quiet country men; they'll fall all over a man like you.'

He laughed. 'Yeah?' She nodded. 'I'll keep that in mind,' he said.

55

THE GARAGE

Then it was Chook in the doorway and she barely noticed the difference. He stood aggressively, the croquet mallet over his shoulder.

'What room can I have?' Chook said. 'Not some weak woman place like Devon's.'

'What do you love? That'll help me decide.'

'I like cars,' Chook said, like an eight-year-old boy.

'I have the perfect place for you. I've got mine in the garage. Come have a look. I told you, I have a '66 Ford Mustang.'

She made sure to take a bottle of whisky with them.

She gave him the keys and let him sit. 'You could die happy right now, couldn't you?'

'Just about,' he said, feeling the wheel, the seat beside him.

'There's not much we do in life that is truly of our own accord.'

'What about my old ladies, ay?'

'They all had to be there, and be weak, for that to happen.

You are utterly powerless, really. The only thing you can control is when you die, if you choose to take your own life. I believe, and messages from the afterlife have confirmed, that the more in control you are at your moment of death, the more powerful your position in the afterlife.'

'You reckon?' He took a long drink from the whisky bottle. 'Bloody beautiful, this car,' he said.

He spoke about his mentor, a man he met decades earlier, a known killer of the 1930s. Things passed from man to man over the decades. Things to keep them safe, get them ahead. 'He had a thing for reputations. I wish he was alive to know I got one myself.'

He'd met his mentor when he used to deliver pies to a mental institution. The man was one of the inmates, wise beyond his placing and against all odds.

'There was some benefit to delivering pies for a living, even though my first wife gave me hell for it.' He passed the bottle to Pera. She took a token sip, then handed it back. 'As if I wasn't already exhausted after a day of delivering pies, and the smell of them got to me after a while, even though I used to love them. Old bitch. Some nights I lay in bed and pictured her cold and dead with her pathetic cotton underwear stuffed in her mouth.'

The man was incredibly tedious except when he was being terrifying.

'It wasn't a bad job, really. The inmates used to give me hell, so I'd call out "Get your rattlesnake pie! Koala bear pie! Get it here, fellas!" knowing it'd upset them. I never felt better about myself than when I was around those losers.

'They wouldn't let me deliver to the women's ward after a

while; too disturbing for the women, I was told. Even the sight of a man could set them off. Shame, because some of them didn't mind a quick feel, a quick peek at the knickers. It wasn't all bad.

'And I met my mentor. He did what he did but not everything they said he did. He made the mistake of choosing young women, and not whores either. I learned my lesson from that. People care about good girls. You gotta choose victims no one cares about.'

'People care about everybody, don't they? They don't like anyone to be killed.'

'They don't care much about old ladies. Old ladies might as well be dead already.'

He went into a long and boring story about all his mentor had taught him, ending with, 'Always walk funny when you walk away from a crime. That's what a witness will notice.'

Chook was a tedious man. He always told his stories filled with dull detail. Did his mother tell him he was interesting?

'Go on,' Pera said, and he did, another twenty minutes of it.

In the end he sighed. 'Why don't all women listen like you? It's not hard, is it?' and Pera thought that was the most pathetic, deluded thing he'd said. Some men were perfectly happy with the fake stuff; they didn't care what else happened so long as you kept the illusion up. These were the ones who could pay for sex and think it was mutual desire.

But she'd listen to their stories for a thousand and one nights if it kept her alive.

'You've probably heard of my mentor. He was famous. Killed half a dozen girls in the thirties in Melbourne.'

'My sister died then. But her boyfriend did it,' Pera said.

'They probably tried to pin it on my guy. He had at least two pinned to him he didn't do. People taking the opportunity to knock off a difficult daughter, that sort of thing. He had a lot of good advice. He reckoned if I ever got caught I should act like an idiot. You know, mentally. They can't hang an idiot, he reckoned. He said it right to the minute they strung him up.'

Pera realised this was the man her husband had spoken about. The man he wanted to blame for her sister's murder.

He finished the last of the bottle, tipping his head back to get it all. 'Get me more,' he said, his speech slurred. His eyes drooped.

'You have a nap,' Pera said.

She waited until she heard him gently snoring, then leaned over, opened Chook's window a crack, and turned on the ignition. He shifted slightly but didn't awaken.

She got out of the car and carefully connected the hose to the exhaust, then slipped it through the car window.

56

THE STAIRS

A feeling of serenity came over the house, as if a window had been cleaned of years of grime and the sun allowed to shine through. If she believed in the afterlife, she'd say she had set Chook free, allowing his ghost to roam where it wished. If ghosts did roam, she hoped his took a moral turn. Otherwise she'd have to keep these men alive forever.

If he was a different man, she could have congratulated herself for taking him out of his misery but she didn't think he suffered misery at all. Certainly not regret or guilt.

She felt ill, but there had been no blackout, nothing but clarity. Surety. He took the place of her sister Charity; that made sense.

There was only one ghost she believed in.

She had pictured him from the moment she knew she was pregnant. A mess of red hair, strong little legs. Five years old and no interest in school or books, no interest in anything but running and climbing and laughing at jokes.

This child never was, outside her imagination, but she knew him so well. She didn't believe in ghosts but she believed in him, stomping up and down the stairs, leaping to miss two and then three steps, falling with a tumble, bouncing up unhurt – how could she be imagining that? It wasn't possible.

Sometimes the ghost was a baby, waiting at the bottom of the stairs since she fell to the bottom of the stairs herself, was pushed, since Joseph pushed her and watched, laughing, as she rolled down the steps and by the time she could stand, the baby was lost.

How old would he be now? Thirty? Thirty-one? He would have been here with her, perhaps, visiting with his family. It was lucky, then. What if The Men had come, with her grandchildren here? She could not bear that. Imagine what they would have done.

Thank God that child was never born.

Wayne came and sat by her on the stairs. She said, 'Ike and Alex are out there, whispering about you. You're already on the outer.'

'I'm not. Ike's my mate.'

'No, he isn't. You're dead weight, like Devon. You need to protect yourself.' She shivered.

'Why were you so mean to me when I was a kid?'

'Because you were a little shit,' she said. She tried to be good to kids; she remembered what it meant to have an adult talk to you with intelligence. What a difference it made. But Wayne was always awful.

'I'm really sorry, Wayne. I felt so protective of your

grandmother. She pretty much saved my life, you know. I don't know where I'd be if she hadn't taken me in in those early days.'

'You didn't have to protect her from me. You were both so mean to me,' he said, and in the muted light he could have been eight years old.

'We wanted the best for you. Your poor dad didn't cope well with life and all the adult bits.'

'Leave Dad out of it. He had it tough. He had a shit childhood.'

He didn't have it tough but Pera didn't say this. She didn't want an argument.

A large silver van pulled into the driveway and a tall, muscly man climbed out.

'It's Byron,' Ike said. 'Coast must be clear.' He looked at Pera. She glanced up the stairs. She could hide. If Byron didn't see her, she could hide somewhere and they'd all drive away.

Ike hopped from one foot to the next. She hadn't seen him so nervous. Frightened, almost.

'Byron?' she said. 'Maybe Byron doesn't need to see me. I can go upstairs. Let you all get on with it.'

He shook his head.

She wrapped her arms around herself. 'Please . . . don't tell him I'm here. Let me be.'

'Yeah, no big deal,' Ike said, totally distracted, barely listening. She tried to walk up the stairs but he stopped her.

The front door opened with a bang. Byron had a heavy footfall, as if he was stamping but it was his massive presence.

'Where the fuck are youse?' she heard.

'In here, mate,' Ike called out, his eye on Pera. He looked slightly panicked and she glanced around for a place to hide but it was too late. It terrified Pera that Ike was so frightened of his own brother. She'd seen no fear in him before this.

Byron walked in. He was tall, imposing. He wore a tight long-sleeved T-shirt which didn't conceal his strength at all. 'Who the fuck is this?'

'This is Pera. She lives here. She's okay.'

'No, she's fucken not.' Byron stared at her, unblinking for a minute or two, then threw down a pile of newspapers onto the kitchen table. 'Check it out, boys. You're famous. Front page news.'

There were pictures of the postcards he'd sent from all over the country, pretending to be them.

Pera felt a ridiculous disappointment this wasn't her fame.

Alex came running down the stairs. 'Mate!' he said, and the two embraced, manly hugs, punches in the arm. It made sense these two would be friends.

Byron read a headline aloud, his finger running along the words.

'He's a bit slow,' Ike said. 'Too many beatings. He'd cop a lot of them because he was such a shit and never learned to keep quiet.'

'I was protecting you cunts,' Byron said.

'Yeah, good job, man,' Ike said.

They started talking about the escape, bigging themselves up, leaping up and down. The violence of it, even in re-enactment, was terrifying. Pera tried not to make a sound, tried not to draw attention to herself. She'd slip out if she could, at least get to a room away from Byron. But as she was slowly sidling to the door, Byron said, 'Where you off to?'

'I was going to find a book I've got. It's about Ruby Sparks, one of the world's great prison escapees. I thought you might like to read it. Or look at the pictures.'

Ike snorted. She'd taken a risk, saying that. But she figured Byron already had her in his sights. He already planned to kill her. All she could do was try to upset his equilibrium, maybe get him to make a decision in her favour by mistake.

'So where are the other blokes? Byron said. 'That little shit and the old cunt?'

'I done Devon,' Ike said. 'The old cunt is somewhere about the place.'

'You had to,' Pera said.

She felt loose on her feet, dizzy. 'A chair, please,' she said. Ike helped her to the Free Spirit Room, where she sat herself down. 'It's all too much for an old lady,' she said.

Ike watched her, his lips twitching. 'You remind me of someone and I've figured out who. There was this old bloke used to hang around the pub, pretty much wherever my dad and his mates were. He was in a wheelchair and they'd have to roll him around, get him upstairs, all that crap. I used to think he was a pain in the arse. I'd have to get him drinks, beers, whatever, and he'd snarl this thank you that sounded like fuck you. I always thought he was some sad loser who used to be somebody.'

His lips twitched again. He sat close to Pera, their knees almost touching. She could smell layers of scent upon him, from the soap she had in the bathroom to the faint smell of fireworks and garlic.

'Turns out,' Ike said, his voice low and clear, 'this guy was the Big Boss. Biggest fucken boss in town. He coulda had me killed on a whim.' He clicked his fingers.

'It's good he didn't,' Pera said. 'He must have liked you all right.'

'That's who you remind me of,' Ike said, and she knew things had shifted.

'I'm not the boss of very much. My own little domain here. There's nothing else I control. I wish I was a big boss. I'd have plenty of money.'

'Don't cry poor,' he said, and she saw she'd offended him.

'No. I'm sorry. I've had a lucky life as far as money goes.' She knew he was smart enough to understand the value of what she had.

She'd spent years studying people as they came through on tours and they were so predictable. They'd hug their children when she talked about children dying. Women asked how she met her husband. She knew how people behaved. But these men were different. They didn't follow the rules.

57

THE FREE SPIRIT ROOM

Pera, Ike, Wayne and Alex sat together. Byron stood. She took in three bottles of Coke out of the fridge, for mixers. One slipped out of her hand and crashed to the floor, making them all jump but Wayne the hardest, spinning around as if someone was about to shoot him. He was paranoid and frightened, now that Byron was here. Pera felt the same, felt herself shivering.

Alex touched her face. 'Oh, dear. Oh, dear.' He squeezed her cheeks together with his strong fingers, reached up and touched her teeth with his other hand. 'Oh, dear.'

'Tell Byron about what happened to your husband,' Wayne said, to cover himself. 'She's hard arse, mate. And we know what she did, so she's not telling anybody about us. You'd last a day inside, Grandma. Two, tops.' Every time they called her grandma, she knew she had a chance.

'I shouldn't go to prison! I killed him out of pure pity. No man should feel so sad and I couldn't help him.' Her throat caught as it rarely did when talking about her husband. She missed Joseph, or what he could have been. They should have grown old together and he should be growing peas and beans and telling her funny stories. If he hadn't been an artist, or if he'd been an undeniably good one, that's where they'd be.

His sad sense of failure was insurmountable, though, so here she was.

Byron looked at her with raised eyebrows. 'You really did that? Killed your old man?'

'He's got a built-in bullshit detector,' Ike said. 'He always knows when you're lying.'

'And when you're shit scared and pretending not to be. And when you want it and you reckon you don't. Ay? It's my superpower.'

Around Byron, Ike shrank into himself, tried to make himself invisible.

'Where is that fucken creep Chook?' Ike said. 'I don't trust that man.'

'Haven't seen him. Probably fucking a cow or something,' Wayne said.

'She hasn't got any cows,' Ike said.

'He doesn't care what he sticks it in. He would stick it in Devon right now if he wasn't otherwise occupied,' Wayne said.

'That rich kid was your boyfriend, was he? I woulda thought he was more Ike's type,' Byron said. He still stood while the others sat. Always on edge. Alert.

'No way it'd happen to Ike. Remember that one time?' Wayne said. 'Man, that even made me feel sick, and I've worked in an abattoir.'

Byron said, 'That weak cunt? Mummy's little favourite? He loves it. The rougher the better.'

Pera saw Ike clench his teeth, the muscles in his face contorting. Something was wrong between the brothers.

'What's going on there?' she asked Wayne quietly.

'You don't wanna know. Let me say I'm glad I never had a big brother. I woulda killed him if I was Ike. The shit Byron put him through . . . Hey, maybe Chook died of the curse,' he said, louder. 'He was in that room with the rest of us and Devon's dead already.'

Pera said, 'I've never seen such a thing. I always say it is cursed because people love a good scare. Love being frightened. But I never believed it until now. But then I'm never with tour groups in the hours or days after. It might well be some of them pass away.'

'Bullshit, Grandma,' Ike said.

'Seriously, where is Chook?' Byron said. She wasn't about to answer that question truthfully. She hoped none of them went to the garage.

'I'll find him,' Ike said.

'Yeah,' Wayne said, and they both left the room. They seemed glad of the excuse. Alex ambled after them, heading in a different direction.

'Did he leave?' Pera said. 'Maybe he's bringing reinforcements. Someone else to talk to.'

Byron laughed. 'You won't be talking to anyone, Pera. I'll cut your tongue out first.' It was the first time Byron had used her name and it terrified her. But she thought, *At least I have a name. They'll know who I am when they find me. I might die but I'll die with dignity.*

The actress's brother, who had died alone in her basement. He died without dignity. Any life that ended in guilt, shame, without love; that was an undignified death.

If no one cared you were dead that was undignified too. There was a certain beauty in a dignified death. There were so many variations of beauty.

Pera had planned her own funeral already. Paid for, guest list made, song list made. There was nobody else to do it for her.

It would be a noble death for Pera. A death of her choosing.

Dying alone wouldn't be an option for her. Too many people coming and going. In the month she shut down the place she was always away, holidaying with her school friends or sending postcards, at least. If Claudia and Isabel didn't hear from her after a month, they'd call, come around, get the police to visit. She thought of this now, with The Men standing so close she could smell the difference in each of them. She had done such a good job convincing everyone she'd gone away; no one would look for her before then.

'Do I frighten you?' she asked.

'I've never been scared,' Byron said. 'Not even of my old man when he was going off. I always kept scissors nearby, even though Mum got the shits when she could never find them when she needed them. I stabbed him in the thigh once. He was so blind drunk he woke up the next day covered in blood and no idea how it happened. Walked with a limp after that. It was easier for Mum and my brothers to get away from him, so it was good for that.'

'Are you frightened now?'

He looked startled. It hadn't occurred to him that he should be frightened but it was true. He was more in danger now than he ever had been.

Byron grabbed her wrist, tight, holding on like a manacle. 'What are you on about? Ay? We can burn this place down and everything in it. There'll be nothing left. You should be the one who's frightened.'

She couldn't bear that to happen. Her house was a repository for precious things. A museum. The threat of its destruction terrified her.

She said, 'I'm surprised to see what sort of man you are. I'd imagined a very different one from Ike's description. You're actually a very intelligent man. If I were a few years younger you might even have liked me.'

'You're not bad,' Byron said, 'for an old lady.'

She realised she'd lessened the impact with this so pushed the buttons again.

'Ike called you impotent. Such an odd thing to say, but they found it very funny.'

'Did he?' Byron said. He didn't react beyond that, and she realised he didn't know what the word meant. She raised a little finger and flopped it in demonstration.

'The fuck did he.' He shifted his jeans across the crotch.

It was like stretching a rubber band and letting it go. He left the room.

58

THE BOOT ROOM

'Oi, cunt,' she heard. Ike and Wayne sat on the back steps that led to the Boot Room, where she kept shoes and an array of sporting equipment.

She could see the three men from the Free Spirit Room window.

Byron stretched an arm to wrap his large hand around Ike's throat.

'You've forgotten, haven't you?' Ike twisted under his grip as he reached the other hand to grab Ike's genitals. 'You've forgotten every fucken thing I ever taught you.'

Ike kicked out, an inefficient blow that served only to give him less purchase on the steps.

'Really?' Byron shifted his grip to Ike's shoulders and tried to turn him around. Ike clung to the stair railing.

Wayne stood up. He gripped his hands together around the handle of a croquet mallet that lay on the bottom step, and aimed. He missed Byron's head, got his neck, but it was a hard enough blow to make Byron slump, weakening his grip enough so Ike could throw him off, down the four or five steps where he landed on his back in the gravel.

A moment later he lifted himself onto his elbows. 'Cunts,' he said, but before he could stand Wayne had handed over the mallet and Ike was on him.

Beating.

He tried to crawl away but Ike did not pause. There was a rhythm to his work; the only thing that changed was the sound as the blows landed.

Pera felt focused, watching them. There was no blankness for her. She thought about setting these men loose on those who'd hurt her or annoyed her, like the hairdresser Marcia who was so rude to her and the butcher's wife, who'd been terrible so long ago. She wouldn't do it but she wished she was that sort of person.

There were others on the list.

She had never seen such violence, such fury.

Ike squatted in the grass, heaving with exhaustion. A light wind lifted leaves and carried them over Byron's body, where they swirled and rose and fell.

Ike's hands dripped with blood. Blood and muck up to the elbows, his face splattered with it, his hair.

Before long he roused himself and had Wayne help him carry the body to the chapel.

They walked back, shoulder to shoulder, not speaking. Pera put a bucket of ice and six beers on the veranda and they sat there, still shoulder to shoulder, and drank. Pera wrapped ice in a tea towel for Ike's knuckles, because he'd bare-fisted by the end of it. Wayne brought the garden hose over and they washed off most of the gore.

Alex appeared. He eyed the stains on Ike's shirt. The ice on his hand. The absence of Byron. He said, 'Good one.' Shrugging, as if to say, *Another friend gone, oh well.* He walked over to the chapel and came back with Byron's gun tucked into his waistband. Pera saw Wayne's eyes flick to it.

Ike was close to Pera, pressed up against her, and she could feel his quick, panicked breath, feel the heat in his hand as he placed it on her shoulder.

Pera said, 'You had to do it. It was the only way to be free of him.'

Ike's hands vibrated. She could tell he was exhausted, that he had expelled every ounce of energy.

'You need to rest,' she said to him. He was grey about the eyes, slumped in a comfortable chair.

'You know, I like you. I like you more than that lot.' Ike indicated with his head *there, those men.* 'Don't run from me.'

'I really won't, Ike. I'm part of it now. I've told you things no one else knows. I don't want you telling anyone. We're on the same side now.'

'Each one you kill, you have to kill another to atone for that one,' Ike said.

He relaxed, his shoulders sinking, his body already at rest. He seemed cut adrift; with Byron gone, what was next? Byron had directed Ike for so long.

Wayne was too agitated to rest, bouncing on the balls of his feet, running to look in the chapel every few minutes as if disbelieving what happened. She had him sit under the tree. She wanted to take a photo of him, capture the moment of him under her family tree where all the lost photos were taken. She snapped one, and one of Byron, lying across the floor of the chapel. He was barely recognisable as a man, let alone himself. Justine, she thought. He can take the place of Justine in purgatory.

She sat next to Wayne under the tree. 'You need to arm yourself, Wayne. You need to be prepared. You think Ike will want to share any this? He's done for Devon and Byron. He's probably done for Chook too, been missing for hours. Maybe he had Alex pull all his teeth out.'

'Arm myself with what? Ike's got a gun. So has Alex. You think I should go get your knife set?'

She wasn't sure if he was joking so didn't laugh. 'Listen, Wayne. I'll tell you something no one knows. I have my own weapon stash.'

'Where?'

'In the Underhistory. The family used hunting rifles to defend the place. And after that my father used them to hunt rabbits. I know where they are but you'll have to get them. There are tunnels, and blocked doors I can't shift. *You'll* be able to.'

She gazed at him steadily.

'If you get a gun you'll be able to take over. No reason why you can't stay here for as long as you like. No reason at all. You can help me with the place, just the two of us.'

'I'm not touching Ike. He's the only mate I've ever had.'

Sad.

'Alex, though. He's awful, Wayne, and you know it. He would slit your throat at the slightest provocation. And I couldn't stop what he'll do to you afterwards . . .'

Wayne screwed up his face, looking like the boy she'd once known, who'd sat on his grandmother's front step watching the other kids play cricket in the street. 'Show me,' he said.

59

THE UNDERHISTORY

They walked through the house to the door under the main stairs, and down to the Underhistory.

'There's a stack of chairs over there under the window,' Pera said, and Wayne untangled the pile and brought her one to sit on. 'Garden chairs, from the olden days. Isn't it funny that these cheap things would survive but my mother's beautiful armchairs were destroyed?'

'Hilarious,' Wayne said. 'I should tie you up.'

She shook her head. 'Where do you think I'm going, Wayne? You and I are in this together.'

'Jeez, it stinks down here,' he said.

It did stink. There was the smell of decay, of wet dirt, of mould, of damp. Of old papers and mouse droppings, dead things because things died down there.

She pointed to a door in the far corner, blocked by broken furniture. He moved it out of the way. 'Through there, I think. You'll come out in another room. After that you'll have to go through the tunnels, some of the ceilings collapsed when the plane hit. This place is like a labyrinth.' She gave him detailed instructions and he walked through the cleared doorway.

Being alone was a relief; she could relax, stop forward-thinking for a moment. She hadn't daydreamed in hours, hadn't thought of the past, dwelt time there.

It was cold, bone-chillingly so, and she wished she had her cardigan. She'd soaked in a lot of sun (and she could see the glorious light coming in through the small, high window, if she twisted her neck slightly) but that soon leached away.

She closed her eyes and tried to rest. She was so terribly tired, so exhausted, that she could sleep here, sitting upright in the cold, foul cellar.

He must be in the tunnel by now. She could hear him calling but she imagined he was quite constricted so he couldn't shout loudly.

It wouldn't be long before Ike came to look for them and she wanted to be ready.

Time passed. Her teeth chattered. She wished she'd convinced Wayne to hand over his fleecy jacket but he'd need it where he was. She told him to be careful of ghosts under there, that the dead liked the dirt, they liked it underground, and hated to be disturbed.

'How's it going?' she called through a vent near where she thought he was.

His answer was muffled but she thought she heard the word 'ghost'.

'Is it cold?'

'Fucking freezing.'

'The coldest bits? You're probably crawling over ghosts. You'll feel colder, they feel warmer for a minute. The bugs who live under there LOVE that.'

'There's no bugs.'

'They're black. If there was light down there they'd shine. Can't you feel them crawling? You'll see it when you get out. Slimy trails all over your body. They get into your clothes. They like to . . .'

'Like to what?' He'd moved further along. He was whimpering now, a precursor to crying, and even though she despised him as weak and pathetic she was still surprised at how quickly he turned to tears.

And then she didn't hear him for a while.

Wayne emerged from the doorway, filthy, and carrying a hunting rifle.

'You did it!' she said.

'You sound surprised.' He tested the weapon.

'Go find Alex. You get him and then we'll think about Ike.'

She knew these men's crimes; she had no sympathy for any of them.

'Go on,' she said.

She didn't want to go back upstairs but it was so cold in the Underhistory. She climbed onto one of the garden chairs and tried to budge the window, thinking she'd be able to fit through if she could climb high enough. It was stuck, though, long-ago paint dried badly.

When was the last time she was seen out and about? Would people look for her? They only expected her once a week or so, or randomly. Pera's mouth was dry and she needed to go to the toilet. She was hungry. Would they let her starve to death? Did she deserve that? She'd always thought she deserved to die of starvation, after what happened to her animals after the plane crashed into her house.

60

HOME OF THE RANGE (THE KITCHEN)

Time passed. She lost a few hours, going by the change of light, which was a blessing but also a waste. She must have slept, because a loud noise woke her.

She stood with difficulty, her legs shaking. Slowly she climbed the Underhistory stairs. She felt lost, unsure what to do next, then hunger drove her to the kitchen.

A man sat at the kitchen table, facing away from her. From the back of his head it looked like Wayne; that bad haircut, like a mullet but even worse.

'Wayne?' she said. There was no response.

She walked around to touch his shoulder and saw that he would not ever be responding again. There was a gaping wound in his chest, still glistening with blood. His mouth was nothing but a red hole and she saw, to her utter horror, that he had no teeth.

Beside him lay the useless hunting rifle. Her father's gun, she remembered him shooting rabbits with it, and rabbit stew for dinner. They all hated rabbit stew, even her father, especially the way Cook made it. She felt momentary guilt at placing such a useless weapon into such a stupid man's hands. How could he possibly have believed that a gun that had lain in a cellar for half a century would fire? That ammunition that had been damp just as long would be any use? He was never going to be able to defend himself.

'You're free now, Faith. Purgatory will let you go.'

Pera sobbed. She suddenly regretted the trick she had played. Wayne was dead. Alex was alive. And she was left with him, to deal with him alone, when everything about him terrified her.

'There you are,' Alex said. He stood in the doorway and she thought he'd grown.

'Wayne turned out to be a waste of space. Most blokes do, in the end. Call me the fucken tooth fairy. Fuck him.' He walked over to Pera, pressed his hand on her shoulder to make her sit.

His fingers moved into her mouth and pressed her teeth, he held them between his fingers, wriggling, wriggling . . .

'They're not in there too solid, are they?' he said. 'They'll come out easy.'

'You'll save me the dental bills,' she said, stunned that she could speak.

She struggled to move, but Alex straddled her, held her wrists with one hand. He was heavy. She felt as if her thighs were flattening.

'What we could do,' he said, 'is call some of your lady friends. Get a party going.'

'Marcia would come. She does hair,' Pera said. 'Although she had a bit of a thing with Wayne a while back so you might not like that.'

Alex took his hands off her shoulders, stood up, and looked around. He blocked her vision but she could hear a low hum of excited conversation.

'Where'd they come from?' he said.

Pera stood up. The kitchen was empty; the chattering noise was the birds outside, cawing and cooing like women with cups of tea to drink and peas to pod.

'They came with you,' Pera said. 'Every last one of them piggy-backing on to you everywhere you go. No wonder you're such a ladies' man, with all these ladies hanging around you. And the men are lady-boys anyway, aren't they?' She rose. 'Let me make you something to eat,' she said. 'And we can chat.'

'You're always feeding us, feed feed feed like we're geese getting fattened up.'

She laughed. 'I'm not! I like to feed people. Wait here; I'll bring something.'

She could lock herself in the larder where the freezer was. Maybe push some of the big tins up against the door and wait it out. Wait until Alex and Ike left. She'd have food. She could melt ice to drink. She still needed the toilet, but she could use an old can—

Alex followed her, close behind, into the larder.

She opened the lid of the freezer, peered in. His hand moved around her waist up her side, her neck, to her chin. She had her back to him and she felt frozen in place, stopped in time.

'Reach in there, Alex. Right underneath I remember there's some chocolate profiteroles. Just for us. We won't tell the others.'

'I'm watching my weight,' he said. 'Gotta keep in shape for the loving, right? All those girls dying to fuck me.' He thrust his groin around, grinding air. She could see Byron's gun in his waistband. His hands were in her mouth.

'Go on,' she said, and she smiled broadly and pressed back against him. 'We can have a romantic dinner.'

He reached in. 'Further,' she said, 'right underneath,' and once his head was right there, in the right place, she slammed the freezer door down with every ounce of strength she had.

He didn't even grunt; he slumped, face first, into the frozen goods, tipping over so that all she had to do was lift his legs and fold him in. Close the lid. Pile tins and bags and everything she could on top to hide him and also to make sure he couldn't get out, as if he'd come to life and walk. 'For Hope,' she said. 'That's Hope out of purgatory.'

She sobbed. After a while she lifted the lid, shifted things aside, took a photo of him there. Then she got a knife from the kitchen, slid it up her sleeve, and headed back down to the Underhistory, via the first-floor toilet where she found blessed relief.

61

THE UNDERHISTORY

'Is Wayne down there? Where is that cunt?' Ike called down the steps.

'He's stuck in a tunnel,' Pera called up, her teeth chattering. If Ike didn't know where Wayne was, she wasn't about to tell him.

Ike came down the steps.

She called out, 'Keep going. Did you find it? Come on, mate.' She rolled her eyes at Ike. 'Someone could go after him but it's pretty tight in those tunnels. Some collapsed when the plane hit. He'll be scratched up. It's full of broken stuff in there. We used to throw all the broken crockery and glasses under the house. I have no idea why. Maybe Mum once said it warded off evil? I really can't remember. If he's stuck, you could go and pull him out by his ankles.'

'Fuck that. I'm not going in any tunnel. He'll be fine or he won't be. What's he doing, anyway?'

'He's finding some of my treasures. He'll share, I'm sure,' Pera said. 'He told me he would share.'

'Did he just? Wayne, you cunt. Are you there?' No answer.

'Maybe we should tie you up. Leave you down here,' Ike said.

'Oh, Ike. You don't need to do that.' She wrapped her arms around herself. Her shoulders slumped. She tried to decide if it was better to give in, let it happen, or to fight one last time. There was no way she'd beat him on strength, which was all that mattered. She sighed. 'You really don't.'

It was cold, always cold, and she felt faint and thought about the father who'd fainted when he saw the rat king. It felt like a lifetime ago.

'We love the cellar, don't we, boys? Reminds us of all those fun times. I think the record was two days, wasn't it?' Ike tapped his temple, as if trying to remember. Pera couldn't tell if he was lying or not. And who he thought he was talking to. His dead brother, perhaps.

Ike laughed. 'People love that shit. We used to bullshit the teachers; say our parents locked me in the cellar for days.' He snorted, half-laughter, but shifted his eyes as if thinking of all he didn't tell their teachers, all the stuff that really did happen to him. He seemed exhausted, as if he'd like to curl up and sleep. Pera wanted to comfort him. She hugged him briefly and he resisted then sank into it; no one had hugged him like that for a long time. If ever.

'Wayne's got a gun now,' Pera said. 'You'll have to watch him.'

'You will, you stupid bitch. He hates your guts, haven't you noticed?' He grabbed her by the arm. 'Let's go find him then. Which way did he go?'

Pera led him to the door that Wayne had cleared hours before. 'He went through here. He's looking for my treasure. Perhaps he's found it by now.' Pera grabbed a torch; she always kept a box of them, ready to go.

Ike snickered. He dragged her through into an empty room that had once contained old furniture, and then on and on, through more doors and empty rooms. Pera had never explored this far into the Underhistory. Sometimes she saw hatchways in walls that led to the tunnels. She wondered if she could get to one, scramble in and crawl her way to freedom, but Ike's grip on her arm was too strong.

Eventually they came to a dead end. A room full of mouldy boxes, lined with shelves.

'Wayne, where are you, fucken shit?' Ike called.

'Maybe the ghosts have already taken him,' Pera said. She sat down heavily on the floor. Ike began to fling open boxes. He swept some ancient paint cans from a rickety shelf.

There was a concealed door behind.

There was no handle on the door but Ike levered it open. 'Is this what you've been hiding? Is this where the treasure is?'

'This is where the secrets lie,' Pera said. She'd never seen the door before. The room beyond was dim; Ike lit his cigarette lighter, and the light from the basement window seeped in.

'Stinks,' Ike said. 'What is that?'

Pera wrinkled her nose. 'Old air. No one's been down here forever. I don't even know if my parents knew about it.'

'Where's this treasure, then?' Ike said. He pulled Pera forward to another door, this one caked in thick dirt. There was a heavy iron bolt across the latch, now corroded and easy to slide back.

Inside, the smell was worse.

Pera turned on her torch, so there was plenty of light to see what lined the walls.

Skeletons.

Skeletons tangled up, arms around each other. Some alone. One lying flat, arms outstretched, as if reaching for help. Dried flesh clung to some of the bones, and the clothing lay flat. There were tall skeletons and small. One tiny one. Pera started to cry, holding her hands 30 cm apart. A tiny, tiny skeleton, a baby.

A stopwatch rested near the skull of one of the smaller skeletons, as if they had died listening to the comforting tick. Cut into the wall behind the skeleton was a tunnel hatchway.

Pera sobbed now, thinking she knew who they were.

That scratching noise. They'd thought it was rats. But it wasn't. It wasn't. Pera couldn't bear it.

'Why you crying?' Ike asked. 'These have been dead fucken years.'

'They tried to escape,' Pera said. 'The people who lived in our sheep shed. They only found five bodies, I knew there had been more of them.'

'What they doing here?'

She remembered when she had run away from the Bees, back to the house, when Young Bobby had found her. She had heard rats scratching under the ruins of the burning house. Not rats.

'The tunnel.' She went to the hatchway and looked into the darkness. The soldiers had found a collapsed tunnel under the ruins of the sheep shed. Phar Lap had led his people to safety, only to trap them in a room locked from the outside. 'My friend and I used to play in the tunnels.'

'Must have been your fault, then.'

And for the first time she said, 'No, it wasn't. It wasn't up to me to save them.' She was letting herself out of purgatory. A huge weight lifted. She no longer felt guilty. Not just people telling her; she really understood it wasn't her fault.

Ike bent down to pick up the stopwatch and held it to his ear. 'Still ticking!' he said. 'That's fucken insane.'

Pera put her hand out for it but Ike put it in his pocket. His hands were unsteady and he kept licking his lips as if they were very dry.

'You know, Ike, I never said, but you remind me of my husband. Which means,' she said, 'you could take his place if you want.'

'Fuck off,' he said.

'Oh! Not here. Not as my husband, silly boy. But in purgatory.'

Ike snorted and bent down, lifting scraps of clothing away from a skeleton, tossing bones aside. He pulled a ring off the bony hand. 'At fucken last, what is it, gold?' He tucked it in his pocket.

Pera drew the knife from her sleeve. She thrust the knife into the atlas of his spine, right in the dent at the base of his skull, and twisted it. She didn't know she knew how to do that but there you go. She felt her heart beat, almost tugging at her, and her eyes misted over as he slumped to the floor.

'And *that*,' she said, 'is for Joseph.'

She took the stopwatch and a coin she found in Ike's pocket. Then she took a Polaroid photo of him, his hands folded over his chest.

She heard voices, young people, laughing and chattering. Looking out of the front door, she saw it was the young man who helped her with her horses; bringing his friends for a party, she guessed, and the thought both delighted and terrified her.

Moving as fast as she could, she called out, 'I'm here! I'm here after all!'

Once again, bodies were lined up in the gravel driveway of Sinclair House. And she was the sole survivor. The remains of the Italian family were there too, alongside Devon, Chook, Wayne, Ike and Alex. It made a dramatic front page of the newspaper.

62

THE PRAYERFUL PLACE (THE CHAPEL)

'We're going to finish our tour in the Chapel today. I need to warn you that we have a problem with the ghosts. They want to get out, you see, and the only way they can do it is to try to frighten you all. *Please* don't be frightened. Don't let them piggyback their way out.

'I've got them all buried here. All the men who died that week. No one else would have such evil creatures but I took them in. I buried them here. Are they happy? I don't know. They're awfully good company, though. Their ghosts linger. You'll be aware, I can almost guarantee that.'

'This is where they dumped Byron's body. I'm not going to tell you the state it was in, but I do have pictures. I have pictures of all of them in here, and mementos, as well.'

Pera showed the tour group her photo album. There were many, many pages in it.

'And if you're really quiet now, you might hear Ike calling from the tunnel below. It's very faint. Some people can hear him calling for help.'

They were silent, dead silent. Pera closed her eyes, listening too. 'Help me, Pera. Please.' It was not lost on her that this echoed what Joseph had said as he died.

'Up the stairs and around the back, I think it's time for some morning tea,' and she led the silent group on through all the ghosts and memories and the things that made her alive.

ACKNOWLEDGEMENTS

I've written this a dozen times in my head. At every stage of the manuscript, from the discovery of the old postcards that started the story, through a fellowship and a residency, to publication, supported by friends, family and peers; there's a lot of love in this book.

So! Thanks to:

Peter Ryan, for buying the postcards and keeping them in a cupboard for ten years before donating them to a school fete, where:

Robyn Campbell found them and insisted they belonged with me. Both have always supported me and my writing.

The Museum of Australian Democracy at Old Parliament House, for providing me with a year-long Research Fellowship. Most of the novel was researched here, and Pera's house was built in my mind, as was Pera herself. Thanks in particular to Toni Dan and David Jolliffe. David, one of the world's greatest librarians, sent so much good stuff my way I almost named a character after him, but didn't have the heart to turn him into a bad guy.

Shane Carmody, who led me through The Savage Club in Melbourne, which helped inspire a number of elements of the story (and gave me great dinner party material).

Katharine Susannah Prichard House in Perth, where I received a three-week residency. I finished writing the book in those magnificent, obsessive days.

Maggie Hodges, good friend and beta reader who said, 'You are NOT done, my dear.' She was right; I had another four or five drafts to go.

Debbie Gibbons, a long, long-time friend and beta reader, who always has insightful things to say and makes me laugh a lot.

My writing friends near to home and around the world. They've supported, inspired and provoked me. Thank you, all of you.

My *Let the Cat In* podcast team J Ashley-Smith and Aaron Dries. You make me laugh and keep me sharp and I treasure every conversation.

Cat Sparks, Rob Hood, Dan O'Malley, T.R Napper and J.S. Bruekelaar: Brilliant writers, great friends and you've all helped make me a better writer.

Angela Slatter, ever-generous, for introducing me to the world of Viper via the amazing

Miranda Jewess, a bright, shining, brilliant star, who helped me make the book what it is, as did the whole Viper team. Working with you all has been inspiring and exciting.

My dad, whose love of reading I inherited, and whose joy at seeing my work in print makes it all worthwhile.

My mum, whose creative spirit and freedom of thought I also inherited.

My sister, who has never stopped believing in me and is a miracle.

James, Mitch and Nadia . . . you are the best family an eccentric writer could ever have, you wonderful, wonderful people. I love you.

ABOUT THE AUTHOR

Kaaron Warren was inspired to write *The Underhistory* when she discovered a bundle of old postcards in a junkshop written by famous Australian artist Sir John William Ashton to his son. Years after Ashton's death, his widow Lady Winfreda was the second victim of the infamous serial murderer John Wayne Glover, known as the Granny Killer. The stories of both Ashtons can be glimpsed in the book. Warren is the author of the novels *Slights*, *Walking the Tree*, *Mistification*, *Tide of Stone* and *The Grief Hole* and the short story collections *Through Splintered Walls*, *The Grinding House*, and *Dead Sea Fruit*. She has won a Shirley Jackson Award, as well as multiple Australian Shadows Awards, Ditmar Awards and Aurealis Awards. She lives in Canberra, Australia. Find her on X @KaaronWarren.